City on a Hill

City on a Hill

—⚏—

PARABLES OF
THE CARPENTER

Kenny Kemp

HarperSanFrancisco
A Division of HarperCollins*Publishers*

HarperCollins books may be purchased for educational, business, or sales promotional use. For information please write: Special Markets Department, HarperCollins Publishers, Inc., 10 East 53rd Street, New York, NY 10022.

HarperCollins Web site: http://www.harpercollins.com
HarperCollins®, ®, and HarperSanFrancisco™
are trademarks of HarperCollins Publishers, Inc.

FIRST EDITION
Designed by Joseph Rutt
Frontispiece illustration by Kenny Kemp

Library of Congress Cataloging-in-Publication Data
Kemp, Kenny.
City on a hill / by Kenny Kemp. — 1st ed.
p. cm. — (Book two in the Parables of the Carpenter series)
ISBN 0–06–008265–8 (cloth)
1. Jesus Christ—Fiction. 2. Bible. N.T.—History of Biblical events—Fiction. I. Title.
PS3561.E39922C57 2003
813'.54—dc22 2003067562
04 05 06 07 08 RRD(H) 10 9 8 7 6 5 4 3 2 1

A city that is set on a hill cannot be hid.
Matthew 5:14

City on a Hill

Visions and Reality

Jeshua walked up the winding dirt path, eyes on the ground. His curly dark hair was wet against his neck and his feet squished in his sandals, but it felt good to be clean after a long, dirty day at work. He had hoped the bath would also refresh his mind, but it hadn't. Something deep inside of him ached, a familiar, heavy tiredness that rested upon his shoulders, pressing down on him. At such times he had to get away to think, to ponder, and to pray.

The streets were deserted, and the setting sun cast a long blue shadow out in front of him. As he passed the small adobe houses, he could hear conversation, occasional laughter, and the squeals of children playing. The smell of barley bread and mutton stew filled his nose, making his stomach flip-flop in anticipation, but there would be no dinner for him tonight.

On the outskirts of town, the Nazareth spring bubbled in its granite basin. Jeshua cupped his hands under the flowing water and drank a long, cool draft. Straightening, he turned back to his village. With forty small adobe and sandstone homes, a few commercial buildings, winding dirt streets, and terraced fields on the surrounding hillsides, Nazareth sat like dregs in a cup, a poor town of poor people.

"Ho, Jeshua!" yelled a child. Jeshua turned, and a trio of boys scampered by, beating the ground with sticks and chasing a ball made of sheep's wool wound with string. Jeshua raised a hand to wave, but the boys were already past him, laughing as they chased the crude ball down the winding street.

He turned and continued on up the hill, turning to the right when the road forked. Each step was an effort. He leaned heavily on his staff, surprised at how weak he felt. Throughout his life, a gray melancholy had occasionally settled upon him, and he had borne it stoically, but it was coming more frequently now, and lasting longer. When he was a little child in Egypt, he would sit on the riverbank in Alexandria and watch the dirty, slow-moving Nile pass and would be filled with an overwhelming sense of doom. He would look upriver, expecting a bank of dark clouds to come sailing around the bend like a dark galleon bound for an unknown sea. He would stand, rooted to the spot, unable to flee, awaiting its arrival, shivering in anticipation and fear. Later, he asked their old magus friend about the image. The soothsayer studied his star charts and then knelt and took the young boy in his arms. Jeshua was surprised when he felt sobs escaping the old man, who held him so tightly Jeshua could barely breathe. Then he released Jeshua, wiped his tears away, and smiled gamely. "On your way," was all he said.

On your way, thought Jeshua, taking another painful step. And here he was, these many years later, still on his way to meet the coming darkness. He imagined it like a bank of unseen storm clouds just beyond the horizon. The cold winds preceding it raised the hair on his neck, filling him with dread and chilling him to the bone.

He pulled his cloak tighter. The magus had no advice for him. His mother tried to salve his melancholy with herb poultices and whispered recitations of happier memories. His father tried to take Jeshua's mind off the darkness with work and play. But only God could lift the burden and release Jeshua from the darkness, giving him hope once again, even for a short time.

But these days God was silent. His voice had always been like the touch of a feather on skin: delicate, almost imperceptible, easily dismissed as the passing wind. Jeshua had to train his mind to listen to the Spirit as he had trained his ears to hear the far-off call of a hawk. It was a skill that needed constant attention, and the only place he could practice it was far from people and the sounds of life. Yet even as he separated himself from others, especially his own family, it became more difficult, though his parents and siblings gave him strength in the most unusual and unexpected ways. A laugh from little Miriam would erase a dark thought. A tussle with his brother Simeon would remind him that life was struggle but it was also joyful. A kind word from his father would fill his heart, and he would remember the great capacity for love that existed in the people he loved.

At such times he *knew* what he was here for: he was here to gently blow on the cooling coal of love until it flared into flame, filling the world with the fire of God's love.

Yet at other times, when the darkness came, he found it difficult to see his path. But even at such times, when he wandered through his life much as others did, lost and directionless, the tiny Voice still whispered to his soul. God had not left him entirely alone; he was not without tools. He had been blessed with a great, surpassing gift—the gift of love, and in every prayer he uttered, he thanked the Lord for the spring of kindness that welled up in him whenever he met a stranger. And the fount was even stronger when the person felt unimportant or beaten or just plain worn out. Jeshua knew how it felt to be weary; he was weary most of the time these days. The darkness was coming, and he wondered if he would have the strength to face it.

At the crest of the hill, the dirt path wound between a stand of sturdy red oak and slender, oily-leafed terebinth trees, and when it curved to the east, toward the Tiran Valley and Tiberias, he left it and climbed up on the boulders that bounded the road. A goat trail appeared and he followed it, the sun glinting on the horizon to his right. After a few minutes, he found himself on a rock shelf looking south out over the Jezreel Valley. He sat with his back against a pine tree. Many leagues to the west, he could just make out the towering heights of Mount Carmel. As he watched, the sun slipped below the horizon, and for five glorious minutes the bottoms of the fluffy clouds were a bright pink, then orange, then red, and then the sky turned purple, then a cobalt blue, and the evening star shone in the west.

The sunset had lifted his spirit, but the heaviness soon returned. He bent his knees and clutched them, rocking slowly, trying to clear his mind in order to hear the still, small Voice. Shadows filled the valley like broth in a bowl. In the distance, at the foot of Mount Carmel, the fires of the tiny village of Meggido became visible. Jeshua rubbed a spray of pine needles between his fingers and cupped his hands over his face, inhaling the sweet smell, but still the weariness would not leave him. The wind sighed in the trees, and he heard the distant voices of shepherds calling their flocks home. In the valley below, he could make out a wagon slowly transiting the Jezreel road. Fires glowed in a dozen little settlements. He looked up again, hoping for an answer, but the arc of heaven was silent.

"What's happening?" he whispered.

In answer, the wind sighed, and fell silent.

Jeshua bowed his head on his knees and prayed.

He dreamed.

He was standing by the pine, looking out over the Jezreel. It mirrored the summer night sky; thousands of torches and cooking fires lit the darkness below, and a great pall of smoke hung low over encampments where two great armies faced each other, awaiting the dawn, a black slash of no-man's-land separating them. From his elevation, the layer of smoke hung below, making the scene hazy and unreal. Banners hung lifelessly in the still night air, and distant voices called out the watches.

His mind's eye seemed to fly low over the camps, where hopeless, grim-faced men sat staring into small fires, thinking about the morning and the doom that awaited them. In large tents generals met, consulting maps, hearing reports of troop strength, and planning strategy. Strange wheeled vehicles with arrow-shaped projectiles atop them collected dew in the darkness. Each projectile bore a seal of three red interlocking arcs, and Jeshua knew they would kill thousands when they were hurled into the sky in the morning.

Then Jeshua saw the dark backdrop behind the props on the stage below. The armies were going to battle because of *him*—he was why tens of thousands of husbands, sons, fathers, and brothers would go to their deaths in the morning.

He shook his head, trying to dislodge the idea. This was the immense black shape that had been moving toward him all his life. It had finally cleared the mist and come into plain view. Soon, his very name would become a sharp sword, dividing the world into two bitterly opposed camps—those who believed his message and those who reviled against it. The situation was doubly disconcerting—those who would fight in his name would no more understand his message than those who opposed and hated him. No one would understand, but they would fight anyway, for that is what men did—they fought over land, over women, over property, over ideas, and even over religion.

Jeshua stretched his arms out and lifted his voice. "I only want you to love each other."

They did not hear. In the valley below, the soldiers went on cleaning their strange metal weapons, the huge silver projectiles remained aimed at the silent, starry sky, and the generals continued seeking out their enemy's weaknesses. The sons of God had finally managed to create weapons to wage the ultimate battle, and when it was over no one would be left alive. Blood would flow like the dark Nile, filling the deep, narrow valley. It would happen here, in this place, in a not-too-distant future.

Jeshua closed his eyes and slumped to the ground, burdened with the dark knowledge. He shook his head dismally.

For a long time he sat there, crushed under the burden. Each gasping breath came raggedly. What could he do? How could he stop this? Jeshua looked up and whispered into the dark night sky, "Father, must it be so? Is there no other way?"

The wind sighed through the trees.

"Then why am I here? You gave me the gift of love, a message of hope, yet they will use my words as weapons against each other. *I* will be the reason for the hatred and the killing. Please, bring me *home.* I cannot bear it." He hung his head and tears streamed down his cheeks. "Is that what you sent me here to do—to destroy the world?"

He awoke.

Dawn was glowing in the east. The valley below was a quiet, pastoral scene of small fields, crooked roads, and tiny settlements. No armies, no terrible weapons, no battle lines.

And no answers. He'd prayed most of the night, to no avail. The dream still haunted him, and he slowly got to his feet, cold and aching. The sun glinted on the horizon.

I will keep asking, he thought, picking up his staff. *But I'm tired.*

He trudged up the trail toward home, to begin his day.

• • •

"I'll be done early," said Joseph, dipping his bread into the broth.

"You always say that," said Mary. She placed a plate of figs on the table and turned away.

"And I'm always right," said Joseph. He took her hand and pulled her back to the table. "Aren't I?"

"Not always," said Mary. "You said once, long ago, that someday I would be rich and have many servants."

The boys laughed. Judah, the older one, tall and broad shouldered, with light hair, nudged his younger brother James. Joseph said, "But you *are* rich. Look about you. See the wealth of children I've given you?"

Mary laughed. "*You* gave me? I think it's the other way around."

She turned, but Joseph still held her hand and pulled her back. "Ah!" said Joseph, brightening. "But you also have servants, which, by a miracle, are also your children!"

"I'm not a servant," said little Miriam, who was combing out her dark hair.

"Miriam," said Joseph. "Get the other plate of fruit."

"All right," said Miriam.

Joseph watched her go and smiled. "There: riches *and* servants."

Mary swatted at him with her apron, but he still held her hand. She scuffed her bare foot on the dirt floor, then kissed him on the cheek and said, "You're right, Joseph. I am rich."

Joseph felt the dirt floor under his feet as well, saw that the fine furniture he labored on never stayed at their house, and regretted the impoverished life he had given her. He let go of her hand, but Mary grasped his again. "Thank you for reminding me," she said.

"And I am richest of all," Joseph said, looking up at her. He turned and nodded at Judah. "You have a full day. Go now." Judah got up and left. Joseph then turned to James. "Finish sanding the frame. The mirror will be here tomorrow."

James nodded and turned back to his breakfast. Joseph cleared his throat. Miriam nudged James in the ribs, and James looked up. "Now," said Joseph. James jumped up, grabbed a piece of bread, and pinched Miriam as he went out.

"Ow!" whined Miriam, rubbing her arm. "He pinched me!"

"James!" shouted Joseph, but James was already gone. Joseph sighed. "Remind me again why we do this," he said, looking at the table of dirty dishes and Miriam pouting.

Mary rubbed Miriam's arm gently. "For love, dear husband." And still she held his hand.

Joseph looked up at his wife. "For love then," he said and kissed her hand, and finally they released each other.

Judah stood by the line of clay water jars, his arms crossed across his chest, thunder in his hazel eyes. Five of them, all full. His father stepped through the doorway, and Judah turned. "I said I'd get to it, but look!" He pointed at the jars.

Joseph peered into them. "What's the problem?"

"They're *full!*" said Judah. "Jeshua always does this!"

"Does what?"

Judah picked up his toolbox. "Makes me look like I'm not doing my part!"

Joseph frowned. "I doubt he intends that, Judah. He's just being helpful."

"But it makes me look bad."

Joseph clapped Judah on the shoulder. "Then you must have your revenge."

Judah blinked, surprised at his father's suggestion.

"Revenge against whom?" came a voice. They turned. Jeshua was approaching, carrying a sloshing water jar on his hip. He set it down by the others.

Judah pointed. "You!"

"Me?"

"Yes!" shouted Judah. "Why do you always *do* this?"

Jeshua shook his head. "The secret's finally out. I do it because I hate you."

"There it is," said Joseph, laughing. He put a hand on Judah's shoulder. "He does your chores because he despises you. But that's all right— we all hate you, Judah."

"I see what's going on," said Judah, shaking his head. "You're trying to cheer me up."

"Do you need cheering up?" asked Joseph.

"About Dinah!"

Jeshua nodded to Joseph. "He's too smart for us."

Judah whirled on Jeshua. "I don't want you doing my chores anymore, understand?"

"Fine," said Jeshua, raising his hands. "But I didn't do your chores. I just filled that last jar there, which I emptied last night for a bath."

"Then who did?"

"Some evildoer," said Joseph ominously. "Beware."

Judah scowled. "I'll find out who it is, I swear it!" He stomped off down the lane.

Joseph and Jeshua both turned. In the window of the small carpenter shop, James's dark head quickly disappeared. Jeshua smiled at Joseph and picked up his toolbox, following Judah out the courtyard door. Joseph turned and walked into the workshop. James was sanding the mirror frame. As he passed, Joseph pinched him on the neck.

"Ow!" yelled James in mock pain, making a show of rubbing his neck.

"Evildoer indeed," said Joseph, turning back, a smile on his face.

Jeshua passed the Nazareth spring, where a line of women waited to fill their water jars. Judah had already passed them, trudging on ahead. "Jeshua!" called out a woman. "Jonah says he saw you up on the Jezreel overlook last night. What were you doing up there?" she asked, winking at him. "Pining for a sweetheart?"

The other women smiled. Jeshua was indeed taking his time getting married. He was well beyond the usual age, and some doubted he ever would; others predicted the solitary life of a Nazirite for him, like his cousin John.

Jeshua was odd, of that there was no doubt. He was given to midnight walks and to disappearing for days at a time. He would be seen wandering along the ridge line overlooking the Netofa or Jezreel valleys or just standing in a grove of trees, hands clasped behind his back, chin raised, eyes closed, the sunshine dappling his face.

And beyond that, he was a *mamser*, born illegitimate, and many people in the village would not even speak to him. Others countered that

Joseph may have married Mary a little too late for decency but that was not Jeshua's fault, and so they ignored the circumstances of his birth. But everyone thought he was strange: a young man who had always seemed older than his years; a loner given to long, solitary walks and disappearances; a fellow who, even when he laughed, seemed somehow melancholy, as if he were carrying a secret weight.

"I was stargazing," said Jeshua. "A new moon is the best time, you know."

"And what did you see in the stars, Jeshua?" asked another woman.

Jeshua surveyed the line of women. He knew they thought him strange at best, and a *mamser* at worst. None of them knew his heart, and for an instant last night's terrible dream returned full force. He shook his head to clear it and reached deep inside for a kind response. "I saw a line of women, as bright and beautiful as the Milky Way, teasing a poor laborer, making him late for work."

"A prophet!" laughed a woman.

"Not much of a prophecy," said another.

Jeshua shrugged. "It's the best I can do. After all, I'm just a carpenter." He turned and trotted up the road, following Judah, the tools in his box jingling as he ran.

A thin old woman with long gray hair shifted the water urn on her hip. She watched Jeshua and whispered to herself. "We shall see."

"What was that, Esther?" asked another.

"He's an odd one, that Jeshua," said Esther.

The women all nodded wisely.

Jeshua caught up with Judah as they approached the summit of the hill. Judah said, "I'll catch whoever did it, you know."

"You?" laughed Jeshua. "You couldn't catch a snail!" He broke into a run, passing his younger brother.

Judah also ran, and because he was taller than Jeshua, he quickly closed the distance between them. "I can catch you, old man!"

They raced to the large, twisted pine tree on the top of the hill and leaned against it, winded. Beyond, spreading out to the north, was the Beth Netofa Valley, the richest farmland in Galilee, ten miles north to south, fifteen miles east to west. Green with new crops and dotted with hamlets and a spiderweb of roads, it was the fertile breadbasket not only of Galilee, but of all Palestine.

"Look!" said Judah, pointing. "A caravan!"

A line of animals moved along the road toward Sepphoris, the capital of Galilee, which perched on a hill in the middle of the valley, the walled city occupying the flattened summit and the poorer homes dotting the hillside below.

"The city is growing fast," said Judah. "How many live there now?"

"I've heard over ten thousand."

Judah whistled. "All those buildings: the *cardo*, basilica, the king's palace."

"Don't forget the theater," said Jeshua. "You know, we should go sometime—see one of those Greek plays. Wouldn't that be exciting?"

"You know what Father would say about that."

"He would say we're grown men who can make our own decisions," said Jeshua. In the distance, on top of the hill, the sun glinted off the white marble theater seats, and the maroon canvas sunshades fluttered in the cool morning breeze.

I would love to see a play, thought Jeshua.

TWO

Kings and Subjects

Herod Antipas leaned on the marble balustrade and looked out across Lake Gennesaret. He was a tall man with high cheekbones, short reddish-brown hair curled close to his head in the Roman fashion, and a deep olive complexion that marked him as an Idumean, the Hebrew-Canaanite mix of people who herded flocks in the deserts of southern Palestine. His neck ached from sitting all morning, listening to entreaties from friend and foe alike. To think he had wanted this! To be constantly harangued for favors, to listen to oily sycophants call him Sire or Your Lordship or Mighty One with barely concealed contempt in their voices.

My dungeons are already too small, he mused.

He shifted his toga and focused on the boats plying the blue water. One in particular, close to shore, was tilting madly, the men hauling in a great net of silver fish. Antipas wished he were out there, his back aching from physical work and his mind as empty as a dried pomegranate.

At that moment one of the men in the boat looked up and saw him. He nudged his companions, and in a moment all three stared up at the king's high tower, the forgotten fish flailing about in the overburdened net.

Antipas raised his hand and waved.

As one, the men went back to work, hauling in the net and emptying it into the boat. Then two of them got on the oars and rowed away as fast as they could, the third manning the tiller.

Antipas let his hand fall to the marble balustrade, turned back, and pulled aside the heavy curtain, entering the gloom of his throne room.

Oil lamps cast a pale yellow light. He sat on the carved ivory throne, kicked off his sandals, and leaned back, wishing he were with those fishermen right now, working hard, telling stories, laughing. He would win them over, for he not only knew a great many stories, he also knew how to work.

One of the immense throne room doors creaked open. Antipas peered through the haze of incense smoke and saw two men silhouetted in the doorway.

Antipas lowered his head, feigning sleep.

"I think he's asleep," whispered one of the men.

The other laughed and strode toward the throne. "He never sleeps!"

Silhouetted before Antipas was a tall, silver-haired man in a golden toga. His companion, a short and exceedingly fat man, remained in the doorway.

"Sleep is for old men, babies, and unwary travelers," said Antipas. "Which are you?"

The man placed his right hand on his heart. "Hail, Caesar."

"In my own throne room, you should hail *me* first." Antipas nodded, and the fat man at the entrance left, closing the door behind him. Darkness filled the room again.

"Then hail King Herod Antipatros!" said the tall man cheerily.

"Open the drapes," said Antipas. "Before I accept an honor, I like to see who gives it."

The man pulled the heavy damask curtain aside. "Your Lordship," he said, bowing.

"Marcus Pertinax," said Antipas flatly, "only you have the nerve to mock a king."

"But as you always remind me, Sire, you are *not* a king."

"I will be king of all Palestine one day, not just tetrarch of an obscure backwater."

"Your father began his march to greatness by governing Galilee."

"I am also on that march," said Antipas.

"Be careful what you desire," said Marcus. "Your older brother was prefect of Judea, and look what happened to him."

"Archelaus was a fool," said Antipas. "The emperor promised him the kingdom if he would just maintain order. But he sacked two high priests and outraged the Sanhedrin. He deserved what he got. No, he got better than he deserved. Banishment is an incomplete punishment—death is so much more final."

"True," said Marcus. "A banished prefect can still stir up trouble."

"Speaking of which," said Antipas, "what trouble did you come to stir up today?"

"No trouble, Sire, I assure you."

"Good. I'm in no mood for it. I've been badgered by beggars all morning."

A hurt look crossed Marcus's face. "But, Sire, I—"

"What *is* it, Marcus? You obviously want *something* from me. Just ask it straight out."

Marcus cleared his throat and hesitated. Then, "Your Lordship—"

"Ye gods!" howled Antipas, shaking his fist at the heavens. "Save me from subtle men!" He glared at Marcus.

"Antipas—"

"*Herod* Antipatros, Marcus. If you're going to ask me for something, use my full name. It gets my attention without being smarmy."

Marcus took a deep breath. "Herod Antipatros, I have a request." He looked warily at Antipas, who nodded. "Sepphoris is a beautiful city, the jewel of Galilee. That is, it is until you finish Tiberias, which is coming along magnificently, if I may say so."

"Do you know why I despise palace talk, Marcus?" interjected Antipas. "It's like smearing oil on a dagger—it only makes it go in more smoothly, which is little consolation to the victim."

Marcus felt warm trickles of sweat running down his back. His friend, or the man who once *was* his friend, had changed in the last few years. Though he himself was older than Antipas, Marcus felt like a child about to be punished. And yet he had done nothing wrong. "When Tiberias is finished, it will outshine Jerusalem."

"It will outshine Alexandria," said Antipas flatly. "Ask your favor."

"Sepphoris has a great theater, a temple of Jupiter, a colonnaded *cardo*, and a palace fit for the emperor himself—"

"It's still my palace, I trust?" asked Antipas.

"Exactly as you left it, Sire. But that is why I am here today."

"So you are building a palace of your own?" asked Antipas. "Your glorious villa is not good enough for you?"

"Yes!" said Marcus. "But I'm building an administrative center."

"An 'administrative center,'" mused Antipas. "Not a palace?"

"Oh, no, Sire . . . just a simple basilica."

"Where you will reign as ethnarch."

"I wouldn't say *reign*, Your Lordship—"

Antipas held up a finger, silencing Marcus. "No one reigns who does not desire it. I do not begrudge your ambition, Marcus, so long as it doesn't interfere with mine. I made you ethnarch *because* of your ambition."

"I am doing my best, Sire."

"I do not doubt it. But I suspect you have money troubles." Marcus nodded. "And so you come to me. How much do you need for your palace—I mean, your 'administrative center'?"

Marcus straightened his back. "Fifty talents."

Antipas frowned. "That's a great deal of money."

"I will guarantee your return," said Marcus. "We both shall profit by this."

"I know *you* will," said Antipas, and Marcus looked up sharply. "But I do not mind, so long as the coffers of Tiberias are filled as well."

"They will overflow," said Marcus.

"Then you have your boon. But remember, *I* have your promise. We shall see who possesses the more valuable coin."

Marcus bowed low once again, discretion binding his tongue, and quickly exited the throne room. Out in the corridor, he closed the door and leaned heavily against it, shaking his head. "By Jupiter, I hate that man," he whispered.

Neri, his fat, red-faced scribe, looked up at Marcus in dismay. "So you didn't—?"

"Fool," said Marcus, straightening. "Of course I got it. Did you expect me to fail?"

"No, Sire, but I thought it might take longer."

"It isn't how long it takes, but how much it *costs*," said Marcus. "And it cost plenty." He started off down the hall.

Neri snapped his fingers. "Oh, I forgot. I have the tax census for the king. May I—?"

Marcus didn't lose a step. "Be quick about it! I want to be back in Sepphoris today!"

Neri turned and placed his shoulder against the door, opening it.

The throne room was dark except for a slit of sunlight between the balcony curtains. Antipas stood in the light, his back to the doorway. "Sire? It's Neri."

Antipas spoke. "Come here." Neri approached the king slowly. The parchment shook in his quaking hands. The king turned suddenly. "Are you a part of this conspiracy?"

Neri blanched, taking a step back. "What conspiracy?"

Antipas crossed and bent over the little fat man. "What is Marcus up to?"

"I . . . I don't know what you mean, Sire."

Antipas scowled. "Sure you do. We both know Marcus hasn't the skill to run Sepphoris, so that leaves you, Neri. You're a smart man, so tell me, what is your master plotting against your king?" Neri's lower lip quivered. He shook his head. Antipas frowned. "You're not going to cry, are you?"

"No, Sire." Neri blinked a tear away and tried to stand taller.

"Good. Can't stand snivelers." He studied Neri. "You will obey your king?"

"Yes, Sire," said Neri.

"Then I want to know how Marcus spends the money I just gave him."

"A basilica, Sire—"

Antipas raised his hand. "I suspect otherwise. And you, as my faithful servant, are to be my eyes and ears."

Neri's hand went involuntarily to his right ear.

"What is it?" asked Antipas.

Neri pulled his hair back, revealing a knotted, purpled scar where his ear once was. He had lost the ear many years ago in a beating by a former master, along with the hearing in it.

Antipas grimaced. "All right," he said, gesturing for Neri to cover the scar. "You have another ear, one that works, do you not?"

Neri nodded.

"Then use it, or you may wind up completely deaf, understand?"

"You will know what I know, Sire," said Neri, his voice shaky and thin.

Antipas waved him away.

Neri found himself out in the corridor, his back against the door, his heart racing. He heard footsteps. Summiting the stairs was an entourage

led by a silk-clothed man even shorter and fatter than Neri was. He
wore a bright red turban and was followed by several dark Nabateans,
bronze-skinned merchant caravaners out of the Negev Desert in Arabia,
with fierce, kohl-lined eyes above bristling black beards.

Neri touched his forehead in greeting as he walked toward the stairs.
The turbaned man passed him, gesturing in like fashion. At the head of
the stairs, Neri turned and watched the man speaking quietly to his
companions outside the king's door. One of the Nabateans noticed him
and gave him a menacing look. Neri turned and scurried down the stone
steps.

A knock came on the door, and Antipas turned. "Enter," he said. "If you
must."

Two tall Arabs opened the great doors, and a little plump man in a
red turban strode into the room, his hands raised in greeting. "Peace be
unto you, my lord Antipas!" said the man. Behind him, one of the
Nabateans carried a heavy, ornate gold chest.

Antipas smiled. Some days it was good to be king. "And unto you,
peace!" he said. "How are you, Azariah?"

THREE

The High and the Low

Judah and Jeshua walked the three miles from Nazareth to Sepphoris and entered the Via Principia, the wide road that paralleled the aqueduct, winding up the steep hill toward the city's southern gate. The road was crowded with Greeks, Romans, Nabateans, Syrians, and even tall, glistening, black-skinned travelers from Upper Egypt. They passed through the gate. From the parapet above, a soldier in full armor looked down impassively at the surging throng. Judah had not seen Dinah at the spring this morning. He wondered if perhaps she had come to Sepphoris with her mother or older sister. He looked around for his beloved, then caught himself.

She was *my beloved,* he thought. *No more.*

Jeshua called out, "Judah!"

Judah threaded his way through the crowd toward Jeshua. "Sorry. I was just thinking."

Jeshua smiled.

"And not about what you think."

Jeshua nodded, not saying a word.

"Well, it's not," said Judah.

"Shall we go?" asked Jeshua.

Judah followed him up the broad, stepped street. Although the hilltop was level, every city street leading to the forum was punctuated with broad stone steps. One had to watch one's feet to keep from stumbling. Once on the forum, they passed the curved theater walls. Through the doorway Judah could see the row upon row of marble seats, enough for four thousand people.

At the southern end of the forum, surrounded by marketplace stalls, stood the massive triumphal arch, built to commemorate the defeat of the Parthians by Herod the Great. A frieze capped the arch, depicting Herod thrusting a spear into Antigonus, his rival, even though no such thing ever happened. To the left was a Roman temple honoring Jupiter, with a large splashing fountain fronting it. Many years ago, before it was finished, Judah had sneaked inside the temple. He had skirted the columns until he saw the giant unfinished statue of Jupiter, surrounded by scaffolding, the bearded god holding a thunderbolt in his right hand and what looked like the tablets of Moses in the crook of his left arm. His massive chest was thrust out, his chin was raised imperiously, and his brow was noble and stern. Judah had never seen a statue before, and it literally took his breath away. He must have stood there gawking at it for a long time, because he didn't hear footsteps approaching. Then someone tapped him on the shoulder, and he looked up into a white-bearded face, not unlike the face of the statue. "You admire my work?"

Judah had stared up at the man, then back at the colossal statue, then turned and fled the temple.

He had not been inside the temple since, but he ached to see that statue again, even if it was an abomination. Judah never saw the old sculptor again, though whenever he came to Sepphoris he looked for him among the people in the forum.

Judah stepped to the side to avoid a blanket spread on the ground displaying jewelry. Greek and Roman merchants displayed their wares near the temple, while the Jews placed their stalls far on the other side, by the multistoried theater.

Before them rose the massive hulk of the new basilica. They'd been told to call it the administrative center, but to Judah it looked like a palace, easily six stories high, fronted by six immense fluted columns standing on a wide, marble porch, which was topped by a triangular pediment. Twenty broad stone steps descended to the granite-paved forum below. Dozens of giant, raw marble blocks dotted the forum, awaiting their turn to be shaped.

Jeshua and Judah threaded their way between the blocks and joined the crowd of workers at the foot of the steps. Marcus stood up on the porch, wearing a purple toga, his long, flowing silver hair glinting in the morning sun. He looked like a king, even though he was merely the administrator, or *ethnarch*, of Sepphoris. "You have your assignments," said Marcus grandly. "Be patient—you will be paid."

"When?" came a voice.

"Soon!" said Marcus, going back inside the basilica, followed by his rotund scribe, Neri.

"The Devil take him," said Zoar, the worker representative. He wore a brown tunic cinched at the waist by a braided leather rope, which he often used as a goad for slow workers. He was a tree trunk of a man, with deep lines in his tanned face, and though he was shorter than most, he was a powerful force, always at the front of any line of working men, sweating and swearing profusely, respected and hated by all. He ran a hand through his short, dark hair. "I won't work another day for free, building Rome's courthouse."

"But it will be *our* courthouse," said a worker.

"Nonsense," said another. "Our courthouse is there." He pointed at the old wooden two-story synagogue on the far side of the theater, now looking like a dilapidated impostor across from the impressive marble basilica.

"Fools!" snapped Zoar. "Buildings don't grant justice." Then he noticed Jeshua at the back of the crowd and crossed his arms across his massive chest. "I suppose you're going to oppose me on this, Jeshua."

"I haven't had breakfast yet," said Jeshua. "Let me chew on what you've said for a while first."

The men laughed. Zoar pushed his way through the crowd and faced Jeshua squarely. "Then chew on this: Marcus promised we'd be paid a month ago. Then he promised us last week. Now he says we will be paid this Sabbath."

"He may surprise us yet," said Jeshua.

"Or we may surprise him."

Jeshua raised a cautioning hand. "Let's not be hasty."

Zoar spit on the ground. "Do you enjoy groveling before Rome, Jeshua?"

"Zoar," said Jeshua mildly, "I can't see how insulting Rome will get us our money."

"Yet you insult *me*—your representative."

"If that's what you felt," said Jeshua, "I apologize."

"So you admit it?"

"I simply counseled patience," said Jeshua. "Certainly we can wait a few more days."

"*You* can wait," said Zoar. "*I* have a family to feed."

There were nods of agreement from several of the men.

"If he said *we*, he means *we*," said a voice, and everyone turned. It was Barak, who stood head and shoulders above every other man in the crowd. If Zoar was a tree, Barak was a mountain, as chiseled as granite, with long, straight, dark hair and a bushy beard.

Zoar squinted at Barak. "I didn't ask for your opinion."

Barak strode forward, his ever-present iron-headed maul held loosely in his left hand. He stood toe to toe with Zoar and looked down at the man. "My opinion is as good as yours. Patience is no crime. Go beg Marcus for our money—that's your job—but don't tell us what *we* must do. It makes *me* impatient." He shifted the maul to the other hand for emphasis.

"I am your representative," said Zoar. "If I say we strike, we strike!"

"When the time comes, we will," said Barak.

"All right," said Zoar. "If we aren't paid by next Friday, we strike. Is that acceptable to *you*, Jeshua?"

Jeshua said, "What are your work assignments, Zoar?"

Zoar glared at him. "There is only one change: Jeshua, you're in the cisterns. Enjoy yourself." He strode away. A murmur arose from the men, who knew the danger of the dark caverns being excavated under the basilica floor. Only the least skilled laborers worked down there; Jeshua was known as a gifted artisan, or *tekton*.

Judah scowled after Zoar. "The cisterns! Why that—"

Jeshua looked up at the sun, which was burning through the morning cloud layer. "At least I'll be cool down there. See you at lunch."

"Jeshua!" said Judah, but Jeshua had already picked up his box and was heading away.

Rabbi Sadoc was exceptionally tall. His green eyes were deep-set under bushy gray eyebrows, and his long and narrow nose topped thick, fleshy lips. His thick, gray-flecked hair defied his attempts to keep it under his tallith head covering. From his upper-story synagogue office window, he looked out across the forum at the new basilica, where the worker meeting was breaking up. He turned at the sound of a door opening. "You're leaving?"

Ishmael, the bald, broad-shouldered man in the doorway, nodded. "He just got back from Tiberias. I'll speak to him soon. But I wish it were you instead of me. You have the skills to deal with the ethnarch that are simply beyond me."

"He would never deal with a rabbi. You're the reason he is involved at all."

Ishmael shook his head. "Whenever you say something like that, Sadoc, I just remind myself to believe the opposite." He closed the door.

Sadoc could hear him chuckling as he descended the stairs.

FOUR

Widows and Judges

The widow Esther bent and placed a small stone next to the others on the top of the round stone blocking the sepulchre entrance. By the Sabbath, there would be seven stones, and the cemetery keeper would clear them away and she would begin again next week. And the week after, and the week after, for the rest of her long, lonely life. She blinked tears away. It was too hard, living without Ezra. She straightened and retied her hair, which the wind had pulled free, winding the long white strands around the bun to secure it. She picked up her varnished cane and slowly picked her way down the rocky path.

Last Sabbath evening, she sat behind the latticed *mekhitsa* partition at synagogue with the other women. When the men's voices were raised in song, she wanted to get up, hobble down the center aisle, and shake her fist at God, demanding answers. Instead, she remained seated, crying into her kerchief, as Rabbi Sadoc held the Sefer Torah high overhead, his eyes closed, praying the *Musaf* benediction: "Cry unto the Lord with all your heart, and He will hear you!"

When the rabbi finished and replaced the scrolls in the Ark, Esther wiped her eyes, a new resolve forming in her heart. She *had* cried unto the Lord, but now that her grieving time was ending, she would also cry unto the ethnarch.

She lined up the last stone with the others on the lintel of Ezra's tomb. "I will never forget," she whispered, "what that evil man did to you, Ezra. Never."

Esther turned and left the tiny cemetery, trudging down the hill to Nazareth, to meet the boy who would carry her on his donkey to Sepphoris. And though her feet did not touch the ground until they reached the forum at the top of the Sepphoris hill, she was still tired from the long, bumpy ride. She handed the boy a shekel and turned to face the basilica, which glinted brightly in the morning sun. Raising her chin, she crossed to it, and scaled the broad marble steps.

Outside it was hot, but the cavernous interior was cool. Esther walked slowly across the peristyle hall. At the foot of an immense fluted column, a man was mixing plaster in a wooden trough. "I'm looking for the ethnarch," she said, her voice echoing in the large, dark chamber.

He cocked a thumb over his shoulder. "Back there."

Esther continued toward a double doorway at the end of the hall. Passing through it, she found herself in a room not quite as large as the main hall but still immense, with a ceiling more than fifty feet above, dotted with skylights. Fluted pilasters, columns projecting only slightly from the marble walls, lined the room, and the floor was tiled in gray speckled granite. Before her, a raised platform was taking shape, workmen hewing giant slabs of white marble into curved sections that would form steps up to a half-circle-shaped dais. Esther guessed the ethnarch would sit up there on a throne, pronouncing judgment. Off to the right was a small doorway, through which Esther saw a man poring over parchments piled high on a table. The sound of her cane tapping on the floor as she approached announced her arrival. Neri looked up. "May I help you?"

"I'm here to see the ethnarch," said Esther.

Neri noticed the way her lips trembled when she spoke. "Is he expecting you?" he asked gently.

"No," said Esther, steeling herself, "but I am expecting him." She began walking down the short hall toward the ethnarch's private offices.

"Madam, you cannot—"

Esther turned the corner, quickened her pace, and entered the room where Marcus lounged on a chaise, eating figs from a bowl. Marcus looked up. "May I help you?"

Neri burst through the doorway. "Sire, I'm sorry—"

"It's fine, Neri," said Marcus, setting the figs down and standing. "I am not busy."

Esther looked up at the tall man with the long silver hair and felt her knees start to buckle. Neri caught her and guided her to a chair, a look of surprise on his face. When she was seated, Marcus sat on his chaise and leaned forward. "How can I help you, Mother?"

Esther clutched at her cane. "I am Esther, of Nazareth. I have a petition."

"Very well," said Marcus. "Neri, fetch your stylus and we will hear this good woman's petition."

Neri exited. Esther looked around. Upon a nearby table were a number of scrolls and parchments. She had always been impressed with writing. Ezra had been able to cipher a little, enough to make him a wealthy man. But his education had proven insufficient to protect him from evildoers. She felt her anger rising, displacing her grief, giving her a bitter strength. She met Marcus's gaze. "My husband, Ezra, was an olive oil merchant. But he is dead now."

"I'm sorry," said Marcus.

Neri ran back into the room, holding a stylus and an inkwell. He settled in at the table, his stylus poised over a blank piece of parchment.

Esther continued, "My story is not so complex that we need to waste much parchment on it." She looked over at Neri, who was already scribbling furiously.

"Go on," said Marcus.

"A business partner cheated my husband out of everything. I only found out after he died, when this man took our warehouse and gave me this." She handed a piece of parchment to Marcus.

"Ishmael of Rimmon," read Marcus.

Neri looked up.

"You know him?" asked Esther.

Marcus shrugged. "Everyone knows *of* him, at least. What did he do?"

"Ishmael also presses oil. He sells the first pressing to synagogues, but he sold the residue to my husband for second pressings. All was well, until the residue got to be of very poor quality and there was less and less of it. Ishmael said it was due to poor crops, but I knew it was because he was selling it elsewhere."

"You're getting all of this?" said Marcus. Neri's stylus hadn't moved since he had heard Ishmael's name. He dipped the stylus and started writing again.

Esther's eyes filled with tears. "He made Ezra sign another contract, which was worse than the first."

"Sounds like an unfortunate, if legal, arrangement."

"That's what I thought," said Esther, wiping her eyes. "But the terms got so bad that Ezra was afraid to tell me about them. He just signed whatever Ishmael put in front of him."

"Most unfortunate," said Marcus, a trace of boredom entering his voice.

"And then, that," said Esther, pointing at the parchment on Marcus's lap. "That's the last one."

"I see," said Marcus.

"That's not Ezra's mark on it," said Esther.

Neri's pen stopped. Esther looked up at Marcus through her tears. Marcus said, "You're sure?"

"It couldn't be."

"Why?"

"Because Ezra couldn't hold a spoon, much less a stylus, a full month before he died. This is dated just a week prior to his death. It's a fraud."

Marcus said nothing but examined the parchment closely for the first time.

"Ishmael has taken everything except our home. He said I should be grateful, because the house was part of the contract too. And now my warehouse is full of his workers, a bunch of dark, evil Nabateans. The press runs day and night, even though just a month ago Ishmael said there was no oil. And now I must live next door and every day see the man who cheated my husband!" She broke down, sobbing into her tallith.

Marcus nodded gravely.

Esther looked at Marcus through her tears. "Will you give me justice?"

Marcus stood and guided Esther to the door. "I'll do what I can," he said. She sobbed as she walked down the hallway, and not until her crying was no longer heard did Marcus turn back to Neri, tossing the widow's parchment to him.

"Do you think it's a forgery?" asked Neri, holding the parchment up to the light.

Marcus reached for the figs and popped one into his mouth. "You know Ishmael."

As she descended the basilica steps, Esther could hardly feel them under her feet. She was exhilarated after her meeting with the ethnarch. *Such a kind man,* she thought. She wiped the last of her tears away and squinted into the bright morning sun.

And now, for the first time since Ezra's death, she felt happy, knowing the ethnarch would punish Ishmael and restore both her property and Ezra's good name. After Ezra died, Ishmael had stood before the warehouse doors, holding up the forged contract and stating in his booming voice that Ezra had been losing money for years and that he, Ishmael, had taken pity and advanced him great sums of money. "I am sorry," he had said, "but now I must collect what is due me."

Esther had looked around, horrified, as her neighbors clucked their tongues and whispered to each other. They had been in her home, eaten at her table, knew the life she and Ezra lived, and they mistook simplicity for poverty. They'd never know how much Ezra gave to the Temple, or how often he would slip a drachma or two into the hands of a beggar without even Esther knowing, until it was time to buy something and she would discover they had no money left. She chided him for his too-generous nature, but she secretly admired him for it. He was much less attached to money than she was, of course, because he was a man—he had always been able to make a living. But she was a woman, trapped in his shadow. She could never survive without his name and a healthy portion of good fortune.

And now they are both gone, she thought, descending the steps.

She picked her way between the huge marble blocks, many taller than she was. To her left was Rabbi Sadoc's synagogue. An idea suddenly came to her. She headed for the synagogue and was about to open the door when it suddenly opened outward. She stepped back and nearly toppled over, when a thin, bony hand grabbed her wrist. She looked up into the narrow, angular face of Rabbi Sadoc. "Careful!" he said, placing his hands on her shoulders to steady her.

"Oh, my!" she said, surprised. "I almost fell."

"I almost made you fall," said the rabbi. "That would have been a sin, wouldn't it?" he smiled.

"Well, you caught me, so we're back where we started."

"Then let's start there," said Sadoc. "How have you been, Esther? I have been meaning to stop by and visit, but I've been very busy."

Esther waved the thought away. "Don't worry. The women are keeping me busy. I haven't had a moment's rest since Ezra died. I'm absolutely dead tired."

Sadoc smiled at the unintended joke. "Well, what can I do for you?"

"I stopped by to thank *you* for all you've done."

Sadoc was surprised. "What have I done?"

"You know," said Esther, "what you *do*. Leading the people. Teaching us the Law. Explaining it to us. I also came to make a small donation."

"But you have so little, Esther, since you lost your press."

Esther nodded. "That's temporary. I just spoke to the ethnarch."

"Did you?" said Sadoc, leaning forward.

"Yes, and he said he would get my property back from Ishmael."

Sadoc almost felt sorry for the foolish old woman. "All things work out according to the Lord's plan," he said. "You believe that, don't you?"

"Yes, I do, and that is why I'm making this offering, to show my faith." She reached into her coin purse and withdrew a shekel and handed it to the rabbi, who tried to look impressed.

"Thank you," he said. "You are most generous."

"I know it's just a mite, Rabbi," said Esther. "But there will be much more when the ethnarch is done with that swine Ishmael."

Sadoc gave her his most sincere look. "I'm sure."

"Well," said Esther, "I must go. Thank you, Rabbi, for your time."

"And thank you for your generosity," said Sadoc, placing the coin in his money pouch and jingling it. "May the Lord bless you."

"He will," said the widow, turning with a flourish and descending the steps.

• • •

Ishmael's estate lay near Rimmon, a village in the eastern hills overlooking the Netofa Valley. It took him twenty minutes of hard riding westward on his gelding, up the main road toward Sepphoris, before he saw anyone else's land, and he never failed to stop at the low rock wall that marked the borders of his property and look back over his shoulder.

He had worked for many years to amass his estate, and his craggy, bronzed face showed it. His vineyards were prospering, and this season's barley sprouts were greening the rolling hills. Ishmael's horse snorted, breathing heavily, and he leaned forward and stroked the animal behind the ears. "Look," he whispered, pointing to the next hilltop. "Soon you will have to run all the way up there before I let you rest, for no one rests while they are on my land." He smiled and touched his leather-wrapped riding crop against the gelding's hindquarter. The horse moved ahead at a canter, and Ishmael pulled back his head covering, enjoying the early morning sun on his brown, bald head.

He was a big man, though not exceptionally tall. His strength lay in his broad chest and powerful arms. He'd worked the wine and oil presses himself—he still did, occasionally—and never ceased to relish the power he felt as sweat broke on his upper lip. Though the circlet of hair on his head was still a dark brown, his full beard was going gray at the corners of his mouth, and he considered shaving it, like the men of Sepphoris did, but they were Greek and Roman, and he was a Jew. A simple thing like shaving would bring down judgment and outrage by his own people, and though he secretly scoffed at religious things, he nevertheless kept the rituals. He was a practical man. Most of his servants were Jewish, and his own devotion to the Law made his rule less onerous for them. In the end, he considered all religions simply tools, much like a rake or a shovel or his riding crop. Sadoc, the Sepphoris rabbi, had taught him that. Sadoc used religion to gain wealth and power in the city; Ishmael had used it to gain the obedience and respect of the laborers on his estate.

By now he had summited the hill, and the entire western Netofa spread out before him. Sepphoris was a tiny dot on the horizon, far across the undulating farmland, but it shone like a crystal in the sun's slanting morning rays. If their plan did not go awry—and Ishmael was smart enough to imagine a hundred ways it could—he would soon own most of this valley, and then Antipas would have to recognize his position and power. Marcus could have Sepphoris, but Ishmael wanted nothing more than the land in this rich valley. He was impatient for that to happen, for though Ishmael's stomach was flat from exercise and a careful diet, his appetite for property was insatiable. He would not rest until he owned the road that ended at the king's own doorstep. And then, who knows—perhaps the road would continue on even there.

He made good time to Sepphoris and gave the reins of his black charger to the stableboy, then turned toward the city center. Striding up the winding cobblestone streets, he heard the forum long before he saw it, for it was the marketplace of all of Galilee. As he stepped onto the granite flagstones that paved the immense square, he estimated the number of people selling and buying at more than five thousand.

Ishmael had a meeting with Marcus this morning, one to bookend his meeting with Rabbi Sadoc yesterday. If things went well, he would soon be rich enough to own every shawl, gold bracelet, and toga in the square, indeed, in all of Galilee. He threaded his way between the marble blocks scattered in front of the basilica and admired the sounds of labor: chisels ringing on stone, the grunting as men hoisted a granite lintel as thick as an oak trunk up onto two doorway plinths, the scraping of trowels spreading plaster across the interior walls. He had to admire Marcus's ambition—it equaled his own, but thankfully, it paralleled it and did not conflict. Their arrangement would not last long were that not the case, for Ishmael had no doubt that the Roman's hunger for property was as insatiable his own. But Marcus craved the urban centers, and Ishmael hated the press of people in the cities. So they agreed to divide the proceeds of their plot between city and countryside, and Ishmael couldn't be happier with the arrangement.

As he climbed the steps of the basilica, Ishmael glanced over at Sadoc's wooden synagogue, so shabby looking now nestled between the immense stone walls of the theater and the rising marble of the basilica. And there stood Sadoc in the doorway, bidding good-bye to an old woman, who slowly moved away, leaning on her cane.

Ishmael topped the steps and walked across the broad porch, past the low but rising facade wall, and into the darkness of the basilica nave beyond. He strode across the immense inner hall, entered the courtroom proper, and entered Marcus's private offices. There was Neri, as usual, bent over his parchments, his nose inches from the text, scribbling away.

Ishmael said, "Good morning, Neri. I'm here to see the ethnarch."

Neri looked up, surprised. "Is he expecting you?"

Ishmael smiled at the fat little man. "Neri, don't you know Marcus's schedule? That's your job, isn't it?"

Neri went back to his writing. "Among a thousand other things, yes," he muttered.

Ishmael smiled and walked down the hallway. In his private offices, Marcus lay on his chaise, eyes closed, fingers laced across his stomach, snoring quietly.

Ishmael shook his head. Only a government official could nap in the morning. He looked around and saw a globe-shaped glass paperweight on the table. He picked it up, feeling its heft. "Well, did you get it?"

Marcus, who had obviously heard him enter, smiled, his eyes still closed.

Ishmael whistled. "All of it?"

Marcus opened one eye.

"You really think he believed you needed fifty talents for *this?*" Ishmael gestured around.

Marcus sat up. "Why not? It's what *he'd* do with it! But we're building something more impressive than a basilica—we're building a kingdom!"

Ishmael smiled. "I think fifty talents will convince even the greediest holdout that he should sell." Ishmael pushed the papers aside and leaned against the heavy oak desk. "You know, Marcus, I've been trying to buy those estates for twenty years, offered fair prices, but they would not sell."

"Perhaps they knew what it would mean if you owned the entire valley," said Marcus, smiling. "The king himself would tremble."

Ishmael shook his head. "I always worry when you start talking about the king, Marcus."

Marcus smiled. "How does a king rule, Ishmael?"

Ishmael shrugged. "By threat of force."

"And by respect for property."

"Respect for property?"

"It is his sharpest sword," said Marcus. "You and I prosper because we trust that our property will remain ours. Without that trust, there is chaos and civil war. Therefore, as long as you get *legal* title to the lands, the king will respect it. He will have to."

"And he will never know where I got the money?"

"How will he find out?" laughed Marcus. "I have just as much to lose as you do. The money was loaned to *me*, after all."

"Indeed. But I can't help wondering what you're getting out of all this. The land in the valley will be mine. What will you get?"

Marcus stood and placed both hands on Ishmael's shoulders. "My dear Ishmael! I will have Sepphoris, the jewel of Galilee. What more could a man want?"

"The world isn't large enough for your wants, Marcus."

"*Our* wants! With our alliance, we will control all of western Galilee. Let Antipas build Tiberias into a monument to his own vanity. While he does, we quiet little mice will nibble up the rest of his kingdom and, in due time, wrench it away from him."

"And if you are wrong?"

"I have other friends beside you, Ishmael."

"Such as?" asked Ishmael.

"Calpurnius Piso, our neighbor to the north, in Syria." Marcus took the glass paperweight from Ishmael's hand and held it up. "The world is a big place. Not everyone loves Herod Antipas as we do."

Ishmael had barely left when Neri heard whistling from inside Marcus's chambers. The ethnarch rarely whistled, and Neri thought as he bustled down the hallway, *Now is as good a time as any.*

Marcus was leaning against the oak table, turning the glass globe over and over in his hands, smiling to himself. When he saw Neri, he hid the smile, and the last whistled note died. He frowned at his fat scribe. "What do you want?"

Neri went to the table and began ordering the parchments and papers. Marcus stood aside and watched, wondering if Neri had been listening in on his conversation with Ishmael. He'd neglected to shut the door as he usually did when sensitive matters were being discussed, and he could kick himself for his lapse. But as he watched Neri stacking the parchments, his forehead beaded with sweat and his pudgy cheeks red with effort, Marcus had to smile. Neri was probably too stupid to even guess at what Marcus and Ishmael were hatching.

"Were you eavesdropping, Neri?" asked Marcus absently, still tossing the glass globe from one hand to the other.

Neri looked up, shocked. "No, Sire! Never!"

"That's good," said Marcus, smiling. "I'd hate to find out you were unfaithful to me."

Neri's mouth dropped open. After all this time! All the years he'd served the ethnarch, to still be doubted! Then he remembered the king's command to spy on Marcus, and he lowered his eyes and silently cursed his untenable position. How could he serve two masters? He looked up at Marcus again. "I wasn't eavesdropping, Sire." It was the truth, but the intensity with which Marcus was looking at him made him wish he *had* been listening in. Something important had just transpired and he'd missed it. Neri knew from long experience that missing *anything* that mattered to the ethnarch would cost him dearly. His hand went to his ruined right ear.

"Quit fiddling with that!" said Marcus. "It's disgusting."

Neri's hand dropped limply to his side. "Yes, Sire."

Marcus turned away and looked out the tall, narrow window. In the distance, above the red tiled roofs, the king's flagpole rose into the sky. When the king was in Sepphoris, his maroon and gold standard flew from that pole. It was bare now.

Behind him, he heard Neri puffing, still moving things around on the desk. Marcus tapped his foot impatiently, wishing the scribe would finish and leave. Then the noise stopped and Marcus turned, expecting Neri to be gone. Instead, the little scribe stood before him, his arms overflowing with yellow parchments, his splotchy red face screwed up into what passed for a smile. "Sire, I have a favor to ask."

"What is it?" said Marcus, sitting down on his chaise, surveying the girth of his servant, wondering when the man found the time to eat as much as he needed to maintain such an impressive waistline.

"Well," said Neri, looking at the floor, "as large as your boon from the king was, I was hoping that you might see fit . . ." He seemed to run out of words. Neri never thought he'd get this far before Marcus cut him off. But Marcus was simply sitting there, watching him. "I was going to ask you, if you could spare it, for a . . . for a . . ."

"A loan?" said Marcus.

Neri nodded.

Marcus smiled and said, "How much?"

Neri, though long rehearsed, still forgot his lines. "I was hoping, Sire. I mean, thank you, thank you, Sire. You are most generous."

Marcus nodded. "How much?"

Neri gulped. "Twenty-five denarii."

Marcus didn't flinch. "That's a lot of money, Neri. What is it for?"

"I'm finishing my house, Sire."

"A private bath is costly," said Marcus.

Neri looked up. No one had seen the plans. He nodded sheepishly. "Yes, Sire."

"Will I be invited?"

"You are always welcome in my humble home!"

"Not so humble after this," said Marcus, reaching into his pouch and handing Neri a golden denarius. "The rate is twenty-five to one now, so this should equal. Spend it wisely, Neri, for it is just a loan. And I will be repaid."

Neri took the coin and said, "Yes. I promise."

Marcus shrugged. "That is all one can ask." Neri turned to go, but just as he was almost out the door, Marcus said, "But you wouldn't mind, would you, Neri, if we put our little transaction in writing? Why don't you work up a contract?"

Neri nodded as he walked down the hall, arms full of parchment. "I'll get right on it."

Sniveling toad, thought Marcus, leaning back in his chaise.

Corrupt viper, thought Neri as he put the bundle of parchment on his table.

FIVE

Profit and Loss

The next morning, Ishmael got up before the sun and rode his horse to the highest promontory on his estate, high up on the southern hills. He'd had a stone tower built there, and he liked to sit on its uppermost platform and survey his domain. He looked to the east, where Joram bar Ehud's estate bordered his. He'd been trying to buy Joram's property for five years now, but Joram set his price ridiculously high.

But in just a few days, Joram would have his price, and Ishmael would have Joram's land. When you had fifty talents to spend, haggling over a few denarii seemed ridiculous. Now that he had access to the king's money, there were a half dozen other properties at this end of the valley and a few more in the western valley that would soon be his. And then it would take him half a day to ride all the way across his land!

Yet as he sat on the upper platform, swinging his legs and watching the sun peek over the eastern ridges, a tiny doubt tickled the back of his mind. He couldn't put a finger on it, but he knew he had missed something. Something important. He sat there until the sun was full up, but he couldn't place the doubt, though with each passing moment he was more sure of its importance. Then it showed itself, and Ishmael went white. "My name will be on the deeds!" he whispered quietly, looking to the east, half expecting to see the king's cohort to appear, riding up the road from Tiberias.

"My name!" he repeated, shaking his head.

His doubt, now visible in the light of dawn, pointed directly at Marcus. He ran a hand over his bald head. Now he saw it clearly, the real risk in this scheme. If it failed, his head, not Marcus's, would be severed from his neck.

Ishmael stared into the sunrise, pondering the image.

Ishmael rode slowly down the long, sloping road toward his house, deep in thought. Tall cypress trees lined the path like sentries. In the distance, near the main house, he saw workers hauling water and feeding the animals. A group of men walked toward the fields, their hoes and rakes over their shoulders. They all stopped and knelt when he passed by. Ishmael gave them a cursory glance and continued toward the dooryard. When he was through the wide gate, he turned right to the stables. And there, standing in the doorway, dressed in much too fine a linen cloak, was Hanock, his chief steward, his back to Ishmael. He was shouting at someone inside, tapping a leather-wrapped riding crop against his thigh.

Ishmael scowled. He had begun to dislike his chief steward not long after the man took the five talents he'd given him last year and multiplied them into ten. With his newfound wealth, Hanock then began to dress in silk and linen. That didn't bother Ishmael. What bothered him was that Hanock also began to imitate him, to copy his manner and tone of voice. He made friends with Ishmael's friends and even once addressed him as "Ishmael" and not as "Master." He got a fierce beating with Ishmael's crop for that indiscretion.

But when Ishmael saw Hanock strike another servant with a riding crop exactly like his own, the dislike fermented into outright hate.

"Why hasn't it been done?" yelled Hanock to someone inside the stable. There was no response, but Hanock forged ahead. "I've told you a thousand times, I want my horse ready *every* morning! When you saddle Ishmael's horse, saddle mine as well. I have important things to do."

"Like what?" asked Ishmael.

Hanock turned quickly, almost falling over in the process. He hid his riding crop behind him and bowed low. "Oh, nothing, Sire. Just business in town."

"What kind of business, Hanock?"

"Nothing important, just . . . you know, things."

"Have you finished the ledgers you promised me two days ago?" asked Ishmael.

Hanock's fleshy face burned crimson. He was a stout man, with narrow shoulders and a prominent belly. His graying hair was ordinarily lifeless, but he took great care to curl it in the current Roman fashion. "They're almost done, Sire." He wiped a pudgy hand across his forehead, which glistened with sweat.

"Well, when they're done, you can go to Sepphoris, but not until. Understand?"

Hanock nodded.

Then suddenly Ishmael had a revelation. He smacked his crop against his thigh. "The ledgers can wait." He jumped off the horse, handed the reins to Hanock, and started toward the house. "Saddle your horse—you're going to Sepphoris after all."

He went inside. Hanock watched the door, expecting Ishmael to come bursting out any second to reverse his prior command. His master had been that changeable lately. When a minute passed and Ishmael did not reappear, Hanock turned back to the stable. The stable master, a small, wiry youth named Naaman, stood inside, holding a bridle, also watching the door for sign of Ishmael.

"I told you: saddle her up!" shouted Hanock, whipping his crop through the air.

Inside the house, Ishmael went quickly to the alcove where he kept the books and ledgers. He pulled out a piece of parchment and dipped a stylus into the inkwell. He paused a moment, then began writing furiously, a smile on his face. When he finished, he folded the parchment, grabbed a nearby candlestick, and poured out a dollop of wax onto the parchment, pressing his signet ring into it, sealing the letter.

Back outside, he strode across the dooryard. Naaman was saddling Hanock's horse, a tawny brown mare. Hanock was watching impatiently, his arms folded across his ample stomach, scowling at the man. "Here," said Ishmael, thrusting the parchment into Hanock's hands. "Take this to Marcus."

Hanock almost dropped the missive. "The ethnarch?"

Ishmael turned to Naaman. "You're going too."

"Why?" asked Hanock. "I don't need him."

"You might."

"What for?" complained Hanock. "I can find Sepphoris by myself."

Ishmael scowled at Hanock. "Just do as I say. No arguments."

• • •

"Naaman! Laggard!" shouted Hanock.

Naaman let the horse's hoof drop and looked up the road, where Hanock sat on his horse in his expensive green silk cloak. Naaman waved. "It's just a stone."

"Then let's *go!*" shouted Hanock, shaking Ishmael's letter. "The ethnarch is waiting!"

Naaman mounted and rode toward Hanock. "Coming! Sorry!"

"You *are* sorry," said Hanock, surveying the skinny stableboy as he pulled up alongside. "Haven't you learned anything from me?"

Naaman considered spooking Hanock's mare, just to watch her bolt and throw the steward to the ground. Instead, he touched the pouch hanging on the leather cord around his neck, feeling the small round stone inside. "Not much, I guess."

"Last summer, Zerah and I invited you to invest with us, but you were too proud. In the end, we got rich and you got a beating." He shook his head. "You'll never learn."

Naaman nodded, but Hanock was wrong. Last summer, when they finished digging the well, Jeshua showed Naaman where his lost talent was buried, then paid him a another whole talent for his labor. Naaman then tossed one coin into the well as an offering to God for saving his life in the well cave-in two days earlier. The other coin he gave back to his master Ishmael, who had loaned it to him in the first place. Ishmael beat him soundly for his trouble. In the end, the only thing he took from that orchard was the small, black stone in his pouch, a reminder of Jeshua and his own change of heart.

He had high hopes that day, almost a year ago, that just as everything inside him had changed, so would the world outside. He had suffered Ishmael's beating without bitterness and was surprised when he found he felt no jealousy for Zerah with his four talents or Hanock with his eleven. He congratulated both men, much to their shock, and then limped out of the room, feeling the sticky blood on his back from Ishmael's crop.

His heart had changed, but his life hadn't. He was still just a stable master. Hanock was richer than ever and twice as cruel. When he discovered Naaman had stopped beating the stableboys, Hanock took it for laziness and whipped them himself. Then he whipped Naaman just for fun.

"Are you listening?" shouted Hanock, smacking Naaman on the thigh with his crop.

"Ow!" yelled Naaman, brought back to the present. "What?"

"I asked you a question!"

"Sorry. What was it?"

"I said, 'When are you going to oil the tack again?' It's hard and cracking." He pointed to his stirrup.

"I oil it weekly, Sire."

"Then oil it twice a week! Do I have to do *your* job as well as mine?" He glared at Naaman, who lowered his eyes. "You're learning after all. Good." Hanock spurred his horse ahead, kicking up dust.

They crested the hill, and the Netofa spread out before them. Despite his stinging thigh, Naaman smiled. It was a nice day, and if Hanock would stop hitting him, it might turn out to be a beautiful one.

"Naaman!" shouted Hanock, in full trot, several rods ahead. "Laggard!"

By the time they began their ascent up the Via Principia, Hanock's temper had cooled, replaced by a growing anticipation. The ethnarch! He'd tried to peer into the parchment's open ends, but the writing in Ishmael's hurried scrawl was cramped and impossible to read. In the end, he reluctantly tucked it inside his toga, wondering what it contained. An introduction to the ethnarch, certainly. Perhaps even a recommendation. Maybe even a commendation. He smiled.

Naaman rode alongside his master, wondering how Hanock could smile, given the circumstances. Hadn't Ishmael sent him to see the ethnarch? Hadn't Hanock heard about the ethnarch's vicious nature? How could he be so relaxed?

Many questions, but only one answer. It was certain that no matter what happened, when Hanock's meeting with the ethnarch was over, he would either be so fearful for his own life or so proud of his own abilities that he would never consider Naaman's request. Naaman decided that to wait until then would mean the end of his dream, so he took a deep breath. "Sire?"

"What is it?"

"You've made wise investments," said Naaman truthfully.

Hanock snorted and dismounted. He squinted at the slight young man. Naaman's sandy, fine hair had receded to the crown of his head. It should have made him look older, but his narrow, unlined face was still that of a youth, barely out of his teens. "What do you want?"

Naaman nodded. "I need a loan."

Hanock dropped his horse's reins and began walking up the narrowing Principia, which was crowded with people. Naaman scooped up the reins and pulled both horses forward. After a few steps, Hanock stopped and turned. "Hold out your hand." His riding crop tapped his thigh.

Fearing the worst, Naaman did as he was told.

Hanock withdrew a large, silver coin from his purse, placing it in Naaman's palm.

Naaman gulped. A whole talent! All he needed were a couple of denarii. "Sire, I can't—"

"Quiet!" yelled Hanock. "Don't you *dare* tell me it's too much! Last year when Ishmael gave me *five* of them, how scared do you think *I* was? A lifetime's income in my hands, and no idea what to do with it? You thought multiplying it was easy, didn't you?"

"No, I never—"

"Shut up!" whispered Hanock hoarsely, noticing the people watching them. "Well, now the tide has turned. And you'd better not bury this coin, or I'll do worse than Ishmael did. You won't get off with a few stripes this time."

Naaman stared at the coin in disbelief.

Hanock leaned in, his breath hot on Naaman's face. "You act like a changed man. I see you trying to impress people with your humility and soft speech. But I'm not fooled. I know you. I know who you *really* pray to up there in your loft." He pointed at the coin. "There's your god, Naaman. Let's see if he answers your prayers!"

Hanock grabbed the reins of his horse and walked away. A boy was standing nearby, his eyes on the coin in Naaman's shaking hand. When Naaman looked up, the boy saw tears welling in his eyes and howled with delight. "He's crying!" he shouted. "Look at him! He's rich and he's crying!"

Naaman lashed out at the boy with the reins. The boy backed away, mocking Naaman's posture, crying, "Woe is me! I'm rich but I'm so sad! Poor me!"

Naaman trudged up the road. Humiliation burned his cheeks like a brand. He could still hear the boy jeering behind him. Hanock had disappeared. The city gates loomed before him, and he was soon pressed into a crowd surging through the entrance. As he passed under the arch, the sunlit *cardo* rose up the hill before him, a long, stepped street lined with vendors of every sort.

Suddenly, Naaman stopped, clutching the coin to his chest. What if he was robbed? There were probably a dozen men in the street watching him right now that would slit his throat if they knew what he had in his hand. He looked around wildly, not knowing where to turn, and stumbled ahead, certain he would be set upon at any moment. He tripped, scraped his knee on the stone curb, and fell, rattling his teeth.

He got to his knees, still clutching the talent in his fist, tasting blood. He felt a sob rising in his chest and gritted his teeth to suppress it. Closing his eyes tightly, he willed himself to be calm, but the fear was rising inside him like water at a boil.

Then a hand touched his shoulder. Naaman pushed it away.

"Can I help?" came a voice.

Naaman shook his head, his eyes squeezed shut. Then a hand lightly touched the crown of his head and a warmth flowed into him. Naaman's heart stopped pounding. His hands, pressed to his wet eyes, stopped shaking. He raised his head and opened his eyes.

A man was kneeling before him. Naaman looked up at him.

"Jeshua?"

They sat on the edge of the fountain near Jupiter's temple. Jeshua turned the silver talent over and over in his hands. Naaman sat glumly by, spent from telling Jeshua his sad story. "I haven't changed after all, I guess."

Jeshua looked up. Once again Naaman felt that piercing look that in another man's eyes would betoken judgment, but in Jeshua's eyes it was an equally intense compassion. Still, Naaman knew Jeshua could not entirely disagree with his assessment of his life.

"So Hanock thinks he has cursed you with this," said Jeshua, holding the coin up.

Naaman nodded.

"We should all be punished so." He handed it back to Naaman and added, "He has underestimated you, Naaman. It seems a common fault."

"What do you mean?"

"Well," said Jeshua, looking around at the crowded marketplace. "How many of these people do you know?"

Naaman scanned the crowd. "None of them."

"And how many know you?"

"None of them."

"Perhaps not even *you* know you."

"But I *do* know me!" cried Naaman. "I have no skill with money. What can I do?"

"What did Hanock do, in the beginning?"

"He went to see Ocran, a financier who works in the bank." Naaman nodded at the great columned building to the left of the basilica.

"Ah," said Jeshua, "I've heard of him. Not entirely honest, but he's not as schooled in evil as he is in money."

"Aren't they the same thing?"

"Money is not evil," said Jeshua, "though it makes a sharp sword in a wicked man's hand."

"What if he cheats me?"

Jeshua put a hand on Naaman's shoulder. "Then he does."

"No guarantees?" lamented Naaman.

Jeshua smiled. "I will guarantee you this: we rarely learn the same lesson twice."

"That's not very encouraging," said Naaman. "But thank you. It was lucky you came along."

"Lucky?"

"Maybe *fortunate* is a better word." Naaman paused. "But perhaps *an answer to a prayer* is the most accurate."

Jeshua smiled. "Wise as a serpent, harmless as a dove."

Naaman shook his head. "What does that mean?"

"Good luck with Ocran." Jeshua stood and walked across the forum. Naaman watched him go, noticed the mantle of dust on his shoulders, the streak of mud on his left calf, and the worn sandals.

Naaman reached inside his tunic and withdrew his money pouch. He removed the black stone and laid it in his palm. It was so much smaller than the talent, worth nothing in an exchange, and yet he'd traded his old life for this small stone, which was warm from his body heat. He held the silver talent in his other hand. It was big and precious and cold, the profile of the emperor Tiberias on one side, the Roman eagle on the other. But it was just a stone too.

He balanced the two stones in his hands for a moment, then put the talent in the pouch and tucked it inside his tunic. He examined the small, black stone. It *was* worth more than the talent—his heart told him so. He clutched the stone in his hand and looked thoughtfully at the bank.

Marcus was not at the basilica. The ethnarch's scribe, Neri, asked a lot of questions about who Hanock was and who sent him. When Hanock said he was Ishmael's chief steward, Neri just looked at him thoughtfully. After a long moment, Neri said the ethnarch was lunching at home. "I'll take you there."

"I know where it is," countered Hanock.

Neri gathered up a stack of papers. "I need to talk to him anyway." He came around his desk and led Hanock out of the offices. As they walked down the basilica steps, Hanock's stomach did somersaults. With every step he became more certain he was in terrible trouble. Why else would the scribe take the time to personally deliver him to the ethnarch?

When they finally approached Marcus's huge limestone villa, with its grand parapets and red tiled roof, Hanock fought the impulse to run. Neri knocked, and a dark, severe looking Nabatean opened the door and frowned at them. "It's lunchtime," he said, scowling.

"He has a visitor. From Rimmon, is that right?" asked Neri, looking at Hanock.

"He's eating," said the Arab.

"Tell him this man represents his friend Ishmael. I'm sure he'll see us."

The man sighed audibly and motioned them inside. The entry floor featured a colorful mosaic of Neptune with his trident, standing in a clam shell. Neri gestured for Hanock to go ahead. Instead of walking around the mosaic, as anyone respectful of Roman religion would, Hanock walked right over it, his eyes on the marvelous tapestries and luxurious furnishings in the great room beyond. Neri snorted at the man's lack of manners.

"Neri!" came the ethnarch's voice. "Can't you see I'm eating?" Marcus appeared around a corner. When he saw Hanock, he stopped. "And you are?"

"Hanock, Sire. Chief steward of Ishmael. He sends his regards and this." Hanock held the parchment out in his shaking hand.

Marcus took the parchment and motioned Hanock toward a pair of facing white divans. Marcus sat on one and opened the letter. Hanock sat on the other. Neri stood behind Hanock. He was not about to miss any more meetings, especially if they involved Ishmael or one of his emissaries.

Marcus read the parchment, then stood and walked over to a wall sconce, where a trimmed lamp was burning. He lit the edge of the parchment and dropped it into a bronze brazier, where it flared as it was consumed. He turned back to Hanock. "So you represent Ishmael."

Hanock nodded.

"The letter said you have his complete confidence."

Again Hanock nodded, pleased at the knowledge.

"I know of you. You have done well with your investments. What was it you made of the talents your master gave you? There were five, weren't there?"

"In the end, I multiplied them into eleven talents."

Neri inhaled sharply, and Marcus nodded. "Doubled, and then some."

Hanock nodded.

"And what did you buy with your profits?"

"A winepress in Cana. Houses here in Sepphoris. Livestock. Land."

Marcus nodded. "Ah. Land."

Hanock didn't know what to say. He nodded.

Marcus considered Hanock, then turned to Neri. "Get us something to drink, Neri."

Neri turned around. The dark-skinned Nabatean stood like a statue in the vestibule. Why didn't Marcus send him? Neri gestured toward the servant, but Marcus shook his head. "Something cool would be nice."

Neri turned toward the hallway. The kitchen was at the far end of the villa. *Getting rid of me,* he thought bitterly as he walked down the hall. *So they can plot in private.*

Back in the main room, Marcus leaned forward. "He told you about the fifty talents?"

Hanock almost swallowed his tongue. "Yes," he lied.

"He told you what to do with them?"

Hanock nodded slowly.

"The money is in the bank," said Marcus, withdrawing a large key on a silver chain from around his neck. He handed it to Hanock and whispered, "Above all, be discreet."

Hanock took the key. At that moment, Neri bustled into the room, carrying two large glass tumblers of red wine. Marcus stood, gesturing for Hanock to put the key away. Hanock tucked it into his toga and turned to receive the glass of wine from Neri, who looked flushed and more than a little irritated.

Marcus clinked his glass against Hanock's. "To Ishmael's wisdom."

Hanock nodded and drank.

Hanock fully intended to go straight to the bank, to see the money, but he was too afraid. What had he gotten himself into? By simply standing there and nodding, he had been thrust into something terrifying. Fifty talents was a lifetime's worth of money, even for a rich man. And what was Marcus expecting him to do with it? Invest it? In what? And why him? He had to think this over. Something was not right.

And Marcus wasn't the least of his concerns. His own master, Ishmael, had sent him into the lion's den without even a word of advice or caution. If he could have read Ishmael's letter, he might have been able to discern Ishmael's purpose. But the letter was in ashes now, and Hanock couldn't make a move until he knew more.

He walked to the stable behind the baths and retrieved his horse. He had a long ride home and he was glad. He needed the time to think.

SIX

Old and New Friends

It was Sunday, the first day of the week, and Arah got an early start with his chores. He hoisted the heavy water urn onto his hip. He'd only recently grown tall enough to carry it this way. He was proud of his height, though he believed he was still too thin. But he was finally doing the work of a man, and next year's bar mitzvah couldn't come soon enough for him.

He walked toward the house and reached for the door catch. He never touched it without thinking of Jeshua, the carpenter from Nazareth. Even though Arah was only a servant in this house, he felt that the great red mahogany door Jeshua had built was somehow his too, and he took pride in it. Over the last two years he had acquired several tools to place in the rough-hewn toolbox he'd built, to go along with the scraper Jeshua had given him. Often, late in the evening, Arah would organize his tools: the maul, the chisel, the rasp file, the knife, and the scraper. As he did so, he thought of Jeshua, wondering where he was and what he was building.

Once, almost a year ago, Master Eli brought word that he'd seen Jeshua at the synagogue in Cana. He didn't say more, only that Jeshua had asked about Arah. The news had made Arah very happy. He told his master that if he saw Jeshua again he should ask him to come visit. Eli had laughed and said, "I'll give him your message, Arah. Is there anything else I can do for you?"

Arah blushed, but old Eli placed his hand on Arah's shoulder. "I miss him too. I invited him, but who knows when he can come? He must work, you see."

Arah wondered when he would see Jeshua again. He had many questions, especially about prayer. He often prayed as Jeshua had taught him,
talking plainly to his Heavenly Father and then listening for an answer.
Sometimes he felt comforted, but mostly it seemed he was talking to the
air. He wanted to ask Jeshua how many prayers one must pray before
God answered them.

As Arah touched the mezuzah on the doorpost, he heard commotion out in the road. Turning, he saw a large caravan cresting the hill. A
fat man wearing a red turban rode atop the lead camel. In five steps Arah
was across the dooryard, shouting, "Azariah!"

Arah ground to a halt before the camel, winded.

Azariah squinted down at him. "And who might you be, young
man?"

"It's me! Arah!"

"No, you must be mistaken," said Azariah, frowning. "The Arah I
know is just a young boy, no taller than me—when I'm on the ground,
of course."

"But it's *me!*" affirmed Arah, helping Azariah off the camel, which
had knelt down.

Azariah brushed the dust off his cloak and put both hands on
Arah's shoulders. "No, can't be. Much too tall." Then he snapped his
fingers. "Perhaps you're his older brother?"

Arah was beside himself. "I don't have a brother."

"Well, then," said Azariah, "then it can't be you, can it?" He looked
around the dooryard. "I don't suppose old Eli is around, is he?"

Arah frowned. "Arah would know, if he was here, but as you said, he
isn't."

"And what are you doing here, Son?"

Arah let out an exasperated sigh. "Talking to myself, I guess." He
turned away.

Azariah grabbed his sleeve, turning him back. "You're not as good at
being teased as you used to be, my boy."

Arah looked at the dirt at his feet. "I'm not used to it, I guess."

"It's the price you must pay to earn your present," said Azariah.

Arah looked up. "Present?"

Azariah reached into the leather pack on the camel's back and
brought down a small chest. It was made of black wood, richly inlaid

with filigrees of gold and silver in curious arcs and swirls, mesmerizing in their complexity. He magically produced a key and slipped it into the lock, opening it. Inside were a number of precious stones, dusky red and opalescent green and honey yellow and brilliant white. Azariah dug through the gems and found what he was looking for. He raised his hand, and Arah saw a silver ring featuring a smooth, milky blue stone. He handed it to Arah, who held it up, turning it this way and that.

"It's called tourmaline, I think," said Azariah. "It has traveled very far to find you."

"It's beautiful," said Arah. "Is it valuable?"

"Not so valuable as gems go, but it reminded me of you."

Arah looked up. "Why?"

"Because it's blue like the sea."

Arah nodded. Last time Azariah had come by, after dinner the two of them had sat on the low stone dooryard wall watching the sunset. Arah had asked if, in his travels, Azariah had ever met anyone who could interpret dreams. Azariah shook his head but said, "Why don't you share the dream with me? If I meet a soothsayer, I'll see what he says about it."

Arah had related a dream he'd had several times: He was in a small boat on Lake Gennesaret with his father. They were fishing, casting the net and hauling it back in. The sky was a cloudless blue, and the sun re-flected brightly off the still water. There was nothing more to the dream, nothing to even really wonder about, yet he'd had it at least five times. He felt a dream that came back that many times must have a meaning, yet he was unable to discern one. It puzzled and disturbed him and made him feel he was missing something important. "What does it mean?" he'd asked.

Azariah had leaned forward and clasped his hands together, think-ing. He didn't speak for so long that Arah almost asked him again, but then he straightened, turned to Arah, and said simply, "Water is life, Son. You and your father were out on the water. You are alive."

"And so is my father?"

"He's alive, Arah. His soul is, at least. Believe it."

Arah felt a catch in his throat. He'd been orphaned for many years now, and the image of his dead father never left his mind for very long. His appearances in Arah's dreams led Arah to believe his father's spirit had something to say to him, but in the dream his father never spoke to him; he just smiled. Arah nodded, unsure. "I try to believe, Azariah. I do."

"That is all you *can* do, Son."

Jeshua leaned into the pry bar, but still the stone would not budge. He armed sweat away and turned to his co-worker Ibhar. "I can't get this alone. Help me."

Ibhar backed away, raising his bony hands. Jeshua shoved the bar between the rock and wall and pried until the handle was flat against the wall and his knuckles were bloody. Then he let the bar drop, sucked blood from a cut, and crawled out of the narrow alcove.

"There isn't room for me in there," said Ibhar defensively.

"Well, it's not coming out anyway," said Jeshua, his hands throbbing. The lamp flame flickered in the faint, dusty light. Just then, another loud report came from above and the room shook. "It's not safe down here when they're moving stone up above," said Ibhar, looking up and getting a face full of dirt for his trouble.

Jeshua shook his head. "It does seem like a lot of trouble, just to bury two men."

"So, now that you've been in Hades for a while, what do you think of it?"

"I thought it would be hotter," said Jeshua, looking back over his shoulder. Ibhar was eyeing the entrance to the small cave. "I could use some help in there," said Jeshua mildly.

Ibhar nodded but didn't turn. His eyes were still on his escape route. Dirt rained down on them as another marble block thudded above.

Jeshua turned back to the stone, which bulged out into the small cavern. As big as a wine cask, it should have come out by now—and would have, in Jeshua's estimation, if Ibhar would lend a hand. But the rail-thin man wasn't inclined today, or any day, as Jeshua had seen.

Jeshua jammed the bar back into its socket. Ibhar had been in the cisterns a month, Jeshua just a couple of days. Jeshua knew he could not fully appreciate the terror and darkness down here in that short time. All the cistern workers considered themselves condemned men, though only one man had died on the job thus far, and that was because he fell off a scaffold aboveground. No one had been buried alive. Yet.

Kneeling, Jeshua pushed on the pry bar, gritting his teeth. Suddenly, the rock shuddered and tumbled out of its socket, hitting the ground with a resounding thud. Ibhar cursed and dived for the doorway, kicking the lamp over. From outside, Jeshua heard him yelling, "Cave-in! Cave-in!"

Jeshua groped for the lamp in the darkness. "I'm all right."

Soon a lamp lit the doorway. Ibhar poked his head inside.

"Over here," said Jeshua, beckoning. "Look."

Ibhar crawled in with the lamp. There, split like an apricot, was the stone, and in its center a cavity sparkling in the yellow lamplight.

"A geode!" said Ibhar.

Jeshua lightly touched the faceted crystal spires, which refracted purple and blue.

"It's good luck," said Ibhar.

Jeshua felt his toes, where the stone had grazed them. "That's for certain."

Just then Judah appeared in the doorway. "Jeshua! They said there was a cave-in! Are you all right?"

"I'm fine," said Jeshua.

"Are you hurt?"

"No," said Jeshua, waving him forward. "Look what we found."

Judah stepped forward. "A geode!" he exclaimed, running his hands lightly across the crystals. "This is valuable."

"How valuable?" asked Ibhar.

"Look! The stone split in two perfect halves," said Judah.

"How valuable?" repeated Ibhar.

Jeshua said, "Whatever we get for it, we'll split between us."

"Equally?"

Judah frowned at Ibhar. "Did you help him dig it out, Ibhar?"

Ibhar looked at the ground and said nothing.

Jeshua said, "He helped."

Judah took the lamp and held it up before Ibhar's face. "Did you?"

Ibhar shook his head.

Judah shoved the lamp at him. "Take this, like you'll take my brother's generosity. Unearned."

"Now, Judah," said Jeshua.

"I'm glad *you're* not hurt, Jeshua," said Judah, scowling at Ibhar.

"So am I," said Zoar. They all turned. Zoar's stocky form filled the doorway. "Dead workers cost money. What have you found here?"

"A geode," said Jeshua.

"Pull it out." Judah and Jeshua rolled the stone halves out into the larger cavern. A dozen workmen stood about, holding torches. Zoar examined the stones, running his fingers over the crystal cavity. "This will make a nice ornament for the ethnarch's home."

"It's Jeshua's," said Judah.

"And mine," squeaked Ibhar.

"It belongs to the ethnarch," said Zoar. "You were working for him when you found it."

"Roman law says any treasure found by a worker while digging for another purpose belongs to the worker," said Judah.

Zoar waved the idea away. "This isn't treasure. It's just a rock." He nodded at two men, who brought a wheelbarrow over. They hoisted the two halves of the stone into it and carted them away.

"That's not fair!" exclaimed Judah.

"Do you like it down here, Judah?" asked Zoar. "Because this hole can accommodate you too."

"I don't care—"

"Wait," said Jeshua, stepping between Judah and Zoar. "He's got no say in the matter. Do you, Judah?" Their eyes met. Judah was angry, but finally shook his head. "Good," said Jeshua, turning back to Zoar. "No one was hurt. That is sufficient for me."

"Wisdom, for once," said Zoar. He turned to the other men. "While I have you gathered here, I have something to say. As I foresaw, we were not paid last week. The Sabbath is just five days away. Only a fool would believe we will be paid then." He glared at Jeshua, then turned and disappeared into the darkness.

Judah turned to Jeshua, but Jeshua raised his hand, silencing his brother. "I'm too tired right now—can we argue about this later?"

Judah let out an exasperated sigh. "Maybe Zoar's right about you." He stomped away.

"So Zoar is really taking the stone for himself?" asked Ibhar.

"Yes," said Jeshua, "but there might be another one. Let's go look."

Ibhar backed away. "I'm not going back in there. That was too close," he said, looking at the low-ceiling cavity, now completely dark, like the maw of some monster, white stones protruding from the walls like sharp teeth.

Jeshua furrowed his brow, took the lamp from Ibhar, got down on his knees, and entered the cavity. Ibhar watched him disappear into the monster's mouth.

At the end of the day, on the road home, Jeshua and Judah picked their way around mud holes. A midday cloudburst had drenched the city and countryside alike. And though the bank of gray clouds had moved on to the east, Judah remained glum. Jeshua, for his part, was happy to be out in the fresh air after a long day choking on limestone dust in the cisterns. The sun was setting, creating a collage of oranges and reds against the fleeing clouds. Jeshua grabbed Judah's arm and said, pointing at the horizon, "Look. Isn't it glorious?"

Judah nodded, and his eyes went back to the road at his feet.

Jeshua looked at Judah. "She can't stay mad at you forever."

"Apparently she can."

"Deep connections make for strong feelings."

Judah shook his head. "She said I make her sick."

Jeshua nodded. "Judah, what's the opposite of love?"

"Jeshua, please. Don't start."

Jeshua stopped to watch the sunset. Judah continued on a couple of steps, then turned back. He put his toolbox down and looked back at his brother, noticing the layer of white limestone dust that powdered the shoulders of his tunic. Even though for five years Judah had been a full head taller than Jeshua, when they stood like this he still felt smaller.

Jeshua shielded the sun's rays with his hand. "It's so beautiful."

Judah took a breath. "I guess the opposite of love is hate. Right?"

"Wrong," said Jeshua, still looking at the horizon.

"Then you tell me."

"I think you know, Judah."

Judah exhaled sharply. "I'm too tired for riddles."

"Humor me, Judah. It's important."

"Isn't everything you say?" said Judah testily.

Jeshua's face showed hurt. Without a word, he picked up his toolbox and started down the road. Judah grabbed his sleeve, stopping him. "I'm sorry. I didn't mean that."

Jeshua looked at him. "It must be hard being second oldest."

"It wouldn't be so bad if I wasn't second to *you.*"

Jeshua nodded.

"See?" said Judah. "Like that! You're so . . . so . . . infuriatingly *agreeable!*"

Jeshua couldn't contain a smile. "Would it make you feel better if I argued with you?"

"Frankly? Yes!"

"Well, I'm trying to, Judah. I asked you a question. You answered it, and I said you were wrong. How much more disagreeable would you like me to be? Should I toss you in a mud hole? Twist your arm and pluck out your hair? Call you names? What? I just want to know what evil I have to do to you to get on your good side."

"Quit mocking me. I'm serious."

"Yes, you are. Too serious. So answer the question, and let's get on with this fight. What is the opposite of love?"

Judah shook his head. Anything to get this over with so he could go home, lie down, and suffer his broken heart in peace. "You tell me."

"It's indifference," said Jeshua.

"How is that?"

"Love is an intense emotion. So is hate. But indifference is the absence of emotion. You just don't care—you know, the way you're feeling right now about what I'm saying."

"So you're saying that because Dinah is angry with me, I should be glad? Thanks."

"She has strong feelings for you. If she didn't, she wouldn't be losing sleep over it."

Judah looked up. "She's losing sleep?"

"Her little sister told me. Dinah is moping around, not doing her chores, angry at everyone. Sounds like you, and you're in love. *Ergo,* as the Romans say: she must be in love too."

"Maybe, but I don't think she's in love with me."

"She is, but sometimes pride overshadows love."

"Pride?"

"You embarrassed her in public that day, Judah."

"I thought I was being romantic, giving her that laurel garland," said Judah. "How can she be mad at me for telling her I love her?"

"You did it in front of your friends. She probably thought you were doing it for show. Or maybe she isn't ready to hear about love yet. You must be patient."

"Patient? It's been two weeks, and she hasn't spoken a word to me!"

"She might be testing you, to see if you can wait a little."

Judah scowled and kicked at a stone. "Who is she to test me?"

"She's the woman you love. Seems to me she has every right to test your love. It's quite a risk for a woman to give her life to a man."

"What's risky about me?"

The distant jingling of bells interrupted Jeshua's answer. At this time of evening, most of the traffic on the road flowed out of Sepphoris, toward Nazareth and Cana and the other small villages surrounding the capital. But here came a long line of camels and horses, all wearing colorful woven blankets with golden piping. Leading them was a small, round man dressed all in red, from his turban to his pointed shoes. Alongside him rode a boy on a black and white horse. Jeshua and Judah stepped off the road to let the entourage pass. Jeshua sat on a rock, massaging his aching calves.

"Jeshua?"

Jeshua looked up. The caravan had stopped, and the boy on the mottled horse was gaping at him, a silhouette in the setting sun. His curly hair formed a nimbus around his head, but there was something familiar about the tenor of his voice. "It's me, Arah!" said the boy, jumping off the horse and running to Jeshua, hugging him tightly.

Jeshua pulled away and looked at Arah, who was almost as tall as he was. "Arah! What a surprise!" He turned to Judah. "Judah, this is Arah, from Eli's estate, in Ruma."

Arah smiled proudly. "I'm going to Sepphoris with Azariah." He turned and helped Azariah off his kneeling camel. Azariah approached Jeshua and touched his forehead, bowing low. "Peace be unto you, Jeshua bar Joseph."

"And unto you, peace," said Jeshua. "Have we met?"

Azariah shook his head but took Jeshua's hands in his. "Arah has often talked about you, but, alas, he lied."

Arah's jaw dropped. "Azariah! I never—"

Azariah raised a hand. "He said you were twelve cubits tall, strong as three oxen, smarter than thirty rabbis, and more handsome than I."

"All are true, except the last part," laughed Jeshua.

Arah relaxed. "I'm helping Azariah for a few days in Sepphoris."

Jeshua nodded at the horizon, which glowed a pale orange. The sun had disappeared behind the rolling hills. "Then we'd better not keep you. You have a ways to go tonight, and there are robbers on the road."

Arah smiled. "Azariah doesn't fear robbers."

"Yes, I do!" laughed Azariah. "But fortunately, my men do not." He nodded at his Arab servants, each of whom was tall and muscled and fearsome looking.

"Where are you going?" asked Arah.

Jeshua pointed south, to where the road wound up the mountainside. "Nazareth."

"You still live there?"

"Yes," said Jeshua. "With my parents, sisters, and brothers."

"We've got a brother about your age, Arah," said Judah.

"Can I come with you?" Arah blurted out. He turned to Azariah. "May I take my leave?"

Azariah looked at Jeshua. "Are you coming to town tomorrow?"

Jeshua nodded. "Yes. And we'd love to have Arah stay with us, if it is acceptable to you, Azariah. You too are welcome."

"It is out of my way. I need to be in Sepphoris for the market early tomorrow morning. But take Arah with you. He wears me out with his questions. Perhaps you can take a turn answering a few."

Judah clapped Jeshua on the shoulder. "It's his specialty!" Then he turned to Arah. "You aren't in love, are you, Arah?"

Arah blushed and shook his head.

Dinner was a raucous affair. It usually was, at Joseph's house, with so many children and so little space. Looking around at the tiny rooms surrounding the small, dirt courtyard, Arah was genuinely surprised. He had imagined that Jeshua lived in a grand stone house, with ornate furniture, heavy brocaded tapestries, and many servants. But it was a simple mud-brick home, neatly stuccoed and clean, but no bigger than the servants' quarters where Arah lived on Eli's estate. Indeed, Arah was disappointed when he saw the home's main entrance. It did not boast a fine, dark mahogany door, with black iron hinges and locks, like the one Jeshua had built for Master Eli. It was just an old, worn oak door, badly scratched on the outside, hanging by tired-looking leather hinges. At that moment Arah finally accepted the fact that Jeshua was just a carpenter, and he was greatly disappointed. He'd built him up so large in his mind that Azariah's joke on the road about his being twelve cubits tall was not far off the mark.

As Arah unbridled his horse in the tiny stable, Joseph came out of his workshop across the courtyard. He put his hands on Arah's shoulders and looked into his eyes for a long moment before pronouncing his judgment. "He's hungry!" he said, hugging Arah as if he were one of his own, then leading them all into the dining area.

Once seated at the low table, Arah was surprised at the ritual that unfolded. It felt like a seder, which in Jewish homes take place but once a year, at Passover. The boys, Judah, Joses, and James, sat on one side of the rectangular table. The girls, Salome, Sarah, Miriam, and little Hannah, sat opposite them. Joseph and Mary occupied a third side, and Arah and Jeshua had the fourth to themselves. The candles on a small menorah were lit, and Joseph reached for Mary's hand. Soon Arah felt a small, warm hand take his, and he and saw little Miriam looking up at him, her face framed by tight, dark curls and her eyes bright with curiosity. He squeezed her hand gently. On his other side, Jeshua took his hand.

"Your guest, Jeshua," said Joseph.

Jeshua bowed his head and prayed.

In later years, Arah would often reflect on that prayer. It was like no prayer he'd ever heard. He could not remember the words, but he never forgot the way it touched him. Beyond the darkness of his closed eyes, Arah thought he sensed a brightness filling the room. If he opened them, he fully expected to see God himself sitting across the table. Arah's fingertips tingled, and he remembered when he last felt this much love. It was the day they finished the front door at Master Eli's estate. Reuben, the prodigal son, had appeared in the distance, trudging down the dusty road, shoeless and dirty. Eli saw him, threw down his staff, and jumped over the low stone wall, running toward him. He scooped Reuben into his arms. As Arah watched the joyful reunion, it was as if he himself were once again in the arms of his own father. As Eli hugged Reuben, crying his name over and over, tears spilled from Arah's eyes, for he couldn't help but hope that someday he would feel his own father's arms around him.

Finally, when Arah could resist no longer, he opened his eyes. Everyone's head was bowed except Joseph's. He was looking thoughtfully at Jeshua, who prayed with his eyes closed and his luminous face turned upward. When Joseph felt Arah looking at him, he closed his eyes and bowed his head again.

When Jeshua finished praying, little Miriam said, "Ow!"

Arah turned. Miriam was massaging her hand. "Too hard," she said, but she was still smiling up at him.

"Sorry," said Arah.

After dinner Joseph gave the boys their evening chores. Joses complained but went to the workshop to put another coat of stain on a piece of furniture. Judah went outside, and Arah heard him shout something about water jars. The girls cleaned up and disappeared, except for Miriam, who hung around Arah and Jeshua, smiling.

"That's enough," said Mary, gesturing at Miriam. "Leave them alone."

Miriam ran from the room. Jeshua said, "You have an admirer."

"And you have a wonderful family, Jeshua."

"Thank you," said Mary from behind him.

Arah turned quickly. "I'm sorry. It is *your* family."

Mary smiled and brought them a plate of honeyed barley cake. Arah took a square, as did Jeshua. Just then James's voice came from outside. "Mother! It's the widow Esther."

Mary went to the door. Esther appeared, her thin, frail form bent over her cane. "Esther!" said Mary, embracing the little woman. Both Jeshua and Arah stood, and Jeshua guided Esther to his chair. Arah nodded at Mary to sit, but Mary bustled around, finding a pitcher of water and a cup, which she filled and gave to Esther, who seemed to delight in the attention.

Esther took Jeshua's hand and held it tightly, looking up into his face. "I wanted you to know. I've been to see the ethnarch—five times now, every day in fact—and he is putting my affairs aright."

Jeshua looked at Mary, whose face showed doubt. She nodded at him to sit, and he did so. "I'm very glad," said Jeshua. "The ethnarch. Now that *is* something."

"I'm quite sure he will settle Ezra's matter with that viper, Ishmael."

"I hope so," said Jeshua, "but Ishmael is a wealthy man—he's bound to know the ethnarch."

"So?" asked Esther.

"Well," said Jeshua gently, "the ethnarch is not exactly a friend to the Jews."

"What Jeshua is trying to say, Esther, is that you mustn't get your hopes up too much," said Mary, patting the old woman on the shoulder.

Esther looked around in surprise. "I cannot believe what I'm hearing! A great injustice has been done. The Lord has promised to avenge our enemies if we are faithful, and I have been. I attend synagogue, I keep the commandments, I am generous with my offerings. I'm doing my part—faith can move mountains, you know."

Jeshua nodded. "But moving a mountain can take a long time, Esther."

"And Ishmael is made of the hardest stone," added Mary.

"Rabbi Sadoc said I would receive justice soon," said Esther.

"Rabbi Sadoc," repeated Jeshua.

"Yes," continued Esther, leaning in. "You know how much I admire you, Jeshua." She patted his hand. "I have never doubted the story of your miraculous birth. I've seen the kind of man you've become, and even though you haven't studied, I think you're as wise as any rabbi. So I'm surprised. I expected you to confirm what Rabbi Sadoc told me. Are you saying he's wrong—that the Lord will not grant me justice?"

Jeshua shook his head. "No, but you must be patient—"

"Patience is a virtue," said Esther. "But now it's time for justice, don't you agree?"

Jeshua looked at her for a long moment before he slowly nodded.

"You're always in our prayers," confirmed Mary.

"Then I cannot be denied," said Esther, taking her cane and getting to her feet.

"I'll see you home," said Mary, grabbing a shawl and leading Esther out into the darkness.

Arah turned to Jeshua. "Miraculous birth?"

Jeshua shook his head, waving the comment away.

James ran into the room, beckoning Arah. "Arah! Come here!"

Jeshua touched Arah's arm in warning. "He's not to be trusted, Arah," he said gravely.

"Jeshua!" countered James. Then, to Arah, "Come on. I want to show you something!" He grabbed Arah and pulled him from the room. They ran across the courtyard and exited the far end. "Someone's coming!" hissed James, pulling Arah into the shadows. They hid behind a gnarled olive tree across the street and peered out, James on one side and Arah on the other. "It's Judah!" whispered James.

Judah was approaching, lugging a heavy water jar. He entered the courtyard, set it down near a half dozen others, and called out to the darkness, "The jars are full and *I* did it! Hah!" Then he strode into the house.

James chuckled. "I've been playing a trick on my brother. I'm filling the water jars."

"What kind of trick is that?"

"He thinks I'm doing it, but he can't prove it," laughed James. "But now, they're going to start *emptying* themselves! He'll be so mad!"

Arah shook his head. "Why do you want to make him mad? What did he do to you?"

James looked at him in dismay. "He's my *brother*, Arah."

Later, when they were getting ready for bed, Arah and James climbed up the ladder to sleep on the flat roof because the house below was full. The sky was full of stars, and the waxing quarter moon hung just above the eastern horizon. The boys spread their blankets and lay down. "What did that lady mean about Jeshua's miraculous birth?" asked Arah.

James shrugged. "We're not supposed to talk about it."

"But Jeshua is a friend of mine."

"Then ask him about it," said James, looking at the sky.

Arah let out a sigh. "You know he won't tell me. Please, won't you?"

James got up on one arm, facing Arah. "All right, but you can't tell anyone. Promise."

"I promise."

"Well," said James, "Jeshua was born in a little town near Jerusalem called Bethlehem."

"Never heard of it," said Arah.

"Several rich and wise men came to see him, even though he was just a baby. He was lying in a manger, with Mother and Father."

"They were all in a feed trough?" asked Arah, teasing.

"No!" said James, chuckling at the image. "Only Jeshua. They were staying in a stable because the inns in Jerusalem were full. It was during the census, where they count everyone."

"Oh," said Arah, still wondering what was miraculous about that.

"Anyway, the men brought gifts of gold and spices. Mother still has the little wooden chest that contained the myrrh."

That's nice, but it's not miraculous, thought Arah.

"There was a star," said James, leaning back and lacing his fingers behind his head, looking up at the dazzling night sky. "In the east. Brighter than any other. And it moved."

"Was it a falling star?"

"No," said James. "It didn't fall. It traveled along the sky, like the moon does, until it stopped right over where Jeshua was asleep."

Arah looked up at the field of stars. At that moment, in the corner of his eye, he saw a falling star angle across the black sky and disappear. "That's miraculous, I guess," he said, humoring James.

"And there were angels," said James flatly.

Arah sat up. "What?"

James shrugged. "Angels. They were singing."

"You're lying!" said Arah.

"I am not."

"Then whoever told you this was lying. Nobody sees angels anymore."

James shook his head. "My mother did. So did my father."

"I don't believe you," said Arah.

James shrugged. "The angels told them about Jeshua's birth and even what to name him. His name means *Jehovah is salvation.*"

Arah lay back and looked up at the stars. James was the same boy who an hour ago was playing pranks on his brother Judah. Now he was telling Arah that Jeshua was born amid traveling stars and choruses of angels.

"Is it true?" asked Arah, still looking up at the twinkling stars.

"Well, you know Jeshua," said James.

I thought I did, thought Arah, his mind whirling.

Arah dreamed the dream.

They were in the little boat on Lake Gennesaret. The sky was a vibrant, uninterrupted blue. His father tossed the net into the cool water, and both of them pulled it in, straining in the hot sun, the light reflecting off the water, sweat dripping down their bare backs.

The net was full not of fish but of tiny, sparkling stars. Arah reached for one that was brighter than the rest. It moved away from his fingertips, slipping through the net interstices, until it was free in the cool, undulating water, receding until it disappeared, winking out.

It was a traveling star, like Jeshua's.

SEVEN

Eyes and Ears

Approaching the crest overlooking the Netofa Valley, Arah couldn't
help sneaking a look at Jeshua. Just think of it! Choruses of angels,
singing hosannas at his birth! And wise men, laden with precious gifts,
appearing in the doorway of a hay-strewn stable, then kneeling to present little chests of gold and vials of rare ointments to Mary, who held a
child to her bosom whose name had been selected by God himself! Arah
wondered if Jeshua had any memory of the event. Was he a baby like all
babies, who gurgled and suckled mindlessly at his mother's breast, or did
he have understanding even at that early age?

Jeshua walked along, deep in thought. Arah wanted to ask him
about these things, but something restrained him. He knew if he asked,
James would get in trouble for telling him the story. He also knew
Jeshua would probably just shake his head and shrug or, worse, say
something that Arah wouldn't understand.

Just then, Jeshua looked up. "I've missed you." He reached out and
touched Arah on the shoulder.

Arah's eyes inexplicably filled with tears. He blinked them away. "I
missed you too."

"Are you still praying?"

The boy nodded. "But the answers are slow in coming."

Jeshua's eyes got a faraway look in them. He nodded. "They certainly are."

• • •

As they walked up the colonnaded *cardo* in Sepphoris, Arah's excitement became contagious. Even Judah, who was still moody about Dinah, had to smile as he watched Arah running up the street, weaving in and out of the columns. Arah eyed the delicate blue crystal for sale in one shop, the fine leather goods in another, the beautiful linen robes in a third. He'd never seen so many people in one place in his life. "How many people live here?" he asked Judah.

"Maybe ten thousand."

Arah shook his head. "All Jews?"

Judah said, "No. Greeks, Arabs, Syrians, a few from a place called Gaul. And Romans."

"Mostly Romans," said Arah, looking around at the number of people wearing togas. He stopped as they emerged into the wide forum. "What's that?" he asked, pointing at a tall, columned building with a golden statue perched above the pediment apex.

"That's Jupiter's temple."

"Who's he?"

"He's the king of the Roman gods. They've got a god for everything: home, hunting, business, agriculture, the sea and water, even war."

Arah frowned. "And we've only got one."

Judah said, "But I've seen their god. He's just a big statue, inside that building."

"Like in the Temple in Jerusalem, where Jehovah lives?" asked Arah.

Judah shook his head. "Jehovah doesn't *live* in the Temple. He isn't a statue, either."

The forum opened up before them. Grocers' stalls lined the perimeter of the great square. Every sort of fruit and vegetable was for sale, and long wooden tables were laden with fresh fish. They walked between rows of merchants, finding it difficult to hear each other above the din of the marketplace. Hawkers shouted their prices, shoppers haggled in loud, angry voices, two minstrels sang a sad dirge about a lost love, and above it all, the clang and clash of iron on stone on the other side of the forum, in front of the new basilica.

They were almost out of the marketplace, and still Arah had not seen Azariah. Then he glimpsed a flash of red to his left, turned, and spied Azariah's immense turban. The small man was looking up at a customer, a tall man in a white toga. They were arguing over something the man held in his hands. Before them were several tables, draped in colorful tapestries, full of all manner of trinkets, cookware, fine silks, and leather goods. As he drew closer, Arah saw that the man was holding several strands of delicate gold chain.

Azariah shook his head, made to turn, and saw Arah. He took the gold chains from the man and waved him away. The man left, disappointed. But Azariah was in good humor. He bowed before Jeshua and Judah and said, "Why don't they simply rob me on the road?"

"No sale?" asked Jeshua, watching the man in the white toga walking away.

"He'll be back," said Azariah, putting the chain back into the little black chest held out for him by one of his servants. Then he turned to Arah. "Did you pass the night well?"

Arah nodded.

Judah leaned forward. "If only he had slept. It was nearly as loud there as it is here!"

They all laughed. Azariah turned to Jeshua. "Something I forgot to ask you yesterday. It seems you and I have a mutual acquaintance. Do you know a Samaritan merchant named Zebulon?"

Jeshua nodded. "We met at the Qelt Inn last fall. How is he?"

"He had nothing but the highest praise for your work, as well as your *other* powers."

"What powers?" asked Arah.

Azariah looked intently at Jeshua. "He said you healed many hearts at the inn."

Jeshua turned to Arah. "One evening Zebulon brought in a traveler he'd found on the Jericho Road who'd been nearly killed by robbers. He was healed, thanks to the Master of the Universe."

Azariah nodded. "He said you had a great deal to do with his healing."

"I just bound his wounds," said Jeshua, "nothing more."

"No, my humble friend," said Azariah. "There was much more. The robbers blinded him in one eye. Zebulon said he was healed because of *your* prayers."

"A prayer can change a life," said Arah, remembering Jeshua's prayer last night.

"Look," said Jeshua, eager to change the subject. "The ethnarch."

They all turned. Marcus and Neri stood on the broad basilica porch. They made a comical pair: the ethnarch, tall and regal, and Neri, next to him, round and red as a pomegranate.

"Surveying their domain," snorted Azariah.

"We should get to work," said Jeshua.

Marcus said, "Call me when they're ready to raise the next pillar. I want to watch."

Neri nodded as Marcus turned to go. Just then, a man dressed in a simple white worker's tunic by the fountain pointed directly at him. Next to him was the red turbaned man Neri had seen in the king's tower a few weeks ago. Also present was another *tekton* and a tall, dark-haired boy. Soon all four of them were looking at him. A chill coursed down Neri's spine. As he watched, the two *tektons* bid the merchant good-bye and turned toward the basilica.

A cold hand on the back of Neri's neck turned him around and steered him behind a column. He peeked out. The merchant had his back to him, talking to the boy. The taller, light-haired *tekton* was entering the alley between the basilica and the bank, but the other worker, the dark one with the short curly hair, was heading toward the basilica steps. Neri pulled back, his pulse racing.

He wanted to step out from behind the column, stride confidently down the steps, and speak to the man, but he was afraid. He almost laughed. Afraid? Of what? A lowly worker? And a Jew, besides, from the look of him. What did Neri have to be afraid of?

He almost stepped out into plain sight when the cold hand squeezed his neck firmly and turned him around again, guiding him into the cool darkness of the basilica. As he walked across the dimly lit interior, Neri wondered, *What in Zeus's name is going on here?*

Sadoc stood behind the curtain, peering out at the forum from his upstairs window. Marcus and his scribe, Neri, were on the basilica porch. When Marcus turned to leave, Sadoc focused on the scribe. He knew very little about Neri. Ishmael spoke of him in derogatory tones, saying he was Marcus's toady and therefore worthless as a contact.

Ishmael had a tendency to quickly size people up and dismiss them, but Sadoc was a much better student of human nature. Even though his chosen career was outwardly nonpolitical, he knew that everything was political. In order to ascend the ladder of power, one had to know powerful people. And he had carefully worked to do so. Ishmael was one of his conquests. But it was difficult to get to know the ethnarch. If Sadoc was ever seen at Marcus's villa or walking up the steps of the new basilica, word would get around so quickly that the Sanhedrin would probably convene that very night to sanction him.

No, he could not risk the rumor that he was friendly with the Roman administrator. The Jewish mob trusted only those who despised and hated the Romans. And so Sadoc had to be subtle. He used Ishmael as his connection with Marcus, which rankled him. Ishmael was clever, but he was quick to judge, and he missed many nuances and subtleties. Sadoc did not.

Sadoc could not dismiss Neri as blithely as did Ishmael. Something about the man interested him. Neri always bowed and scraped and walked a humble step behind Marcus, but Sadoc noted that Neri also whispered discreetly into the ethnarch's ear. Only a fool would believe that Marcus was the ruler he pretended to be. He spent little time tending to his duties. While he attended the theater and the coliseum chariot races and vacationed on the beach at Caesarea Maritima, Neri no doubt worried over the day-to-day matters of governing Sepphoris. The proof was in the city itself. It ran smoothly, and since Marcus was rarely around—except at formal occasions—Sadoc knew Neri must be the power behind the judgment seat. And Sadoc must somehow get to know him.

So he watched Neri from behind the heavy damask curtain. Neri, in turn, was watching a group of people conversing near the temple fountain. The group became aware of Neri's interest and soon broke up. The merchant and the boy continued talking, and the two Jewish *tektons* started toward the basilica. Neri turned and stepped behind a porch column, peeking out. One worker disappeared between the basilica and the bank, but the other walked to the foot of the basilica steps and looked right at the column Neri was hiding behind.

Sadoc smiled. From his vantage point, he could see both Neri and the worker. Neri appeared to be agitated. The scribe ran a hand across

his face, then turned and fled inside the basilica. The *tekton* stood for another moment at the foot of the steps, then turned away.

Sadoc wondered what had just transpired. Was Neri afraid of the
worker? If so, why? Sadoc made a mental note to discover the identity of
the man who had intimidated the ethnarch's scribe with a mere glance.

Then Sadoc looked up and was shocked to see the ethnarch himself
in an upper-story basilica window, looking directly at him.

And smiling.

Sadoc ducked behind the curtain. He waited until the ethnarch's face
disappeared from the basilica window, then went quickly downstairs,
grabbed his staff, left the synagogue, and strode across the forum. Why
was the ethnarch in that window? What had he seen? What did Neri
know? And who was the worker who seemed to be everyone's focus?

Sadoc strode past the curve of the theater walls, toward the bubbling
fountain and the array of goods carefully arranged on tapestries draped
over wooden tables. Azariah was talking to the tall boy, giving him a
couple of coins and pointing toward the *cardo*. The boy tucked the coins
inside his tunic and trotted off. Azariah turned as Sadoc approached.

"Azariah!" said Sadoc. "I thought that was you! How long have you
been back?"

"Just got in last night, Rabbi," said Azariah, adjusting his turban
self-consciously.

Sadoc looked the merchant over. "I see you've adopted the dress of
the eastern provinces. I thought you were Nabatean at first."

"Business reasons," said Azariah quietly. "No one wants to traffic
with Jews, you know."

"Except other Jews," winked Sadoc.

Azariah shrugged.

"I understand, my friend," said Sadoc, putting his thin, bony hand
on Azariah's shoulder.

Azariah looked up, pleased, then reached into his tunic and withdrew a money pouch. "I won't be here for the Sabbath, so . . ." He
placed five denarii coins in Sadoc's hand. "I've had a successful trip."

"Oh?" said Sadoc, pocketing the coins. "Where have you been?"

"All over. Petra. Samaria. Tiberias."

"Tiberias?" said Sadoc. "I heard the ethnarch was just there a few
weeks ago."

Azariah nodded. "Three weeks. I saw him there, along with his scribe, who was skulking around the throne room when I arrived."

"Skulking?"

"I recognized him, but I don't think he knows who I am. Just as well. I'm suspicious of men like him. They profit by telling their master what he wants to hear and soon forget the difference between the truth and a lie. But the master must know the difference, if he wants to remain the master."

Sadoc smiled and nodded. "You are a good judge of people, Azariah."

Azariah shrugged. "It's my business."

"I wish I had your talent," said Sadoc. "I'm always being taken advantage of."

"Well, you come to me for business advice," laughed Azariah, "and I will see you on spiritual matters."

"That would please me greatly, friend." Sadoc bowed and turned away.

Azariah watched the lanky, almost bone-thin rabbi stride across the forum, his dark cloak billowing out behind him as he walked, his long staff punctuating his steps. *That wasn't just a chance meeting*, he thought. Just minutes ago, the subject of Sadoc's interest, Neri, stood on the basilica steps, looking at them. Now Sadoc appears, asking questions about the man.

I wonder what kind of web that old spider's spinning? thought Azariah.

Hanock stood just inside the solid bank doors. A year ago, the bank was one of the most impressive buildings in Sepphoris. Now, compared to the new basilica going up next door, it was just another collection of fluted columns atop marble steps.

The bank was mostly empty. Doors along both side walls led to offices, where the money changers worked. Only a few were open this early. Hanock saw a man pouring a bag of tiny black quadrans, the least valuable coin of the realm, into a large clay jar. Another passed him carrying two large bags marked with the silver denarius symbol, a day's wage in the empire.

Hanock fingered a gold denarius in his purse, enough to live on handsomely for a month, food and lodging and all. But the coin was nothing compared to the wealth in any one office he was walking past. And every coin in the changers' offices could be multiplied by ten and still not equal the fifty talents Marcus had entrusted to him, now sitting in the darkness of the stone vault below this building.

Suddenly the image of being buried alive under a mountain of drachmas, shekels, kordantes, and prutahs filled Hanock's mind. He saw himself gasping for breath, kicking, trying to push himself up through a cold ocean of glittering coins. They covered his eyes and stopped his ears and filled his mouth, the tinny taste of silver and the acid taste of gold melting on his tongue, until he suffocated, the wealthiest man in the world, drowned in prosperity.

"Hanock?"

Hanock turned. Ocran stood before him, tall and dark, his soft features not hiding his feral nature. He extended a strong yet soft hand to Hanock. "Are you all right?"

Hanock nodded. "I'm fine."

"I'm so glad." Ocran gestured toward a large door at the rear of the hall. They passed through it and turned right toward another, smaller door, which was guarded by two soldiers with sharp lances. The soldiers glared at Hanock as they passed.

"Never mind them," whispered Ocran as they descended the stone steps. "They do that to remind you what you're doing here."

"I don't need reminding," said Hanock.

They continued down until they stood on a landing. Ocran lit a torch from a wall sconce, and they entered the outer chamber. A man in armor sat in the darkness, a sword across his lap. He stood, and Hanock knew why he had been sitting: he was too tall to stand erect in the low room. Yet Ocran, who was also very tall, could walk upright without bending. The guard's face was clean shaven, as was his head, which glistened in the torchlight. His neck was thick and corded, and his shoulders were those of an Atlas. With a massive hand, he picked up his stool and held it while Ocran and Hanock passed, then set it back down in front of the door and sat, his back to them, once again staring blankly ahead.

The vault was a large room with many cells carved into the granite walls. Each cell had a black gate secured with an iron lock. Hanock withdrew a large key that hung on a leather cord around his neck, inserted it into the lock, and opened the gate. They stepped inside the alcove, and Ocran held the torch higher. A bronze-banded, ornately carved wooden chest filled the alcove. Hanock produced a key and opened it. Soon, Ocran's torchlight was multiplied by the golden talents lying in the chest on a bed of black velvet. He let out an appreciative whistle. "What do you have in mind?"

"Something . . . audacious. Something impressive."

Ocran shook his head. "Hanock, this money is already audacious and impressive. Didn't the ethnarch tell you what to do with it?"

Hanock frowned at Ocran. "They want me to buy property in the Netofa."

"They?"

Hanock silently cursed himself. He'd almost given his master away. This morning, before he rode to town, Ishmael had pulled him aside and cautioned him yet again about keeping his name off any document he might sign. Hanock had nodded. He liked the idea of letting people believe he alone was in charge of the fifty talents. He reminded himself to be more careful. "The ethnarch," he said casually. "And his scribe. You know. *Them.*"

Ocran nodded, but the question still remained in his eyes. "I know of several properties that are available."

Hanock shook his head. Ishmael had given him a list of people he was to see, estates he was to try to purchase. Hanock still had the list tucked into his tunic, but on the way to Sepphoris this morning, after he'd scanned the names, a wonderful and daring thought had occurred to him. Real property would not multiply the investment quickly enough. The estates Ishmael had in mind were impressive, but they were just land, and the increase in their value would be incremental at best. And sometimes even land lost value, as Hanock knew—he owned a building that burned down last fall, the fire taking its value with it into the smoky sky.

But what if he surprised them all and found a way not just to increase the investment but perhaps to double it? He'd done it before. It wasn't too hard, but you had to keep your wits about you. He imagined himself standing before the ethnarch, flanked by not one but two large chests containing a hundred or more golden talents. Hanock smiled. At that moment, he knew he would never feel Ishmael's crop on his back again. He would bid his master good-bye and join the ethnarch's trusted inner circle. And after that, who knows? He might even advise the king one day.

"Hanock?" Ocran's voice interrupted the delightful image.

Hanock turned to the tall financier.

"I said I knew of several valley estates that are available."

Hanock dismissed the idea with a wave of the hand. "I don't need your advice on this matter."

Ocran leaned forward, his face lit by the reflected light of the coins. "Do you remember when we first met, over a year ago?"

Hanock nodded.

"I told you then that I'd made several men wealthy. Do you know how I did that?"

Hanock looked at him blankly.

"By giving them *advice*, which they *took*. You became one of those men, Hanock."

"Yes, but that was *then*. Things are different now."

"Not different at all," said Ocran, picking up a coin. "In fact, the more money one can lose, the more conservative one should be. I know. I've been trading for twenty years."

Yes, and look at you, thought Hanock. *In just one year I've earned more money than you've made in ten.* "This is a great opportunity," said Hanock, shifting his belt around his ample belly. "If I prosper, I may count the ethnarch as my friend."

Ocran laughed. "Hanock, you're a *servant*. You forget yourself."

Hanock glared at Ocran. "No, Ocran, you forget yourself. *You're* the servant—you're here to serve *me*."

"I am trying to. Let me ask you a question: Why do you think the ethnarch would entrust a fortune to a servant when right next door to his basilica is a bank full of experienced financiers?"

"There is only one answer," said Hanock. "He obviously sees talent in me that you lack."

"You really believe that?"

"Of course," said Hanock, taking the golden coin from Ocran. "You fellows are good at counting other people's money. I don't see much skill at multiplying it. It's true, last year you gave me a few good ideas, but I was the one who found the winepress. You came in with me on that deal, as I remember. And since then, I've given you more advice than you've given me. This morning is a mere formality. I asked you to meet me here because I wanted to hear it from your own mouth."

"Hear what?"

"That you have no ideas." He put the coin back into the chest and closed the lid, locking it. He turned and left the cell.

Ocran followed, and Hanock locked the door behind him. "You're making a great mistake, Hanock."

"More expert advice?"

"One more question," said Ocran, holding the torch up so he could see Hanock's round moonlike face clearly. "Has it ever occurred to you that the ethnarch may have other schemes in motion, scenarios in which you are a victim?"

Hanock laughed, not altogether convincingly.

"Because—and I say this with all due respect, Hanock—I cannot imagine why he would entrust his fortune to such a fool as you unless he wanted that fool to fail." He handed the torch to Hanock and strode from the chamber.

"But can't you pay them *something?*" pleaded Zoar. "The workers must *eat,* after all."

Marcus turned and glared at him. "They'll be paid when *I* decide. Right now I have bigger problems. I've got a ship at Caesarea that won't unload its cargo without payment. I still owe the marble merchant for *his* latest shipment. The workers can quit now and get nothing, or they can work a while longer and get everything that's owed them. It's their decision."

"But it's been weeks—"

Marcus raised his hand, silencing him, then took a seat on his chaise. "Did you think the coins I quietly slip into your hands come without any effort on your part? Your job is to quiet the workers so I don't have to hear their complaints."

"But I can only threaten a strike for so long before they call my bluff."

"What about this other worker who always opposes you, the one who counsels patience?"

Zoar's face darkened. "Jeshua. He's as predictable as sunrise, but fewer and fewer men are siding with him. Soon he will be alone and I'm afraid the workers will demand action."

Marcus nodded. "I'm glad you fear, Zoar. Instill some of that in your men."

"Sire, empty bellies make for rash judgments."

Marcus sighed heavily. "You eat well enough. And you should be more concerned about *my* judgments, Zoar. What if I should judge it time for the workers to know about our arrangement?"

Zoar went white. "You wouldn't—"

"Not if you do your job and let me do mine." Marcus turned away and began sorting through a bowl of plums for a ripe one.

Zoar stood there for a long moment, then turned and exited. He trudged down the hallway, his mind tilting madly one way and then the next. He passed Neri without a word—a rare thing, for he usually had a snide remark prepared for Neri's one good ear—and went out into the courtroom, where Barak looked up from his labors, saw the look on Zoar's face, and surmised the outcome of the meeting. Barak cursed loudly, dropped his iron maul with a loud clatter, and stormed from the room.

Neri watched Zoar walk away with his head down and was puzzled. He'd seen the man leave meetings with Marcus before, but never as a beaten dog. Angry, cursing, or triumphant, but never defeated. Neri trotted down the hall. Marcus was looking out the large window at the king's palace, the stone towers golden in the morning light.

"Are you going to pay them?" asked Neri.

Marcus didn't turn. "In due time."

Neri took a great chance then. "Sire, why don't you just pay them out of the money you got from the king?"

Suddenly, Marcus turned and backed Neri into the corner. He grabbed the man's ear and pulled him close. "Now you listen to me, you little swine," he hissed. "What I do with that money is my business. Not yours, not theirs"—he nodded toward the courtroom—"not anyone's! And if you bring it up again, I'll disembowel you and hang you by your intestines!" He let Neri's ear go, and Neri stumbled back, banging his head on the wall.

Stunned, Neri left the room. A goose egg was rising on the back of his head. He touched his ear and was not surprised when he saw blood on his fingertips. He pulled out a kerchief, placed it against his bleeding ear, and sat down at his desk to think.

Marcus's meeting with Zoar made one thing abundantly clear: Marcus had not borrowed the fifty talents to finish the basilica. And with the appearance of Hanock, whom Neri knew to be a fool, it also became clear that Ishmael, who knew Hanock best, was working some mischief against Marcus. Marcus had to see this, so why had he gone along with this, giving the money to Hanock?

Then suddenly, the knot on Neri's head ceased to throb and the pain in his ear subsided. Clarity filled his mind like a cold liquid, causing him to catch his breath and hold it. In a flash of insight, he knew the true purpose of the loan: Marcus indeed was plotting against the king, as Antipas had said. What Neri couldn't fathom was how giving fifty talents to Hanock would further that plot. Neri shook his head in disbelief. Didn't Marcus know he was placing his head on the chopping block?

And that meant Neri would be the one beheaded.

EIGHT

Open and Closed Doors

Judah lugged the empty jars to the spring. He hadn't taken on this chore for nothing. Even though carrying water was women's work, he had his own reasons. He first saw Dinah at the spring a year ago, when her family moved to Nazareth. Her father had died, and her mother, according to custom, had been taken in by her in-laws.

Dinah, slender and green eyed, was standing in line that cold fall morning, a kerchief pulled tightly over her long black hair, waiting her turn to fill her jar. Judah caught her eye before she demurely turned away, and he felt her eyes on his back as he walked up the road.

The next morning, he grabbed the water urns from his sister Sarah and said, "Let me," leaving her speechless, standing in the courtyard. Dinah wasn't there that morning, and he was afraid she had just been visiting, but she reappeared the day after and smiled at him when he passed her with his filled jars. He was so surprised that he stumbled and sloshed water all over himself, causing the women in the line to laugh. One nudged another, and soon they were all looking from him to Dinah, though Judah saw none of this. Humiliated, he continued on his soggy way home, but his heart was as full as the water jars. She had smiled at him.

From that time onward, that was their routine: Dinah smiling at him at the springs and Judah aching to speak to her but prevented from doing so by convention. It wasn't until a full month later that his mother was introduced to Dinah's mother, Tarah. Judah just happened to be loitering nearby. Mary introduced him, and Tarah looked at him in a way that revealed that his name was already known to her. Tarah then introduced Dinah to Mary as Judah stood by, smiling but saying nothing.

After that, when they met daily at the Nazareth spring, Dinah would nod at him and he would nod back, their eyes speaking but their mouths silent. One day Judah accidentally spilled water on her sandals, giving him a chance to say, "Sorry."

"It's all right," she had said, wiping her foot dry.

Yes, it is, thought Judah, grateful for his clumsiness.

From then on, the trickle of words flowed, more added daily, until a torrent spilled out whenever they saw each other at the springs. Their time standing in line was but a moment, and they parted ways with many questions unasked and answers unspoken. Their throats were parched in anticipation of the next meeting, and each drank of the other's company as if it were a draft of the coolest, sweetest water imaginable.

They became very close, considering the social impediments for young men and women, which meant proximity but not contact. Dinah was never out of sight of her older sister or mother, and Judah was rarely permitted to stray from his father's workshop during the day to see her. But he made good use of his time there carving little things for her. He once carved a little bird out of oak and painted it black, giving it to her.

"What does it mean, the raven?" she asked, turning it over in her hands, admiring the delicate carving of the wings, the steely look of the bird's eye, and noble set of its beak.

"It reminded me of your hair," said Judah, not knowing how to make the truth sound any better than just saying it. "It's black," he added, feeling foolish.

"It's beautiful," she said, holding it to her breast and looking up at him.

Judah thought his knees would buckle.

And so he was shocked the day he finally got up his courage to tell her his true feelings as he placed the woven laurel garland on her head. The words had no sooner left his mouth when she turned and stormed away. His friends were as surprised as he was, and nobody could fathom what he'd said wrong.

Since then, he hadn't even seen her at the springs. This cool, misty morning, he stood glumly in line, tapping one of the empty clay jars with his toe, thinking. His turn came, and he dipped a jar in the granite basin, then filled the other one. He turned from his task and hoisted both jars onto his hips and started home. Then he saw Dinah at the rear of the line with her mother, looking right at him, an empty jar on her hip. Their eyes met and she looked away.

Crushed again, Judah put his head down and continued on past her another few steps.

Then something inside him stopped his footsteps. He put his jars down and turned. Without a word, he walked back to Dinah and snatched the empty water jar from her. He strode to the head of the line and filled the jar, then took it back to Dinah and shoved it into her arms, elbowed the woman there aside, without a word. Then he scooped up his own jars and left, his shoulders hunched angrily.

Everyone gawked at Dinah, whose face burned crimson. "Well, I . . ." was all she could say.

Her mother patted her arm and finished the thought. "Men."

Esther placed a stone on the entrance to the sepulchre. "I'm not giving up," she whispered, "so don't you worry, Ezra. Your good name will be restored."

She turned away. Her knees were giving her trouble again, as was her back. She attributed her aches to the many bumpy cart rides she'd made to Sepphoris over the last few days to see the ethnarch. She could hardly bear to go out of the house anymore, and not just because of her aches but also because she would undoubtedly encounter Ishmael's workers in the warehouse next door. Yesterday, she looked inside and her heart fell. When Ezra was alive, Ishmael had maintained that there was little oil available for second pressings, but now the press turned day and night, and the stacks of filled oil casks rose higher and higher. She was so dismayed at the sight that she immediately hired the boy to take her to Sepphoris again on his donkey cart so she could talk to the ethnarch.

She had seen him almost daily since their first meeting almost a week ago. The first three times he had met with her and listened intently to her story, but yesterday he was not there, or so his scribe said.

She left that day, dejected, walking slowly across the great, dark basilica hall, her eyes on the floor, which featured intricate mosaics of commercial life. She was watching the artisans setting tiles into a mosaic of a huge cornucopia spilling out fruit and grain when she heard voices and looked up. The ethnarch was walking across the hall, followed by a group of men in togas. Esther moved to intersect his path. He seemed unsurprised to see her. "How are you, Esther?" he said, stopping momentarily, bowing deep.

"I am fine," said Esther. "I was wondering—"

"I haven't yet made a decision in your case. As you can see," he said, gesturing about, "we are very busy here. Check back next week." Without waiting for an answer, he continued on.

"Sire!" cried Esther, surprising herself. "Won't you please grant me justice?"

Up on the scaffolds, workers stilled their trowels, dripping with white plaster. Down on the floor, the hod carriers froze in midstep, and the mixers stopped swirling the plaster in the big wooden troughs. The ethnarch's entourage stopped too, looking back at her, as surprised as she was at her outburst. Only Marcus continued on, raising his hand. "Justice? Of course!" He disappeared through the courtroom double doors amid the laughter of his companions, who obviously knew a definition of the word *justice* that escaped Esther.

Esther looked around. The plasterers were once again slathering the walls, the hod carriers were hoisting full mortarboards onto their shoulders, and the artisans were carefully placing the next glazed tile into place in the mosaic. And once again, she was invisible.

Recalling the incident, Esther set her jaw. "I'm not invisible," she said, slowly picking her way up the hill between the tombs. She knew she shouldn't pester the ethnarch so often, but she felt compelled to see him, to beg for justice and, barring that, for mercy, just as she felt compelled to attend synagogue, to light her tiny bronze menorah, to recite her anxious prayers, and to place the chalky stone on Ezra's tomb. All of it was designed to earn a blessing from the Master of the Universe.

"I have faith, Lord," she said, looking up at the sky, which was full of white, fluffy clouds. "And I know you're watching."

So this morning, the very next day after her humiliating encounter with Marcus in the basilica hall, she once again stood watching the *tektons* working on the cornucopia mosaic and tried to calm herself. Her heart beat time in her narrow chest, and she felt sick to her stomach. She

was an old woman, important to no one, without means or money, and
yet here she was, about to plead for justice once again. If Ishmael had
robbed *her,* she could have let it go. The money was not important so
long as she had a piece of bread she could gum and clean water to drink.
But he had cheated her husband of his good name. The villagers in
Nazareth now thought that wicked Ishmael had helped Ezra, not stolen
from him, and so the warehouse was now rightfully his. She had long
felt the envy of some in town whose husbands were not as industrious as
Ezra, and she'd heard the rumors that Ezra had gambled away his fortune. The thought filled Esther with dismay. Ezra had never thrown
dice—not in his entire life!—and the only reason Esther didn't have a
nicer home was that Ezra put his money back into the business or quietly and unobtrusively slipped some into other people's pockets, often
without their even knowing it. Yet people talked, and she was experienced enough with human nature to know that some people actually
enjoy the misfortune of others, relishing it like a good meal because secretly they want an excuse for not doing more with their own lives.

    Yet even as she thought this, she felt guilty. Some people had good
luck to go along with their industry. Ezra did. So when it came time to
share their blessings, he always made sure they did, because only God
knew who deserved good fortune and who did not. Better to give to all
and let the Lord judge the receiver, even as he judged the giver.

    Oh, if only the Lord were judging Ezra's case right now! His good
name would be restored and the people of Nazareth would finally know
what a good man he had been. She had promised God that when—not
if—the business was restored, she would expand her generosity, even toward those who secretly delighted in her misfortune.

    What more could he ask of her?

    But then a cloud crossed before the sun and the interior of the basil-
ica went even darker, casting a shadow across her hope. Why should the
ethnarch care? Jeshua, in his gentle way, had told her as much. "He is no
friend to Jews," he had said, and though she hated to admit it, she had
seen it herself in the ethnarch's cold, gray eyes. Jeshua had also said the
ethnarch was undoubtedly a friend of Ishmael, and if that was so, then
he was no more inclined to grant Esther's petition than to invite her over
to his villa for dinner. The thought made her angry, and her heart,
which fluttered with anxiety and fear before, now thumped a bitter, even

cadence. She pushed Jeshua's warning away, preferring to remember that he had agreed with her that faith can indeed move mountains, even if it takes a long time.

Time is all I have left, she thought, making her way to the rear of the basilica and entering the courtroom. The white marble-stepped dais was nearly finished. The entire room was paved with huge granite slabs, and if not for the skylights overhead, it would have been very dark inside. But the dais itself glowed like a diamond under the skylight directly above it. Turning to her right, she entered the ethnarch's offices. Neri was sitting at his desk, writing on a parchment. She delicately tapped the doorjamb with her cane.

Neri looked up, and a cloud crossed his face. "Esther, please! It does no good to come here every day. You'll just anger him."

"But I need an answer to my petition. It's been long enough, hasn't it?"

Neri laid down his stylus and steepled his fingers. He took a breath and measured his tone. "Do you have any more evidence in support of your petition?"

"Do I need more? Isn't the fraudulent contract enough?"

Neri heaved a sigh. "Please, Esther, go home. The ethnarch will make his decision in due time. You must be patient—"

"If the ethnarch will tell me when he intends to resolve my case, I won't return until then. But he hasn't—he just ignores me. And it's not fair!" She struck the ground with her cane for emphasis, the metal tip ringing on the marble floor.

"Neri, what's going on?" came a voice.

Marcus was rounding the hallway corner. He spotted Esther, and she saw the effort it took for him to put a smile on his face. In that instant, all her hopes were dashed. There was no mistaking that smile—it was the same smile she saw on Ishmael's face the day he'd shown her the fraudulent contract.

Marcus said flatly, "Esther, what is it today?"

"My cause is just," said Esther. "You know it and I know it. Even your scribe knows it."

"It's a difficult decision. I'm duly considering your—"

"I know your heart now," said Esther, standing as tall as she could, looking up at the ethnarch. "And I bear witness that God's punishment will fall upon you and your house—so watch your head!" And with that, she turned and left the office.

Neri and Marcus looked at each other in dumb astonishment for a moment, and then Marcus burst out laughing. Even Neri couldn't resist a chuckle at the incongruity of the tiny, shriveled old woman threatening the ethnarch.

Esther hobbled blindly across the courtroom, her ears ringing with their laughter. She passed through the doorway and trudged between the immense columns of the hall nave, shaking her head at her foolishness. She had lost control and sealed her fate. One moment of anger had made up the ethnarch's mind, if it wasn't made up before.

Outside, she sat on the bottom step of the basilica, buried her face in her hands, and cried. A bell was struck, and the workers' clatter ceased. From the marketplace, food vendors were wheeling carts toward the construction site. The smell of roast meat and hot bread filled the air, along with the fragrance of split melons and ripe fruit.

Esther looked up through her tears, the movement around her a blur. It was only a matter of time before Ishmael pushed her out of her home, and then where would she go? She had no money, and she and Ezra had no children to take her in. She closed her eyes and lifted her chin heavenward. "Lord," she whispered, "what shall I do?"

But no answer came, and she opened her eyes. And there, crossing her field of vision, were two men dressed in sleeveless tunics, cinched at the waist. One was Judah bar Joseph—she knew his tall, muscular build anywhere. The other man was black with dirt. It wasn't until he smiled at the other that she recognized him. "Jeshua!" she called.

Jeshua and Judah turned and saw Esther. Judah whispered, "She'll want one of your answers, Jeshua. I don't envy either of you." He slapped Jeshua on the back and walked away.

Jeshua threaded his way between the great blocks of stone and approached Esther. "Have you had lunch? Please, come join us."

"He turned me down," she said, her voice catching with emotion. "Did he say that?"

Tears glistened in Esther's eyes. "He laughed in my face!"

Jeshua sat down next to her on the low step. He put his arm around her shoulders but said nothing. Esther leaned against him, her frail body heaving with sobs.

After a long time, her tears spent, Esther looked up at him. "Maybe I did pester him too much. Maybe I made a nuisance of myself. But the Torah says we should call upon the Lord in all things and he will hear us. Have I done wrong?"

"The ethnarch is not the Lord," said Jeshua.

Esther blinked. "What should I do?"

"Have you considered what justice is costing you?"

"Costing me?"

Jeshua nodded. "Anger—even righteous anger—can hurt us even more than the injury did."

"Are you saying I should forgive Ishmael? After what he did?" Esther pulled away and stared at Jeshua.

"I'm just saying anger destroys."

Esther slowly got to her feet and leaned on her cane. "Jeshua, I know your counsel is well intentioned, but you have a lot to learn about the world. Not everything can be solved by forgiveness. Evil must be battled, and justice comes at a price. My eyes might be failing, but I've kept them open all my life. Perhaps you should open yours."

She turned and walked away.

Jeshua studied his clasped hands, thinking.

"Look about you!" said Esther, and Jeshua looked up. "Wickedness! Mammon! And *you're* building it!" She turned away and continued on.

Jeshua looked up at the basilica facade.

Sadoc strode across his office, angered by the rapping on the door. "Riva, I told you to leave us alone!" he said, opening the door brusquely. "Esther!" he said, surprised.

"I thought I heard voices."

"No, it's just me," said Sadoc, leading her to a chair. He sat down opposite her.

"Am I disturbing you?" asked Esther, noting the open scroll on his desk.

"I was just reading. Jeremiah."

Esther nodded. "I was just quoting him myself! What a coincidence!"

"He's very . . . *portentous.*"

"Oh, yes," said Esther. "But though he's gloomy, there are morsels of hope."

Sadoc leaned forward. "Such as?"

"Well," said Esther, "he counsels us to pray always, and God will answer our prayers."

"What a wonderful thought," said Sadoc.

"And that's why I'm here," said Esther. "You remember my petition with the ethnarch."

Sadoc nodded. "The 'snake' Ishmael."

"That's the least of his nicknames. You know the ethnarch, don't you?"

"Not really. I'm just a poor rabbi, Esther, nothing more."

Esther said, "But you are a member of the Sanhedrin. He will listen to you."

Sadoc pursed his lips. "I don't know if he will, but I will try."

"Thank you, Rabbi," said Esther, her strength returning, along with her hope. "I knew you would give me good counsel. Unlike some others."

Sadoc helped her up and led her to the door. "What others?"

"Just a friend who said I should forgive that viper."

"Let the sinner repent, and then show him mercy. Any other way mocks the justice of God."

Esther beamed up at Sadoc. "You're exactly right! Thank you for your counsel!"

"Don't mention it," said Sadoc, shutting the door and leaving her on the landing.

Esther made her way down the stairs, her spirits buoyed. At the foot of the stairs, she heard voices coming from the rear of the building. She passed between the facing rows of synagogue benches. Through a rear door, she heard Sadoc's wife, Riva. Entering the kitchen, she saw Riva and her oldest daughter standing at a table, kneading bread dough. "Riva!" exclaimed Esther. "Your husband is the most wonderful man!"

Sadoc shut the door and turned. "You can come out of your hole now."

Ishmael stepped from behind a curtain. "I didn't appreciate the 'snake' remark."

"Just quoting," said Sadoc, settling into his chair, lacing his hands behind his head, stretching luxuriously.

"You love this charade, don't you?" said Ishmael. "Pretending to be the caring shepherd?"

Sadoc shrugged. "She isn't giving up, Ishmael. You should know that."

"Why should she? Now that she has you on her side," said Ishmael. "Foolish old woman. I almost feel sorry for her." He smiled.

"Me too," said Sadoc.

Jeshua munched a piece of bread, but his attention was on the synagogue, where he'd seen Esther enter a few minutes before.

"You think she'll get better advice from *him?*" asked Judah. "Everyone knows he's a hypocrite—all he cares about is money."

"That doesn't make him a hypocrite," said Jeshua, watching the rabbi's office window for movement. He saw none, just a burgundy curtain moving in the breeze.

"Meshach, the chief elder of the synagogue, says Sadoc won't give the men a complete accounting of the offerings he receives."

Jeshua said nothing.

"You think he'd lie about that?" asked Judah.

"Rumors are easily spread," said Jeshua, shrugging. "I like to give people the benefit of the doubt."

"And look where it's gotten you—working in the cisterns."

"Work is work, Judah," said Jeshua, still focused on Sadoc's window.

"But there are different *kinds* of work, Jeshua. Your talents are wasted down there!"

"Don't worry about me."

"I'm not worried *about* you," said Judah. "I'm worried *for* you."

Jeshua stood, ignoring the remark. He walked across the forum, keeping his eye on Sadoc's upper window. He was upset at how he'd left it with Esther. He'd had nothing helpful to say, and now she was talking to the rabbi, getting the advice she should have gotten from Jeshua.

Or perhaps getting bad advice, which was more likely, in Judah's view. Esther was intelligent, but since Ezra's death her actions had been swayed by grief. When he heard about her daily visits to the basilica,

Jeshua admired her courage and resolve, but as he'd told her, constant entreaties might work with the Lord, but with men there is no such guarantee. And yet his biggest fear was that the rabbi would counsel Esther to stop pleading with the ethnarch, which Jeshua believed was also bad advice. There might be other ways to keep the ethnarch focused on her plight without angering him. He wanted to discuss them with Esther, so he cut his lunch short and hurried over to the synagogue.

He pulled the massive synagogue door open and entered the vestibule. Beyond the balcony pillars was the meeting hall. Rows of wooden benches faced each other. In the middle was the table, or *bimeh*, where the Torah scrolls were rolled out and read. To his right was a stairway, which led to the rabbi's upstairs office.

Jeshua removed his muddy sandals and placed them just inside the great door, then began climbing the stairway, wondering what he would say. He didn't want to interrupt their meeting, but he wanted to give his point of view to Esther. He also wanted to finally meet Rabbi Sadoc, about whom so many people had such strong and conflicting views.

At the top of the stairs, he stopped and dusted himself off and leaned toward the closed door. If Esther and the rabbi were in deep conversation, he would not disturb them, but if they were finishing up, perhaps he might join them for a moment. He was about to knock when a loud voice came from within. "I tell you, he suspects something!"

A quiet voice responded, "What could he possibly suspect?"

Jeshua straightened. The loud voice was a mystery, but the soft voice must be the rabbi's.

"He doesn't trust me!" boomed the loud voice. "We were discussing how we would buy up the valley estates. He made a big show of generosity, telling me I could have them all—all he wanted was Sepphoris. It was so generous, so out of character, that I suspected something right away."

"Such as?"

"Think about it! *My* name will be on the deeds," said the loud voice.

"Ah!" said Sadoc. "He is grooming a scapegoat."

"Exactly," said the adamant voice. "So I sent Hanock to get the money from Marcus—he will purchase the lands, and it will be his name on the deeds, not mine."

"Is Hanock the one you helped make all that money last year?"

"The very same fat fool. Back then, I told Ocran to be on the lookout for him, to help him out. I guaranteed him a portion of the proceeds. Hanock thinks it was all his doing."

The rabbi let out an impressed whistle. "Very clever, Ishmael."

Jeshua blinked. Ishmael—could this be the same Ishmael Esther so despised? Was Esther even in there? No, she couldn't be. They were talking about things they would never permit her to hear. *Or me,* he thought. He turned to go, but something held him in place.

"A name on a deed is nothing," said Sadoc breezily. "I shouldn't worry about it."

A chair leg scratched on the floor. "You'd worry if it was *your* name on the deed," hissed Ishmael.

"Yes, but as a rabbi, I'm not allowed to—"

"Oh, shut up!" growled Ishmael. "Everyone is protected except me!"

Sadoc lowered his voice. "Speaking of protection, has Marcus received a reply from Calpurnius yet?"

"I don't know. He hasn't said anything."

"Let us hope he does, Ishmael. A letter guaranteeing protection from Antipas would be more valuable than a hundred golden talents right now."

Jeshua finally forced himself to leave. He crept silently down the stairs, feeling like a thief at one step and an innocent man escaping execution at another. He was grateful when he was once again in the vestibule. He hurried through the doors, going right out into the street, taking several steps before he remembered his sandals. He retrieved them and skirted the building front, looking up to see if anyone was on the balcony. Fortunately, the space was empty.

He hurried across the forum. Though his lunch had been cut short, he had plenty to digest.

Neri stepped behind the big porch column, watching the artisan leave the synagogue, carrying his sandals. Late yesterday, Neri made some inquiries and learned that the man's name was Jeshua, of Nazareth. Also yesterday, a few minutes after he resisted the urge to go down and speak to this Jeshua at the foot of the basilica steps, Neri had walked back across the basilica nave and stood behind a wooden crate on the porch.

Jeshua had gone, but a moment later he saw Rabbi Sadoc striding across the forum, heading straight for the red-turbaned merchant's stall near the temple fountain.

Neri watched them converse, and an important detail was added to his meager store of knowledge: the rabbi and the merchant were friends. He also knew this much: a play was unfolding before his eyes. The actors were taking their places on the stage. In addition to the two main players—Marcus and Ishmael, who, owing to their frequent meetings, were clearly up to something—there were now at least three minor characters: Rabbi Sadoc, the turbaned merchant Azariah, and the *tekton* Jeshua.

Neri watched as Jeshua, still carrying his sandals, crossed in front of the basilica and disappeared. Then there was movement to his left, and Neri turned and saw Ishmael leaving the synagogue. Ah! So Jeshua had just left a meeting with Ishmael and the rabbi. Perhaps he was not a minor player after all. Neri drew farther back into the shadows and watched Ishmael turn down a side street. From the way Ishmael carried himself, Neri knew his visit with Sadoc and Jeshua had been a successful one.

Neri turned and ducked under the facade wall scaffolding behind the porch pillars and walked into the gloom of the basilica nave. He cataloged on his fingers the cast as he knew it thus far: Azariah, the merchant he saw three weeks ago at the king's palace in Tiberias; Sadoc, the Sepphoris rabbi; the *tekton* Jeshua of Nazareth; the greedy landowner Ishmael; and the ethnarch himself, Marcus Pertinax. Though Neri had not seen all of them in the same room, he was convinced they all had parts in the same play.

And it was beyond time for Neri to leave the audience and choose a part for himself, or he most certainly would be cast as the fool.

NINE

Risk and Reward

Hanock crested the rise, and Ishmael's estate came into view. The grand two-story stone house was surrounded by fruit trees, pastures, vineyards, and farmland. The twin lines of cypress trees led down the hill toward the house. Dozens of workers labored in the fields as he passed. Hanock couldn't help but notice that most of them turned away when they recognized him.

He didn't care. He was not chief steward to be liked. And anyway, his days trapped on this estate and under Ishmael's painful crop were quickly drawing to a close. As he thought of his future, the familiar tightness in his chest returned. He pondered his encounter with Ocran in the bank vault. Ocran's prediction that he would fail gnawed at him. Ocran certainly had more experience than Hanock, but he could not deny Hanock's strongest argument: if the ethnarch had wanted Ocran's experience, why did he choose Hanock? Ocran had had no response to that, but later Hanock realized that he himself had no answer, either. Why *had* the ethnarch entrusted fifty talents to him? True, he had made money in the last year, a great deal of it—so why was his heart beating so fast?

After their meeting two days ago, Hanock had found himself walking the streets of Sepphoris, trying not to think about Ocran's foreboding words. But the more he hid from them, the more they festered in his mind, reminding him that luck had played a large part in his success last year in multiplying the five talents Ishmael had given him. He wondered if that luck would revisit him now. He strolled idly through the forum's market stalls and down the *cardo* toward the city gates, turning his situation over in his mind. Finally, he stood under the eastern city gate, where the *Decumanus,* the main east-west street in town, met the trade road coming up the hill. He looked out across the Netofa Valley and shrugged his shoulders, and for the moment, the doubt left him.

He turned back toward the forum and started mentally listing his contacts, people he could talk to about investments. He still had Ishmael's list of valley estates tucked inside his tunic. He would go that route— the slow, incremental route—only if no better opportunities presented themselves. As he walked among the swirling, colorful crowd and savored the smells of baking meat and bread, he felt certain he would find a better way to invest the ethnarch's money than in mere real estate. In a city this big and vibrant—the largest city in Galilee—there had to be someone who could help him make the ethnarch a great sum of money.

Throughout the day, Hanock had spoken to a number of financiers. Ocran was not the only banker in Sepphoris, and once word got out that the two had parted ways, other candidates had approached Hanock with suggestions. Some of the schemes were downright lunatic: a gold mine in Idumea—how could he manage a venture so far away? A ship filled with furs from Gaul would soon be landing in Ptolemais—who needed furs in Palestine? An old man who pointed a gnarled finger at Hanock and told him that he could take him to see the Delphic oracle, who would answer all Hanock's questions—for the right price.

Hanock laughed. The oracle was a myth, if she ever existed at all. Breathing vapors from a crack in a rock and prophesying. He might as well go to a synagogue and pray as travel all the way to Greece to watch some old hag sniff smoke and tell him his fortune in rhyme.

In one aspect, though, Ocran might be right. Perhaps Marcus was using Hanock as a shield, but a shield against whom? Ishmael was in on the deal, which is how Hanock got involved. Certainly Marcus would not abuse his friend Ishmael, would he?

But the initial, nagging question still haunted Hanock as he walked the Sepphoris streets: Why did Marcus choose him? Why didn't he just give Ocran the money? There was still only one answer that made sense: Ocran was too conservative, and Marcus wanted a quicker and larger return. Perhaps this was a sort of test of Hanock's abilities: Would he act tentatively, as bankers like Ocran would, or would he be audacious and obtain an impressive return?

That *had* to be it! It was a test, and now both Ishmael and the ethnarch were watching him carefully to see what he would do. Well, he would surprise them both. This was his greatest opportunity, to invest *someone else's* money. He must not shy away from the challenge.

All day yesterday Hanock had met with what he began to think of as "investment suitors," men who practically kissed his hand for the opportunity to pitch an idea. Word had traveled fast, and it was soon known that Hanock had a small fortune to invest. No one, as yet, had figured out that the money belonged to the ethnarch, though Hanock wondered how anyone would not discern that fact almost immediately. This realization only confirmed his disdain for the men who courted him as he sat in the restaurant facing Jupiter's temple, listening to one eager salesman after another. And since there was nothing to do as he listened but eat and drink, by sunset he was filled to the brim with lamb and barley bread and also drunk as a pressman.

He had stumbled off to bed at the inn, fallen into a dreamless sleep, and awakened this morning with eyes so bloodshot he could barely see. He had refused breakfast and stumbled down the narrow cobbled street to the baths, where he'd wrapped a soft towel around him and leaned back in the *tepidarium*, the warm room, soaking his feet in a bowl of warm saltwater, awaiting his turn in the *caldarium* itself.

It was midmorning, so the baths were almost empty. Hanock was glad. His head ached, and all he wanted to do was sit here quietly with his fingers laced across his distended belly and keep his eyes closed against the painful light.

Then he heard movement and opened his eyes. A man entered the room. He was tall, well proportioned, and had skin the color of copper. His hair was short and black and curled tightly around his head. He had a broad, smooth forehead above eyes of the deepest brown, with flecks of gold in the irises. He wore a turquoise earring. He nodded at Hanock and sat down opposite him.

"You're not from around here," said Hanock, stating the obvious.

"How did you guess?" laughed the man, revealing the most perfect set of white teeth Hanock had ever seen. And since he was a foreigner and had not heard of Hanock's fortune, Hanock was able to steer their conversation away from finance. They got into a long discussion about the man's travels that extended from the *tepidarium* to the *caldarium*, through their massages, and on to the dressing area.

The man hailed from Egypt, but he was not Egyptian. His father was a Roman centurion, originally from Germania, far to the north and west. Hanock had heard of Germania, and wanted to know what it was like to live in ice and snow. The man laughed—he had never lived in Germania but was raised in Egypt, as he'd said. His mother was a Nabatean noblewoman. From his youth he'd traveled extensively with his father, from Babylon in the east to Hispania in the far west, where he said the land closed in on the Middle Sea and then opened up into an ocean that was even larger. "It goes on forever," he said, "to the ends of the earth."

"Forever, you say?" asked Hanock.

The man nodded. "And all part of the empire, for now."

"What do you mean, 'for now'?"

The man shrugged. "Things change."

Hanock nodded, though he was doubtful Rome would ever pass away. He'd seen the cohort garrisoned in Tiberias, five hundred tall, well-trained soldiers marching in perfect cadence, armed and armored, carrying standards bearing the emperor Tiberias's profile. Ten cohorts comprised a legion, and Rome had a dozen or more legions scattered around the world. He doubted an army that large could ever be defeated.

His new friend was a trader. "For example," he said, pulling off a gold ring and holding it up. "In Judea gold is rare, but in Egypt there are many mines, and the temples there are built of solid gold. Likewise, here in Judea olive oil is plentiful, yet in Egypt olive oil is as rare as gold is to you. The trick, then, is simple: gold to Judea, oil to Egypt."

"And money to you," said Hanock. "Sounds very neat."

"There are occasional difficulties."

"Difficulties?"

"Pirates and brigands on the high seas, angry storms that sink boats, untrustworthy captains, greedy port authorities, and so on. But when potential pirates see that every hand on my ship looks suspiciously like a legionnaire, well, let's just say that a higher percentage of my goods reach their destination than of any other merchant you're likely to meet in this little country."

Hanock felt his heart jump. He was beginning to think—no, he was well past thinking; he was *hoping*—that this was the man he'd been searching for. But he must not appear too eager. "So what brings you to Sepphoris?" he asked casually.

"I've a ship in Ptolemais. We just unloaded a number of horses from Greece. Incredibly strong, beautiful horses. They're headed for buyers in Phoenicia, where the chariot races are particularly popular."

"My master—I mean, my *partner*—is a great collector of fine horses," said Hanock, ready to kick himself for stumbling so.

"Is that right?" said the man. "Then he would appreciate these animals. Black as night, swift as the wind, calm as a cat by a warm fire. But, alas, they are all spoken for. Perhaps on a future trip."

"You'll be bringing horses again?"

"Every journey has a different cargo, a different destination. My next trip is, shall we say, much more lucrative and less delightful to the nose than this one." He laughed.

Hanock leaned forward.

The man smiled. "Coins."

"Coins?"

"I trade in coins: Roman denarii, Greek talents, Syrian drachmas. Coins wear out and must be replenished. Though many countries mint their own, Roman coins are still the preferred currency of the empire."

Hanock fingered the denarius in his pocket, trying to feel the emperor's face on it.

"We will be bringing a large quantity of coins to Palestine next time we come."

"Why you? Can't Rome transport the coins itself?"

"Certainly, but Rome usually ships the coins in its own well-marked galleys, and so they are obvious targets for pirates. But my ships are smaller, more maneuverable, and faster. We can more easily slip through the pirates' nets. And for our troubles, we are paid handsomely."

"If I may ask," whispered Hanock, "how much is 'handsomely'?"

The man surveyed Hanock carefully, then smiled. "Twenty-five percent."

"For shipping coins?"

The man nodded. "Without standardized money, there is no commerce. Rome knows this. We are the insurance for the empire's banking system. We purchase the new coins in Rome, transport them around the world, and are paid a premium for our efforts at our destination. Indeed, I often think twenty-five percent is too little for the great risks we take. But we rarely fail, and I've yet to lose a shipment this year." He nodded and leaned back proudly.

Hanock smiled. As soon as he left today, he would go to the temple of Jupiter and make a sacrifice.

The man said, "I have dominated our conversation. I never asked what you do, friend."

"I am in coinage as well. In fact, I have a number of coins that I wish to invest. Perhaps in a voyage to Rome."

"I'm pleased to meet you," said his companion, bowing deeply. "My name is Ahmad."

They parted shortly thereafter, but not before agreeing to meet early the next morning to travel to Ptolemais to see Ahmad's ship. If things went well, they would finalize their agreement.

Now, turning into the dooryard of Ishmael's estate, Hanock could barely contain a smile. All the way home from Sepphoris he had sung, and though his voice was more like the croaking of a frog than the lilt of a lark, he lifted it anyway, singing over and over an old drinking song he knew. It occupied the miles, and he never tired of it, though he must have sung it twenty times.

He dismounted and walked his horse into the stable. One of the boys ran over to receive the reins. Hanock looked around. "Where is Naaman?"

The boy shrugged and led the horse away. Hanock looked up at the loft, where he knew Naaman would sometimes laze. "Naaman?" There was no answer. "If you're up there, you'd better come down." Still no answer.

He looked around. Luckily, Ishmael's big black horse was gone. All the way home, Hanock had weighed the wisdom of telling his master about his encounter with Ahmad. He had finally decided to say nothing—yet. For one thing, their arrangement was not yet confirmed. For another, he still felt the list of Netofa estates Ishmael had given him rubbing his skin inside his toga. He knew his master's preferred investment was in these properties, but since he also knew he was being tested, he now saw the list as little more than a suggestion and perhaps a challenge. Would he be aggressive and audacious, or would he be timid and predictable? Hanock couldn't wait to see the look on Ishmael's face when he found out that Hanock had added twenty-five percent in value in just a few short weeks! He would have to admit—finally—that Hanock was indeed his peer in terms of handling money.

Hanock almost giggled as he left the stable. He hadn't even pictured yet what the ethnarch would say at the news! Hanock started humming the drinking song again, this time visualizing the ethnarch's jaw dropping as Hanock opened the second chest, full of golden talent coins.

After changing his clothes in his quarters, down at the end of the row of servant rooms, Hanock went around the back of the house to the press building, where the laborers were filling casks with new wine. Hanock's assistant Zerah was supervising, and the stable master Naaman stood by him, holding a piece of parchment. Zerah looked at the uncharacteristic smile on Hanock's face, and his eyes lit up. He drew close and whispered, "You have a grand secret, don't you? Is it about the talents?"

Hanock wagged a finger at him. "Why should I let you in on it?"

"If you don't wish to tell me, then don't," said Zerah, turning away, pouting.

Hanock frowned. He respected Zerah even less than he did the stableboy Naaman. At least Naaman had a semblance of a backbone. Zerah was always fawning over him. "You know, your attitude makes it very hard for me to feel generous toward you."

"I'm sorry," said Zerah, recovering his usual manners. "I'm very happy for you. Really."

"I never forget my friends," said Hanock. "Or my enemies."

Naaman looked up. His eyes were not soft and pleading like Zerah's. He'd given up hope of ever getting back on Hanock's good side again. The man lived to torture him, and Naaman was tiring of it. He straightened and looked Hanock in the eye. "And I never forget my lenders."

Hanock had forgotten about the talent he'd loaned Naaman. A sudden anger flared, and he took a step toward Naaman. Through gritted teeth, he said, "I want it back."

Naaman glared at him. "You put no deadline on its return."

"It was mine to give and now it's mine to claim."

"That's not what Ishmael says," said Naaman.

"You told the master?"

"He said it was a great opportunity and that I should not squander it."

"He did, did he?"

"And he told me that I should be grateful, so thank you. Your generosity is legendary."

Out of the corner of his eye, Hanock saw Zerah smile. That last phrase was Zerah's usual, obsequious response to Ishmael, always uttered with complete insincerity. To hear Naaman use it with Zerah's approval was a betrayal of the most vile sort. "Take care, stableboy," snarled Hanock. "That talent coin I loaned you has two sides. No matter what happens, Ishmael will know I am indeed generous, as you say. But if you lose it, not only will I know, but he will know as well, and that is something you do not want."

Naaman nodded slowly. "As I said, your generosity—"

"Shut up!" howled Hanock. "Shut up! All of you!" He looked around. A dozen workers stood watching, their faces purposely blank. Zerah looked judiciously at the floor. Only Naaman smiled at him, which filled Hanock with rage, but all he could do was point his crop at the little runt and stare at him, trembling with anger. Then he turned on his heel and walked away.

Shortly after Hanock left, Naaman excused himself. He walked behind the press building and slumped down against the wall, his heart pounding and sweat pouring off him like a summer shower. He looked down at his hands, which were shaking as if with palsy, wondering what demon had possessed him to talk so rudely to Hanock.

And then he remembered he still had no idea what to do with the talent Hanock had cursed him with. If he should lose it, or fail to make as much with it as expected, Hanock would beat him and cast him into prison. If he multiplied the talent, Hanock would undoubtedly strip him of the profits and fire him. Either way, he would not be working for Ishmael much longer.

He grasped the coin in the pouch around his neck and knew he had nothing left to lose.

TEN

Ropes and Blades

The Sabbath came and Jeshua's family prepared for dinner. Simeon and his wife were not present, as they usually were. They were in Caesarea Maritima, picking up a shipment of wood for the furniture Joseph and Simeon were building for a restaurant in Cana.

Judah, as usual, was grumbling. The water jars that in the past had so mysteriously filled themselves were now being emptied just as mysteriously. He looked around on the courtyard for telltale water splashes, but the packed dirt was dry. Sunset was fast approaching, and he muttered to himself as he hurried to the spring, where he filled the six jars once again. Dinah wasn't there, and for that he was glad: he was too angry to talk to anyone. When he got back home, he was going to wring James's neck.

So after placing the jars outside the kitchen door, he marched into the central living area. James was puzzling how to untie a knot in a rope as Jeshua watched. Judah yanked the rope out of James's hands and scowled. "I've had enough of your pranks."

Jeshua said, "He's been with me since we came home from work."

Judah shot Jeshua a hard look. "How did you know what I meant?"

Joseph was sitting by the fireplace, working on sketches for the restaurant furniture. Without looking up he said, "Judah, *everyone* knows what you meant. I'd think that by now you'd have come to appreciate the special kindness underlying these pranks, as you call them."

"But the jars are being *emptied* now!" wailed Judah. "I almost broke the Sabbath filling them."

Joseph frowned at James. "A joke is one thing, but leaving your mother without water on the Sabbath is *wrong*. Don't let me hear of it again."

James shook his head. "I didn't empty them—honest!" When he looked around and saw no one believed him, he ran outside.

"Happy now?" said Joseph to Judah. "Thank you for starting the Sabbath off so pleasantly." He turned back to his parchment.

Judah handed the knotted rope to Jeshua and sat down next to him. "It isn't funny anymore," he whispered.

"I told you, he was here with me," said Jeshua, turning the rope over in his hands. "You filled the jars when we got home. I didn't empty them, and neither did James."

"Then he has an accomplice," growled Judah. "I'm tired of this."

"So are we," said Joseph. "So solve it, once and for all, or I'll find enough work for all of you that you won't have any energy left for pranks."

Joses, two years older than James, entered the room. Judah pointed at him. "Are you in on this too?"

Joses said, "In on what?"

Judah turned back to the fire. "Surrounded by conspirators," he said darkly.

Outside, James stood in front of the full water jars, thinking.

"Jeshua!"

Jeshua stirred on his pallet, turning over.

"Jeshua!" came the emphatic whisper again.

Jeshua opened his eyes. Someone was leaning over him. He blinked. "What?"

Judah motioned for him to follow. They crept out of the room, careful to avoid the other boys' sleeping pallets. It was cold and Jeshua could see his breath. Judah opened the door, and there in the courtyard stood Ibhar, Jeshua's cistern digging companion, shivering in a light cloak. Ibhar whispered, "Something's going on. I thought you should know."

Jeshua reached to pull Ibhar inside the house, but Ibhar held his ground.

Judah whispered, "Tell him what you told me."

Ibhar leaned toward Jeshua. "At quitting time, I overheard Barak talking with some of the other workers. They were whispering, but you know me, I have good ears. They're planning something for tonight."

"What?" asked Jeshua, a chill moving up his spine.

"I think they're going to destroy the basilica."

Jeshua looked at Ibhar for a long moment, his jaw set. "I'm going."

Judah was incredulous. "You're joining them?"

Jeshua turned to go back inside. "No. I'm going to try to stop them."

Judah grabbed Jeshua's sleeve. "But it's the Sabbath!"

Jeshua gently removed Judah's hand from his sleeve. "Can you think of a better day to try to save lives?"

He went inside. Judah watched him go, then turned to Ibhar, who just shrugged.

They trotted across the undulating valley floor, the road a silver path under the nearly full moon, which had reached its zenith and was now moving toward the western horizon. Jeshua estimated that it must be well after midnight. He touched his side, feeling the stitch there. He hadn't run the three miles to Sepphoris since he was a boy. A cold sweat sheened his forehead. A headache thumped at his temple, and his legs, usually strong, stumbled often. The land surrounding them had begun to take upon itself the characteristics of the Jezreel Plain, where he had dreamed of the mighty opposing armies. A heaviness settled on his shoulders, slowing him even more. Judah looked back over his shoulder, perplexed at Jeshua's slow pace. Even Ibhar, with his long, spindly legs, was keeping up. Why was Jeshua falling behind?

As they started up the steep Sepphoris hill, their pace slowed to a fast walk. Ahead, looming white before them, was the tall city wall. As they approached, Jeshua knew something was amiss. The iron-banded gate stood ajar, and the sentries, always atop the wall parapets, were nowhere to be seen.

They slipped under the gateway arch and entered the long, stepped *cardo*. The columns on either side of the street looked like soldiers in formation, reminding Jeshua of the cohort in Tiberias, six hundred strong. Ten times that many Jewish workers were not a match for such an army. Yet before the cohort could make the forty miles to Sepphoris, the hundred Roman soldiers encamped at the Sepphoris crossroads north of the city would be wiping the blood off their swords. Jeshua's temple pounded with the sound of clashing iron, and he couldn't clear the terrible image of the Jezreel armies from his mind. It made each step an effort.

They stopped where the *cardo* opened out onto the forum, its scores of wooden market stalls shuttered for the night. To the left, the bath chimneys steamed; to the right, the curved theater porticoes waited for a new tragedy to unfold.

"Listen," said Judah, grabbing Jeshua's arm.

There were voices. They followed the sound toward the basilica and hid behind the temple fountain. Across the open forum, beyond the scattered chunks of marble, at the foot of the basilica steps, a dozen torches burned, one held high above the others.

"Barak," whispered Judah.

Barak was talking to the men in a throaty whisper, which neverthe- less carried far on the still night air. "All accounted for?"

"Yes," said Ibhar, stepping out from behind the fountain, causing Barak's men to turn. Jeshua and Judah looked up at him in surprise. "He's here," said Ibhar.

Judah scowled. "Traitor!"

Ibhar couldn't meet Jeshua's eyes. "I'm sorry," he said quietly. "They promised to get me out of the cisterns. I'm sorry." He hung his head and moved a couple of steps away, out of Judah's reach. Barak led the men over to the fountain, and Jeshua and Judah had no choice but to stand and be seen.

Judah looked at the men surrounding them. "What are you doing here? It's the Sabbath!"

Barak held his ever-present maul in one hand and the torch in the other. "It is, and so Rome would never expect what we are about to do. They haven't even posted guards at the gates. Very slipshod of them." He laughed, as did the men surrounding him.

"But the Law!" wailed Judah.

Barak spit on the ground. "Tonight, we are the Law. The Lord will understand."

Jeshua shook his head. "What I don't understand is why you sent Ibhar after me. You knew I would oppose this."

"Yes, we knew that," said Barak. "There are still a few who agree with you, who believe we should wait—wait until we starve. But once they learn you helped us destroy the basilica, they will join us. You see, everyone also knows how difficult it is for a Roman sword to distinguish between an innocent Jew and a guilty one."

"I won't help you, Barak," said Jeshua evenly.

Barak shrugged. "Doesn't matter. You can deny you helped us, but your presence here argues otherwise." He set the head of his heavy, iron-headed maul on the ground in front of Jeshua, the handle sticking up into the air. "Pick it up."

Jeshua ignored the maul and looked from one grim-faced man to another. "Have you all considered the consequences of your actions?"

"Another sermon from the rabbi," grumbled someone.

"We already went to synagogue tonight!" said another.

The men laughed.

"Quiet!" growled Judah. "You brought him here, now let him speak."

"Yes, speak on, Jeshua," said Barak. "Because no matter what happens tonight, I know you'll stand by us. I know you that well."

"Then answer my question," said Jeshua. "What are the consequences?"

Barak pointed at the building. "A great tumble of stone and not a man within fifty miles who will lift a finger to rebuild it."

Jeshua pushed past Barak, scaled the basilica steps, and stood on the broad porch between two immense marble columns. The men arrayed themselves on the steps below him. "If you pull this building down," he said evenly, "you will also bring down upon your own heads the wrath of Rome." He pointed to the north. "From the crossroads, a hundred soldiers."

"We'll fight," said Barak, resting his maul on his shoulder. "We match their number."

"Yes, but then tomorrow, six hundred more from Tiberias. And in a few days, perhaps an entire legion from Damascus—six thousand soldiers. We will all die—don't you remember the zealot revolt?"

Barak spit on the ground. "I do."

Jeshua nodded, continuing. "When Judas bar Ezechias barricaded the city, Varus, the governor of Syria, put Sepphoris under siege, planning to starve the people into submission."

"But they couldn't," said Barak, looking out across the men's faces. "Because by night, the zealots would sneak out of the city and kidnap sentries right off the Roman picket lines. Judas would have the soldiers' arms and legs hacked off and hurled back over the wall at the Romans."

"Good idea," said a worker. "Saves arrows."

The other men laughed. Jeshua waited for their good humor to subside, then continued. "But Judas was finally captured. They brought him before Varus, bound with strong cords. He stood there, apparently beaten, saying nothing. But when the soldiers stepped back, he lunged at Varus, slicing his neck deeply with a blade he held secretly in his mouth."

"Served him right," said Barak, nodding.

"But Varus didn't die," said Jeshua. "Holding a bloody compress to his neck, he calmly ordered Judas's tongue to be cut out. Then they quartered him alive, as he had the captured legionnaires. And when Judas died, they cut his head off and placed it on a pike atop the city wall. They crucified the rebels and sold their families into slavery. Then they burned the city to the ground and sowed the hilltop with salt."

"My father died in that revolt," said Barak.

Jeshua nodded. "In the end, what did they accomplish, those brave zealots?"

The crowd was transfixed. Jeshua's face seemed to glow brighter than the torches, even as darkness haunted his eyes. Barak looked around at the men. He could feel their anger curdling to fear. "They have us under siege *now!* We'll starve if we do nothing!"

The men looked at Jeshua, who reached inside his cloak and brought out the rope he'd been knotting earlier for James. It was a complex mass of tightly woven strands as big as a man's fist. "Untie this," he said, handing it to Barak, who turned it over in his big hands, trying to loosen it, but it was no use. "Use this," said Jeshua, producing a serrated knife. Barak grabbed the blade and quickly sawed through the knot. The rope fell on the ground in a dozen pieces.

Barak gave the knife back to Jeshua. "What does that prove?"

Judah picked up one of the rope strands and handed it to Barak. "We are the rope."

Jeshua dug the knife blade into the space where a fluted column met its square marble base. Soon the blade was notched and bent. He handed it to Barak and nodded at the rope in Barak's hand. Barak set to work, but this time no amount of sawing with the damaged blade would sever it. With a final, angry curse, Barak looped the rope and pulled the blade against it, straining with the effort. The blade suddenly separated from the haft, opening a jagged gash on his thumb. "Ow!" he said, sucking the wound and glaring at Jeshua.

Jeshua handed Barak a kerchief. "We will always be the rope."

Barak picked up the broken knife blade. "So how do we dull the Roman edge?"

"Where is Zoar?" asked Jeshua.

"He wasn't invited."

"Then who leads? You?" asked Jeshua.

Barak unraveled one end of the cut rope. Soon, the length was separated into a dozen thin strands. "If I led, this is what would happen," he said, taking Jeshua's useless blade and sawing easily through the strands, one by one. He handed the blade back to Jeshua. "No. You must lead us."

The sky in the east was beginning to lighten; morning was only an hour away. The men were watching Jeshua with expectant faces. His temple still pounded with the headache, though it had receded a little. He looked at Barak. "If I lead, what will *you* do?"

Barak put a hand on the hilt of his sword. "I will keep *my* blade sharp, just in case."

When the men left and their torches sputtered on the dewy ground, Sadoc stepped out from behind the curtains onto the balcony. The sloping basilica roof was tinged with the bluish light of dawn. Once again, his sharp eyes had not failed him. The workers had come very close to violence, but this *tekton* Jeshua had restrained them with a speech that Sadoc both admired and feared. Admired because of its simple, powerful eloquence; feared because the eloquence was not his own.

Standing there in the spreading dawn, Sadoc eventually found something to smile about. The workers had gathered to destroy the basilica, but the chief Jewish worker, a man named Zoar, whom Sadoc knew in passing from synagogue, had not been present. Over the months, Sadoc had learned the identities of most of the men who labored on the abomination across the square and had cultivated one or two as informants, just in case. Not much had come from these contacts beyond revealing the pay conflict the laborers had with Marcus. Obviously, the fruit was not yet ripe. But at this moment, Zoar's absence from this midnight meeting said something about Zoar's relationship with the men he represented. Had he fallen from favor? Was he still the ethnarch's tool, as Sadoc suspected? And if not, would Zoar be amenable to a contact now?

Sadoc didn't know the answers to these questions, but the fruit was growing heavy on the vine. It would soon be ready for plucking. Sadoc promised himself he would be in the vineyard when that time came.

ELEVEN

Stones and Coins

It was Sunday morning, the first day of the week, and once again Naaman sat on the low fountain wall fronting Jupiter's temple, turning the talent coin over and over in his hands. More than a week had passed since he had sat here with Jeshua, who had found him crying in the *cardo*, the victim of a devilish crime.

Naaman shook his head ruefully. "We should all be cursed so," Jeshua had said, and he was right—the silver talent coin truly was a great opportunity. But Jeshua didn't know Hanock, who was not lying when he said he'd see to it that Naaman rotted in the king's dungeons if he failed to return the talent with interest.

For a brief moment, Naaman considered burying the coin, as he had the other one in the orchard where Jeshua had been digging the well. Of course, that would defeat the purpose of the loan, wouldn't it? He ran a hand through his thinning hair and shook his head. Last time, he almost lost the buried coin. When he returned a few nights later to retrieve it, he couldn't find the stone marker he had so carefully placed over the location. Panic gripped him, and thus began a series of events that culminated in having his life saved by Jeshua in the well cave-in and then receiving not one but two talent coins as payment for helping dig the well. He'd given one to God as a thank-offering and returned the other to Ishmael, who beat him bloody for not multiplying it.

But in the end Naaman was richer for the experience. Ironically, losing the buried coin was the best thing that had ever happened to him. He met Jeshua, and Jeshua not only saved his life but changed it as well.

A few stripes from Ishmael's crop were a small price to pay to have one's eyes opened and one's heart remade.

There was only one thing to do. Naaman stood and led his horse toward the bank. A slender, dark-haired boy with a patchy tuft of hair on his chin was sitting on a block of marble in front of the bank, swinging his legs, basking in the sun. Naaman walked over to him and pulled out a shekel. "If you watch my horse, I'll give you this."

The boy nodded, taking the reins. Naaman turned and scaled the broad marble steps. Inside the bank, the sunlight fell through a dozen skylights, landing in bright trapezoids on the polished floor. Through doorways along the walls, Naaman saw the men weighing and changing currencies. He walked slowly, hands clasped at his back, trying to look prosperous. He was wearing his best clothes: a tan linen tunic and a deep blue traveling cloak. He had even dusted off a pair of sandals for the occasion. He searched the crowd for Ocran, and then suddenly, there he was, standing in a shaft of sunlight, wearing a white toga that bared one pale shoulder, looking like some sort of Roman deity. Naaman wouldn't have been surprised if, at that moment, a chorus had begun singing. As Naaman approached, Ocran turned. "Can I help you?"

"Do you remember me?"

Ocran's thin face screwed up into a squint. "Do I owe you money?"

Naaman shook his head.

"Do you owe *me* money?"

Again, Naaman shook his head.

Ocran slapped Naaman on the shoulder like an old friend. "Then we must be meeting for the first time."

"N-not quite," stuttered Naaman. "A year ago, I was here with Hanock of Rimmon—"

Ocran turned on his heel and strode away.

Naaman followed. "Sir!"

Ocran didn't slow his pace. "I've nothing to say to him."

"Neither do I."

Ocran stopped and turned. "You don't represent him?"

Naaman shook his head.

"You didn't come here to plead with me to talk to him?"

"*I* don't even want to talk to him."

Ocran studied Naaman, then snapped his fingers. "I remember you!" he said, picking an imaginary piece of straw off Naaman's shoulder. "The stable master! You got a coin from old Ishmael too, as I recall."

Naaman nodded. So the man *did* remember him.

"I heard you did not multiply your talent." Ocran's eyes twinkled. "Yet I see you survived the beating Hanock said you received from Ishmael."

Naaman felt his face reddening. "Yes, sir."

"So, did you learn your lesson?"

Naaman nodded uncertainly.

"And you're not here representing Hanock?"

Naaman shook his head.

"Good. Because the only thing I want to know about Hanock is that the king has thrown him in the dungeon."

"Why would he do that?"

Ocran decided to be careful about revealing too much to this stranger—perhaps he *did* represent Hanock after all. He smiled. "So what can I do for you?"

Naaman gestured for Ocran to extend his hand, then poured the contents of his money pouch onto Ocran's palm. The big, silver talent rolled out first, followed by the small black stone. Naaman reached for the stone, but Ocran made a fist, pulling it away. "What have we here?" he said, peeking into his hand.

Naaman didn't know what to say.

Ocran handed the talent to Naaman as if it were a mere prutah but held the little rounded black stone up to the light. "Is it valuable?" he asked, turning it this way and that.

Naaman nodded. "Very."

"More valuable than the talent?"

"In some circles, yes," said Naaman.

"Small circles, I would imagine," said Ocran, handing the stone to Naaman. "But this," he said, taking the silver talent, "is another story. And what do you wish to do with it?"

"Multiply it."

"Ah," said Ocran, "that is the trick, now, isn't it? Multiplying it. That would involve *risk*." He said the last word in a deep, rumbling voice. "And where did you get it?"

"My master gave it to me."

"A lie. Ishmael is not stupid twice."

"No, not Ishmael," said Naaman. "Hanock."

Ocran handed the coin back to Naaman. "Be gone." He turned and started away.

Naaman grabbed Ocran's sleeve. Ocran turned slowly, astonished that this manure shoveler would dare touch him. "Please," pleaded Naaman. "Hanock gave it to me—but he did it to punish me."

"Some punishment," said Ocran, taking the coin and holding it aloft. "Anyone want to be punished by having this coin?" he shouted to the entire bank.

A dozen hands went up, along with laughter and shouts of, "Here!" "Me! Me!" and "I'll take it!"

Ocran saw the desperation in Naaman's eyes. "It's a trick. Give it back to him."

"He won't take it," said Naaman. "And if I don't multiply it, he'll throw me in prison."

Ocran studied Naaman for a long moment then said, "Perhaps I *can* help you." He looked thoughtfully at the talent, and a bitter pleasure— the kind you see on the face of young boys who are watching a fish flop around in the boat, dying—lit his face, which at that moment was half in and half out of the light. One of his eyes shone with malicious delight; the other was veiled in shadow. The effect was alarming, and Naaman took a step back.

Ocran looked up. "What?"

Naaman was suddenly certain that if he gave Ocran the coin, he would never see it again. He reached for it, but Ocran drew it back. "I said I would help you."

Naaman shook his head, holding out his empty, trembling hand.

Ocran's smile disappeared. "So now you don't want my help?"

"Please," whispered Naaman.

Ocran looked at him as if Naaman had just emptied his bowels on the marble floor. "Fine," he said coldly. "Here." And with that he hurled the coin high into the air. Naaman watched it soar, now sparkling in a light shaft, now lost in shadow, until it hit the floor with a loud, metallic ring and bounced toward the large, open doorway and the crowded forum beyond.

Naaman chased the coin, dodging people, hearing Ocran's distant laughter, "Chase it, stableboy!" Naaman's hands clutched at the empty air, and his heart pounded a counterpoint to the sound of the coin hitting the floor, once, twice, and a third time before it bounced through the open doorway and disappeared. He raced after it, knocking a woman over. On the broad porch, a glimmer of silver hung in the air for an instant like a quartered moon, then Naaman heard another sparkling *clink* as the coin hit the marble and careened upward again.

Things seemed to be moving very slowly. The laughter behind him faded, and silence filled his ears. Eyes in the faces in the forum below reflected the silver coin as it arced slowly through the air. Then time regained its footing, and the coin struck the edge of a marble step and spun crazily off to the left. Naaman dived after it and struck his shin on a pillar base, sending searing pain straight to his forehead, blinding him. As he fell, the small black stone flew from his hand on its own invisible trajectory. Naaman tumbled down the unforgiving marble steps, wrenching his shoulder. He lay crumpled on the stone for a long moment, blindly gasping for air and stunned by the pain. Finally, his vision cleared. A number of people were standing at the foot of the steps, looking intently, not at Naaman, but at something else.

Naaman followed their line of sight and saw the dark-haired boy holding the reins of Naaman's horse in one hand, and the large, silver talent coin in his other upraised hand, grinning at his deft catch. The crowd began to clap and cheer. Naaman stumbled to his feet and limped down the steps toward the boy, who laid the valuable coin in Naaman's outstretched hands.

"Thank you," mumbled Naaman, clutching the coin tightly. "Thank you."

The boy shrugged.

Then a terrible realization came to Naaman. "Where is the other one?"

"You dropped *two* talents?" asked the boy.

"Not money, a stone!" wailed Naaman, looking about at their feet.

"A stone?" said the boy.

Naaman held up the coin. "It's worth more than this!" he said, and his eyes convinced the boy he was not joking.

"What does it look like?" asked the boy, also starting to search.

"Small. Black. Round," said Naaman, now on his hands and knees, ignoring his screaming shoulder and bloody shin.

"Small, black, and round," repeated the boy, expanding his search to the steps above Naaman. "Small, black, and round," he chanted, as if it were a spell.

"Small, black, and round," said Naaman, joining in the incantation.

"Hah!" came the boy's voice, and there, for the second time in as many minutes, he held aloft a valuable prize. The gathered crowd came closer, saw what it was, then turned away.

"Give me that!" Naaman snatched the stone back, then saw the hurt on the boy's face. Naaman handed the little black stone back to him. "I'm sorry."

"It looks like any stone," said the boy, turning it over in his hand.

"It's just a stone. But it's also a memory."

"It remembers?"

"It helps *me* remember," said Naaman, holding his hand out. And once again, the boy gave the valuable back without hesitation. Naaman put it in his pouch.

"Remember what?" asked the boy, helping Naaman down the steps.

"The day my life changed."

"You had a day like that?"

Naaman nodded. "On that day, a man saved me—twice."

The boy's eyes opened wide. "Twice?"

"First he saved my life," said Naaman, "and then he saved my soul."

"How did he do that?"

"I don't know. He just did."

The boy nodded, understanding. "I know a man like that."

Naaman reached into his tunic and held a shekel out to the boy, who shook his head. "I'm just glad I was here."

"So am I," said Naaman. "Without you, I would have lost it."

"The stone?"

"No, the coin," said Naaman quickly, then reconsidered. "No. The stone is much more valuable. Thank you." He bowed. "Shalom. I'm Naaman."

The boy smiled. "I'm Arah."

• • •

The rapping continued. Neri threw down his napkin and strode to the door. Who was bothering him on his lunch hour? He jerked the door open and almost fell over in surprise. There stood Rabbi Sadoc, wearing a gray tunic and a black cloak, grimacing a smile at him.

"Scribe Neri? Am I disturbing you?"

Neri shook his head.

"May we talk?"

Caught off guard, Neri merely nodded and stepped aside.

Sadoc breezed in, remarkably agile for such a tall, angular man. His long face betrayed no emotion as he surveyed Neri's home. The clinking of hammers on stone from the courtyard got his attention, and he raised a bushy eyebrow.

"I'm building a bath," said Neri, motioning for Sadoc to sit on the gold and red striped divan. He went to the courtyard door and shut it, quieting the workmen's clatter outside.

"Ah," said Sadoc, "a bath. I envy you Romans your luxuries."

"I'm Greek," said Neri.

"Of course," said Sadoc gravely. "But the edifice of Rome is built upon a Greek foundation, is it not?"

Neri nodded. What did this cadaver want? His mere presence gave Neri the chills. Neri pulled his cloak tighter around him.

"But of course you know this—I'm just making small talk," said the rabbi, smiling again, which only deepened Neri's chill. "I've actually come to share some information with you."

Neri nodded at him to continue.

"It concerns a midnight conclave that took place on the steps of the basilica last Sabbath evening."

"Who was present?" asked Neri, surprised he'd heard nothing about any such meeting.

"The workers. As you know, my synagogue faces the forum. Late last night, well after midnight, unable to sleep, I was reading in my up-stairs offices when I heard voices. A hundred men were assembled on the steps of your new basilica, discussing its destruction."

Neri's mouth went dry. So the workers had finally run out of pa-tience. "But the building still stands. Did you stop them?"

"Oh, no, my dear scribe, I wouldn't have *dared* to go down there. They had blood in their eyes—you could see it reflected in the torchlight."

"Who, then?"

"I do hope we shall be friends," said Sadoc, idly scanning the drapes and tapestries.

Neri nodded, familiar with negotiations such as this. "Yes," he said, inching forward in his seat, "I have no doubt of it."

Sadoc met his gaze evenly. So they understood each other. "His name is Jeshua."

Neri tried—unsuccessfully, he thought later—to hide his surprise, yet if Sadoc noted it, he gave no sign. "Jeshua," repeated Neri, as if trying out the name. "I may have heard of him." He gave Sadoc a quick glance, but the rabbi was studying his clasped hands.

Then Sadoc looked up. "He was quite persuasive, reminding the men of the zealot revolt many years ago. Are you familiar with it?"

Neri nodded.

"I thought you should know," said Sadoc, rising.

Neri stood. "Thank you for sharing this with me."

Sadoc bowed low, then walked to the door. He opened it and turned. "I hope we shall speak again, Scribe Neri."

Neri nodded. "The next time as friends, Rabbi."

Walking back to the basilica after lunch, Neri pondered the rabbi's visit. Their short conversation raised many questions, but one stood out from all the others: This Jeshua was in league with the rabbi—Neri had seen him leaving the synagogue meeting last week after his meeting with Sadoc and Ishmael—so why was Sadoc bringing him to Neri's attention now?

Of course the answer was plain: to further whatever Sadoc and Ishmael were up to. They wanted Jeshua to meet Neri.

Well, fine. Neri wanted to meet *him.*

When Neri walked into his offices, Marcus was going through the orderly stacks of parchment on Neri's desk. When he saw Neri in the doorway, he grabbed the scribe by the scruff of the neck and dragged him into his private rooms, slamming the door behind them. He shoved Neri against the big oak desk, scattering papers and scrolls. The cloudy crystal globe rolled toward the edge. Neri grabbed it just before it fell.

Marcus frowned at him. "What's this about a secret worker meeting Friday night?"

Neri turned. "I just heard about it myself, Sire."

"How is that possible?" howled Marcus, halving the distance be-tween them, spittle flying from his lips, his eyes dark with fury. "You're supposed to *know* about these things!"

Neri nodded.

"They almost tore down the basilica!" shouted Marcus, running his hands through his hair and turning toward the window. "I'll have to get rid of them, get new workers. . . ."

"But, Sire, you already employ all the skilled artisans in Galilee."

"Then we'll get Assyrians. Or Phoenicians. I don't know!" Marcus turned around. "By Jupiter's throne, Neri, how could you allow this to happen?" He snatched the glass globe from Neri, turning it over in his hands. Neri thought it would make a good bludgeon and scooted out of the way, putting the desk between himself and Marcus.

"But it didn't happen, Sire," said Neri carefully. "One of the workers stopped them."

"It wasn't Zoar! I'm told he wasn't even invited."

"It was a *tekton* named Jeshua."

"Never heard of him," said Marcus, glowering at Neri.

As they walked between the columns of the great, dark hall, Neri glanced back at Jeshua, who was covered with dirt from head to toe from working in the cisterns. He certainly didn't look like someone who could quell an angry mob. Neri quickened his pace, entering the court-room. To his right, the door to his offices stood open, and he heard voices. They entered and hurried down the corridor. Turning the corner, Neri saw Zoar standing just inside Marcus's doorway. Zoar turned, saw Jeshua, and shouted, pointing, "You're replacing me with *him?*"

Neri nodded at Jeshua, who had to squeeze past Zoar, who re-mained rooted to the spot, glaring hatefully at him. Marcus, who was re-clining on his chaise, nodded at Zoar, dismissing him. When Zoar didn't move, Neri touched his sleeve. Zoar wheeled on the small man. "Don't touch me!" he screamed, spittle flying.

"Leave us, Zoar," said Marcus flatly.

Defeated, Zoar turned and slammed his shoulder into Neri as he exited the room.

Marcus nodded for Neri to close the door, then he pointed at Jeshua. "I'm told you prevented a riot Friday night."

"I thought it unwise to awaken the soldiers," said Jeshua.

"Or me," said Marcus, standing and walking to the window. Outside, the sound of chisels on stone rang out, and below it all, the marketplace murmured. "You're an artisan," said Marcus, turning. "You'd like to finish the basilica, wouldn't you? Beautify the city? Glorify Rome?"

"Only Romans can glorify Rome."

"But you love Rome, don't you?"

"I abide Rome, Your Honor," said Jeshua. "I love Galilee."

"And your men," finished Marcus.

Jeshua nodded.

Marcus began walking a slow circle around Jeshua. When he was behind him, he leaned in and whispered, "Zoar is out. You are the new worker representative."

"And if I refuse?" said Jeshua.

"You won't," smiled Marcus. "You know your history too well: Varus and the zealots."

"What about our pay?" asked Jeshua.

"In due time," said Marcus. "But now, for your first assignment: tell your men that any damage they do to the basilica will be punishable by death, swift and sure."

Jeshua started to go, but Marcus said, "One more thing. Tell them this is *your* fault."

Jeshua set his jaw and left.

Neri shut the door behind him. "I thought you wanted him on *our* side!"

Marcus smiled. "First we crush the grapes, Neri. Then we make the wine."

Neri stared at his reflection in the wineglass. He'd already looked for answers in five full glasses, and still they did not come. He'd made a stupid mistake. In protecting himself from Marcus's fury about the secret worker meeting, he'd let Jeshua's name slip. Then, within an hour, Marcus had fired Zoar and made Jeshua the worker representative in his place—and all this was probably *exactly* what the rabbi and Ishmael wanted: their own spy inside the ethnarch's offices, right under Neri's nose.

Neri put his head in his hands. Sadoc had certainly used him expertly. And the worst part was that Neri still had no idea what scheme was unfolding. All he knew were the plotters: Sadoc, Ishmael, Hanock, and Jeshua.

And what about the many closed-door meetings Ishmael had had with Marcus? Was Marcus a part of this too? Is this where the fifty talents came in?

And most of all: How did this affect the king and, by extension, Neri himself?

Neri's head swirled with facts, rumor, and supposition. He waved the servant girl over. Another glass of wine was needed to sort this out.

Neri didn't leave the restaurant till late afternoon, and when he did, he had to be helped out the door. He leaned against a stucco wall, flushed, trying to focus his eyes. He reached up and touched his ear stump. A beggar approached him with his hand out. "Away, you!" shouted Neri.

"Please," said the beggar, his breath sour with wine, and the momentary connection between the two filled Neri with disgust.

"Off with you!" he shouted, and the beggar shuffled down the street. Neri saw several people watching him. "What are you looking at?" He pushed off the wall and walked down the street with as much dignity as he could muster, but the cobbles rose and fell like the deck of a storm-tossed ship, and he stumbled, grabbing a young girl's arm to steady himself, making her scream. Her mother whirled and saw Neri clutching at her child. She screamed and scooped the child into her arms, backing away from him.

Neri saw the disgust on her face. He hurled himself at the woman, brushing his hair aside and exposing the scarlet, knotted scar tissue where his ear once was. "Is this why you're screaming?" he bellowed. "Am I a monster?"

Someone behind him laughed. Neri turned. A man was standing behind a food cart. "Or am I a clown?" yelled Neri, grabbing his huge belly with both hands and shaking it. "The funny little fat man?"

The man behind the cart continued laughing, but then Neri noticed his customer. "You!" he exclaimed, stumbling forward. "It's you!"

The man reached for him, but Neri took a step back.

"Scribe Neri," said Jeshua, reaching for him again.

"No!" shouted Neri, backing away. "Don't trust this man!" he shouted at the crowd. Then he turned and fell flat on his face. The crowd howled. Neri tried to stand, but his legs were rubber. Someone lifted him up. Neri tried to pull away, but the grip was too tight. He was guided down a side street, leaving the laughing mob behind. Finally, he was leaned up against a wall. Jeshua's face wavered before his eyes.

"You're drunk," said Jeshua gently. "Please, go home."

"I know what you're up to," slurred Neri, pointing his finger at Jeshua. "You and the others. You think I'm stupid, but I'm not—I'm smart." He touched his finger to his forehead as proof. Something was sticky there. He lowered his hand and saw blood on his fingers. He blanched and sank to the ground. Jeshua produced a kerchief and gave it to Neri, who put it against his bleeding temple. "I don't trust you," said Neri weakly, the fight gone out of him.

"We need to find a doctor," said Jeshua, standing.

Neri caught Jeshua's tunic and pulled him back down. The wine had made him by turns wise, then invincible, then angry, and now, finally, weak and afraid. He clutched Jeshua's arm. "Why are you plotting against me?"

"I'm not plotting against you," said Jeshua.

Neri shook his head. "You are! You, Sadoc, and Ishmael. Even the ethnarch!" Tears sprang to his eyes. "I've served him faithfully for ten years! Why does he hate me? I've never cheated him, never stolen from him. I've always worked hard! Why?" Neri trailed off in ratcheting sobs, tears streaming down his flushed cheeks.

"I am your friend, Neri," said Jeshua, placing his hand on Neri's shoulder. "I'm just a common worker—"

Neri looked up, suddenly lucid. "Not true—any fool can see that!" He pushed Jeshua's hand away. "And you think I'm a fool, don't you?"

"I think you're drunk," said Jeshua gently. "Come, I'll take you home."

"No, you won't," said Neri. "You'll take me to Sadoc or to Ishmael. Or to Marcus!"

Jeshua put his hand on Neri's shoulder again. "No. I'll take you home."

"No!" shouted Neri, scrabbling away. "I'll take myself home—when I'm ready." He got to his hands and knees, then stood slowly, trying to keep his balance. "I'm not a fool. I've been running this city single-handed for almost ten years. I'm not a fool!" He was about to say more when he noticed the lines of concern on Jeshua's face. His anger drained out of him, and his shoulders slumped. He hung his head. "I don't want your pity."

"I don't pity you. Please, Neri, go home."

Neri couldn't bear the compassion on Jeshua's face a moment longer. He turned and lurched away down the narrow, undulating street.

The inn was cool and dark, and Neri heard the tinkle of glassware and low voices as well as the hollow sound of dice shaken in a wooden cup. A bald man in a stained apron approached, his hands held out in greeting. "Scribe Neri!" he said. "We haven't seen you here in ages. Welcome!" He guided Neri to a table and nodded at a shapely young woman with dark eyes and long, curly black hair. She picked up a bottle of wine and two goblets and came toward them.

Neri watched her approach. "I'm here on business."

The innkeeper smiled. "And business awaits."

TWELVE

Full and Empty Vessels

Monday morning was unseasonably cold. The sun was barely a glint on the horizon when Judah stumbled out the door and grabbed two water jars. He was halfway to the spring before he noticed they were already full. Feeling stupid, he turned back and checked the other four. Three were full, but one was completely empty. That didn't surprise him; their household used a lot of water, and it was not rare for all the jars to be drained between supper and morning. But *one* empty jar—that was strange. He had seen Salome and Sarah clean up after dinner, using two jars to wash the dishes. So two should be empty, not just one.

Judah scowled. This was James's doing. Last week he'd cornered the boy and threatened mayhem if he kept filling the jars. James shook his head innocently, but Judah simply said, "You've been warned," and turned away.

Then the jars started emptying themselves. Judah asked Jeshua again if he was part of the prank. Jeshua denied it. Even Simeon, who came over for dinner last night with his wife, laughed when he heard about Judah's troubles. "Whoever wants to come over and fill our water jars is welcome to do so!" Everyone laughed except Judah, who gave James a menacing look.

So, first the jars were filled, then they were emptied, and now some were full and some were empty. Judah imagined his tormentor watching him even now, and he whirled around, hoping to catch a glimpse of the prankster, but all the windows facing the small family courtyard were shuttered. Judah picked up the empty jar and headed for the spring, baffled.

On the way, he ran his hand through his hair, smoothing it. Maybe he would see Dinah. Since that day last week when he had abruptly filled her empty jar, she had not come to the spring. There was a line of women at the spring this morning, but Dinah was not present. He would catch no glimpse of her long, black hair peeking out of a head kerchief or her green eyes searching him out.

Disappointed, he got in line. A woman turned back. It was Tarah, Dinah's mother. She noticed him and frowned, then put her water jar down and walked back to him. Judah saw her coming, and his heart sank. "Good morning," he said, his eyes on the ground.

"Judah bar Joseph," said Tarah flatly. "No theatrics today?"

"No, Madam," said Judah. "I'm sorry. I just don't know how to act around . . . Dinah."

"Really?" said Tarah, folding her arms across her bosom. "I would say you accomplished *exactly* what you intended. She was humiliated. Again."

"I didn't mean to—"

"You seem to enjoy embarrassing her. Why is that?"

"I'm not trying to embarrass her!" whispered Judah, looking around.

"No, it just comes naturally, doesn't it? Well, it must stop. Do you understand?"

Judah nodded. "Tell her I'm sorry. Please."

"Tarah," called out a woman. "Your turn!"

"Tell her yourself, young man!" said Tarah, walking to the head of the line. Judah watched her go and felt the eyes of all the women on him. After a moment, he plucked up his courage and walked up to Tarah, who was bent over the stone basin, filling her jar.

"Madam?" he said politely. "May I carry your water home?"

Tarah ignored him. "Very funny."

"Please. Let me carry your water."

Tarah straightened and looked around. The other women were watching with amused smiles. Tarah frowned at Judah, "She's not there, you know. She left early this morning to visit relatives in Cana. So do you still want to help me?"

Judah nodded.

"Well, then," said Tarah, tossing her scarf over her shoulder and thrusting her filled jar into Judah's arms. "Come on." She marched off, and Judah stumbled after her. Cold water sloshed over the lip and drenched the front of his tunic. As he passed the women in line, he saw more than one smiling at him. He tried to smile back but couldn't manage it.

Neri's arm was a cold, dead stone. He moved, and darts of pain shot, screaming, into his forehead. He rolled off the dead arm and clenched his eyes, his head pounding. After a long while, he opened his eyes. The olive curtains glowed pale green. He sat up slowly, his right arm hanging uselessly at his side. For a brief, terrifying moment, Neri wondered if the arm had died during the night. Fear rose in him like bile, and he stumbled to his feet, lurching toward the curtain and yanking it aside. Yellow light filled the room, and Neri forgot all about his arm. Blinded, he shut the curtain and fell back into bed, pulling a pillow over his face.

Images floated across his closed eyes. The dark inn. The greasy innkeeper. Wine. Laughter. The tumble of dice. A smiling woman with long, curly hair. A yellow disk, like a tiny, glinting sun, sitting in the middle of the table.

Neri bolted upright. He was still wearing his tunic, but his girdle lay on the floor like a somnolent white snake. He threw himself at it, pulling at the folds, his good hand scrabbling across the material. "Where is it?" he groaned, pulling the folds of fabric apart. "My purse!" he howled, and his vision exploded into red fireworks. He stood, quavered for a moment, then fell backward, striking his head on the bedpost. As his consciousness fell away, he thought blankly, *Night? Already?*

When he woke, his cheek was pressed against the cold marble floor. A rope of saliva joined his fattened bottom lip and the corner of a tile. For a long time he lay there, studying the shimmering silver thread, his mind retracing yesterday's events. The day had started out bad and had gone to worse: that skeleton of a rabbi telling him about the near riot Friday night, Marcus's firing of Zoar, replacing him with Jeshua, one of the conspirators. The confusion that followed, resulting in too much wine, the jeers of mockers in the street, the encounter with Jeshua—was that by chance? Then the cool darkness of the inn and the warmth of a woman's hand on the back of his neck. The table, the dice, more wine, a gambler grinning at him. The tiny yellow sun.

The denarius. Marcus's loaned denarius.

Neri closed his eyes. Could it be true? Had he lost it gambling? At that moment, a spider scurried across his hand, and he shook it away, striking something. His purse! He grabbed it, got to his knees, untied the drawstring with trembling fingers, and emptied it out on the bed. A couple of shekels, a half dozen assarions, and a solitary, worthless bronze prutah. But no golden denarius, no tiny, shining sun.

I lost it, he thought, over and over, a mantra that somehow, if repeated enough, would reverse itself. *I lost it gambling. Lost it. Lost it.*

"Save me, Zeus," he moaned, collapsing on the bed. "I lost Marcus's money." He pulled a pillow over his face, wishing he could suffocate himself and be done with it, for no matter what happened next, it would be more painful than gasping for breath until your lungs burst and your eyes rolled back in your head and your purple tongue lolled out. *Not Marcus,* he thought, biting the pillow fabric. *Oh, Zeus, anyone but Marcus!*

Hanock strolled along on the wharf at Ptolemais, surrounded by a swirl of people. A half-dozen galleys were docked, with another three or four out in the harbor, waiting their turn at the long pier. He craned his neck, looking for Ahmad's distinctive black galley. Last Friday, when they came here, it had rocked gently in slip number three, and Ahmad took him aboard to see the last of the horses in the dank, smelly hold. There, in the darkness, a huge, black Arabian pranced and shied when they approached.

"High spirited," commented Hanock.

Ahmad nodded. "She's going to Caesarea Maritima. A gift for Valerius Gratus."

"Really?" said Hanock, duly impressed. "You know the prefect?"

Ahmad stroked the horse's mane, calming it. "Gratus is also a part of the upcoming . . . *transaction.*" He winked.

"And there is still room for other investors?" asked Hanock, knowing he sounded eager, but he couldn't help it. During their long morning ride to the coast, Ahmad had refused to talk business or, rather, to talk about this *particular* business. He was full of stories of distant lands and kings and consuls and praetors, yet when Hanock tried to pull details about his next venture, Ahmad seemed uninterested, which only fanned Hanock's desire all the more. By the time they crested the final row of hills and the coastal plain of Acco spread out before them, Hanock was merely going through the motions—he'd already made up his mind to throw in with Ahmad. Hanock still carried the list Ishmael gave him inside his tunic, but the sparkling beauty of Ahmad's black galley gently rocking against the pier and the tangy smell of the port itself convinced him that the audacious and impressive investment he was seeking was right in front of him.

Ahmad took him topside and showed him his private quarters. The bed was draped with thick, colorful, fringed blankets. The wardrobe door stood ajar, revealing a dozen fine togas and cloaks. And in the corner, behind a tall freestanding mirror, sat an ornate carved chest, banded with iron and locked with a heavy padlock. Hanock nodded at it, and Ahmad adjusted the mirror to hide the chest. "It's nothing," he said.

"Certainly," said Hanock, trying to appear worldly, even as the floor shifted under his feet and he remembered he'd never been on board an oceangoing vessel before.

"Occasionally, there are profits," said Ahmad breezily. "Now look here." He unrolled a large map, which showed the Middle Sea and the countries surrounding it. Ahmad pointed out Egypt in Africa, then moved his finger up to Sicily and the boot-shaped Italian peninsula, then over to Lusitania and Gaul and up to a distant island called Britannia. He tapped the island. "They eat human flesh there."

Hanock's mouth dropped open. "They don't!"

Ahmad nodded. "It's a big world."

"Where did you get this map?"

"In Rome. Here. It's yours," said Ahmad, rolling up the parchment and handing it to Hanock

"B-but I can't, Ahmad," stammered Hanock. "Won't you need it?"

"I have others."

Hanock held the map reverently in his hands. He never imagined there was a map that showed the entire *world*. And now it was his! Suddenly, his apartments and winepresses seemed insignificant in comparison. He was filled with a sudden, powerful urge. "Take me with you."

"What?"

"Take me with you. To Rome."

Ahmad smiled. "Certainly you've been there before."

"It's been ages," lied Hanock. "I wish to see the City of Hills."

Ahmad smiled. "All six of them?"

Hanock nodded.

Ahmad smiled. "Are you sure you can get away? You said you had a lot to do on your estate."

Hanock had told Ahmad he was the owner of Ishmael's estate when they went out riding the day after they met. Ahmad wanted a closer look, but Hanock said he had to be back to town before nightfall. Ahmad was disappointed and Hanock suspected he doubted his story, so to secure his belief, he took him to the bank in Sepphoris and showed him the golden talents in the underground vault.

When they emerged it was full dark, and Ahmad said he was tired. They bid good evening, promising to meet the following morning and ride to Ptolemais. Ahmad walked off and Hanock was left alone, standing on the bank steps. Ahmad seemed less impressed with money than anyone he had ever met, and it gave Hanock pause. Maybe once you had a certain amount of money, it no longer whispered to you at night, calling you to get out of your warm bed, to take the key from the loop around your neck, to open the chest and examine its cold beauty in the moonlight. Maybe you slept through the night and never dreamed about people plotting ways to steal it from you. Maybe, if a man had enough money, he could live simply, with just a few well-wrought possessions but with many adventures and powerful friends. Ahmad apparently used his money to buy unforgettable experiences among fascinating people in distant, exotic lands.

Hanock wanted that life. He was already becoming bored with property, which was a constant worry. He longed to travel, to leave tenants and winepresses behind, to watch a play unfold in a theater in Rome, accompanied by a beautiful woman who smelled of gardenias.

Standing in Ahmad's quarters in the black galley, he resolved that if fate was going to direct him to Ahmad, he would not resist, and though he himself couldn't go to Rome this time, his money would, and when it returned, he would have enough to buy his own galley and sail anywhere he liked, perhaps even to Britannia, where the savages ate each other and looked out across a slate gray ocean that never ended.

He stood now at the end of the pier and squinted across the sparkling water to see if Ahmad's ship was moored out in the bay. It wasn't. He walked back down the pier, not duly concerned. When he delivered the chest containing the fifty golden talents to Ahmad two days ago for the voyage to Rome, he heard the great black horse stamping down in the hold and remembered Ahmad saying the horse was a gift for Valerius Gratus, the Judean prefect, in Caesarea. Maybe he had gone to deliver the horse. He had, after all, invited Hanock to Ptolemais today see him off. Hanock had readily agreed, eager to smell the salt air again and watch the wind catch the billowing sails, pushing his fortune across the sea, to return greatly multiplied.

Nearing the landward end of the pier, he spied the harbormaster in a wide-brimmed straw hat sitting on a wooden cask, squinting at a piece of parchment while another man stood by, waiting. "It's in order," said the harbormaster, and the man took the parchment and left. "Unload it *now!*" the harbormaster called after him. "Others are waiting!"

"I'm looking for Ahmad's ship," said Hanock. "The black galley."

"He left two days ago. Saturday."

"He said he was returning today, after he delivered a horse in Caesarea."

"Don't know anything about that," said the harbormaster, rummaging through a box at his side. "Ah! Here!" He handed a sheet of yellow parchment to Hanock, who scanned it.

"There must be a mistake," said Hanock, showing the parchment to the harbormaster.

"No mistake," said the man, taking the paper. "The manifest. It's in order."

"But it doesn't mention the horses."

The harbormaster squinted at the paper. "Wasn't any horses."

"There most certainly were! I saw one, the last one. The others had been unloaded already."

"Wasn't any horses," repeated the harbormaster. "The ship came in empty. Didn't load nothing, and then it left two days ago." He put the manifest back into the box.

"There must be some kind of mistake!"

"And it must be yours," said the harbormaster. He picked up the box and walked away. Hanock watched him go, dumbfounded. He turned to slip number three, where Ahmad's ship had been. He had been on it. There were horses—he saw them.

No, he thought, *you saw one* horse. There were no others. Neither had he seen the crew, assuming they were ashore on leave. There was only the great black horse in the hold, the clothing and fine bedding in the state room, the mirror, and behind it, the banded money chest—assuming it *was* a money chest. Hanock sat down on a piling, shaking his head. Everything on board the black galley could have been a prop for a play.

But he might be overreacting. The galley could have been unloaded when the harbormaster wasn't here. After all, he couldn't be at the port twenty-four hours a day. But the manifest said the ship arrived in Ptolemais empty. But what about the horse, the one he *did* see? How did it figure in things?

It was a prop too, just like the clothing and the chest and the mirror. And the map.

Hanock groaned and leaned forward, putting his head in his hands. Last Friday he had given fifty talents to a man who had given him a worthless contract in return and then made up some story about going to Caesarea and then returning to Ptolemais before the trip to Rome. Ahmad was not coming back. He'd just stolen enough money to last him the rest of his life—why should he return?

I don't even know where he's from or his father's name or even one other person in Galilee who knows anything about him.

Beyond tears, Hanock just sat there, head in his hands, slowly shaking it. Stupid, stupid, stupid. Finally, he walked blindly to the stables and waited listlessly while the boy retrieved his gray gelding. Hanock gave him a coin and turned to mount his horse. Then, in a dark corner of the long, low stable, he saw a large, black horse. It was the horse from the ship's hold. "Whose horse is that?"

"My master's," said the boy, "but she's for rent, if you want her."

"Have you rented her recently?"

"Yes. A man who kept her a week. Gave me a shekel!"

"When did he return her?" asked Hanock.

"Early Saturday morning."

Hanock shook his head, unbelieving.

• • •

All day, Zoar had been hunched over the marble, chiseling the acanthus leaves into the column capital. His hands moved rhythmically in short arcs and precise movements, but his mind was far away. All day long he pondered his revenge options, which ranged as far away as the king's throne room in Tiberias and as close as a few inches, his hands pulling the garrote tight around the ethnarch's neck. When nightfall came, he ate dinner quickly, left the house without kissing his wife or children goodnight, and walked the dark streets of Sepphoris, brooding.

Now, standing in the shadow of the arched theater portico, he glowered at the basilica, then glanced at the synagogue, where a lamp burned in a window on the second story.

After two long hours, the lamp finally went out, and shortly thereafter a man exited the main synagogue door, disappearing quickly around the corner. Zoar moved in the shadows toward the synagogue, avoiding the light of the nearly full moon. He grasped the door handle and opened it, moving quietly into the vestibule. He heard footsteps and saw the glow of the candle coming down the narrow staircase. Zoar moved back into the shadows and waited.

When Sadoc stepped onto the landing, Zoar stepped forward. "Rabbi?"

Sadoc jumped and dropped the candle. The room went pitch black. "Who is it?" gasped Sadoc, retreating to the safety of the staircase.

"Shh!" hissed Zoar, stepping forward and picking up the candle. His eyes were already well adjusted to the dark. He handed the candle to the rabbi, who backed up another step.

"Who is it?" repeated Sadoc, his voice quavering.

So the old rabbi was capable of fear. Good. "I'm Jewish—don't be afraid."

Sadoc moved up another step. "That doesn't mean you wouldn't do me harm."

Zoar almost smiled. "I need to talk with you about the ethnarch. I think you will want to hear what I have to say."

Sadoc's quick mind got control, and he willed his hands to stop shaking. He nodded and turned to go back upstairs. "All right. Come upstairs. Quietly."

Zoar followed him, his mind working the new facts about the rabbi into his plan.

Judah climbed the ladder and joined Jeshua on the flat roof. Jeshua was sitting on a blanket, looking up at the band of stars crossing the sky. Judah sat down next to him.

"Ever notice," said Jeshua, "how the night sky is always changing? There are always stars you never saw before."

Judah gave the sky a cursory glance. "I guess."

"Always something new to see," mused Jeshua, leaning back on his elbows.

"Yes."

"A new way of looking at things."

"Jeshua," said Judah, "I understand. Don't beat me up with it."

"Don't worry," said Jeshua, lacing his fingers behind his head. "Dinah still loves you."

"You heard about this morning at the well?"

Jeshua nodded. "That Tarah is formidable."

"She hates me."

"Tarah doesn't hate you—she fears you. She's afraid you'll take Dinah away from her."

Judah laughed. "*I'm* the one who's scared, not her, Jeshua."

"Everyone is afraid of something."

Judah lay back by his brother. "You've never been afraid of anything."

"That's not true."

"Of what?"

"It's not important," said Jeshua.

Judah got up on one elbow. "You always do that—act like no one can understand your problems. I'm not an idiot, you know. I'm smart enough to get myself in trouble with the mother of the most beautiful girl in Nazareth, so don't treat me like a fool."

"All right," said Jeshua, glad to finally share his thoughts. "I'm worried I won't be able to accomplish what I've been sent here to do."

Judah shrugged. "Well, we know it's something important."

"But what?"

"You said it yourself," said Judah. "We're here to learn to love one another."

"Sounds simple enough," agreed Jeshua.

"I've also heard you say that worrying is wasted effort."

"I'm a hypocrite," said Jeshua. "I still worry."

"Me too," said Judah. "I wish loving came as naturally as worrying does."

Jeshua nodded. The familiar burden had pressed down on his neck and shoulders all day, but lying up here on the rooftop with his brother, looking at the stars and pondering the great expanse of heaven, made it recede a little.

"She loves you, Judah," said Jeshua. "Give her time."

Judah sighed, but then he nodded. "And you—give yourself time. When your moment comes, you'll know what to do."

THIRTEEN

Fact and Fiction

Early Tuesday morning, Jeshua heard someone call his name. He dropped his pickax and walked over to the ladder that gave access to the cistern, squinting up into the jagged circle of light. Someone was beckoning him and so he climbed up. When his eyes adjusted to the light, he saw it was Neri. Without meeting his eyes, Neri started off and Jeshua followed, dusting himself off and shaking the dirt from his hair.

Neri led Jeshua around the side of the basilica and then up the broad marble steps and past the immense, fluted columns on the broad porch. At the ever-growing facade wall behind the six columns, they stopped. Above them, workers were using block and tackle to hoist a huge block of stone called a spandrel into place on the wall. Wooden scaffolding filled the arched entranceway, its curved top shaped to support the immense voussoirs, the wedge-shaped stones that formed the curved portion of the arch. When the huge keystone was lowered into place, its weight would support the arch after the scaffolding was removed. The arch would be two stories tall, and eight men would be able to enter abreast under it.

"You'll work up top now," said Neri, still not meeting Jeshua's eyes.

"Scribe Neri, are you all right?" asked Jeshua.

Neri wanted to apologize to Jeshua about his behavior on Sunday, but he didn't know how. His pride prevented him. "Zoar was punishing you," he said, looking up at the arch, carefully avoiding Jeshua's eyes. "Now it's his turn."

Just then Zoar appeared, ducking under the scaffolding. He scowled
at Jeshua and ignored Neri, who took advantage of the awkward moment and disappeared under the archway scaffolding. Jeshua touched
Zoar's sleeve. "Neri says I'm to work with you on the arch."

Zoar jerked his arm away. "I don't want you anywhere near me," he
growled.

"I don't want to fight with you."

"Too late," said Zoar, thrusting his massive chest against Jeshua's.

Jeshua looked up and met Zoar's fierce eyes firmly. His dark eyes did
not contain the fire of anger or accusation, but rather a calm sea of compassion. Zoar took a step back, trying to avert his eyes, but Jeshua's eyes
held him fast. Zoar willed his hands to rise and shield his face, but they
hung limply at his side. He felt himself melting under the scrutiny of
Jeshua's deep, liquid eyes, and a whimper of fear rose in his throat. It
took every ounce of strength he had to stifle it.

"I don't hate you, Zoar," whispered Jeshua. "Please, don't hate me."

Zoar knew that in a few seconds he would be in grave danger of revealing every dark secret in his heart. If he didn't look away soon, he
knew he would be compelled to climb up onto the basilica roof and
shout out every wicked thought he'd ever had and every evil deed he'd
ever committed.

How could he not hate a man who had such power over him?

Finally, Jeshua's eyes let him go. Zoar looked down and saw his
hands clasped in Jeshua's. A tingling warmth was flowing into him,
spreading up his arms. With a jerk, he pulled away. His hands were hot
and red, pulsing with blood, and though he was now free and backing
away, the warmth still moved up his forearms as if he'd thrust them into
a hot bath. His mind shifted between a reptilian hatred and a tiny, growing fear that this wonder would cease; that the warm tendrils that wound
up through his weary muscles like glowing threads would not reach the
cold, empty vault of his heart.

He backed up, gasping for air. Black dots floated across his vision as
if he had been staring into the sun. He turned away, raising the dark
walls around his heart, desperately fending the light off. With the last
reserve of his angry strength, he reached into a cold reservoir deep inside
and scooped overflowing, icy handfuls of bitterness and rage, pouring

them into the dungeon of his heart. The light began to retreat. Then he clasped his hands together and squeezed the tingling, terrible light from his fingertips like a sliver from a bloody cut. Looking down, Zoar almost expected to see drops of sunlight leak from his fingertips and strike the marble floor, hissing like steam.

Finally rid of the painful brightness, Zoar refilled his heart with pain and hurt and jealousy and a grinding, crushing loneliness, stirring the ingredients until they congealed into a black coal of concentrated pain that fueled his bitter world. When his legs would obey, he hobbled down the basilica steps, back bent like an old crone, pressing his cold hands together in a sad parody of prayer.

Jeshua turned away, tears in his eyes.

Last night, Hanock had drunk himself into a stupor after his mind ground to a halt and could think no more. Then worry took the place of thought, and only more wine would chase the fear away. When he was shaken awake at dawn, he had a splitting headache. Now he found himself at the crossroads, south of Ptolemais. One road went east, up over the coastal range and down into the Netofa Valley and Sepphoris. The other road went south, skirting Mount Carmel and heading to Caesarea Maritima, the Judean capital. Hanock sat on his horse at the crossroads for a long time, considering whether he should ride down to Caesarea and see if Ahmad's black galley was moored there. But he knew that Ahmad was no more in Caesarea than he was in Ptolemais. By now he was a hundred miles out to sea, two chests instead of one sitting behind the mirror in his stateroom, knowing he had made the finest trade of his career: a man's life for an old map.

Hanock looked up the Sepphoris road, which wound up the craggy hillside, disappearing into a copse of pines. If he took that road, he would have to face the ethnarch. In fact, before he even came to the coast, he had foolishly made an appointment with Marcus for this afternoon to inform him of the importation plan. Now he would have to tell the ethnarch what had happened, and by tomorrow morning he'd probably be dead. And it wouldn't do any good to run to Ishmael. He remembered the terrible, bloody beating Ishmael gave Naaman for not multiplying one talent. Only old Hades himself knew what Ishmael would do to someone who not only failed to add to a sum of money but lost it entirely.

Fifty talents. For a brief, shining moment, Hanock had been one of the richest men in Galilee. Now he was the poorest, because even his own life didn't belong to him anymore.

He looked again at Mount Carmel, where myth had it that the prophet Elijah battled the prophets of Baal and Asherah. The mountaintop was wrapped in a gray caul of clouds. Rain drizzled onto the dark evergreen forests on those precipitous heights. Perhaps he could disappear into that deep forest. But no, Marcus would find him and take him to the king, who would impose his favorite punishment, and within very few days Hanock's head would be on a pike above the Sepphoris gate.

With no other choice, Hanock turned toward Sepphoris. Perhaps Marcus would only throw him in jail. Maybe Ishmael would intercede on his behalf, though he doubted it. He looked down at his shaking hands, willing them to be still, and gulped back the acid taste of fear. The trip to Sepphoris on this cool spring afternoon would be his last. He goaded the horse forward. Perhaps he would run into a band of brigands, who would rob or even kill him, but his luck had run out. There were no robbers on the road today—he had an appointment with the ethnarch, and nothing would prevent it.

Many miles farther, in the midst of the rolling Netofa farmland, when the road forked again, the gelding wanted to continue east, toward Rimmon. Hanock had to yank the reins hard to get the horse to turn south toward Sepphoris. The Roman garrison occupied the junction, fortified battlements surrounding mud brick barracks. Beyond the high earthworks, he could hear the clash of armor as the men trained. Two sentries stood at attention before the wooden gates, the purple plumage on their helmets bristling proudly. Their lances pointed upward, and they stared impassively at him as he passed.

Before him, Sepphoris rose like a colorful crown on an rolling emerald plain. On either side of the road the land was tilled, fieldstones piled up to form low walls, workers weeding the green shoots of wheat and barley. The road, straight as an arrow to the foot of the hill, pointed directly at the king's palace and its jutting spires high up on the flattened summit. Hanock stopped, considering whether to go on to Sepphoris or to go home and beg for Ishmael's mercy. At that moment, the horse started forward again, and Hanock almost laughed out loud. "You know his mercy as well as I do—you've felt his crop!" He thought of all the times Ishmael had beaten the servants bloody. He'd seen the gleam of delight in the master's eyes as he laid into them, relishing each stroke of the leather-wrapped switch, heard the swish as it cut the air just before cutting their flesh. He'd even felt Ishmael's foul breath on his own neck, panting as he worked up a sweat, etching bloody grooves across his back. Hanock reached under his toga and found the raised line of a scar, remembering his last lashing almost a year ago. When Ishmael finally tired, Hanock jumped to his feet and ran out of the house and across the dooryard. He didn't stop until he'd put the stable between himself and Ishmael's vengeful crop. He collapsed into a haystack there, sobbing in pain and humiliation. Thankfully, it was dark—that is, until a lamp approached and Naaman revealed himself.

"Are you all right?" asked Naaman. Hanock pressed his palms to his eyes to squeeze the last tears out, got to his feet, and strode toward Naaman, knocking the lamp from his hands. Naaman stumbled and fell backward. A wooden rake lay nearby. Hanock picked it up, grabbed Naaman by his skinny arm, and pulled him to his feet.

"Please, please, please," was all Naaman could say. His thin hands scrabbled at Hanock's meaty forearms to no avail. And with each "please," Hanock let the rake handle fall. He told himself he'd stop when the wood splintered, but it didn't, and the beating went on and on. Finally, Naaman's eyes rolled up in his head and he passed out, crumbling like a sack of grain. Hanock stood over him, exhausted and exhilarated, his shirt sticking to the bloody cuts on his back. He looked up at the night sky and howled, cursing God, then slumped down against the stable wall and stared numbly at Naaman's immobile body, emptied out of all emotion.

Naaman almost died from that beating, and when Ishmael found out, he lit into Hanock again, breaking two crops across Hanock's already bloody back.

But none of that mattered now, for Ishmael was the least of Hanock's problems. In a few minutes he would see the ethnarch, and once Marcus inflicted his punishment, Hanock would pray to the God he had cursed for the sting of Ishmael's crop.

Reaching the foot of the hill, the road began winding up between the jumble of mud-brick houses. Hanock felt his fine silk toga whisper across the scars on his back. *It will be a shame to ruin this garment,* he thought distantly. *It's much too fine to be covered with blood.*

"You *what?*" roared Marcus.

Hanock knelt on the mosaic entry. "I lost it," he repeated.

"All of it?" shouted Marcus.

Hanock nodded.

"By Jupiter! Get up!" yelled Marcus, kicking Hanock hard in the side. Hanock got to his feet. He dared not look the man in the face. "And why are you bare chested?" asked Marcus. "What happened to you?"

Hanock pointed at the bundle at his feet. The silk toga lay there, folded neatly. As he turned, Marcus saw ropy white scars on Hanock's back. "Put it on. Are you mad?"

Hanock shook his head and donned the toga.

"Who is this Ahmad?"

Hanock shrugged, and Marcus slapped him. Hanock almost raised his eyes then but kept them on the ground. A fellow Jew would never humiliate him that way. He might beat him or lash him or even hit him with a closed fist, but he would never slap him. His face stung and he felt his blood rising, but he kept his gaze focused on the mosaic of Neptune, who cradled a trident in the crook of his massive arm. "He said he was a merchant," said Hanock.

"Where is he from?"

"He mentioned Damascus, Jerusalem, Alexandria. And Rome. I think he lives in Rome."

"You *think?*" howled Marcus. "You don't know?"

Hanock shook his head.

Marcus turned away, running his hands through his long silver hair, looking like he might go mad. He spoke haltingly: "Gone. Fifty talents! A *merchant* from Rome in a black ship. A dream! A nightmare! Can't be. Can't be. Save me, Apollo. . . ." He pointed at Hanock. "How long ago?"

"What?"

"When did you last see him?"

"Three days, Sire."

Behind Marcus, Neri sat on a divan, his head cradled in his hands. Marcus turned. "Any ideas?"

Neri shook his head miserably.

"Well, one thing is certain," said Marcus, facing Hanock once again. "We must find this Ahmad. I'll send a message to Caesar in Rome."

Alarmed, Neri looked up. Marcus saw his look. "You're right. We shouldn't involve the emperor. Keep this to ourselves. It's enough that Antipas must know. Oh, Minerva, goddess of wisdom, save me! The king!" He sat down and shook his head. "We're all dead men."

Neri and Hanock exchanged troubled looks—Neri because he hadn't counted on losing his head over this, and Hanock because he thought the lost money belonged to Marcus. "It was the king's money?"

Marcus looked up, a feral light in his gray eyes. "It's mine. Do you understand?"

Hanock nodded. At that moment, a tiny flame ignited in his heart—he might live through this after all. Marcus made a much larger target than he did, especially for the king's headsman.

Neri looked at Marcus in dumb astonishment. The ethnarch's foolish slip had revealed everything to Hanock, a man of such obvious stupidity that Neri wouldn't have entrusted a mina to him, much less fifty talents. *Two sides of the same coin,* he thought, looking from Marcus to Hanock. *The currency of stupidity. We've certainly got fifty talents worth of that.*

Then Marcus looked up, and his eyes bored into Hanock. "By Pluto and all his minions, I will not suffer this alone." He turned to Neri. "Cast him into the dungeon."

Hanock was relieved; at least he wasn't going to be killed on the spot. He was about to thank the ethnarch when Neri stood up, shaking his head. "It's not finished. No doors or anything."

"So put doors on."

"But, Sire, everyone thinks the caverns are cisterns. The Jews would never—"

"What do I care?" interrupted Marcus, staring into the distance.

Neri was unsure what to say next. As a Roman who had lived in Galilee for just a short time, Marcus had not yet grasped the delicate relationship with the Jews. The Greeks, Neri among them, who had been here much longer, knew that if the workers found out the cisterns under the basilica were actually dungeons, they would surely riot. "Sire," he said, "this is not a good idea—"

"Just put him there while I decide what to do."

"But, Sire—"

Marcus jumped up and grabbed Neri by the throat, nearly lifting him off the ground. "Another word from you, and neither of you will ever see the sun again. Understood?" Marcus released him and he fell away. Neri held up a hand, acknowledging the order, his face red and his eyes bulging. Marcus turned and whistled.

Though he feared for his life, Hanock almost smiled; given the ethnarch's mercurial nature, the blame for the loss of the talents might rest on the backs of many, not just his. Hanock watched impassively as Neri slowly got to his feet, red faced and gasping for air.

In a moment, two soldiers burst through the sheer courtyard curtains, brandishing their gladii. Marcus held up his hand and they halted. Neri was bent over on the divan, massaging his neck. Hanock knelt to present a smaller target. Marcus pointed at him and said, "Take him to the cisterns." Hanock stood slowly, and the soldiers grabbed him roughly. "And, Neri," said Marcus, turning, "make sure the cell doors are strong. They might need to hold more than one man." He turned and strode from the room. Neri looked over at Hanock.

Unable to hold it back any longer, Hanock smiled.

Ishmael received the message from Marcus by midafternoon, and within two hours he was standing in the doorway of the ethnarch's private chambers, shaking with rage, holding Marcus's missive in his meaty fist. "What's this about my steward?" He slammed the door behind him.

"Please sit, Ishmael," said Marcus, reclining on his cushioned chaise.

"I'll stand, thank you," said Ishmael, shucking his cloak. Marcus noted how muscled the man's bare upper arms were. "You locked him up?" growled Ishmael.

"Just to encourage his memory. He lost a great deal of my money." Ishmael frowned. "How did he do that?"

"He gave it to a seafaring merchant, who has now disappeared."

Ishmael's face drained of color. He leaned against the oak desk. "He was supposed to buy land . . . the estates. I gave him specific orders . . . a list . . ."

Marcus snorted. "Which he ignored, Ishmael."

Ishmael shook his head. "So how much did he lose?"

Marcus pursed his lips. "All of it."

Ishmael sagged. "All of it! How can that be?"

Marcus scowled at Ishmael. "When you sent him to me with the letter of introduction, I assumed he was acting as your representative. Are you now telling me you didn't oversee him?"

Ishmael detected a tone in Marcus's voice he didn't care for. He stood and pointed at the ethnarch. "I sent him to you because you intended *my* name to be on those deeds."

"Of course!" said Marcus. "That was our arrangement. I get Sepphoris and you get—"

"To be the scapegoat, should something go wrong."

Marcus raised his hands. "What are you saying, Friend?"

"I just said it, *Friend!*" barked Ishmael, his chest puffed out and his eyes boring into the ethnarch. "You were going to betray me. If something went wrong and the king found out, I alone would suffer his wrath."

Marcus laughed, a long, hard roar that nearly sent Ishmael lunging across the room to wring his neck. Marcus collapsed on the divan, still laughing, unable to speak. After a long moment, he shook his head and wiped his eyes. "You idiot!" he exclaimed. "I'm the one who borrowed the money from Antipas! What does it matter whose name is on the deeds? I could have hired anybody—you or your chief steward or the Sepphoris rabbi, for that matter!"

The mention of Sadoc's name startled Ishmael, and he looked away for an instant, trying to grasp why Marcus had mentioned him. The momentary glance was not lost on Marcus, who filed it for later consideration. But right now, with Ishmael's beefy hands clutching the riding crop and the man looming over him, Marcus had more immediate concerns. He shook his head, motioning for Ishmael to sit. He modulated his voice, making it smooth and silky. "Don't you see, Ishmael? It was no ploy—I *wanted* you to have those lands."

"As well as the king's wrath," said Ishmael.

Marcus waved the idea away. "Nonsense. We sink or swim together on this. And right now, unless we get to the bottom of Hanock's story, we are both very close to drowning."

"Then let me at him and I'll get the whole story," said Ishmael, whipping his crop through the air. "He wouldn't dare lie to me."

Marcus nodded. "By all means. We might yet find this Ahmad scoundrel, as well as my fifty talents. But if we don't . . ."

"Then the king will find us," finished Ishmael. He looked thoughtfully at Marcus. "It was wrong to accuse you. I'm sorry."

Marcus shrugged and looked at the floor. After silence had filled the room for almost a minute, Marcus spoke emphatically. "Above all, the king must not find out." He looked up at Ishmael for confirmation.

Ishmael nodded. "I agree." He stood. "I'm going to hear the story from Hanock's own mouth—all of it." He struck his crop against his own thigh hard enough to raise a welt, or so Marcus thought, wincing. Ishmael turned, yanked the door open, and left the room. There was a scuffling sound in the hallway and Ishmael shouted, "Out of my way!"

"Neri," barked Marcus, "come here!"

Neri appeared, shutting the door behind him.

"If you're going to eavesdrop, at least don't get caught," said Marcus.

"I wasn't eaves—"

Marcus raised his hand, cutting him off. "He's plotting against me, you know."

"What makes you say that?"

"I'm not a complete fool," said Marcus. "Ishmael is up to something." He surveyed Neri. "And I certainly hope it doesn't involve my trusted scribe."

"Sire, I would *never* betray—"

"Neri," said Marcus, leaning back on the striped chaise, "do you know the story of Herod the Great? How he supported Antony and Cleopatra against Octavian?"

Neri nodded. "Vaguely."

"Aah!" said Marcus. "It is instructive. You see, at that time, Antony shared power with Octavian. They were both fine military commanders who split the republic between them, Antony ruling the east and Octavian governing the west, two lions, each with his own domain. But when the inevitable happened, and the lions began hunting in each other's territory, Herod supported Antony, his benefactor. But Antony was defeated by Octavian's navy at Actium, and thus Herod's life was forfeit. He should have run and hid, yet against all sage advice, Herod boldly went to Rhodes and met with the victorious Octavian. He removed his crown and knelt before the new emperor. The courtiers expected see him killed on the spot, but Herod made no apology, saying, 'As I was faithful to my patron Antony, so will I be faithful to you, Octavian.' Octavian relished Herod's honesty and courage and bade him put his crown back on. He remained king of the Jews and flourished—except in love, which is another story."

Neri nodded, understanding. "His faithfulness was rewarded."

"I always knew you were smart, Neri. I hope you are wise as well."

Neri tried to look sagacious.

"What, then, shall we do if Ishmael is unable to extract any more information from Hanock?"

"Do you know Rabbi Sadoc?"

It was Marcus's turn to be startled, but he shrugged blankly. "Sadoc? Just in passing."

"On the way to the cisterns," said Neri, "Hanock never stopped praying. He's evidently quite a pious man."

"Do you think the good rabbi will help us?"

"I think he would do most anything to get in your good graces, Sire."

"Really?" mused Marcus, remembering Ishmael's interesting reaction to the name just minutes ago. "He's never sought out my friendship."

"Yet I know he would prize it, if it were offered," said Neri.

"All right then," said Marcus, rising. "In the end, we'll have knowledge from two sources, and we will discern more than just the truth about the money. We will also know the truth about Ishmael and his friend, Rabbi Sadoc."

Neri left quickly. As he walked across the basilica hall, his mind raced. After such a long time in the desert, the oasis of truth was finally shimmering on the horizon. He cataloged the facts he now possessed: One, Ishmael and Sadoc and Jeshua were plotting against Marcus. Two, Ishmael and Marcus were definitely plotting against Antipas—he had heard as much through the door just moments ago. Under normal circumstances, they would never have made such a slip, but their minds were preoccupied with the lost money. He also wondered how long it would be before Marcus realized what Neri had heard through the door. He shuddered, hoping it was a long time.

Neri ducked under the archway scaffolding and stepped into the bright sunlight of the porch. Jeshua was off to one side, plastering the wall, his trowel moving rhythmically back and forth in a smooth arc. On the other side, Zoar was carving a capital, scowling hatefully at Jeshua.

As he arrived at the bottom of the steps, Neri remembered his own concerns. He touched his girdle, where he hid his coin purse. Certainly, compared with Marcus's missing fifty talents, his loss of a single denarius amounted to nothing. He sighed with relief. It seemed his prayers had been answered, and he intended to sacrifice to Zeus today, right after he spoke to the rabbi.

FOURTEEN

Light and Darkness

As Neri passed, Jeshua felt the scribe's eyes on him. He didn't look up but continued moving the trowel in a short arc, smoothing the white plaster. After Neri continued down the steps, Jeshua once again felt Zoar's angry glare on his back.

Earlier today, when he had held Zoar's hands in his and pushed the light into the burly overseer, Jeshua knew it was his last chance to reach him. Words did not penetrate the man's quick, angry mind. Kindness bore no key that unlocked the man's heart of stone. But perhaps a touch would succeed where the others had failed.

Jeshua had discovered his gift when he was a small child. He was holding his mother's hand, accompanying her to the marketplace in Alexandria. She was smiling down at him, and he felt her love like sunshine on his face. Looking up at her, he squeezed her hand and sent his love back. She suddenly stopped and knelt down in front of him, tears filling her eyes. "Is that how you *really* feel about me?" she asked in a voice choked with emotion.

Jeshua nodded, and her free hand went to her breast. Her breaths came slow and deep, as if she were inhaling a rare, perfumed flower. Her glistening eyes had a faraway look, even though she was still looking at Jeshua and still held his hand. "I never knew . . ." she said, a tear spilling down her cheek, "how much you *loved* me."

They were like that for a long time, Mary kneeling before her small son, tears in her eyes and her face full of light. She looked at his small pudgy hand in hers, then looked back into his eyes, which were also filling with tears. "I love you, Mommy," he said, and she held him tightly. After the tears were spent, Mary pulled back and looked once again into his bright eyes. "The angel was right," she whispered. "You *will* change the world."

I wonder, thought Jeshua, moving the trowel slowly, smoothing the white plaster. Over time, he had occasionally used the power of his touch, though he was careful with it because it was so potent. The last time was last fall, at the Qelt Inn on the Jericho Road. He'd healed the injured traveler, who was brought to the inn by the merry Samaritan merchant. But this morning, when he took Zoar's hands to try to heal him, something terrifying had opened up before him. There was a blinding darkness in the man, an emptiness that was growing, killing his soul, and that emptiness was now feeding upon his hatred for Jeshua and increasing in strength.

In a short life he nevertheless imagined as full, Jeshua had experienced indifference, annoyance, haughtiness, and derision—but never outright hatred. He'd always been able to turn the emotional tide, deflect the dismissive slur, or simply walk away. Most times he could stanch the anger of others and divert their hatred, calming them with quiet words and self-deprecation.

But Zoar was different. Even Achish, the robber who had nearly killed the traveler on the Jericho Road, was not as full of evil, though he'd committed nearly every sin imaginable. And little Naaman, the beaten-down stable master, when Jeshua first met him, was really just a scared, lonely man who had never been loved. And when Jeshua finally peeled away the layers of hurt he'd surrounded himself with, he blossomed like a tender, beautiful flower.

But Zoar's bloom was blighted on the inside. When Jeshua tried to send his love into him, Zoar resisted. *He loves darkness more than light,* Jeshua had thought in amazement, and the world was suddenly darker and more dangerous than he'd ever imagined. He had always believed love would be sufficient to turn every heart, given the chance, but now he doubted, for nothing had prepared him for the gaping, bottomless emptiness that was eating Zoar's soul.

I can't do this, he thought, scooping up another dollop of plaster and slathering it on the wall. It wasn't something he could discuss with anyone, no matter what Judah said, for this was his unique trial.

Father, he silently prayed, the trowel moving slowly across the wall, *help me*. He looked over at Zoar, who was glaring at him even as his maul struck the chisel, his muscled arms glistening with sweat, his brow furrowed with anger, and his eyes cold and hateful.

Jeshua turned back to the wall. *Please, Father, help me light the darkness.*

Neri looked around at the rabbi's office. The dark, ornately carved furniture was large and heavy, befitting the serious matters discussed here. Sin and repentance, punishment, and, Neri also knew, *bribery*. All religions were built upon the idea that you could bribe God with your obedience or your prayers or your generous donations and thereby merit blessings. And since God was an absentee landlord, someone else had to receive the payments. So Jewish rabbis and Roman flamens alike lived well, and Sadoc was no exception.

Sadoc sat behind his intricate table, looking mildly at Neri, waiting. The uncomfortable niceties of greeting were over, and Neri had taken his seat. Now it was time for business. "The ethnarch has a request, Rabbi."

Sadoc's long, narrow face smiled. "I am at his service."

"He requires your help in a matter involving Ishmael of Rimmon. I'm sure you know him."

Sadoc looked thoughtful, and Neri knew a lie was coming. "Yes, he's been to synagogue once or twice. I should like to get to know him better."

Neri noted with grudging respect how carefully the rabbi's words were chosen. Sadoc admitted to knowing Ishmael so Neri could not use their secret conclaves against him. Stating that he would like to get to know him better left the door open for future public meetings without drawing suspicion. He could always say the idea had been given him by Neri himself. Neri would have to sharpen his questions if Sadoc was going to reply to them so artfully.

"I'm glad you are friends," said Neri carefully. "That may help us solve a problem."

"I will help in any way I can," said the rabbi expansively. "I wish to serve the ethnarch."

Again with that, thought Neri. Sadoc must really want to get inside that office and have a private chat with Marcus. Why? Suddenly, another possible conspiracy appeared on Neri's list: Sadoc and Marcus against . . . *whom?* Who was rich and powerful and a mark for scheming men? Antipas? Was Sadoc a part of the Marcus-Ishmael scheme against the king—the one Neri had the least information about? Neri's mind whirled with possibilities.

"It seems the ethnarch entrusted Ishmael's chief steward with a great deal of money," said Neri, watching as the rabbi's bushy eyebrows rose predictably. "Hanock—that's his name—now claims to have given it to a mysterious merchant who disappeared in a black galley from Ptolemais a few days ago."

"Sounds like quite an adventure story."

"Yes, but we don't believe Hanock has told us the whole plot."

"Where is he now?"

"Under the basilica, in a sort of temporary jail."

"In the cisterns?" queried Sadoc, his thick brows rising even higher.

"Yes," said Neri, now even more certain that the whole world would know the true purpose of the caverns. He pushed the thought away. Plenty of time to worry about that later.

"So torture him," said Sadoc flatly.

"What?"

"Get the truth from him. Isn't that what you do?"

"We do not! We don't torture anyone!"

Sadoc rose, raising his hands. "I didn't mean *you*. I meant the empire. The soldiers. They surely have ways of obtaining information from captives. Use them."

Though he was Greek, Neri was a citizen of Rome. When he thought of the empire, he saw great cities with busy markets, glorious palaces, impressive theaters, clean, paved streets, luxurious baths, and life-giving aqueducts. But suddenly, he saw Rome as the Jews did: an oppressor whose improvements they would just as soon live without. "He's not a prisoner of *war* to be tortured," said Neri, standing. "But I will share your suggestion with the ethnarch."

Sadoc became as obsequious as a slave. "I'm so sorry—that's not what I meant at all."

"Your apology is . . . accepted," said Neri, sitting and lacing his hands across his belly. "We prefer more subtle ways of learning the truth. The ethnarch feels that since Hanock is a Jew, he might be more inclined to speak to you, Rabbi."

"Perhaps. But that depends on how devout he is."

"Well," said Neri, "he prayed the whole way to the dungeon."

"Oh, well," said Sadoc, waving it away. "If I were sent to dungeons, I would pray. And hard."

"There is one other thing," said Neri. "Ishmael is one of the richest men in Galilee. He recommended his servant Hanock to the ethnarch. It is not impossible that he had something to do with this so-called loss. Perhaps," he said, leaning forward and lowering his voice, "the whole story about the black galley is an invention."

"Surely Hanock would not allow himself to be thrown in prison just so his master could steal fifty talents from the ethnarch."

Neri looked up. "How did you know the amount?"

"I must have heard it from someone," said Sadoc breezily. "A trove of that size is bound to draw attention."

"The ethnarch would greatly appreciate your assistance," said Neri, still pondering the rabbi's last statement.

"Greatly appreciate?"

"Greatly." Neri stood, bowed, and excused himself, a rich man, if information was currency. As he walked down the creaking, narrow stairway, he knew he'd had the better of that meeting. Sadoc and Ishmael were indeed coconspirators. Ishmael had told the rabbi about the fifty talents. Or Hanock did. Maybe Hanock was in on the Ishmael-Sadoc-Jeshua plot.

Neri felt for his purse in his girdle. It was empty, but for the first time in days, he felt prosperous again. By the time he exited the synagogue, he was whistling.

Sadoc stepped off the ladder and peered into the darkness of the cisterns. Beyond the shaft of light he could see nothing. Then a soldier appeared out of the darkness, holding a small terra-cotta oil lamp, motioning him forward. Sadoc followed him through a rough-hewn arch and down a twisting corridor. They stopped. "He's in there," said the soldier gruffly, handing Sadoc the lamp and turning away.

"Who is it?" said someone. Sadoc turned in the direction of the sound. He was standing in the entrance to a large chamber. Holding the lamp up, he could just make out the latticework of interwoven iron bars. Beyond stood a well-fed man, wearing only a torn tunic.

"Hanock?"

Hanock's eyes reflected the tiny light. "Who are you?"

"I'm Rabbi Sadoc. How are you faring?"

"My master just left. Fortunately, he had only one crop. Give me the light."

Sadoc moved closer, then recoiled. Hanock's face was a bruised mess, one blackened eye swollen shut. His outstretched hands were caked with blood. Sadoc gingerly handed the lamp to Hanock, whose hands trembled as he received it. He held it up before him, the light making his face a grotesque mask.

"I'm here to help," said Sadoc.

"Then give me your cloak—it's freezing down here."

Sadoc drew his cloak tighter around him. "No."

Hanock held the lamp up, illuminating the tall rabbi. "I thought you came to help me."

Sadoc smiled. "If you help me, you'll be out of here and won't need my cloak."

"Help you? *You're* the not the one in the dungeon, Rabbi!"

Sadoc nodded. "It's about the money. What is the truth of it?"

Hanock laughed bitterly. "I told the ethnarch the truth, and he put me down here. My master came, and I told him the truth as well." He held out a bloodstained hand. "A lot of good truth telling is doing me."

"You weren't lying?"

"I would have lied to stay out of this place! I thought if I told the truth, they'd show some mercy! You know all about mercy, don't you, Rabbi? The kind of mercy that throws a man into the pit, beats him bloody, and then sends a rabbi down to gloat. Go away—but leave your cloak."

Sadoc stepped closer to the bars. "What did Ishmael have to do with this?"

"He recommended me to the ethnarch, that's all. Losing the money was my fault. And now I'm going to die without ever seeing the sun again."

Lightning quick, Sadoc reached into the cell, grabbed the lamp, and jumped back.

"Give it back!" wailed Hanock, grasping for Sadoc, who held the lamp under his face for a moment so Hanock could see his eyes. Then he hurled the lamp against the bars, showering Hanock with oil and plunging them both into darkness. Hanock rattled the bars and shouted obscenities. Sadoc crossed his arms and waited. Finally, when the last sob died in Hanock's throat, Sadoc whispered. "Truth is light."

"Go to hell."

"Listen," said Sadoc, moving a step closer, but still far enough away to avoid Hanock's clutching fingers. "Tell me the truth about your master, and you may yet see the light again."

"I told you the truth."

"But I want to hear *all* the truth, including the part about Ishmael planning everything."

"What?"

"Ishmael plotted to take the ethnarch's money. You are Ishmael's servant, so you went along with him, doing as you were told. *That* truth will bring light to your darkness, Hanock. Perhaps even the sun itself, shining warmly on your face once again."

Hanock muttered, "Ishmael? Planned the whole thing? Just doing as I was told? Yes. Yes, that's it. As I was told. It was his idea!" He grabbed the bars firmly. "Rabbi, it's true. Ishmael was behind the whole thing. I was just following orders. He has the money. All of it."

"Very good," said Sadoc, shucking his cloak and handing it to the two hands reaching from the bars. "No light yet, but a little warmth in the darkness."

Hanock pulled the robe through the bars and clutched it like a lover. "Very nice," he said, putting it on, running his hands across the embroidered wool.

Sadoc moved closer to the bars. "Hanock, listen."

Hanock leaned forward and was suddenly grabbed by the throat by two great, clutching claws, pulling him against the bars, pressing his bruised face into the latticework. Hanock scrabbled at the hands, all tendon and bone, but he couldn't dislodge them from his neck. "Listen," said Sadoc in a calm voice. "Marcus will like your new story, but if you should ever tell the old one again, I promise you the darkness will never end. Understand?"

"I understand," croaked Hanock, gasping for breath.

Sadoc released him, and Hanock crumpled to the cold floor.

Shortly thereafter, Sadoc stood in the doorway of the ethnarch's villa. Marcus smiled. "Do come in, Rabbi."

Marcus noted that Sadoc carefully skirted the polished mosaic of Neptune.

"I have news," said Sadoc.

"Sit down," said Marcus. "Welcome to my home." Sadoc sat and looked around. Embroidered tapestries hung on the walls, ornate geometric mosaics marched around the floor, divans were artfully arranged in small groupings, and sheer, whisper-light curtains framed the wide doorways to the lush courtyard garden beyond. "Pray, tell," said Marcus, sitting opposite him.

"It would appear that Ishmael is responsible for everything."

"So the fear of God finally pulled the truth out of Hanock," said Marcus.

"The fear of *something*, Sire," nodded Sadoc humbly.

"Can I count on your confidence in this matter—especially in terms of Ishmael? He is, after all, a close friend of mine."

"You may have complete trust in me."

Marcus smiled. "As a man of God."

Sadoc nodded. "Of course."

"Then I am truly in your debt, Rabbi."

"And I in yours, ethnarch, for the rare opportunity alone to visit your beautiful villa."

"You are welcome anytime," said Marcus, standing. "I trust this small confidence shall be the first of many, Rabbi."

"My heartfelt desire," exuded Sadoc, standing and moving toward the door. He again walked around the entry mosaic and turned. "If there is anything I can do for you, please do not hesitate to ask. I am at your service."

"Thank you," said Marcus.

Sadoc almost touched the door latch, then turned back. "Oh, there is one small matter I have been asked to inquire about, and it seems appropriate now, given the turn of events."

I knew this was too easy, thought Marcus. "What is that?"

"There is a woman, an old widow from Nazareth—"

"Esther," said Marcus flatly.

Sadoc smiled. "You remember her?"

"How could I forget? She vexes me daily with her petition."

"Her petition against Ishmael."

"She is a friend of yours?"

"She is a generous benefactor to my synagogue," said Sadoc.

Marcus nodded, understanding. "Ah. Well, then. You may tell the good widow that things are progressing in her favor."

"She will be most pleased, and grateful for your wisdom, Ethnarch," said Sadoc. He raised his hand in farewell and exited. The door shut behind him.

Neri appeared from behind a heavy curtain. Marcus turned to him. "Opinion?"

"The man is a snake."

"Yes," said Marcus. "But alas, my house is infested with rats. I need a hungry snake."

"But perhaps this snake is too hungry, Sire."

Marcus laughed. "As we all are, my dear scribe. I trust no one except myself," he said, still looking at the closed door. "And, of course, *you,* Neri."

FIFTEEN

Truth and Lies

It was late afternoon by the time Sadoc left the ethnarch's villa, and low gray clouds overhead shielded the sun, but he still felt buoyant. He had finally made a direct connection with Marcus. He no longer needed Neri or even Ishmael, who would soon join his steward in the dark cisterns. As his footsteps echoed under the curved theater portico, he looked at the grand stone basilica to his left then glanced ahead at his synagogue. His heart sank, not because of the building's shabby wooden exterior but because the pesky little widow Esther was standing on the steps, about to pull open the synagogue door.

Sadoc put a smile on his face and called out, "Esther!"

Esther turned, and her wrinkled face formed a smile. "Rabbi! I was coming to visit you."

Sadoc nodded and they entered the cool darkness of the vestibule. "Please, won't you sit down?" he said, gently taking Esther's elbow and leading her over to a bench. She seated herself and smiled up at him. "I was in town, and a little voice told me you would have good news for me. So I came straight over." She looked up at him expectantly.

Sadoc set his mouth in a straight line. "I'm sorry, Esther. The voice was wrong; the ethnarch hasn't decided your case yet."

Tears filled Esther's eyes. "He isn't going to grant my petition, is he?"

"Have faith, dear sister," said Sadoc, patting her arm.

"I've fasted and prayed," sniffled Esther. "I've seen the ethnarch nearly every day. What more can I do?"

Sadoc nodded knowingly. "You're sure you've done *everything*?"

"What do you mean?" asked Esther, dabbing at her eyes with her kerchief.

"Well," said Sadoc, "when we ask God for something, he needs to know we are serious."

"But I've done *everything* I can think of, Rabbi!"

"Yes, yes," said Sadoc. "But there is always something we've forgotten."

Esther stared at him blankly. "I can't think of a thing."

"Faith is acting as if what we ask for had already been granted."

"What does *that* mean?"

Sadoc shrugged, saying nothing. Esther tapped her cane on the floor, thinking. Sadoc was about to give her the answer when she looked up. "Oh! You mean I must act *now* as if God had already answered my prayers."

Sadoc nodded. "And what were you planning to do if the ethnarch granted your petition?"

"I was going to make an offering at the Temple. Are you saying I should go now?"

"It's a long way to Jerusalem, Esther."

"Yes, it is," she said, but she was warming to the idea. "It would take the rest of my savings, and I'd have nothing to come back to, but that would certainly be a show of faith." She looked at Sadoc, whose face showed doubt. "What is it, Rabbi?" she asked.

"It might be a little . . . *extreme*," said Sadoc. "God doesn't want you to starve."

"But faith requires action—you said so!"

"Yes, but God doesn't want us to injure ourselves in the process."

"So what do I do?"

Sadoc stood and walked up the center aisle of the synagogue, brushing his hand against a worn bench. "God is everywhere," he said, looking up at the leaky skylight far above, now covered with a canvas tarp to keep out the rain.

It took almost a full minute, but then Esther's cane struck the floor decisively. "You're right—I don't need to go to the Temple. I can do something *now*, right here in Sepphoris."

"Do what, dear?" asked Sadoc.

"I'm going to make that same donation to *your* synagogue, Rabbi!"

"You are most generous," said Sadoc, crossing and taking Esther's hand. "God will surely bless you."

"He already has—he sent me to you!" She smiled toothlessly. "The little voice was right after all."

Sadoc nodded, smiling.

Behind the six immense porch columns, the facade wall now rose over ten feet high. High up on the interior scaffolding, Jeshua and another worker muscled another immense spandrel into place. In the nave below, several Greek artisans were shaping marble voussoirs. As Jeshua watched, one of the artisans walked several times around a rough stone, moving his hands across the marble, tracing the golden veins with his fingers. Then he placed his chisel carefully, reared back with his maul, and struck the chisel decisively. A large shard of marble fell from the block, ringing on the floor, leaving a perfectly smooth plane on the voussoir.

Jeshua climbed down and ducked under the wooden archway scaffolding. Out on the porch, to his left, Zoar was sanding a leaf motif on the capital he'd been working on all day. "I'd like to work with the Greeks carving the voussoirs," said Jeshua. "Learn how they do it."

"No," said Zoar flatly, turning back to his work.

"Why won't you release me?"

"Because you wish it," barked Zoar, throwing his hammer and chisel on the ground and stomping away. He ducked under the arch and went to the water barrel, dipping the ladle. He looked back and saw Jeshua standing in the entrance, watching him. Zoar glared at him until he turned away. Then Zoar looked up at the wooden scaffolding, which now rose high above the wall itself. How different that wall looked since his meeting last night with Rabbi Sadoc!

Initially, he'd gone to see the rabbi merely to complain. In synagogue, the rabbi was generally critical of Roman public works, but he'd specifically declaimed against the basilica. Over the course of his harangue, it had become obvious to Zoar that the rabbi would be sympathetic to his anger at being fired by Marcus. But when they'd sat down in Sadoc's darkened office, and the rabbi cupped his hand around the candle, reducing the light to a mere glow, Zoar knew the rabbi had something on his mind as well. Over the course of the next hour, they'd talked about the basilica, spiraling in as if from a great distance, first discussing its architecture, then moving in closer to a conversation about its purpose, which was interrupted by a fierce, whispered diatribe by Sadoc about the arrogance of the Roman occupiers, building a courthouse directly across from a synagogue! Then the circle had tightened even more, and Zoar realized Sadoc's true intent, which coincided so neatly with his own rage.

By the time they had concluded their meeting, Sadoc had drawn from Zoar the building's prime weakness: the facade wall behind the six porch columns was not supporting the stone roof. It was merely decorative, designed so that if the immense entrance arch ever failed, then only the wall itself would collapse—it would not bring down the entire building.

But what a collapse it could still make! And, if properly executed, as the facade wall fell, it might topple an interior column or two, columns that *did* support the roof above—and within seconds the basilica would be reduced to a pile of rubble.

At that, Sadoc had leaned back in his chair, thinking. Zoar had leaned forward. "Wouldn't that give them a surprise?" he'd asked the rabbi.

Sadoc had nodded, a smile forming on his fleshy lips.

This morning, Zoar examined the facade wall with new eyes. When the time was right, he would see to it that a half dozen spandrels were placed high up on the scaffolding, directly above the arch. And when the scaffolding gave way, the immense stone blocks would crash down on the arch, dislodging the keystone. And when it fell, the entire wall would collapse, burying whoever happened to be under it at the time, and he hoped that would include Jeshua.

Yet though he wanted nothing more than to be rid of Jeshua, he needed to keep him close for now. Neri had put him on his crew, and Zoar was smart enough to know there had to be a reason beyond Neri just wanting to torment Zoar. He wondered if Neri knew of his plan.

Nonsense, he thought. *If he knew, I'd be in the dungeons right now instead of up here, planning his death.* No, Neri didn't know, but he'd placed Jeshua with Zoar for a reason, and Zoar had to keep Jeshua near until he knew what that reason was, no matter how uncomfortable it was being around the man. Through the archway, he watched as Jeshua bent over a mixing trough, stirring rhythmically. No, he would not let Jeshua work with the Greek stonemasons. He would keep him on his own crew. And when the planks gave way and the stones rained down, Jeshua would finally know who had the *real* power.

Outside on the basilica porch, Jeshua stirred the plaster thoughtfully. Zoar didn't want him around, yet he wouldn't ask Neri to move him elsewhere. That wasn't like the man. And Neri said he was punishing Zoar by putting Jeshua on his crew. But Jeshua felt like *he* was being punished. Was he wrong about the scribe? He believed there was integrity in the man, but his actions were perplexing.

Someone tapped him on the shoulder. He turned. There stood Ibhar, covered with white limestone dust. It peppered his hair and hung from his scraggly beard, forming a mantle on his narrow shoulders. "You look like a spirit!" laughed Jeshua.

Ibhar didn't smile. "I have to talk to you."

"I can't right now."

"Now!" whispered Ibhar, looking around furtively.

Jeshua nodded, and they ducked under the archway, going inside the basilica. Zoar had climbed back up on the scaffolding and was supervising the placement of several large voussoirs on the planking above. Jeshua led Ibhar to the water barrel and dipped the ladle, handing it to his dusty friend. Ibhar took a long drink, then ran a hand across his mouth. "They've built a cage in one of the cisterns. There's a man in it."

Jeshua pulled Ibhar behind a column. "Who is it?"

"I don't know. I only got a glimpse before they took us off to work elsewhere. Then someone came and started beating him. He was screaming so loud, I thought they were killing him!" He shuddered.

"Is he a worker?" asked Jeshua.

"I've got to go," said Ibhar. He dashed toward the entrance. Jeshua turned and saw the source of Ibhar's fear. Zoar stood not five paces away.

"Who have they put in the cisterns?" asked Jeshua, approaching him.

Zoar reflexively stepped back, then caught himself and held his ground. "How should I know? You're the worker representative."

"Did you know we were digging a dungeon all this time?"

"What does it matter?" said Zoar. "They pay, we work. It's all the same."

"Is he one of us?"

"He's not a worker."

"I mean, he might be a Jew."

Zoar turned and walked away. "I don't give a damn if he's the Messiah!"

Evening was falling, and Arah was heading for his special place, up on Gilead's Hill, which overlooked Eli's estate. He figured by now God had to believe him—he had been praying daily for two years, exercising faith. But no answers came. Maybe it was as Micah said: "There's no telling how you've offended God." Arah searched his conscience and made a list of his failings: sloth, jealousy, talking back to the cook, teasing his little sister, ignoring his mother's pleas not to tease her, and so on. Depressed, a few days ago he mentioned his list of sins to old, bald Micah, who said, "Easier to stop the Jordan than to stop sinning. God made us this way."

"So if he knows we're going to sin, why does he punish us for sinning?"

Micah frowned. "You saw that carpenter from Nazareth a few days ago. This one of his ideas?"

"No," said Arah. "I made it up myself. I don't understand."

"Not for us to understand. It's for us to obey."

"And sin, I guess," said Arah, scuffing the hard dirt with his toe.

Micah smiled, his one tooth gleaming. "Well, at least you're doing *part* of what you're here to do. Work on the part about obeying."

Arah continued up the path. When they read Torah in synagogue, in passage after passage the pattern was repeated. God would get angry at people's wickedness and kill everybody. Then, humbled, the survivors would repent and obey for a time. Then, as they were blessed and prospered, they would sin again, and God would punish them all over again. Arah wondered how *anyone* would ever get into heaven. At such times, he felt his spirit shrinking and feared that by the time he was Micah's age, his tiny, wicked soul would rattle around in his body like a pea in a gourd. By then he too would probably be convinced that you could never please God, no matter how hard you tried. It was a depressing thought.

Yet as he crested the hill, the setting sun full in his eyes, he knew this was not the same god Jeshua talked about. Arah wondered if Jeshua's god was the God of the Sefer Torah or if he was someone else. If he was another god, then Arah was committing idolatry and his soul was in peril. And yet Arah couldn't bring himself to pray to Micah's god. Since Micah's god knew he would sin again, no matter how repentant he was at this moment, he was at best weak-willed and at worst a liar. Either way, that god surely would not allow him into his heaven.

So instead, he prayed to Jeshua's god, the one who understood that sinning was a natural part of life. The one who wanted Arah to just do his best, no matter how often he failed. If Arah was praying to the wrong god, then so be it. He couldn't imagine being happy in heaven with Micah's god anyway.

He found his usual place under the tall sycamore tree and sat down, leaning against the smooth trunk. Before he he'd met Jeshua, he would prostrate himself on the ground and pray like everyone else, but he'd stopped doing that when Jeshua told him that God was our father. It just didn't seem right to have to throw yourself on the ground before your own father. Wouldn't he rather you just talked to him?

But then Arah wondered why Jeshua's god was so slow to hear his prayers. *If he really is my father*, thought Arah, *then why won't he answer me?*

Then Arah remembered something. When he was little, he ate a whole loaf of barley bread slathered with butter and honey. He got sick and threw the whole thing up. His mother dabbed his sweaty forehead with a wet cloth, saying too much of anything was bad. Arah put his chin on his knees and wondered if that was true of prayer as well. Could you pray too much? Did Jeshua's god get tired of hearing us always begging? And didn't he know before we asked what we were going to ask for? So if he knew what we wanted, and knew what we needed, why didn't he just give it to us?

"Because you don't ask in faith," Jeshua had said as they'd walked to Sepphoris last week, after Arah had shared his concerns with the carpenter.

"But you said faith is a gift," said Arah. "But to get it, you have to already have it. How is that possible?"

Jeshua smiled. "That's called a paradox, Arah. But don't worry, everyone is born with enough faith—a little bit of leaven will raise many loaves."

"How do I know if I have faith?"

"Before you go to bed, you always fill the water jars, don't you?"

Arah nodded.

"Why?"

"I get switched if I don't," said Arah.

"Not if there's no tomorrow."

"But there's always a tomorrow."

"How do you know?"

"Because there always has been," said Arah. "Why wouldn't there be a tomorrow?"

"So you believe tomorrow will come."

"Yes."

"Well, faith is believing in something that is true but as yet unseen, like tomorrow."

"So believing is having faith?"

"That's part of it. But even more important, you must *act* upon that belief. You fill the jars because you believe tomorrow will come and the water will be needed. You're exercising faith."

"Because if I don't, I'll get switched," laughed Arah.

Jeshua shrugged. "What matters most is that the jars get filled."

Arah smiled, thinking of Jeshua. How he had missed him! Even though Nazareth was only a few miles from Eli's estate, Arah hadn't seen him in two years, and now, after his visit with Jeshua and his family, he missed him more than ever. Talking with the dark, curly-haired carpenter was like drinking cool, clear water. It filled him up and made him want to be a better person. He couldn't explain that to someone like Micah, who only saw Jeshua as a negative influence. Maybe when you get old, your mind becomes comfortable with things as they are, even if they're wrong. Change is uncomfortable, like sleeping on someone else's pallet—the lumps are in the wrong places.

The red sun slid behind the hills, and the low ceiling of clouds went orange and pink. Arah closed his eyes and bowed his head. "I have faith, Lord," he whispered. "I miss my father. You could send him back and we could talk. I have so many questions. There must be a reason why you don't. Maybe you can tell me what that reason is, because I don't think it's fair that you get him all to yourself, while my sister and my mother and I don't get him at all. I know I don't have a right to ask you for anything, but Jeshua says you're my father, so I'm asking anyway."

The cool wind sighed through the trees, stirring the leaves. Distantly, a crow screeched, followed by a dog barking, then there was silence again. The wind moved across the long green grass, sweeping along in a wide swath, disappearing over the top of the hill. Arah opened his eyes. The sky was turning purple and shadows filled the valley.

Arah looked heavenward. "I'm just trying to keep the jars full."

Working by the light of a single lamp, Jeshua gently stroked the donkey's coat with the stiff brush. Sounds of laughter and conversation drifted through the open windows surrounding the courtyard. Jeshua looked up and saw Joseph standing in the stable doorway.

"You could use more light," said Joseph, entering.

"There's enough light."

"And more than enough darkness. Are you all right?"

Jeshua nodded. "I'm just a bit . . . overwhelmed."

"Sepphoris?" asked Joseph.

Jeshua shrugged. "Among other things."

Joseph put his hand on Jeshua's shoulder. "The darkness?"

"It's getting worse. There's a worker in Sepphoris who wishes I were dead."

"You've encountered this before," said Joseph, "and you've always managed to reach them."

"Not this time," said Jeshua. "I touched him, and the darkness in his heart almost swallowed me." He shuddered. "I could not heal him."

"You can't heal everyone, Jeshua."

Jeshua's eyes glistened. "Why not?"

"Because people are free to choose. God isn't a puppeteer and we his marionettes. You once told me that choosing right from wrong is the whole point of this life. I've thought a lot about that, and also about something else you said: that God is love. And so I cannot imagine our Heavenly Father not having a plan to reclaim those who choose poorly."

"What do you think that plan is?"

Joseph looked into Jeshua's eyes. "You, Son."

Jeshua nodded slowly. "Perhaps that is the burden I feel. I'm afraid."

"Jeshua?"

Jeshua looked up. Joseph recited the angel's words. "'Fear not, for behold, I bring you good tidings of great joy, which shall be unto all people. For unto you is born this day a Savior, which is Christ the Lord.'"

Jeshua hung his head. "But how will I do it?"

Joseph took the tiny clay oil lamp from the windowsill, cupping it in his hands. "See this? So small, yet it banishes darkness from an entire room. This tiny flame is love."

"But that light can be extinguished," said Jeshua, pinching the flame out, plunging them into darkness. "The love of men grows cold."

Joseph took Jeshua's sleeve and led him out into the courtyard. The full moon was rising in the sky, casting distinct shadows even in the darkness. "Yet still there is light."

"And when there is no moon?"

"Then there are the stars. You've said God's love will always light the darkness."

"What other wise things have I said?" asked Jeshua, noticing for the first time that the burden he'd felt since his encounter with Zoar this morning had lifted a little.

"Here's one," said Joseph. "Light and truth, when combined, equal wisdom."

"I said that?"

"Maybe that's why I'm here," said Joseph. "To remind you. You said we all have light within us, the desire to be truthful and do good. And if we try, we can change the world—"

"And God will give us the wisdom to know how," finished Jeshua. "But you are wrong about one thing, Father. I didn't teach you this. You taught me. And *that* is why you are here."

They embraced and Joseph whispered, "You will have the wisdom when you need it, Jeshua. I know it."

SIXTEEN

Twists and Turns

Ishmael rode along, lost in thought. He'd been too easy on Hanock yesterday. The steward's fanciful story about a black galley and the mysterious Ahmad was a child's tale, and Ishmael would bleed the truth from him today. Ishmael knew his time was short; he'd seen the pitiless look on Marcus's face. He'd spent a long time this morning preparing another crop to work the truth to the surface. The switch was long and sturdy and wrapped tightly with a long strip of leather.

He looked up. The road crested the hill near a stand of oak trees. As he watched, four horseman appeared. Soldiers. They saw him and stopped. The purple plumes on their galeas fluttered in the breeze. They didn't move but just sat, watching him.

Under normal circumstances, Ishmael would not have feared the sight of a Roman soldier—or even a cohort of them. He was, after all, a friend of the ethnarch. But seeing them sitting there on their large black horses in full battle armor filled him with dread. He goaded his horse forward and was soon within a few rods of the soldiers. "Ishmael of Rimmon?" said one of them. Ishmael nodded. "The ethnarch commands your presence. Are you armed?"

Ishmael slowly reached for his short sword in its scabbard. The soldiers' hands went to their swords. Ishmael's sword clattered to the ground. One of the soldiers dismounted and walked toward him, picking up the blade. He tucked it into his belt and mounted his horse.

"Anything else?" asked the first soldier. Ishmael shook his head. "To Sepphoris, then," said the soldier, wheeling his horse. Ishmael spurred his mount onward, following the first soldier. The other three fell into place behind him. "The ethnarch is looking forward to seeing you," said the first soldier.

Ishmael forced a smile. "And I him."

At lunch yesterday, when Naaman had told Hanock's assistant Zerah about what happened with the financier Ocran in Sepphoris on Sunday, Zerah had scoffed. "He did all right by me and Hanock."

"Something about him was wrong," said Naaman. "He looked at me as if I were a sheep at shearing time: Is the wool nice and soft? Will it bite me if I nick it with the razor? You know, like I was a *thing*."

Zerah laughed. "Thing or not, if you don't get your share, he doesn't get his. The more money he makes for you, the greater his portion. It's in his best interests not to misuse you."

"But what if he could misuse me without any consequences?"

"What do you mean?"

"I mean," said Naaman, leaning forward, "who cares if a stableboy gets sheared?"

"You could always complain to the ethnarch."

"You know what Master Ishmael says about him. He'll probably throw me in jail, just for spite."

"Like Hanock," shivered Zerah.

Naaman nodded. News of Hanock's plight had reached the estate yesterday, shortly after Marcus threw him in the dungeon. Ishmael immediately saddled his black stallion and galloped off to Sepphoris. He didn't return until late, and when he did he was angry. He grabbed a bottle of wine and shut himself in his private rooms. No one saw him for the rest of the evening, but a servant boy heard cursing and things breaking against the walls.

As Naaman rode along the road with the morning sun warming his neck and shoulders, he shivered as well. *Poor Hanock,* he thought, wondering how he'd managed to lose all that money. Zerah said it was five hundred talents. Not even the king had that much money, said another servant. "I think it's more like twenty talents," said another, but even though a man could live comfortably for the rest of his life on that much, Naaman thought twenty talents was probably too little, five hundred too many. Someone said Hanock gambled it away, but Naaman didn't believe that, either. Hanock was a miser—he wouldn't wager a talent in a dice game or waste it on a woman.

But regardless of how he had lost it, he had indeed lost it and was now in the ethnarch's dungeon under the basilica. Naaman felt bad, but he had to admit that as long as Hanock was in prison, he couldn't very well throw Naaman in jail. Reminded of his plight, Naaman found his hand going to the money pouch. What was he going to do with this coin?

Another estate came into view. A low fieldstone wall surrounded the dirt dooryard, and a flowering grape trellis arced above the gate. Beyond, an old, gnarled olive tree shadowed a well. Thirsty, Naaman turned his horse toward the house. He dismounted and opened the trellis gate. "Hello?" Behind him, across the road, on the crest of a rolling hill, he could see a half dozen men working the fields, weeding the seedlings. He heard voices from somewhere, the delighted squeal of children. Just then a small girl ran around the corner of the house, chased by an older girl, both laughing. They ran across the dooryard toward Naaman and jumped over the low wall, shouting, heading for the fields on the other side of the road. Naaman watched them go, his hand still on the gate.

"Who are you?"

Naaman turned. An old man, very broad, very tall, and very gray, stood in the open doorway, his thumbs thrust into his broad leather belt.

"A traveler, sir," said Naaman. "Shalom."

"What do you want?"

"To water my horse," said Naaman. "And perhaps have a swallow myself."

The man turned and whistled. Naaman heard footsteps, and a boy appeared in the doorway, his face hid in shadow. The man said something, then disappeared inside the house. The boy stepped forward, and Naaman's jaw dropped. "Arah?"

"Naaman?" said Arah, coming forward. "What are you doing here?"

"I'm headed to Sepphoris," said Naaman. "I stopped for a drink."

Arah led Naaman across the dooryard and pushed the waterskin over the well edge and quickly withdrew it. Naaman took a long drink while Arah led his horse to the water trough at the side of the house. "Why are you going to Sepphoris?" asked Arah.

"Business."

"If you're going to throw more money around," laughed Arah, "I'll come along."

Naaman had to smile, remembering how they had met. "I hope it doesn't just get tossed away, like last time," he said, patting the coin purse hanging around his neck.

"Do you still have the little black stone?" asked Arah. "Can I see it?"

Naaman removed the stone from the pouch and handed it to Arah, who studied it closely. "I have something like this," said Arah, giving the stone back and turning toward the house. "I'll show you." He disappeared inside the house.

Naaman led his horse over to the low fieldstone wall and sat, closing his eyes, enjoying the sun on his face. "Here it is!" said Arah, appearing again. He had one hand behind his back, his eyes twinkling with a secret. "Guess what it is."

"It's a stone," said Naaman.

"No, but it's related to something right in front of you."

Naaman looked around. "But all I see is stone: the flagstones around the well, the stone wall I'm sitting on, the stone stoop, the stone house."

"You see but do not comprehend," said Arah.

Naaman cocked an eyebrow. "You speak like an oracle."

"Then I will tell you your future: you will not guess my riddle."

"False prophet!" laughed Naaman. "You say it's not stone?" Naaman tossed his little black pebble from one hand to another. "Is it alive, like an animal or a plant?"

"Not anymore."

"Not anymore," mused Naaman. "But it once was?"

"Yes. Long ago."

Naaman looked around, dismissing everything that was made of stone or was still alive. It couldn't be Arah's clothing, because cloth had never been alive. It couldn't be leather, like a sandal, because the boy was barefoot. There was no food to be seen. The urn by the door was made of clay. Naaman's eyes held on the immense door. It was red mahogany with a rounded top. Just then, the two little girls jumped the low wall by him and ran into the house.

And the door they ran through opened *in.* Naaman had never seen such a thing. He glanced at Arah, who nodded, seeing the line of Naaman's sight. "Is it the door?" asked Naaman.

"Close enough!" shouted Arah, pulling Naaman across the door-yard, being careful to keep one hand out of sight behind his back. As they approached the door, the workmanship revealed itself. Delicately cut panels, meticulously joined. Naaman touched the surface—the varnish was as thick as honey. A black iron door handle gleamed, and he noticed a small window at eye height. He peered through it but couldn't see anything.

"The shutter is down," said Arah, stepping behind the door and raising it. "Now look."

Naaman did, and he could see Arah's eye on the other side. The boy came around the door. "Do you know what it is?"

"Couldn't be the door, for it lacks nothing. It's a masterwork, complete in and of itself. What could you possibly have that could add to this marvel?" Arah held his hand out. In his palm was a little cylindrical clay vial with a cork stopper. "What's that?" asked Naaman.

"Oil," said Arah. "For the hinges."

"For the hinges," repeated Naaman. "But how is that like my stone?"

"Well," said Arah, unstopping the cork and reaching up, tilting the vial slightly. A drop of olive oil fell onto the upper iron hinge pin. "I helped Jeshua build this door—"

"Jeshua? Jeshua who?"

"Jeshua bar Joseph. Do you know him?"

"I don't know his father's name. The Jeshua I know is from Nazareth, though."

"That's him!" said Arah, holding up the vial. "He's the one who gave me this!"

Naaman opened his hand, revealing the little black stone. "Arah, that is the same man who saved my life. And this is how I remember him."

They looked at each for a long moment, their wonder turning to smiles, and then they reached out and hugged each other, united by a small black stone, a tiny terra-cotta oil vial, and a carpenter from Nazareth named Jeshua bar Joseph.

• • •

"Good luck in Sepphoris," cried Arah, waving. "Say hello to Jeshua for me!"

"He'll be surprised to know we've met."

"I doubt it—and don't worry about investing it," called Arah. "You'll do fine!"

Naaman touched his coin pouch. There, against the larger shape, was the small rounded contour. Jeshua's stone. There was a reason he had stopped at Arah's this morning, and it wasn't just to get a drink of water. A satisfying warmth filled him. He took a deep breath of the cool morning air and goaded his horse into a trot, eager now to be on his way.

"You cannot do this!" shouted Ishmael as he was led away.

"Reconsider your story," called Marcus.

"But it's the truth!" shrieked Ishmael as the guard pushed him out of sight.

Neri shut the door. "It's a great risk, Sire."

"But which is more fearsome? Ishmael's anger or the king's?"

"But how will this help?"

"If Ishmael is free, he can do me a great deal of harm," said Marcus, pacing. "Of course I don't believe that nonsense the rabbi came back with about Ishmael being involved in Hanock's loss. I trust Sadoc even less than I trust Ishmael. But I've got to blame someone for the lost money!"

"And you're sure the king won't believe Ishmael?"

"Antipas needs me; I doubt he even knows who Ishmael is."

"How long will you keep him in there?" asked Neri.

"Long enough to figure this out. I spoke to Ocran yesterday, and he told me about his argument with Hanock in the vault. Late last night, I got word from the harbormaster at Ptolemais. There was indeed a black galley and a man who answered the description of this Ahmad. Riders are on their way to Caesarea to see if the galley is there."

"What if it's not?"

Marcus scowled. "Of course it won't be there! But a black galley is not invisible. I've offered a reward for information about it. We'll find it, and I'll flay the thief myself. But all this takes time."

"And so Ishmael will wait in the darkness of the dungeon."

"We'll give him a lamp," said Marcus. "We're not barbarians."

Naaman was standing at the front of the basilica, looking around for Jeshua. He wanted some advice, or at least encouragement, on how to invest the talent Hanock had given him. Time had passed—too much time—and he needed to get on with it. The luxury of fear was gone; he needed to be courageous.

He was about to turn away when he heard shouting coming from the building. Instinctively, he stepped behind a large marble block. Two soldiers ducked under the archway scaffolding. Behind them came Ishmael, followed by two more soldiers. His hands were tied behind his back. "This is an outrage!" he shouted, looking over his shoulder. Naaman expected to see the ethnarch, but the arch remained empty. At the bottom of the broad steps, the soldiers turned to the right, leading Ishmael into the alley between the basilica and the bank.

"Naaman?"

He jumped a foot into the air, whirling around. "Jeshua! You scared me!"

Jeshua nodded toward the entourage of soldiers. "Isn't that your master, Ishmael?"

"Yes," said Naaman. "Where are they taking him?"

"I would guess the cisterns. They already have one man in there."

Naaman nodded. "Hanock. Now Ishmael. I may be next."

He turned to go, but Jeshua caught his sleeve. "Wait—" Then Jeshua stopped, looking at something over Naaman's shoulder. Naaman turned. Marcus was now striding down the basilica steps with Neri trotting close behind. Jeshua released Naaman. "I've got to see about this," he said, walking an intercepting line toward Marcus.

Neri saw him first and waved him away. "No time now!"

"Who is in prison?"

Marcus didn't break stride. "None of your business, *tekton*."

Jeshua grabbed Neri, stopping him. "The workers will want to know."

Neri waited until Marcus had walked out of earshot, then pulled his arm from Jeshua's grasp. "Be careful, Jeshua. You did me a favor, now I will do you one. The ethnarch is looking for scapegoats—you just saw one being taken to the cisterns."

By now they had been joined by a dozen men with tools in their hands. "We didn't agree to dig dungeons, Scribe Neri," said Jeshua.

"What's the difference?" said Neri, annoyed. "You get paid the same!"

"We haven't been paid at all," said Barak, elbowing his way toward the front of the crowd, towering over everyone else. His iron maul was slung over his shoulder. He looked like he could bring down the basilica himself if he swung it hard enough.

"Is that what this is about?" asked Neri. He looked around, saw he was alone, and nodded, lowering his voice. "I see your concern."

"What we need to know," said Jeshua firmly, "is if you *share* it."

"Your pay is late, that's all. Some troubles."

"What kind of troubles?" asked Barak.

"Nothing that concerns you," said Neri, backing away, stumbling, finding himself up against Zoar, whose arms were folded across his chest. Zoar glared at him silently. Neri turned and found himself once again face-to-face with Jeshua.

"Your troubles concern us," said Jeshua.

"Just a small problem," said Neri. "The ethnarch will solve it. I really must go."

"When do we get paid?" asked Barak.

"And don't say 'soon,'" said Zoar.

Neri looked up at Jeshua, pleading silently for help.

"When?" asked Jeshua mildly.

"Come see me!" said Neri, pushing past Jeshua.

The men reached to grab Neri, but Jeshua raised his hand. "Let him go." The men parted, and Neri made it through the press of bodies—now numbering more than twenty—and escaped into the emptiness of the forum. He didn't even look back as he waddled quickly away.

"Well?" said Zoar.

"I guess I'll go see him," said Jeshua.

"When?" asked Barak.

"As soon as he gets back," said Jeshua. He left the group and crossed to Naaman, who was still standing behind the marble block. "Do you know what this is all about?"

"The ethnarch's money, I think," whispered Naaman. "He loaned a great sum of it to Hanock, who lost it. Now he is blaming Ishmael."

"You should go to them," said Jeshua.

"Down there? In the dungeon?"

"They might need your help."

"It serves them right!" said Naaman, astonished at the suggestion. "You know what they've done to me!"

Jeshua looked at Naaman but said nothing.

"They both beat me!"

Jeshua just looked at him.

"Why me?"

Jeshua put his hand on Naaman's shoulder.

"I'll end up in there too, you know," said Naaman weakly. "And you don't even care."

"I *do* care," said Jeshua. "Remember?"

Naaman turned away. Yes, he remembered. He remembered how he had treated Jeshua last summer, how he had accused him of theft, knowing full well that he didn't steal the buried talent. And he remembered how Jeshua had saved his life in the well cave-in. "All right," he croaked miserably. "I'll go."

Jeshua nodded. "God will be with you."

"I hope so," said Naaman, turning back. "Because I can't face those two alone."

The soldier lowered the basket of food to Naaman, who stood in the darkness at the foot of the ladder with his hands upraised, resisting the urge to scurry back up to the surface like a frightened rat. He hated darkness and cold and had been in a cave only once in his life—and that was to stand in the doorway of the sepulchre where they had placed his grandfather's body after he died. Now, as he stood in the darkness of the cisterns, a shiver coursed down his spine and his nostrils flared, searching for the smell of rotting flesh. He jumped when a hand appeared out of the darkness and grabbed him. "Over here," said a gruff voice. Naaman hugged the basket tightly and followed the soldier, who took three steps and ducked inside a dark oval. Naaman followed, one hand brushing the rough wall, the other clutching the basket. After two or three turns, the passage opened up and someone said, "Who is it? Marcus?"

"No," said the guard. "It's the emperor."

"Curse you!" shouted Ishmael's voice. "Tell Marcus I demand to be let out!"

"Oh, I'll tell him, Sire," mocked the guard. "Make it quick," he said to Naaman, then left.

"Who goes there?" came Ishmael's voice.

"It's me," quavered Naaman, not daring to move. He had no idea how big the room was or where he stood in it or whether there was a drop-off one step in front of him.

"Me, who?"

"The cur, Naaman," came Hanock's voice.

"Who?" asked Ishmael.

"The stableboy," said Hanock bitterly. "Come to gloat, no doubt."

"Where are you?" asked Ishmael.

"By the entrance," said Naaman. "Is it safe to cross? I can't see a thing."

"What could be safer?" laughed Hanock. "We're shut up like locusts in a jar, drying out for frying."

"What do you want?" asked Ishmael.

"I came to see if I could help," said Naaman, and Hanock laughed.

"Shut up!" said Ishmael.

"Sorry," said Naaman.

"Not you, Naaman. Hanock."

"Oh," said Naaman, making his way slowly across the floor, testing each step. He held the basket out in front of him like a shield. "I brought food."

"We need a lamp," said Ishmael. "Hanock's nearly mad with the darkness."

"You just got here, Sire," said Hanock. "We'll see how you do in a couple of days."

"Don't mind him," said Ishmael. "How did you find out?"

"I saw you coming out of the basilica," said Naaman. "I was in town. On business."

Hanock laughed. "That reminds me, Naaman. Tell the guards to get started on another cell. I'm not sharing my lodgings with a thief."

"What's this?" asked Ishmael.

"Remember the talent I loaned him?" said Hanock. "He'll lose it soon, and when he does, he'll be joining us."

"I won't lose it," said Naaman.

Hanock laughed again. "Ah, but you will, Naaman, you will. People don't change."

Ishmael's voice came hard and fast. "Pray that isn't true, Hanock, for while I may tarry here a day or two, unless you recover the ethnarch's money, they will carry your bones out of here."

Silence from Hanock.

"I have food," said Naaman, reaching into the basket. "It's not much, but I didn't have much money." He held out a piece of flat bread.

"Liar!" hissed Hanock. "He's got a whole talent!"

"Don't give him any," said Ishmael, his hands stretched out. He found the bread and took it, then tore off a piece, tasting it. "Ah, it's fresh. Very good."

"Give me some!" shouted Hanock. Naaman reached into the basket and got another piece of flat bread. He slowly made his way toward Hanock's cell. Suddenly, a pair of hands grabbed him, pulling him against the hard iron bars. "Got you!" exulted Hanock. "Give it here!" He groped at Naaman, grabbed the bread, threw it back into his cell, and soon had his hands around Naaman's neck, choking him.

"Help!" squeaked Naaman, scrabbling at the hands on his neck.

"Hanock!" boomed Ishmael. "Let him go!"

Naaman couldn't breathe and began to see little white dots moving in the darkness. With great effort, he raised his foot, found a place between the iron lattices, and kicked at Hanock with all his might. Hanock fell backward to the ground, and Naaman was free.

"You broke my leg!" howled Hanock. "Coward!"

"Shut up," said Ishmael. "You got what you deserved. Naaman, are you still alive?"

"Yes," coughed Naaman, bent over on the rough stone floor.

"Then come here. I told you not to give him anything and look what happened."

Naaman groped around for the basket and its contents, being careful to stay far away from the labored breathing coming from Hanock's cell.

"You'll pay," hissed Hanock.

Naaman put his hand on the two oranges, the small bag of dates, and something sticky. "The honey!" he lamented. "You broke the jar!"

"Where is it?" shouted Hanock.

Naaman shook his head. "Ruined. All of it."

"Nonsense!" said Hanock. "Give it to me!"

"Hand me your bread and I'll soak some of it up."

"My bread?" said Hanock suspiciously. "So you can keep it? No."

"I'll give it back," said Naaman, picking shards of pottery out of the honey. "It'll be full of dirt, but—"

"I don't care!" said Hanock. "I haven't eaten! Scoop it up, give it here!"

"Give me your bread," said Naaman.

"No!" shouted Hanock. "It's a trick!"

"Fool!" shouted Ishmael. "Can't you see he's trying to help you? Why, I cannot fathom. Here, Naaman, here's my bread. Put a little honey on it."

Naaman took Ishmael's bread, dipped it in the honey, and gave it back. "Thank you," said Ishmael.

"Me! Me!" shouted Hanock.

"You had your chance," said Ishmael, munching the bread. "Mmm. Tasty."

"Naaman! Give me some!" cried Hanock.

"He doesn't deserve it," said Ishmael. "Think of what he's done to you. He beats you. I've seen your scars. Worse than I ever gave you, Naaman. When I punished you it was deserved. I may have been harsh, but I was trying to help you. Hanock beats you out of pure hatred."

"You knew!" shouted Hanock. "You told me to lay into them!"

"Ignore him, Naaman," said Ishmael gently. "Come closer. Let's talk."

"I'm hungry!" whimpered Hanock. "I'm sorry, Naaman. I was just following orders—*his* orders! Don't believe him! He's subtle. Crafty! Look at what he's done to me!"

"You did this to yourself, you scoundrel," said Ishmael. "I'm locked up in here because you refused to follow my specific orders. And I will watch them carry your dead body out of here, Hanock. Believe it."

Hanock started to cry, a pitiable, croaking sound that made Naaman want to stop his ears. "Not my fault! I did my best."

In spite of the memories Ishmael was dredging up, Naaman pitied Hanock. He reached into his basket and found the jug of wine, still intact. "Here's a drink, Hanock."

"Where?" said Hanock, his voice catching.

"None of your tricks," said Naaman. "Or you won't get it. Understand?" He could just make out Hanock's white forearms reaching through the bars, grasping the air.

"Where is it?" whined Hanock.

"It's a wine jug, too large to fit through the bars. I'll hold it up for you to drink."

"Not very wise," counseled Ishmael.

"I'll be good," said Hanock.

Naaman moved closer to the bars. He could just make out the gray oval of Hanock's face pressed inside a square of lattice, his mouth open. His hands grasped the bars below tightly. *Stupid, stupid, stupid,* thought Naaman as he moved slowly forward. He lifted the jug, and the hands shot out, grabbing it, pulling it to him, but the jug was too large to fit between the bars. "A trick! It's too big! I can't drink it!"

Naaman wrestled the jug back. "I told you, I'd have to pour you a drink."

"Sorry," said Hanock. "Once again. Please." He pressed his face against the bars. Naaman held the jug up. Hanock opened his mouth, and Naaman, more by feel than sight, poured the wine into it. A few sputters, and Hanock managed to swallow most of the stream. The rest ran down his chin and chest. Finally satiated, Hanock said, "Enough!" and Naaman raised the lip of the jug. "Aah!" said Hanock gleefully. "Thank you!"

"Give me some," said Ishmael.

"Just one more sip," said Hanock. "I'm so thirsty." Naaman raised the jug, and Hanock grabbed it, dashing it against the bars and shattering it. "Hah! Go thirsty, Master!"

"Hanock!" shouted Naaman, soaked with wine. "Why? There was plenty."

"Let him thirst."

"I told you," said Ishmael flatly. "It was wasted effort, helping him."

"Go to hell, Master," spat Hanock.

"I'll get some more food," said Naaman.

"No," said Ishmael. "I need you to go home. Calm the servants and keep order. But on your way, stop by the synagogue and ask Rabbi Sadoc to bring us food and a lamp."

"I can get those things."

"I know," said Ishmael. "But do this. Ask the rabbi. Understood?"

"Yes," said Naaman. "And I'm sorry, Master. I hope the ethnarch changes his mind."

"Unlikely," said Ishmael. "But others might change it for him. Now, go."

Naaman turned to Hanock. "There's more food and drink coming. Don't despair."

"It is you who will despair, when I get out of here," cackled Hanock.

Naaman turned, groping for the entrance. When he found it, he turned. "I'll be back!"

"Yes, you will," laughed Hanock. "In chains!"

"Shut up, Hanock!" said Ishmael. "Thank you, Naaman."

"The widow to see you, Sire," said Neri.

Marcus was standing on his balcony, looking at the king's empty palace. He didn't turn.

"Perhaps you should consider her petition," said Neri.

"After all her badgering and rudeness? I think not, Neri. Send her away."

"Your Honor, there is a good reason to help her."

Marcus turned.

Neri cleared his throat. Did he really have to spell it out for the man? When no light of recognition lit the ethnarch's eyes, Neri continued. "Throwing Ishmael in prison for Hanock's actions is risky."

"But Hanock came to me as Ishmael's representative. I entrusted the money to him based on their relationship."

"Yes, but Ishmael asserts that Hanock disobeyed his specific orders. Instead of buying the estates Ishmael listed, Hanock gave the money to this Ahmad. And we have no proof otherwise." Neri then held up the forged contract Esther had given them. "With this, however, you have a legitimate reason for jailing Ishmael."

Marcus grabbed the contract from Neri and examined it. His scowl slowly turned to a smile. "I see. Perhaps the widow Esther deserves justice after all. Send her in."

Marcus straightened his toga and ran his hands through his silver hair. He put on his most disarming smile. When the old woman came through the doorway with Neri, he was a paragon of graciousness. "Please, Esther, won't you sit?"

Since her outburst last week, Esther had stayed away from the ethnarch. Perhaps the rabbi had influenced the ethnarch after all. She was glad she had given her last bit of money to his synagogue, even if it meant she hadn't a single mina left for food. But that's what faith was, wasn't it? Having the courage to do the right thing. Surprised at her reversal of fortune, she sat in the chair and blinked at Marcus.

"I have been rude to you," said Marcus. "My apologies."

Esther shook her head. "Oh, no! I'm sorry, Your Honor. I said horrible things! But I was so afraid, so out of ideas, I didn't know what—"

"That's fine," said Marcus, wearying of her apology. "I have considered your petition. I have weighed the evidence and made my decision." Esther leaned forward, her eyes bright. Her frail hands shook on the handle of her cane. Marcus held the contract up, shaking it for emphasis. "This is most certainly a forgery."

"Yes!" said Esther. "Does that mean you'll punish Ishmael?"

"He is already in prison," said Marcus.

"Oh, Your Honor!" said Esther, tears filling her eyes.

"There is justice in the world," said Marcus. "And today, Minerva smiles on you."

"Who?"

"Oh," said Marcus, "you might know her as Athena—goddess of wisdom and truth."

"I recognize only one God," said Esther, confused. "And that is Jehovah."

"Of course," smiled Marcus vaguely. "They are the same."

"No, they're not—"

"What he means," interjected Neri, putting his hands on Esther's narrow shoulders and leaning close to her ear, "is that their *justice* is equivalent. Your petition has been granted."

"Oh," said Esther. No matter what the ethnarch believed, she knew who had blessed her. She would offer sacrifice to Jehovah—let the pagan gods go hungry. "I see," she said, putting on a smile for Marcus.

Marcus watched the moment with amusement. He believed in neither Minerva nor Athena nor Jehovah. *He*, Marcus Pertinax, the ethnarch of Sepphoris, and no one else, had granted the widow's petition.

"I apologize for my badgering, Sire," said Esther, looking at the floor.

"Your persistence did you credit. Indeed, it was a deciding factor in your case."

Esther looked up. "When will I get my property back?"

"In short order," said Marcus. "Neri will draw up the papers." He held out his hand. Esther got to her feet and stared at his hand, uncomprehending.

"Kiss it," whispered Neri.

Marcus raised his chin imperiously, waiting.

"Do it!" said Neri, fearing a reversal in Marcus's rare magnanimity.

Esther took Marcus's hand and touched her dry lips to it, then quickly turned away. "Thank you," she mumbled as she made her way to the door.

"You're welcome," said Marcus.

Down the hallway, after turning a corner and looking back to make sure she was not followed, Esther wiped her lips and spit on the floor. "I'm sorry, Lord," she murmured, glancing heavenward. As she crossed the great colonnaded hall, she promised to make an even bigger sacrifice in Jerusalem once her property was restored. "I had to, Lord," she whispered to herself. "But I know it was you who changed his heart."

After Esther left, Marcus turned back to the window. "Tell our friend Ishmael that I have granted the widow's petition. And tell him also that unless he comes up with my money soon, I shall reveal more crimes in which he is implicated."

"What crimes?"

"Just tell him. He will know what I mean."

Neri left and Marcus smiled. This whole mess might resolve itself after all. He crossed to his chaise and sat, feeling very wise and powerful. But then a thought came. Antipas. Even if Antipas accepted Ishmael as a scapegoat—the king was part Jewish, after all, and believed in such nonsense—his thirst for blood might not be satiated with one offering. He might want more.

The tiny thought grew into a large black doubt. Marcus touched his neck thoughtfully. Fifty talents! The king had never given him a repayment deadline, but he would expect a return at some point, with interest. If that didn't happen, only Jupiter knew what Antipas was capable of.

He crossed to the cluttered table. Pulling out a clean piece of parchment, he settled in his chair, the stylus poised over the blank page. He had protected himself against Ishmael; now he had to protect himself against the king. He dipped the stylus and wrote:

To the estimable Legatus Augusti pro praetore Calpurnius, governor of Syria, greetings . . .

SEVENTEEN

Debt and Forgiveness

His wife shook him awake. "The door!" It sounded like they were battering it in.

Marcus got to his feet groggily. "I'll see to it." Out in the hallway, the servant girl stood, shaking like a leaf. "Go back to bed," said Marcus. She scurried off. As he entered the great room, one of his guards was already there, his sword drawn. Marcus went to the door. "Who is it?"

"The king's guard!"

Marcus nodded at the guard, who turned and disappeared into the courtyard. "Just a moment," he said. If his guard returned in time, he might be spared.

"In the name of the king!" shouted the voice outside. They beat upon the door again.

Marcus turned when he heard footsteps. His personal guards burst from the courtyard garden, brandishing their swords. The banging on the door continued. "They say they're from the king, but they might be impostors," said Marcus. "Ready yourselves." He turned back to the door. "I'm opening. Step back." He lifted the heavy iron bar and pushed the door open. There, on the wide porch, lit by sputtering torches, were twenty soldiers, golden lorica breastplates reflecting the light, galeas pressed low on their heads, hands on their short broadswords. "What is this?" exclaimed Marcus. He looked at the heavy oak door, now scarred. "You've destroyed my door!"

One of the soldiers produced a scroll, unrolling it. Marcus glared at him. "You will be bareheaded before me!"

The soldier looked up from the scroll but did not remove his galea. "A message from the king," he said flatly, and read: "To the honorable ethnarch of Sepphoris, Marcus Pertinax, by order of Herod Antipas, Tetrarch of Galilee and Perea, give heed: your presence is demanded in Tiberias to answer criminal charges."

"Criminal charges?" asked Marcus. "What charges?"

The soldier rolled up the scroll. "That is the message. Prepare to travel."

Marcus heard a sound, turned, and saw his wife fainting into the arms of one of the soldiers, who stood with their blades lowered. As he watched, they once again lifted their swords—and pointed them at him.

"I wouldn't think of going to Tiberias without you," said Marcus.

"Thank you, Sire," said Neri morosely.

The retinue was silent, except for the clip-clop of hooves. The full moon was directly above them. Marcus rode ahead. Occasionally he would turn and look at Neri for a long moment before facing forward again. Gradually, Neri became certain that Marcus knew of the king's command that Neri spy for him, yet Neri had not communicated with the king since their meeting in Tiberias almost a month ago. But that didn't prevent Marcus from casting dark looks back over his shoulder.

The dark Sepphoris hill shrank behind them. *I shall never return*, thought Neri, pulling his cloak tighter, wishing he'd had time to pull on boots instead of sandals. But the soldiers had burst in, shaking him awake. Marcus had stood in the doorway, lit by torchlight, almost smiling as he watched Neri dress and then be hauled outside by the guard.

The road wound up a hill at the eastern end of the Netofa. Evergreen forests closed in on either side, blanketing them in darkness. Their boughs shifted in the cold night breeze, moving silver shadows on the needle-strewn forest floor. Pine scent came crisply to Neri's nose. He wondered what sort of dungeon Antipas had constructed in Tiberias. Would it smell like decay and death?

He feared he would soon find out.

• • •

Marcus pressed his nose against the cold marble floor. The sun was rising, and a sliver of bluish light peeked from under the heavy balcony curtains. Other than that, the room was dark. "Hail, Herod Antipatros," he said humbly.

"Marcus Pertinax," said Antipas. He nodded at the soldiers, who turned and left, closing the door solidly behind them. "Ethnarch of Sepphoris, praetor of the courts, future consul."

Marcus hazarded a look up. Antipas sat on his throne, his face in shadow, but the glow of balcony light illuminated his sandaled foot, which tapped silently. "Yes, Sire?" said Marcus.

"Why do you mistreat me so?" asked Antipas.

"Sire?" said Marcus.

"Raise yourself, Marcus. You know how I hate false obeisance."

Marcus got to his knees. "It is not false, Sire. When the king sends soldiers to my home in the middle of the night, he may trust in my sincerity."

"I suppose so," chuckled Antipas. "Now, I believe you have something to tell me."

"What is that, Sire?"

Antipas drove his heavy oak scepter to the ground, the golden tip ringing on the marble. "The truth!" he shouted. "The truth," he repeated mildly, "is all I've ever asked of you, friend."

"I have failed you, my lord."

"And how have you failed me?"

"The money."

"Yes, the money," said Antipas. "I heard all about it. I waited several days for you to come to me and admit the loss, but when you didn't come, I sent for you."

"I was going to, Sire."

"So you admit you lost it?"

"Not exactly, Sire," said Marcus. "I gave it to a moneylender, and he lost it."

Antipas clucked his tongue. "How big a fool is this man?"

Marcus bent to the ground once again. "Not as big a fool as I, your honor."

"Nor, perhaps, as I, who loaned you the money in the first place. You had not the wit to handle such a large sum, I'm afraid."

Marcus nodded. He would agree to anything if it meant he would get out of this room alive.

"What was that?" asked Antipas.

"I'm sorry," said Marcus. "You are right."

"So you think your king is a fool?"

Marcus's head snapped up. "No! I meant, *I* am a fool! I never meant to say—"

"Peace, Marcus," said Antipas. "I know what you meant. And I daresay you agree with me in all particulars, even if you won't admit it. But you're anxious, kneeling here before the king, knowing your life hangs in the balance."

Marcus nodded miserably.

"Good," said Antipas, standing. "Because it *does.*"

Marcus nodded again, hoping against hope.

Antipas stood and walked down the steps of this throne, crossing to the curtains, drawing them aside. The sun was just glinting on the horizon. He turned back to Marcus. "Now, stand."

Marcus got to his feet and looked into Antipas's eyes for the first time.

Antipas sighed. "You have cost me dearly, Marcus, but I am not in a retributive mood today," said Antipas, "for I am in love."

"In love? With whom?"

"Ah," said Antipas, pointing at Marcus. "You knew I was not talking about my wife."

Marcus cursed himself silently. "I, ah, well . . ."

Antipas raised his hand. "It's obvious we've grown apart. After all, Phasaelis was a political wife, wedded to make peace with the Nabateans. I had hoped she would make me happy as well. She did, for a time." He crossed to his throne and sat down on the marble steps, looking at Marcus. "And I might have continued with her, if only . . ."

"If what?" asked Marcus, glad the conversation was turning away from him.

"Herodias," said Antipas dreamily.

"Your brother's wife? *That* Herodias?"

"I know, I know," nodded Antipas. "Foolishness. 'Just like his father,' the rabble will say. Well, I don't care. I love her."

"But what about Phasaelis?"

"She found out about Herodias and has gone home to Petra."

"How did she find out?"

"True love cannot be hid, my friend. She had her spies, as we all do."

Marcus knew in that instant that Neri had betrayed him. He promised himself he would kill the little fat scribe before the moon waned. The thought almost made him smile.

Antipas was gazing out the bright window. "Phasaelis is gone, and that is that," said Antipas absently. "But Herodias sent word last night that she is divorcing my half brother Philip, to be with me."

"Your star rises," said Marcus cautiously.

"She will marry me, not just because I am destined to rule all of Judea," said Antipas. "She loves me, you know."

Marcus nodded. "Of course."

"So you see, you caught me on a good day. I will forgive your debt—wipe it away."

"All of it?"

"All of it," said Antipas. "Do you find that . . . unsatisfactory?"

"My lord!" said Marcus, reaching for Antipas's hand, kissing it.

Antipas pulled his hand away and wiped it on his robe. "A simple thank-you will suffice."

"I don't know what to say!" said Marcus, his eyes full of tears. "I feared you would cast me into prison, or worse!"

"I am feeling generous. Herodias is bringing a large dowry for our wedding, so I will not miss your fifty talents so much. But there one thing."

"Yes, Sire?"

"You will get no more money from me, Marcus. Not for your basilica, your villa, or your home on the coast. Not for public works or theatrical productions or your private treasury. From this moment forward, you are on your own. Understood?"

Marcus nodded furiously. "Yes. You are right. I deserve this."

"Marcus?"

"Yes?"

"You deserve nothing," said Antipas, his voice like iron. "Remember that."

"Yes, Sire," said Marcus, lowering his gaze.

"I only have a moment," said Neri, rushing into the chamber. "He'll be looking for me."

"Calm yourself," said Antipas. "The servants will give him a big breakfast, with plenty of wine. He will not miss you."

"He misses little," said Neri.

"Neither do you, I trust," said Antipas. "So tell me, what have you heard with your *good* ear?"

Neri's hand almost went to his nubbed ear, but he restrained himself. He took a deep breath, trying to balance the king's command with his fealty to Marcus, however strained it had been lately. "I've tried, Sire, but he is very secretive."

"He will be less secretive in the future," said Antipas breezily. "I've forgiven his debt."

Neri's mouth dropped open. "Why?"

"I keep my own counsel," said Antipas, "but I will tell you this: I want to know what he *really* wanted that money for. It certainly wasn't to finish a building. There must be more to it."

While Marcus was consulting with the king, Neri had been kept downstairs, watched by two of the Roman soldiers, so he had not been able to listen at the doorway to find out what Marcus was saying to the king. But judging from the look on Antipas's face, the king knew many more facts than he was letting on. Either Marcus had confessed to all his doings, or Antipas had other, more effective spies than Neri. He gulped, knowing he must be careful he himself didn't wind up in the king's famous dungeons. He took a breath. "Marcus and a wealthy landowner named Ishmael are indeed plotting something, Sire, but I haven't any details. I don't even know if it concerns you. But the Sepphoris rabbi is involved with them, I believe."

"A rabbi?" asked Antipas, amused. "Truth?"

Neri nodded.

"And what's this I hear about a dungeon filling up?"

"Yesterday, Marcus threw his friend Ishmael in prison."

Antipas leaned forward. "That's a strange way to encourage fidelity to a secret." Antipas tapped his sandal, then he smiled. Neri knew what the king would say before he opened his mouth. "Or maybe it's how Marcus keeps Ishmael from *sharing* the secret."

Neri said nothing.

"Who else is in there with him?" queried the king.

Neri knew it was useless to withhold information the king obviously already knew. "Hanock, Ishmael's chief steward. The one Marcus gave the fifty talents to."

"Ah," said Antipas, leaning back on his throne. "So Hanock, the man who was cheated out of my money—or so he claims—is Ishmael's servant, and Ishmael is Marcus's coconspirator."

Neri nodded.

Antipas studied Neri. "What else?"

Neri racked his brain. Suddenly, an idea came to him. Perhaps he could accomplish something of value here, something more important than rich men squabbling over money and power. "There is one more thing, Sire. Marcus owes the men working on his basilica more than a month's wages. They nearly tore the building down last week, angry at not being paid."

"How does this concern me?"

"An uprising would threaten the peace of all of Galilee."

"Perhaps," mused Antipas, "but when I forgave Marcus his debt, I told him he was responsible for all financial matters in Sepphoris. I will not reverse myself."

"But there may be rioting," emphasized Neri. "The Jews are very angry."

Antipas waved the comment away. "They are always angry. Remind them what happened twenty years ago during the zealot revolt. And tell them to pray history does not repeat itself."

Neri nodded, gulping. "I'll tell them, Sire."

"And keep your good ear open, Neri. It may yet be enough to keep you out of trouble."

Marcus slouched in the saddle, sluggish with wine. Neri rode behind, trying to discern his master's mood. He thought Marcus had nodded off when, suddenly, the man began to sing:

Golden sun on a summer day,
Silver stars on a winter night.
To match my wealth with nature's boon,
Would set my worldly cares aflight.

Marcus could not carry a tune. The breakfast wine had made him happy and not yet sleepy. Now was the time. Neri spurred his horse forward, drawing alongside Marcus. "You know this one," said Marcus. "Sing!"

Neri shook his head. "You're the performer, Sire. I am the appreciative audience."

"And what a *large* audience you are, Neri!" laughed Marcus, puffing his cheeks out.

Neri gave him a pained smile. "The king's reaction was quite amazing."

Marcus nodded, growing serious. "Surprised me beyond words."

"He's very generous," added Neri.

Marcus nodded. "Generous to a fault, our tetrarch. May his name be praised."

"Yes," said Neri. "He is a forgiving soul."

Marcus looked sideways at Neri. "What are you saying? That I'm *not?*"

"Not at all, Sire. Your generosity far exceeds the king's. Everyone knows that."

"Have I been generous with you, Neri?"

"You always have been. I hope you always will be."

"Why wouldn't I?" snapped Marcus. "You saw how I treated that pesky widow. Gave her justice, more than her due."

"Yes," said Neri, "you showed great kindness."

Marcus reined in his horse and glared at Neri. "What is all this fawning? Or do you think I am too drunk to notice sarcasm when I hear it?"

"I am just stating facts. No sarcasm intended."

"Then out with it, Neri," barked Marcus. "What do *you* want?"

Neri screwed up his courage. "I thought that since the king has been so forgiving of your debt, you might look upon my small matter with equal magnanimity."

Marcus scowled. "What's happened? Your bath addition collapse?"

"Worse than that," said Neri. "I lost the money. Gambling, I'm told."

"You don't remember?"

"Not exactly. I was at an inn. There was a beautiful woman and a great deal of wine. And when I woke up the next morning, the innkeeper told me I'd lost the money in a dice game."

Marcus laughed. "Are you sure the woman didn't take it?"

"Yes," said Neri. "She was there when I returned the next day. Several people had witnessed the game, and I then finally remembered what happened." He hung his head in shame.

Marcus howled. "Neri! The punctilious scribe who can account for every lepton I've ever spent! You lost your money . . . *gambling?* I thought you were smarter than that!"

"It's true," lamented Neri, hoping Marcus's mirth would blossom into forgiveness.

When Marcus stopped laughing, a smile still remained on his face. "Fear not, Neri. I will forgive your debt, but you will have to agree to the same bargain I made with the king."

"What is that?"

"You will ask me for no more money, and you must finish the baths on your own, out of your own purse. Is that understood?"

"Yes!" said Neri. "And you shall be my first guest in those same baths."

Marcus looked at Neri. "Imagine, you gambling. You just don't seem the type."

Oh, don't I? thought Neri, pondering the gamble he was taking by spying for the king.

They were both in a singing mood after that. When they arrived at Sepphoris, Marcus asked Neri to fetch Zoar, and Neri bustled off to find him, whistling. When they arrived back in Marcus's offices, Marcus said, "Zoar, take hold of Neri."

Surprised, Neri stepped back, but Zoar grabbed him by both shoulders from behind and held him as Marcus approached. "Zoar, I want you to show Neri the dungeon."

"But, Sire," said Neri, "what have I done?"

"Shut up!" hissed Zoar, shaking Neri.

Marcus raised his hand. "Don't hurt him, Zoar. Not yet. It seems Neri here is a thief. He has stolen a golden denarius from me."

"Monster," said Zoar gleefully.

"Quite," said Marcus, staring into Neri's frightened eyes. "Put him down in the cisterns. The darkness will put his quick mind to work."

"T-to w-work at what?" stammered Neri.

"You just think about it," said Marcus flatly. Zoar hauled him out of the room, laughing. "Don't damage him. Much," said Marcus as they disappeared down the corridor.

"I won't," said Zoar heartily. "Much."

There was the sharp report of a slap and Neri cried out.

Marcus turned back to the window. He would get the information he needed. Neri was spying for the king—how else would Antipas know so soon of the loss of the fifty talents? *Well*, he thought, *now you will spy for me, Neri.* He heard Neri's echoing wail as Zoar cuffed him again, dragging him across the hall as the sullen Jewish workers watched. They were probably thinking that if the ethnarch would treat his own scribe so, what would he do to them if they misbehaved?

Marcus smiled.

It was evening and the warehouse workers were loading the last casks of olive oil onto wagons for transport to Sepphoris in the morning. One of the men looked up and saw a small, bent woman standing in the doorway, holding a lantern. She struck her cane on the ground and cried, "You are all on my property! Be gone!"

The workers turned. One man laughed, then another, and soon all of the workers were laughing. Then a man joined the woman in the doorway, soon followed by another, and the laughter died. Several other men appeared out of the darkness, holding torches, their faces stern. The woman turned to the man next to her. "Jeshua, please."

Jeshua walked into the cavernous warehouse. He held a piece of parchment. The head Arab worker, Salim, put down a heavy cask he was toting. He pointed at Jeshua. "You're trespassing."

"It is you who is trespassing," said Judah, stepping forward to join Jeshua. Several other men stood behind them, each holding the tool of his trade: a sharp spade, hammer, chisel, or pry bar. Their faces were hard in the flickering torchlight.

Esther looked up at Salim. "I don't suppose you know how to read?" she said, taking the parchment from Jeshua.

"I can read," said Salim. "Can you?" He pointed at the sign hanging outside the warehouse bearing Ishmael's name.

"That's coming down," said Esther, shoving the parchment at him. "Here."

Salim looked at the parchment. His men gathered behind him. They were about even in number to the workers behind Jeshua and Judah, but Salim's men had no weapons except grappling hooks and staves. Salim looked at the parchment, furrowing his brow.

"He can't read," said Esther.

Jeshua put his hand on her shoulder to quiet her, then turned to Salim. "Here, let me," he said mildly, holding out his hand. Salim reluctantly gave Jeshua the parchment. Jeshua said, "It says Esther gets her warehouse back—along with everything that's in it."

"How do I know it says that?" asked Salim.

"By this," said Jeshua, giving the parchment back to Salim. "That's the ethnarch's seal. You recognize it, don't you? It's on your bills of lading, right?"

Salim looked at the seal pressed into wax at the bottom of the parchment. He looked at Jeshua, saw the grim faces of the *tektons* standing behind him, and took note of the tools they gripped tightly in their hands.

"You have no business here," said Esther, unable to restrain herself any longer. "Get out!"

Jeshua lightly touched Salim's arm. He could feel the conflict in the man. Salim was struggling with pride and a commitment to his master and concern for his family and fellow workers. Esther's own pride was not making it any easier to resolve this problem without violence. Behind Salim, several of the workers were arming themselves with iron hooks and long wooden poles.

Esther glared up at Salim. "I said, get—"

His hand still on Salim's arm, Jeshua lightly touched Esther's shoulder with his other hand. She stopped in midsentence. She was looking up at the hateful Nabatean with the kohl-rimmed eyes and the thick black beard when suddenly she saw a woman next to him, her face veiled. She held a little child in her arms. Two more little children clung to Salim's legs, looking up at him hopefully. Behind his wife stood another child, a girl, perhaps twelve years old, her face also covered in the Nabatean fashion. And behind her, an old couple, as bent and bowed as Esther herself, their eyes frightened. They were all dressed in tattered, dirty clothing, and the big-eyed children at Salim's feet looked frightfully thin. The baby in the woman's arms began to cry weakly, and the woman quietly cooed to it as she reached out and took hold of Salim's sleeve.

Esther looked up at Salim's dark face, wondering why he gave no notice of the people—obviously his family—that surrounded him. The parchment alone had his rapt attention, but Esther suddenly knew that what she was seeing was what Salim was *thinking* about—all those who depended on him. He was not a savage or a thief. He was a man with a family. He was the provider for all these people, and her decision at this moment might take away what little bread he could provide for them.

Esther blinked and the vision was gone. Salim stood alone, still holding the parchment, his lips pursed in thought. She took a step forward and touched his hand, drawing his gaze. "I'm sorry," she said quietly. "I didn't know."

At her touch, he looked down at her and noticed her eyes glistening.

Behind Esther, Salim saw an old man, his bald head revealing a freckled crown. He was looking at the old woman with great admiration and love. His skin had the translucence of death, and Salim knew he was the man who had once owned this building in which they were standing. The old man reached out and touched the woman lightly on the shoulder, but she gave no indication she felt his touch. Salim saw a dozen other men, as insubstantial as gossamer, working at the press, filling casks with golden olive oil. They moved in the economic cadence of experienced workers, around and through Salim's own men, as well as the Jewish men standing behind the old woman, yet no one else apparently saw them. These were the people who had depended upon the old man, the workers who had lost their jobs when Ishmael took the press over. The old man had died, and only the tiny, wrinkled little woman touching his arm and looking expectantly up at him remained to care for them.

The vision ended. Esther stood before him, her hand lightly on his own, her eyes bright. Salim placed his hand over hers. "I'm sorry about your husband," he said. Esther started at the mention of Ezra. Salim continued, "But we needed work. My family . . ."

Esther felt tears building behind her eyes. She could only nod and say, "I know."

Judah watched the exchange, surprised. Just moments ago, he was steeling himself for a fight when suddenly, as quickly and quietly as a gust of wind, a change had come over both Esther and the Arab. Judah dropped his maul to the floor and gestured for the men behind him to lower their tools. He stepped forward and put his hand on Salim's shoulder. "We work in Sepphoris," he said. "Maybe we can find you work there."

"Really?" asked Salim, brightening.

"And I might be able to keep a few of your men on here," said Esther, surprising herself.

Salim motioned for his men to put down their weapons. He bowed deeply before Esther, touching his fingers to his forehead. "If you give us a chance, you will find we are hard workers." Behind him, his men nodded.

Judah smiled. "We will do what we can. But to begin with, my stomach says it's dinnertime, and employed or not, we all get hungry." He turned to Esther.

Esther looked around and saw nearly forty men looking at her expectantly. "You want me to feed *all* of you? I don't have a single prutah to my name!"

Jeshua held up a silver denarius. "Now you have eight of them."

"That isn't enough to—"

Judah pulled a few assarions from his money pouch. "Will this help?"

"How about this?" said Ibhar, digging into his pocket and pulling out a few coins.

"I have this," said another worker, holding up his money pouch.

Esther looked around. Two days ago, she had given her last mina to Sadoc and had gone hungry since. Now it looked as if she might not starve after all.

Judah collected the money. The Nabateans, not to be outdone by their new friends, opened their pockets, and soon a kerchief was spread out on the hay-strewn floor and a pile of gold and silver coins grew there.

"This should be enough to feed all of Nazareth," said Jeshua.

"Why not?" said Judah, looking around. "Let's celebrate the return of Esther's press!"

A cheer went up from the men. Judah scooped up the coins, pointed at a couple of workers, and together they set off out the door.

Jeshua took Salim's hand. "Peace be unto you. I am Jeshua bar Joseph. Welcome to Nazareth, our home."

Salim touched his forehead respectfully. "And unto you, peace. I am Salim bin Ahmed, of Petra." He looked around at his men. "We are a long way from home."

Esther took his hand and patted it. "Not anymore."

EIGHTEEN

Serpents and Doves

W hen Naaman emerged from the cisterns last night, Jeshua had already left for home. With Ishmael's charge foremost in his mind, Naaman hurried back to the estate. He was more than halfway to Rimmon before he remembered he was supposed to see Sadoc, the rabbi. Hanock's attempts to throttle him had left him so upset that he'd forgotten all about it. Cursing himself, he reined in and debated whether he should ride back to Sepphoris tonight. He looked up and down the dark road. There were bandits in Galilee, and they haunted the Netofa Valley, as elsewhere. *The food I gave them will just have to do for tonight,* he thought, turning for home. *I'll go see the rabbi first thing in the morning.*

And now here he was, standing in front of the basilica, under glowering skies, which reflected the gloom in his own heart. Jeshua was up on the porch, dumping a burlap sack of lime into a wooden mixing trough. He was covered with dust, and his powdered hair made him look like an old man. As Naaman trotted up the steps, Jeshua turned and saw him. "I can't talk long," said Jeshua, leading Naaman down a few steps, nodding toward Zoar, who was high up on the scaffold, supervising the placement of a large spandrel in the wall. When they were out of earshot, he whispered, "What did you find out yesterday?"

"The ethnarch gave Hanock money to invest, and he lost it, but why Ishmael is down there, I don't know."

"Marcus probably thinks they stole the money from him."

"Why do you say that?"

Jeshua remembered the conversation he'd overheard upstairs at the synagogue between Sadoc and Ishmael. "I just think the ethnarch has reason to disbelieve Ishmael's word."

"Why?"

Jeshua whispered. "I don't know enough to say. Did you take them some food?"

"Yes, but by way of thanks, Hanock tried to choke me," he said, rubbing his neck. "He broke a jug of wine just to deny Ishmael a drink. I hope he never gets out of there." He looked at Jeshua. "I know I shouldn't feel that way."

"But you do feel it," said Jeshua, "though you acted otherwise. That's more important."

"I'm on my way to the rabbi's now," said Naaman, turning away.

Jeshua grabbed his arm. "Sadoc's? Why?"

"Ishmael wants him to bring a lamp and some more food."

"Why don't *you* bring it?"

"I have no more money," said Naaman. "Except for the . . . uh . . . loan."

Jeshua withdrew a small purse from his belt. "I'll give you some."

Naaman shook his head. "He wants the rabbi to bring it."

"I don't think that's a good idea, Naaman."

"So should I get the provisions for them?"

Jeshua shook his head. "No. I'll do it."

"You?" asked Naaman. "Why you?"

"Because," said Jeshua, shaking his head, "it's time I found out what is going on here." He turned and climbed the steps and suddenly found himself face-to-face with Barak, who was standing in front of an archway, glaring at him.

"It's Friday. Is Marcus going to pay us or not?"

"I honestly don't know, Barak. You've heard about the men being cast into the cisterns."

Barak shrugged. "What's that to me?"

"Barak, have you ever been in an earthquake?"

"One struck Samaria when I lived there, years ago."

"You know how animals—especially dogs—can sense it coming?"

"They start acting strange. I've heard that. So?"

"So," said Jeshua, gesturing about. "Don't you think everyone is acting a little strange these days? It feels like something's coming."

Barak frowned. "You're right, Jeshua, something *is* coming. Warn Marcus." He turned away, striding down the basilica steps.

Jeshua watched him go. Demanding money from the ethnarch was as useless as begging for it. Marcus would simply repeat his threat to call in the legionnaires, and those who weren't run through with Roman lances would languish in the dungeons Jeshua had helped dig.

He shuddered at the image. In his mind's eye he saw Sepphoris, the glorious city on a hill, aflame in the night sky, orange tendrils of fire licking upward, hundreds put to the sword, thousands left destitute and homeless. All because the ethnarch gave his money to a fool. Jeshua shook his head and for a brief instant considered riding to Tiberias to beg for the king's help. But the idea was ridiculous—why should the king care about the ethnarch's problems? He might even take Jeshua's plea as a pretext for marching on Sepphoris, precipitating the very thing Jeshua feared most.

Jeshua ducked under the arch and entered the basilica. A trickle of dirt fell onto his neck. He looked up. The facade wall now stood as tall as three men, and the curved wedge-shaped voussoirs were all in place, resting on the wooden arch supports. The gigantic keystone sat far above on the scaffolding, awaiting its placement. Once it was in position, its angled planes and immense weight would press down on the voussoirs, securing the arch tightly for generations.

But if the keystone were dislodged, the entire arch would give way, tumbling to the ground, crushing everything and everyone beneath it. And just as every arch had a keystone, every conspiracy had one as well, a key element that gave it power and direction. Jeshua stopped and looked back at the facade wall. What was the keystone in Ishmael's and the rabbi's arch? Was it the same keystone Marcus was chiseling, or were they constructing separate arches?

Jeshua stopped outside the ethnarch's offices, expecting to see Neri at his table, but he was not there. He heard footsteps and stepped inside. Marcus was coming down the hall. He attempted to skirt Jeshua, but Jeshua would not step aside. They stood face-to-face.

"Where is Scribe Neri?"

"He's indisposed," said Marcus, moving to his left. Jeshua moved to his right, blocking the way. Marcus exhaled sharply. "Let me pass."

Jeshua stood his ground. "You chose me as worker representative. Please hear me out."

"What is there to hear?"

"I've been sent to warn you about earthquakes, Your Honor."

Marcus laughed. "Are you an oracle now? Predicting earthquakes?"

Jeshua shook his head. "Any fool could, at this point."

Marcus scowled. "Be careful. There's room for you in the cisterns, along with Neri and the others."

The news of Neri's incarceration stunned Jeshua. Marcus used the moment to slip past him. He turned in the doorway and smiled. "I guess you didn't know."

Jeshua shook his head.

"Add it to your store of ignorance, Jeshua." Marcus strode across the courtroom. Jeshua followed at a distance, still processing the information. At the far end of the hall, Marcus ducked under the facade wall scaffolding and disappeared outside.

Jeshua was about to follow him when Zoar's voice came from above. "Where have you been?"

Jeshua looked up. "Discussing our wages."

"And what did Marcus say?"

The other men had stopped work and were listening. Jeshua looked from man to man. He did not know what to say. "I'm working on it," he finally managed, and ducked under the scaffold, walking quickly down the basilica steps.

"He doesn't know what he's doing," said someone, watching Jeshua go. Zoar smiled.

At the foot of the basilica steps Jeshua looked around, but Marcus was nowhere in sight. He turned to his right and trotted down the alley between the basilica and the bank. As he reached the rear of the building, Jeshua saw a soldier posted at the cistern entrance. He stepped back, thinking, then turned and ran back up the alley to the marketplace, where he bought a bottle of wine, some flat bread, a small oil lamp, and two blankets. When he returned, he gathered his wits, slowed his breathing, and strolled up to the soldier. "Provisions for the prisoners."

The soldier gestured for Jeshua to unroll the blankets. He bent the bread and sniffed at the bottle of wine. When Jeshua nodded his assent, the soldier took a long pull from the bottle. "Not bad," he said, wiping his lips. "Must be his own stock."

"Whose?"

"Neri's."

"He does know his wine."

"He'll like the lamp too. It's as dark as the inside of a cat down there."

Jeshua nodded and hefted the bundle up on his shoulder.

"If there's any wine left over, I'm on duty until the second watch," said the soldier, winking.

Jeshua nodded. "Yes. I'll see to it."

He walked into the entrance. Two of the three cistern holes were covered with iron plates, but a ladder stuck out of the third and Jeshua climbed down it. At the bottom, he struck flint and lit the lamp, holding it up and peering into the darkness. A soldier sat in a corner, watching him. "Scribe Neri?" asked Jeshua. The soldier pointed to his right. From the main chamber, three dark passageways exited. "Which one?"

"Far one," said the soldier. Jeshua almost started for it, then turned back, holding out the jug. "It's his, but I gave a little to the other guard. I thought I should offer you a drink too."

"He's drinking on duty?" asked the man, straightening.

Jeshua grimaced. "I insisted. And it was just a swallow."

The soldier looked at Jeshua, then his eyes went to the bottle. "So long as it was just a swallow, I guess it couldn't hurt. Him or me." He took a long, slow drink, smacking his lips in appreciation and handing it back to Jeshua. "Better save the little fellow a bit."

"Yes," said Jeshua. "The far one, you say?" The soldier nodded, and Jeshua made his way to the passage. He knew it well. It ended in the small chamber where they had found the geode. Yet now, across the chamber entrance, was an iron barred door. Jeshua tapped on it, holding up the lamp, squinting into the darkness. He could not see anyone in the gloom.

"Go away," said Neri's voice.

"Neri? It's me, Jeshua."

"Can't help you," said Neri flatly. "Not anymore."

"I came to help *you*. I brought blankets and food."

"I've got plenty of both."

"I have a lamp."

"I like the dark. Helps me think."

"Neri, what happened?"

Neri approached the latticed iron gate, his round face appearing out of the darkness. "I took a wrong turn. Take care you don't follow me." He turned away.

"Where are the others?"

"What others?"

"Ishmael and his steward, Hanock, the one who lost Marcus's fifty talents."

Neri turned. "How did you find out?"

"It's common knowledge by now."

"Well, I guess now the workers will finish what they started last Friday night," said Neri, frowning. "We're all going to die, Jeshua."

"I pray not," whispered Jeshua. "But I need your word that when this is over, you'll pay the workers their due."

"You'd take the word of a prisoner in a dungeon?"

"I would—if he were you."

"Then you are a fool, Jeshua."

"After you hear what I'm going to tell you, you may change your mind. In any case, you have nothing to lose."

Neri turned, shaking his head. "All right, you have my word, for what it's worth."

"Yesterday, Marcus granted Esther's petition," began Jeshua.

Neri nodded.

"But *why?* It cannot be because he thought her cause was just."

Neri pulled his hair away from his damaged ear, giving Jeshua a good look at it. "I listen and hear; sometimes I comprehend. Marcus granted Esther's petition because he needed a reason to throw Ishmael in prison. He says it's because Ishmael is responsible for the loss of the fifty talents, but I think it's because he has doubts about Ishmael in regard to some scheme they are hatching together."

Jeshua nodded. "I may know something of that. A few days ago, Esther went to the synagogue to talk with Rabbi Sadoc. I don't know him, but I've heard bad things about him, so I followed her, to see if I could help. I was about to knock on the door when I overheard Ishmael and Sadoc talking about a plan Marcus and Ishmael had devised to use the fifty talents to buy up estates in the valley—and squeeze the other landowners out."

Neri frowned. "Well, that's not what happened, according to Ishmael. Hanock gave the money to some seafaring rogue and now it's gone." Neri paused, thinking. "If that was their plan, I can't understand why they were so secretive about it—people buy and sell land all the time."

"But land is power, Neri," said Jeshua. "And Antipas doesn't share power with anyone."

"They wouldn't be that stupid, would they?" said Neri, more a statement than a question. He shook his head, amazed. "And I thought he was just paranoid."

"Who?"

"The king. He ordered me to spy on Marcus. See what he's up to."

"What have you told him?"

"Nothing he didn't already know. What he lacks, I think, is tangible proof."

"Here is where I may be able to help you," said Jeshua, grasping the bars and lowering his voice. "In that meeting I overheard, Sadoc mentioned a letter from the Syrian governor, guaranteeing the conspirators—Marcus and Ishmael—protection from the king."

Neri inhaled quickly. "A letter from Calpurnius? Are you sure?"

"One doesn't forget that name," said Jeshua darkly. Calpurnius Piso was the latest in a long line of overreaching Syrian governors who had all lusted after the riches of Galilee. Antipas's father, Herod the Great, had held them in check for forty years, but when he died and the Galilean zealots revolted, Quintilius Varus invaded, destroyed Sepphoris, and killed thousands of Jews. It took several years and the intervention of Augustus Caesar himself to restore the land to Antipas, who still mistrusted any Syrian governor, and that included the latest officeholder, Calpurnius.

"So Calpurnius is allied with Marcus against Antipas," said Neri, shaking his head in wonder. "And there is a letter to that effect?"

"I believe so. They were waiting on it ten days ago."

Neri paced his cell, then stopped. "I need to notify the king. Will you help me?"

"Will you keep your word?"

Neri thrust his hand through the cell bars and took Jeshua's hand firmly in his. "Yes, Jeshua, I will. On my life."

Jeshua went down the other passageway, searching for Ishmael and Hanock. When he found them he entered, holding up the lamp. "Who are you?" asked Ishmael, taking the blanket Jeshua held out to him.

"A friend of Naaman's. He wanted you to have this too." He handed the lamp to Ishmael.

"Your name?"

"Jeshua bar Joseph, of Nazareth."

"He's the well digger," chimed in Hanock, grabbing the other blanket. "He tried to steal your talent from Naaman last year."

Jeshua didn't say anything.

"Yes," said Ishmael, pulling the blanket around him. "He certainly *acts* like a thief." He studied Jeshua. "And what can we do for you, young man?"

"Don't trust him!" shouted Hanock. "He works for Marcus!"

"Is that true?" asked Ishmael. "You work for our beloved ethnarch?"

"I'm a laborer on the basilica."

"Hmm," said Ishmael, still sizing Jeshua up.

"He's lying," said Hanock. "Tell him nothing."

"I'd tell him anything if it meant getting away from your prattling, Hanock," snapped Ishmael. "But though he's not lying, he's not telling us the entire truth, is he?" he said, holding the lamp up to see Jeshua's face better. "A laborer, you said?"

"Yes."

"What else have you brought us?" asked Hanock.

Jeshua picked up the bottle of wine. "I understand the last one broke. Here's another, only slightly reduced by bribery of the guards."

Ishmael reached through the bars and took the jug, sloshing it. "Here," he said, handing it back to Jeshua, "pour me a little drink."

"Me! Me!" shouted Hanock.

"Not him," said Ishmael. "He broke the last one."

"I heard. So I brought a cup this time," said Jeshua, producing a small wooden cup and filling it. He gave it to Ishmael, who drained it, then Jeshua filled it again and handed it to Hanock, who drained it and then hurled it across the room, where it bounced off the wall. Jeshua fetched it without a word.

"Thank you," said Ishmael. "Pardon our manners. We're not used to being caged like animals."

"I wish there were something I could do," said Jeshua.

Ishmael smiled ruefully. "Do you have fifty talents?"

Jeshua smiled as well. "Sorry."

Ishmael shrugged. "Just keep us in lamp oil, friend, and we shall be grateful. And if you see your employer, the ethnarch, tell him we are looking forward to his next visit." He turned and sat down in his cell. "Thank you for the light."

Jeshua looked over at Hanock, who was glowering at him. "You're welcome."

Dinah and her mother walked past Esther's warehouse. Ishmael's wooden sign lay on the ground, singed black in places. Inside, both Jews and Arabs were working, some loading wagons with casks, others cleaning the large stone oil press under Esther's direction. Tarah called out, "Esther!" Esther turned and bustled over to them.

"I see you got your warehouse back," said Tarah. "We just heard."

"Yes!" said Esther. "We tried to burn the sign, but the paint just smoked. I might build a manure trough with it instead." She turned to Dinah. "So, how is the famous Dinah?"

"Famous? For what?" asked Tarah, glancing at Dinah, whose face was beet red.

"Famous for being loved by all," said Esther. "But most especially by one."

"Well, she doesn't love him," said Tarah flatly.

"That's a shame," said Esther. "He's an impressive young man."

"Impressive?" sputtered Tarah. "Only if you count buffoonery as impressive!"

"Mother," pleaded Dinah, "please."

"All I know," said Esther, "is that he took back my warehouse from Ishmael's ruffians!"

"Was there a fight?" asked Dinah fearfully.

Esther smiled inside. By now, everyone in Nazareth knew how Tarah felt about Judah, though Esther couldn't imagine why she wasn't delighted that Judah would show an interest in her daughter. Esther decided to have a little fun at Tarah's expense. She leaned forward and lowered her voice. "Late last night, Judah and his men came with me to reclaim my warehouse. They stood in the doorway, big and bold as summer thunder, carrying their picks and axes and hammers on their shoulders, ready to fight. The Nabateans grabbed their scimitars. Blood was about to flow. . . ."

"What happened?" asked Dinah, terrified.

"Well," said Esther, barely suppressing a smile, "Judah steps forward and folds those big arms across his broad chest and looks at them with his fierce eyes, and they back right down."

"Judah bar Joseph?" asked Tarah. "*That* Judah?"

Esther nodded. "The very same. But then, the scoundrel did a terrible thing."

Tarah nodded, knowing the story thus far was too good to be true. She glanced at Dinah to make sure she was listening.

Esther shook her fist at the heavens, "Oh! It just boils my blood to think about it!"

"What in the world did he do?" begged Tarah.

"He turns to me and says, 'Now you have to feed them!'" Esther straightened, her eyes narrowed to slits. "Imagine! Feed the men who helped steal my warehouse!"

"He made you feed them?" asked Tarah.

Esther confirmed it with an angry nod. Dinah suppressed a smile.

"So you fed them," said Tarah.

"But that's not all," said Esther. "Judah made me feed *his* men too!"

Dinah laughed and quickly put a hand over her mouth.

"Well!" said Tarah, shaking her head. "I don't see what's so terrible about that!"

"Disappointed?" asked Esther innocently.

"Not in the least!" said Tarah. "Good day, Esther. I'm pleased you recovered your property." She turned and bustled off.

Dinah watched her go, then turned. "Is that all true?"

"Almost all of it," nodded Esther. "Especially the part about Judah."

"That doesn't sound like the Judah I know."

"Oh, it is," said Esther. "But for a young man in love, facing twenty fighting men is nothing compared to facing one beautiful maiden." She squeezed Dinah's hand. "Judah is foolish as a colt, but he'll grow out of it. Take it from an old mare."

Dinah sighed. "I wish he'd grow up faster."

"You just worry about yourself. Remember, forgiveness is a woman's crowning glory." She patted Dinah's hand and turned back to the warehouse. "All of you," she shouted, "get to work! Or no honey on your bread!" The men groaned happily.

"Dinah!"

Dinah turned. Her mother was waiting up the street, her arms crossed, frowning.

NINETEEN

Rising and Falling

It was lunchtime, and Jeshua was eating with Judah and Salim. "Here comes Barak," said Judah, pointing. Barak was walking across the forum toward them. Twenty or thirty men were following him. Judah turned to Salim. "Are you with us?" Salim nodded and whistled softly, getting the attention of his men, who were eating nearby. Barak planted his feet in front of them, crossed his arms, and scowled disapprovingly at the Arab workers. "Well?"

"He still has six hours," said Jeshua.

"Six hours, six months, it's all the same," spat Barak. "He isn't going to pay us because he has no money to pays us *with!* Isn't that true?"

Jeshua nodded. "Yes. I believe it is."

There was a general, unhappy murmur among the workers behind Barak.

"Then that's it!" said Barak, picking up his maul and turning away.

"Wait!" cried Jeshua, jumping to his feet and grabbing Barak's arm. "If you resort to violence, Marcus will call out the garrison!"

Barak slung his maul over his shoulder. "I'd rather die with enough strength to swing a sword than starve to death."

Many heads in the crowd nodded.

"But there are other options," said Jeshua. "We can strike."

"Are *you* calling a strike?" asked Barak, incredulous.

Jeshua nodded. "I would prefer patience."

"No more waiting!" yelled a man at the back.

Jeshua raised his hands. "But if the choice is between tearing down the basilica—which will bring the soldiers—and a peaceful strike, then I will support a strike."

"But what if he refuses to pay us, even after we strike?" asked Barak.

"Things are happening. I don't know exactly what, but if we do not act rashly, Barak, our problem may resolve itself."

Barak spit on the ground. "Go see your master one last time, Jeshua. Tell him to pay us or else." He shouldered his way through the crowd.

"Tell him!" said a worker, following Barak.

"Now!" said another.

Jeshua nodded and started toward the basilica.

"Jeshua!" said Judah, grabbing his arm. "Do you want us to come? Just in case?"

"In case of what?"

"In case the ethnarch . . ." he trailed off, not knowing what to say.

Jeshua put his hand on Judah's shoulder. "Watch yourself, you and your friends. I fear Barak is not done making trouble. And find out where Zoar is. His absence concerns me more than his presence." He turned and walked toward the basilica steps.

Zoar ducked back under the archway scaffolding. He had watched the confrontation from behind a column on the basilica porch. Inside, in the cool darkness, he hid behind a large crate, watching as Jeshua appeared and walked across the empty basilica, heading for Marcus's offices.

When Jeshua had disappeared through the courtroom doorway, Zoar quickly scaled the scaffolding. The spandrels were in place on the topmost tier of planking. The keystone had been lowered into its place just an hour ago, locking the arch. All was ready. He climbed back down the scaffolding, keeping an eye on the courtroom door for sign of Jeshua.

Tonight, when he knocked the shims out from under the support leg, the scaffolding would collapse, and the five spandrels high above would fall against the naked curve of the voussoirs, shifting them just enough to release the weight of the keystone, which would fall, bringing the entire wall down with it. Anyone within fifty feet would be crushed. As he climbed down the scaffolding, Zoar looked up at the long, square

architrave beams spanning the twenty-four pillars of the great hall. If the
facade wall fell against just one of those pillars, it might bring down the
entire basilica.

He stepped off the scaffolding and knelt by a wooden leg. A half
dozen cedar shims were wedged under the leg to level the scaffold. He
glanced over his shoulder. There, leaning innocuously against the closest
fluted pillar, was his iron sledge. One well-placed stroke was all it would
take. The shims would skitter across the marble floor, and within seconds death would rain down from above. He looked toward the arch,
measuring the distance. He would have to move fast to get out of the
building before the stones began to fall. And as the building collapsed
and the smoke billowed out the entrance and down the broad marble
steps, he would be safe out in the forum, watching the demise of his enemies—Marcus, Neri, and Jeshua—in one exciting, cataclysmic moment.

He shivered with anticipation.

Jeshua passed through the courtroom doors. The ornate, carved stone
judgment seat had been placed atop the curved marble dais. The sun
shone down through a skylight, bathing the seat in a brilliant, white
light. Two soldiers stood before Marcus's office, their lances crossed,
blocking the doorway. "I've come to see the ethnarch," said Jeshua, approaching them.

"He wishes no visitors."

"I'm the worker representative," said Jeshua. "It is important—a
matter of life and death."

"No visitors," said the soldier, placing his hand on his sword hilt.

"What's this about life and death?" came a voice, and Marcus appeared in the doorway, carrying a number of parchment scrolls.

"Ethnarch," said Jeshua. "I must talk with you."

"I'm busy," said Marcus, putting the scrolls on Neri's already overflowing table. Several books and papers slipped off and fell on the floor.
Marcus cursed.

"Let me," said Jeshua, ducking under the lances before the soldiers
could react. He knelt and began gathering up the parchments and

scrolls. The soldiers started toward him, but Marcus held up his hand. He watched Jeshua kneeling, picking up the papers, his back to the blades just inches away, oblivious to the danger. *Too much of a fool to kill,* he thought, motioning for the soldiers to return to their posts. Jeshua got to his feet, placing the bundle of papers on the table.

"I told you before," said Marcus, "you must be patient—"

"If you tell the workers about your situation," pleaded Jeshua, "they might understand."

"What situation?"

"That you lost the money you were going to pay us with." Jeshua gestured at the table piled high with Neri's paperwork. "But throwing everyone in the dungeon won't solve your problems."

"How dare you speak to me like this!" barked Marcus.

"If you don't speak frankly to the men, they will strike, and maybe worse."

"Are you threatening me?" shouted Marcus. The soldiers stood outside the door, their hands on their swords, waiting for a gesture from Marcus.

"I am just giving you the information you need to govern wisely."

"Who are *you* to counsel me?" growled Marcus, shaking with rage. "A *tekton?* Tell the workers that if they touch this building or any person in it, I will have every one of them crucified!" His eyes bored into Jeshua.

"When the wind blows, from which direction does it come?" asked Jeshua mildly.

"What?" bellowed Marcus.

"The wind. Whence does it come?"

"What are you talking about?"

Jeshua waited, looking up at the ethnarch.

"From the west, you fool," barked Marcus. "Now what—"

"Not always."

Marcus shook his head. Was the man insane? He nodded to the soldiers. They grabbed Jeshua and held him tightly between them. He did not resist but said, "You're making a terrible mistake."

Marcus laughed. "Tell it to the darkness."

•   •   •

Antipas dismissed the courier and opened the sealed roll of parchment.

> To Herod Antipatros, Tetrarch of Galilee and Perea, greetings.
>   The intelligence you have long sought has finally revealed itself.
> I would deliver it to you personally, but Marcus has cast me into
> prison. I will give you details when we next meet, but suffice it to
> say for now: your long-standing rival to the north is involved.
>   Your humble servant, Neri

"Chuza!" shouted Antipas.

The doors opened and an old man entered. "Yes, Sire, what is thy—"

"Call the military prefect."

Chuza turned and left. In short order, General Actius trotted into the throne room, his sword drawn, looking around as if he thought he might encounter assassins. Antipas was lacing up his sandals. "Actius," he said, "how long will it take you to ready my cohort?"

"To go where?"

"How long?" repeated Antipas.

"An hour, maybe two," said Actius.

"You've got half an hour," said Antipas as he strode past the general.

"A half hour!" lamented Actius. "But, Sire, we cannot—"

Antipas stopped at the doorway and turned. "Tell you what," he said. "Make it an hour, but use the extra time to sharpen your swords. We may be going into battle."

Actius smiled. "To battle! Where, Sire?"

"Sepphoris."

It was midafternoon before Antipas led the cohort out of the city gates. He wore his red cloak, and when he looked behind him, he saw more than four hundred silver galea helms glinting in the sun, their purple plumes dancing, lances pointing heavenward. There were two hundred cavalry, one hundred archers, and another hundred infantrymen, each carrying a newly sharpened gladius. His yellow and maroon standards snapped in the cool breeze, and he relished the awe and wonder on the faces of the Tiberians as they passed.

Antipas looked to the west, where gray, billowing clouds were bunching up on the horizon. He had already sent a few men north to see if Calpurnius's legionnaires were marching south across the Syrian highlands, toward the border. He had sent his fastest rider to the Sepphoris garrison, where he would take fifty men and speed to Ptolemais, in case Calpurnius decided to sail into battle.

And finally, he had sent two riders to Caesarea Maritima on the southern coast, to see what Valerius Gratus was up to. The Judean prefect might be in league with Calpurnius, and if so, Antipas was surely in danger. If not, he'd only have to fight on one front. *Either way, it's well we took the time to sharpen the swords,* he thought, spurring his horse.

Fifty workers saw the soldiers take Jeshua down the basilica steps and around the side of the building. Within minutes Barak had men huddled around him, eager for his advice. "Nothing now," he cautioned. "Give them no warning." The men nodded. "Go back to work, but pass the word. Tonight, at the beginning of the second watch, we will meet inside the theater. No lit torches, but bring your tools. We have one more job to do."

The men dispersed.

Ibhar was climbing up out of one of the other cisterns when he saw the soldiers prodding Jeshua down the ladder sticking up out of another. Ibhar watched him disappear into the darkness, then quickly left. Dashing out of the alley and into the forum, he realized he'd just missed an important meeting. Dozens of men were departing from a central point. His eyes went to the hub. There stood Barak, speaking with two or three remaining men.

A worker grabbed Ibhar's sleeve, whispering, "Second watch, tonight. The theater. Come prepared." He turned away, leaving Ibhar gaping after him.

That was when he started looking for Judah, who was not in the outbuilding on the south side of the basilica, installing doors, as he had been for several days. He asked Judah's co-workers where he was, but the word of tonight's events had already reached them and they were deep in whispered conversation. One pointed toward the marketplace, and Ibhar trotted across the forum. He found Judah haggling with a merchant over a cask of nails. Judah pointed his finger in the merchant's face, speaking low and hard to the man, who frowned in return, shaking his head.

"Judah?" interrupted Ibhar, touching his sleeve.

Judah raised his hand. "One minute," he said. "Two drachmas for the *saton*—no more!"

The merchant shook his head. "Three."

Judah reached into the nail cask. "These aren't made of gold, you know!"

"But they're just as rare," smirked the merchant. "Or you can wait until next week when more will arrive and the price comes down."

"Judah, your brother!" whispered Ibhar, unable to contain himself longer.

Judah turned. Ibhar beckoned him to follow. Judah gave the merchant one last dirty look and threw the nails back into the large keg. "Don't sell it to anyone else!" The merchant held up three fingers, then turned away. Ibhar led Judah out of the merchant's earshot, then faced him.

"They threw Jeshua in the cisterns. Just now—I saw it."

Judah broke into a run, a headlong dash that upset a cart as he passed, spilling the contents. The merchant yelled and was pushed to the ground when Ibhar tripped over him as he ran past. "Sorry!" yelled Ibhar, looking back over his shoulder and colliding with another man who carried a side of meat over his shoulder. "Sorry," recoiled Ibhar, lurching aside. The meat left a bloody mark on his tunic and he grimaced at it as he ran. Looking up, he saw Judah clearing the last of the market stalls, speeding past the fountain, and disappearing between the basilica and the bank.

When Ibhar arrived at the cistern entrance, Judah was already turning away from the soldier posted there. "They won't let me see him," complained Judah. His eyes were full of rage.

Ibhar led him away and whispered, "They're going to tear down the basilica tonight."

Judah turned away, his fists balled.

"Where are you going?" called Ibhar.

"To get answers," said Judah.

As he rounded the front of the basilica, Judah noticed that the men were at their stations, but few were focused on their work. One saw him and beckoned him over. "They took your brother."

Judah nodded. "I know. Why?"

The worker shrugged. "Have you heard?" he whispered. "About tonight?"

Judah scowled. "Suicide. All of you."

The man's concern gave way to hardness. "Grow a backbone, Judah. Time to be a man instead of a lapdog, like your brother."

Judah grabbed the man by the throat and was about to hit him when a voice said, "Save your energy, Judah. There will be plenty of fighting later."

Judah turned and saw Barak. "Why is Jeshua in the cisterns?"

"It is the ethnarch's reply to our demands."

"Can't you see?" complained Judah. "This is what they *want!* Or are you so tall, your head is in the clouds?"

Barak dropped his maul on the ground. "Because I am so tall, I see things you cannot. Storm clouds are gathering, Judah." He looked at the sky, where indeed, dark clouds were moving in from the west. "It will have to rain a week to quench the fire we will kindle tonight."

"You'll get us all killed," said Judah, turning away.

Barak caught his shoulder, wheeling him around. "Choose, Judah. The time draws nigh."

Judah jerked free and headed up the basilica steps. He ducked under the archway and started across the main floor. From high up on the scaffolding Zoar watched him go, mentally adding Judah's name to his victims' list.

Judah marched across the huge hall, entered the courtroom, and veered right toward the ethnarch's offices. Two soldiers stood at rest, their lances blocking the entrance. As Judah approached, they pointed their lances at him.

"I wish to see the ethnarch."

"You shall not pass," said one of the soldiers.

"I must see him!" shouted Judah, causing the other workers in the room to turn and look.

"You shall not pass," repeated the soldier, touching his short sword menacingly.

Judah turned to the workers. "Jeshua is in the dungeon! He needs our help!"

There were at least twenty workers in the large hall. Their mauls and hammers and sledges were more than a match for the two soldiers. But no one moved. In fact, no one would even meet his eyes. He turned back to the soldiers, whose faces how held mocking smiles. He glared at them for a long moment, then turned and walked away.

Behind him, one of the soldiers laughed. "Jews."

"Born cowards," said the other.

As he ducked to go under the arch, Barak grabbed Judah's arm. "Where are you going?"

"To get help to free Jeshua," said Judah, wrenching his arm free.

"No, you're not," said Barak, grabbing Judah's neck with his massive hand and steering him under the arch. "We can't afford any trouble right now."

Judah felt the giant's fingers around his neck. "What about to-night?"

Barak leaned forward, whispering. "For everything there is a season, Judah."

Barak guided him down the basilica steps, turned him to the left, and thrust him into an outbuilding, shutting the only door securely. For the next five hours, he stood sentry, his arms folded across his chest, his huge maul lying at his feet. Inside, Judah sat on the floor, his mind playing out a hundred scenarios of torture and death involving his brother, growing angrier and more desperate by the minute.

Arah was filling the water urns for the cook when he heard shouting from the fields across the road. The workers were pointing to the east, where great clouds of dust boiled above the hills. Someone shouted, "Brigands!" and the workers dropped their hoes and spades, dashing toward the house.

Eli must have heard the commotion, for he appeared on the doorstep a few moments later and squinted at the hills. "Secure the house," he said, waving the workers inside.

"Who is it?" asked old Micah, the last to arrive in the dooryard.

"Perhaps it's Azariah, come from Jerusalem," said Eli.

Arah wanted to tell his master that Azariah was in Sepphoris, but then he realized Eli was just saying that to keep Micah calm. Eli then turned and spoke a few clipped syllables to someone inside the house. In short order, the wooden window shutters were pulled closed and the house was shut up tight. Only the big red mahogany door remained open.

Eli looked eastward again and now saw the flags whipping in the brisk breeze. Soon, lance tips appeared. "The king's cohort," he said.

"How many do you think?" asked Micah, dread in his voice.

Eli scanned the lances. "All of them. Now, go inside."

Micah hurried inside the house, shutting the door behind him. The sound of the iron bar falling into place was distinct. Eli remained on the porch, thumbs hooked into his broad leather belt, watching the army appear on the hilltop and begin its descent toward the estate.

Arah was up in the big olive tree that shaded the dooryard well. From his vantage point, he could easily count the number of soldiers marching in tight formation—over four hundred men. At the head of the cohort rode a man whose horse was festooned with maroon coverlets with gold piping. The horse bridle and reins glittered as if made of gold. The man wore a helm with a tufted spray of red plumage. His armor was a brilliant gold. It must be the king. The red cloaks of the army were a thrilling and fearsome sight, and the clanking of their cuirasses raised a tumultuous din, like the ringing of death's bell. The slanting rays of the late afternoon sun reflected off their armor and blinded Arah like a thousand tiny golden suns.

They were about to pass by the dooryard gate when the king held up his hand and reined in his horse. Eli stood alone on the porch, frowning. He was a tall, broad-shouldered man, quite old but still formidable. He saw himself as a sovereign over his own lands and was not easily intimidated. The king dismounted and raised his hand in greeting.

Eli nodded, but not as graciously as Arah would have expected. A quick glance at the king revealed that Antipas too noted the chilly reception. "I am thirsty," he said, striding under the trellis, shucking his riding gloves.

"We are at your service," said Eli flatly. "Arah!"

Arah dropped from the tree. Startled, a dozen archers notched arrows. Arah froze, crouching, afraid to move. The king turned, raised an eyebrow, and gestured for the archers to lower their bows. "Spies in the trees?" he said, walking over to Arah.

"He is our water boy," said Eli. "Arah, this is King Herod Antipatros."

Arah, unable to move, stared wide-eyed at the king. Antipas bent toward him and whispered, "You're supposed to bow and say, 'I'm at your service, my king.'"

"I'm . . . I'm at . . . your service," said Arah, stumbling over the words.

"My king," said Antipas.

"My king," repeated Arah.

"Good!" said Antipas. "Then let me see some!"

Arah straightened and ran to the well. He hauled the waterskin up and handed it to the king, who drained it in a long, slow draft. He gave the skin back to Arah, burped loudly, and several soldiers laughed. "Thank you, young man."

"You're . . . wel . . . welcome," stammered Arah.

Eli grunted, drawing Antipas's attention. "Where do you ride today?"

Antipas had started toward the gate. "To quell a labor disturbance in Sepphoris."

"Have we need of fear?"

Antipas turned and gave Eli his most commanding frown. "Yes, you do." And with that, he ducked under the trellis, mounted his horse, and spurred it down the road. The cohort clanked into motion, and Eli and Arah stood in silence, watching as hundreds of stern-faced soldiers passed the estate, stirring up once again the great cloud of dust that had just barely settled.

Arah whispered, "Did he say Sepphoris?"

Eli nodded.

"I have to go!" said Arah, running toward the barn.

• • •

Naaman looked through the doorway at the leaden sky. Clouds had obscured the late afternoon sun, and the wind that whistled through the stable was cold. The horses stood silently in their stalls with their heads down. Rain was coming.

As Naaman raked the hay, the money pouch bumped rhythmically against his chest, reminding him of the talent Hanock had given him. With both Ishmael and Hanock in prison, he might soon be unemployed, and the talent would have to sustain him for a long time.

He heard the beat of horse hooves and went outside. A boy at full gallop sped down the wide lane between the tall cypress sentry trees. Before he saw the boy's face, Naaman knew it was Arah. When Arah reined to a halt before him, Naaman surprised both of them by saying, "Is it Jeshua?"

"I don't know," said Arah. "Is it?"

"I have a feeling it is."

"The king and his army passed our place," said Arah, dismounting. "They're going to Sepphoris. I was afraid for Jeshua."

Naaman nodded. "So am I." He turned and ran into the barn.

Arah followed him. "How did you know it was about Jeshua?"

Naaman grabbed a blanket and flung it over a brown mare. "I think this is what Jeshua means by the 'whisperings of the Spirit.'"

Arah nodded. "It tells you things."

Naaman felt the money pouch against his chest. "Yes. Important things."

Arah felt the bulge of the clay oil vial inside his tunic and nodded. "Yes, important things."

TWENTY

Clouds and Rain

A full ten minutes after the quitting bell clanged, Barak finally opened the door. Judah burst by him and ran out into the forum. Most of the workers were already gone, and none of the men who remained would help him rescue Jeshua. Out of ideas and beside himself with fear, Judah did the only thing he could think of—he took off at a run for home. As he cleared the city gates and sped down the sloping road, he could see the Nazareth hills to the south, carpeted with evergreens. As he reached the valley floor, a chill wind blew out of the west, and he shivered in spite of the sweat on his brow. Thick clouds hung low overhead, and everything took on a gray cast as darkness descended upon the Netofa Valley.

As he ran up the Nazareth hill, Judah's mind raced even faster than his feet. He could think of nothing except Jeshua in the darkness of the cisterns, probably hurt, maybe even dead. He entered the village at a full run and burst into the family courtyard, yelling, "Father! Father!"

Joseph appeared in the workshop doorway. "What is it?" Judah stood before him, gasping for breath, unable to speak, but his face bespoke disaster. Joseph turned and called, "James!" James ran into the courtyard. "Get some water!" Joseph led Judah to a low stone bench.

James filled a ladle and gave it to Judah. Judah pushed it away. "It's . . . Jeshua—the dungeons," he finally managed to say.

James's mouth fell open, and the dipper poured water onto the ground. Joseph asked, "Is he all right?" James dipped the ladle again, extending it to Judah, who took it this time and drained it.

"I don't know," said Judah, giving the ladle back. "He went to demand our wages and the ethnarch threw him in prison!"

"He shouldn't have accepted that responsibility," came Mary's voice from behind them. They turned as she approached. "I was afraid for him from the beginning."

"He had no choice," said Judah.

Mary waved the idea away. "We always have choices."

Judah looked up at his father. "There's going to be trouble tonight, during the second watch."

"A repeat of last Friday," said Joseph, frowning. "But no Jeshua to stop them this time."

"Will they kill him?" asked James fearfully.

Everyone looked at Judah, who didn't know what to say. Miriam started crying, her little fists clutching Mary's skirt. Salome, just a year younger than Judah, stood in the doorway, tears filling her eyes. Joseph saw the anxiety mounting. He met the eyes of each person in turn. "Jeshua is a respected *tekton* and the worker representative."

"Why should that stop them?" said Mary flatly.

Joseph picked up Miriam, who was crying softly. He held her close, smoothing her hair. He looked around at his family. "As soon as Judah gets his wind back, he and I will go to Sepphoris to reason with the ethnarch."

"Reason?" asked Mary. "What hope do you have that you can reason with him?"

Judah shook his head. "I tried to see him, Father. The soldiers wouldn't let me."

"Then we'll try again, Son." Joseph turned to Mary. "Get my cloak, please." Mary didn't move. Instead, she looked at her husband for a long moment. To James, it seemed like they were having a silent conversation in which Mary was doing most of the talking. Finally, without a word, she took Miriam from Joseph and went inside the house. Joseph turned to Salome. "We'll need food and bandages, in case he's hurt." Salome nodded and disappeared inside. Then Joseph took off his leather apron and headed inside as well. As he passed James, he said, "Fill the water skin."

James ran into the house and reappeared with a leather bladder and began ladling water into it from the big brown urn.

"It's my fault," said Judah, and James turned. Judah was still sitting on the low stone bench, his eyes filled with despair. James looked down at the ladle in his hands, and suddenly a great fear filled him. When Judah and his father left for Sepphoris in a few minutes, he might never see them alive again. He put the ladle aside and sat down next to Judah, who stared ahead, shaking his head bleakly.

"Before you go," said James, his voice quavering, "I need to tell you something."

Judah ran his hands through his hair, lost in thought. "Later."

"I filled the water jars," said James.

"I know," said Judah. "It doesn't matter."

"But I didn't empty them."

"All right," said Judah.

"She did." When Judah looked at him, James looked away. "Dinah did it. I saw her one day, and she looked so sad. This was after you . . . you know . . ."

"Acted stupid, yes, I know," said Judah, putting his head in his hands.

"And I wanted her to know you were kidding, how you and I play jokes on each other all the time and you were just playing a little joke on her."

"But I wasn't," said Judah. "When I told her I loved her and she was going to marry me, I was serious. I just said it in a stupid way."

"Oh," said James, more confused than ever. "Well, I just wanted her to forgive you for whatever you did, so I told her about my prank, how I was filling the jars. She laughed and said now I should start *emptying* the jars."

"So you did."

"No," said James. "I said you didn't deserve it, but she said, 'He deserves whatever he gets,' and then she said *she'd* do it, to throw you off my trail."

Judah met James's eyes for the first time, and James saw anger replacing despair. "So *she's* been emptying them," said Judah. "Why that little hypocrite! Pretending! The injured feelings and embarrassment! All made up!" He glared ahead angrily.

James felt his efforts were going terribly awry. "No! She really *was* embarrassed!"

"Oh," said Judah. "That makes it better. Thanks, James."

"It's not like that!" said James. "She loves you!"

Judah laughed ruefully. "Sure she does. Look how she shows it."

James hung his head. "She said the same thing about you."

Then Joseph reappeared, wearing his traveling cloak and carrying a bag slung over one shoulder. James jumped up and finished filling the waterskin. Joseph nodded at Judah. "Are you rested enough to go?"

Judah stood. "Yes."

James looked up at his father, but Joseph held up his hand. "No. There may be fighting, and though you're almost a man, you're not big enough yet to fight like one."

"But, Father!"

"Don't argue," said Joseph. "I need you to look after your mother and sisters. Joses is gone to Acco and Simeon is an hour away. We have to go now. You're in charge until I get back, understand?"

James nodded.

"Good," said Joseph. "I trust you to keep them safe."

James turned to Judah. "I'm sorry. The water prank was stupid."

Now that he was going back to Sepphoris with his father, Judah felt better. He pointed at James. "When I get back, I'll get even with both of you."

"I hope so," said James. "Father?"

"Yes?"

"You're going to bring Jeshua home?"

Joseph nodded. "Yes, James, I am."

James nodded. "Good."

Joseph turned to Mary and hugged her tightly. He kissed Salome and picked Miriam up and hugged her as well. Then he strode out of the courtyard, Judah behind him.

"Judah!" called James, running after him with the waterskin. "Here."

"Don't worry," said Judah, taking the bladder. "If I know Jeshua, by now he's got all the guards listening to one of his stories. In the end, they'll be better friends with him than we are."

James nodded hopefully.

By the time the army arrived at the crossroads north of Sepphoris, the sun had slipped below the horizon in a short but spectacular display of gold and reds against the quilt of black clouds that now filled the sky.

Antipas reined in his charger and turned to Actius. "General, take the cohort to the garrison."

"But, Sire," said Actius, "we're here to protect you."

"I doubt I'll need protecting from the ethnarch. Besides, since the days of Pompey, it has never been a good idea to ride into a Jewish city on the Sabbath with Roman flags flying." He nodded at the standards bearing the profile of the emperor, topped with the bronze eagle with its outstretched wings.

"Sire," said Actius, dismayed, "you speak like a Jew."

"I *am* a Jew," countered Antipas. "At least in part. And I know enough to avoid enraging them unnecessarily. Do as I say."

"But you *will* take a contingent with you," added Actius. "Those are narrow, dark streets—perfect for striking and hiding."

"I will take you and twenty men. The rest will go to the garrison and await my orders. If there should be trouble, they are only minutes away."

"I fear for your safety, Sire," said Actius.

"Fear not," said Antipas, smiling. "I expect nothing more than a very surprised ethnarch. This trip is actually for the benefit of our neighbors: Calpurnius to the north and Gratus to the south. Tonight we are premiering a play for them. Keep an eye out for the riders I sent earlier, who will tell us whether our audience is in Ptolemais or Caesarea or both."

"I hope we don't have to fire the city to get their attention," said Actius.

"Certainly not," said Antipas, surprised. "We're putting on a comedy tonight, not a tragedy."

News spread throughout Sepphoris long before Antipas's horse cantered under the tall south gate just after sundown. Doors were locked, lights extinguished, and eyes peered through window shutter slats as the contingent rode up the empty Via Principia. A fine mist had arisen, and fog from the valley crawled up the streets, a silent, gray blanket. The half dozen archers walked slowly through the gathering dark, their arrows notched, looking around uneasily. As they entered the forum, Antipas looked to his left. The Roman flamen stood on the temple porch in his white vestments, a small crowd of worshipers before him. Black smoke rose from the altar brazier, mingling with the low dark clouds. To his right rose the curving theater wall, and before them stood Herod's immense triumphal arch. Passing under it, he saw the new basilica come into view. Antipas reined in his horse. Six fluted columns rose majestically above twenty broad marble steps, gleaming even in the darkness. The building was so big it blocked the view of his palace beyond.

Antipas dismounted and led the contingent across the forum, threading his way between huge marble blocks. A guard appeared on the basilica porch and quickly descended, kneeling before the king. Antipas shucked his riding gloves and asked, "Where are the dungeons?"

"Dungeons, my lord?" asked the guard, looking up.

"Where you're keeping so many of Marcus's friends," said Antipas. The guard pointed to his right. "Show me," said Antipas, and the guard led them down the alley between the basilica and the bank. At the rear stood the cistern entrance. A guard lounging next to the doorway jumped to his feet and unsheathed his sword. Antipas raised his hand and continued past him. "Just a little visit." Actius glowered at the man as he passed.

Inside were three large iron plates covering three holes. "No stairs yet, just ladders," said the guard, grabbing a torch from a wall sconce. "This one." He uncovered the last of the holes. Antipas took the torch and started down the ladder.

"My king!" said Actius. "Let me go first!"

"Nonsense," said Antipas. "Post your guard and wait. I won't be very long." He turned to the guard. "Come with me." He climbed down the ladder, and the guard followed. In the darkness below, Antipas held up the smoking torch as the guard joined him. "Where's Neri?" The guard pointed, and Antipas gestured for him to lead the way. At the end of a long, winding passageway, Antipas saw a gate of interlaced iron bands. "Leave me the key," he said, dismissing the guard. Antipas held the torch higher walked toward the gate.

Neri was sleeping, dreaming of sitting in the Roman baths as Marcus and a score of other men laughed and pointed at him. They were robed, but he was naked as an infant. He bent over and cupped a hand to his good ear to shut out their mocking laughter.

"Neri!" shouted Antipas.

"What?" said Neri, suddenly awake. "Marcus? My lord, I'm sorry . . . "

"Oh, are you?" said Antipas, amused. "So you've changed your mind?"

Neri stumbled to his feet, gratefully noticed he was clothed, and rushed to the gate. "My king! You came! What time is it?"

"Shortly after dark on the Sabbath." Antipas looked around at the cell, clucking his tongue. "What have you done to deserve this?"

"Nothing!" said Neri. "He's gone mad, throwing everyone in prison!"

"Who else is down here?"

"Ishmael of Rimmon and his steward. Also, a worker. I heard them bring him in earlier."

"What did he do?"

"He delivered the message to you! Or sent it along, rather. He's done nothing wrong that I know of."

"What wrongs *do* you know of?"

"I know the details of Marcus's plans."

"It's cold down here," said Antipas, pulling his cloak around him. "Let us discuss this upstairs, in the ethnarch's new 'administrative center.' I should like to see his reactions when you tell your story."

Neri fetched his sandals. "I hope you brought your cohort with you."

"Do we need them? Isn't it just you and me and Marcus?"

"I told you: today is the deadline for paying the workers," said Neri. "Was anyone in the streets?"

Antipas shook his head. "No. Everyone is shut up in their cozy holes like mice."

"I hope they stay there," said Neri.

Antipas unlocked the gate and opened the door. Neri was about to step through when Antipas put his hand on Neri's chest, stopping him. "One thing, Neri."

"Yes, Sire?"

Antipas bent and looked the little scribe in the eye. "I have just released you from prison. I trust you will be suitably grateful." Neri nodded. Antipas turned with a flourish and walked down the passageway. As he headed for the ladder, he said to the guard, "Bring the others—let's have a party!"

When Antipas and Neri arrived at the foot of the basilica steps, followed by an unnaturally quiet Ishmael, a stunned Hanock, and a bruised Jeshua, they saw Marcus waiting for them up on the wide marble porch. "My king!" said Marcus gaily. "What a nice surprise."

Antipas laughed. Five of his soldiers stood in a semicircle behind Marcus, their hands on their sword hilts. The man had to be congratulated for his nerve, facing his audience with such aplomb. Antipas scaled the steps, keeping his eyes on Marcus's face, waiting for the change, and when Marcus saw Neri and Ishmael behind Antipas, even an actor as good as Marcus could not hide his disappointment. "You've freed the rats from their holes," said Marcus flatly.

Antipas smiled. "Let's just say I'm the broom that sweeps the house clean of all pestilence." He brushed past Marcus and ducked under the archway scaffolding, disappearing inside the building.

Neri came next, keeping a soldier between him and Marcus, but Marcus leaned around the soldier and hissed, "You've done it now, Neri."

Neri said nothing, ducking under the huge arch.

As Ishmael passed, Marcus took his arm. "We can still reconcile, my friend."

Ishmael yanked his arm away. "I left my blanket down there for you." He shoved Hanock, who preceded him, through the archway and followed him inside.

Marcus turned back, saw Jeshua, and grabbed his arm. "What happened to you?"

Jeshua's face was bloody and bruised. "You did, Sire."

"I never intended *that*," said Marcus, recoiling.

"So says the child who starts a fire that burns down his own house."

Marcus dropped his hand from Jeshua's arm, and Jeshua walked under the archway. Marcus turned and saw the soldiers, waiting.

Just then the first raindrops fell, splashing on his bare head. Marcus pulled his cloak around him and ducked under the arch.

It began to rain.

TWENTY-ONE

Lightning and Thunder

Raindrops splashed on the stage floor. The group of men moved back under the overhanging proscenium, where it was dry. At the rear of the theater, high up behind the last row of tiered seats, Zoar quietly slipped through a large door and trotted down the aisle toward the stage. He joined the group there, whispering, "The king is here!"

Barak looked up. "How many soldiers are with him?"

"Fifteen or twenty. The rest are at the garrison. He emptied the cisterns and arrested Marcus. They're inside the basilica now."

Barak pulled his wet hood back. "What are they doing?"

"Who cares?" exclaimed Zoar. "This is our chance! Now we can make our wishes known directly to the king!"

"What about Marcus?" asked Barak, confused.

Zoar shook his head at Barak's stupidity. "The king doesn't bring a cohort with him to pay a social call! Can't you see? Marcus is out!"

"What shall we do?" asked a worker.

"First, we secure the gates—no messengers to or from the garrison. That will buy us some time."

"Our plan was to topple the basilica," said Barak, recovering his wits. "Not go to war against the king."

"We're not going to war," said Zoar. "We're just getting his attention."

"How?" asked a worker.

"We outnumber his guard. We surprise and disarm them. Then we have the king all to ourselves. He'll have to listen to us. No one gets hurt and we get our money. Simple."

"Madness," scoffed Barak.

"Don't be a coward," said Zoar flatly.

Someone gasped.

Barak grabbed his maul by the handle and held it out before him, the iron head pointing at Zoar, a position no other man could maintain for more than a couple of seconds, yet Barak held it half a minute before he spoke. "Cowards take hostages. Brave men fight out in the open."

"I said nothing about hostages or fighting," countered Zoar. "Antipas doesn't want a war any more than you do, Barak. He'll pay us, just to be rid of the headache. Besides, he longs to be loved by his people. What better way to obtain that love than to intercede on our behalf by deposing a corrupt ethnarch? When it's over, we'll build him a triumphal arch, just like his father's. Everyone goes home happy."

"We should wait," said Barak doubtfully. "Think this over."

"I thought you were tired of waiting," said Zoar. He looked around at the gathered men, their dark faces gaunt and angry. His time had arrived. "We will never have another chance like this. The king, practically alone, here in Sepphoris! The alternative is slow starvation. Is that what you want?" One by one, the men nodded their assent. Zoar's eyes finally met Barak's.

"No killing," said Barak. "Just talking, like you said."

Zoar smiled. "Absolutely. Gentle as lambs."

And just like that, Barak was deposed, though he didn't realize it until the meeting broke up and four groups of men left the theater, keeping to the shadows as they moved quietly toward the city gates.

The southern and eastern gates were closed and soldiers patrolled the parapets atop the tall stone walls. Joseph said the other two gates were probably shut as well. No lights burned from the poorer homes outside the gates—they were shut up tight as tombs. Rain had begun to fall. Judah motioned for Joseph to follow him. They climbed stairs up the side of the whitewashed aqueduct and entered the shallow sluice, sloshing along, bent low, hoping the parapet guards had taken cover from the rain and would not see them approaching. Ahead, the water entered a round opening in the wall, disappearing into blackness. "I wish I had a sword," whispered Judah as he knelt and crawled into the opening.

"I wish we had a light," said Joseph, following. "Where does this come out?"

"The basin behind the tannery, right off the Via Principia."

"Oh, right," said Joseph, remembering the tall, square building with no windows. "I always wondered what that was."

Judah crawled along in the darkness, up to his elbows in the near-freezing water, which seemed to be rising. He wondered if it would fill the pipe entirely and drown them.

"I wish we had a boat," came Joseph's voice behind him.

"A paddle too," said Judah, squinting into the blackness.

"Don't need a paddle," said Joseph. "The current's strong."

They finally emerged from the pipe in a rush of water and fell out into the large basin on the cistern roof. The giant wooden wheel, used to raise the water to the next level, sat motionless, dripping. Judah pointed at the city wall behind them. A soldier stood atop the wall with his back to them, looking down the Via Principia, that wound up the Sepphoris hill.

Judah put his foot on the great wheel. It moved, and one of its buckets emptied out with a splash. The soldier on the wall turned, and they ducked for cover. When they dared look again, the soldier was walking away, along the parapet. Joseph and Judah carefully scaled the wheel, and this time got up without incident. Soon they were sloshing along another channel in calf-deep water, following the aqueduct's curving path, until they reached the next cistern and the next water wheel. There they descended by ladder and stood, sopping wet, in a dark, narrow alley.

Suddenly they were grabbed from behind and their hoods were pulled back. Before them stood Ibhar, Jeshua's cistern co-worker. "Judah!" he exclaimed. "How did you get inside the city? The gates are closed."

"The aqueduct," said Judah. "What's going on?"

Ibhar led them under a porch, out of the rain. "The king is here, and he's got everyone in the basilica. Jeshua too."

"Jeshua!" said Judah, starting off.

A burly worker named Kemuel grabbed Judah. "We've already made plans."

"What plans?" asked Joseph.

"You weren't invited for a reason, Judah," said Kemuel. "Barak thought you might interfere."

"You're following *him?* You're all mad!"

"We're not mad," said Kemuel. "We're angry, and we're taking action."

"You're cutting your own throats," said Joseph mildly.

Kemuel scowled at Joseph. "No one asked your opinion, old man."

"Please, Kemuel," said Ibhar, "they're my friends."

"Then you tie them," said Kemuel, tossing Ibhar a rope.

They were brought into the theater by the lower door at the rear of the stage. "I wondered when you would arrive, Judah," said Zoar, who had been consulting with several other men. "And who's this?" He pulled Joseph's hood back. "Your father?"

"Peace be unto you," said Joseph.

"Peace be unto us all," said Zoar, his eyes like flint, "when this is over."

"Untie us!" shouted Judah.

"Quiet!" said Zoar. "Or Kemuel will gag you."

"We came for Jeshua," said Joseph. "We'll take him and leave you to your destiny."

"Speaking of destiny," said Zoar, "do you think you'll escape yours?"

"Release us!" said Judah, shaking with rage.

"Or what?" asked Zoar. Judah glared at him. Zoar nodded to Kemuel, who produced two kerchiefs and gagged both Judah and Joseph. "Since they won't participate in the play," said Zoar, "let them watch from the audience." Judah's and Joseph's feet were bound, and then they were dragged toward the edge of the stage and pushed off into the open area in front of the first row of seats. They hit the stone floor hard and lay stunned in a shallow pool of water, the rain cascading down on them.

Zoar turned to Kemuel. "Watch them," he said, turning and leading the other men up the stairs. As Zoar and the men stole single file out of the main door, they stayed in the shadows of the arched portico. Across the forum, barely visible through sheets of rain, a half dozen soldiers huddled on the protected basilica porch, a lone torch lighting them. The workers trotted off to their assigned destinations. Zoar peered around one of the portico pillars, toward the synagogue, looking for the lamp burning in Sadoc's office window. The lamp was a signal that after the facade wall fell, Zoar would find refuge in the synagogue. Then, a few days later, Sadoc would see to it that Zoar and his family were taken to a small town near the Phoenician border. As he had hoped, the lamp was burning in the window. Zoar smiled, pulled his hood down over his brow, and made his way through the shadows toward Jupiter's temple.

Lightning forked above the earth and thunder rumbled. For a brief instant, the forum was lit like noonday, and the huge marble blocks looked like white pieces on a dark game board. The soldiers took another step back under the basilica pediment, out of the driving rain.

Sadoc had seen Zoar's men moving stealthily under the theater portico. When he saw Zoar's face appear from behind a pillar, he stepped back into shadow. After a moment, Zoar turned and left. Sadoc pinched out the lamp flame. A tendril of gray smoke rose from the wick, backlit by another flash of lightning. Sadoc pulled his cloak around him, fending off the chill. He still had not decided whether or not he would answer Zoar's knock after the man destroyed the basilica. Sadoc sat at his desk and pondered his options, all of which were favorable.

They stood under one of the aqueduct causeway arches, watching the soldiers patrol the wall parapet above the Via Principia. "They've shut the main gate," whispered Naaman. "How do we get in?"

Arah thought. If this gate was closed, they all were. He looked up. Water coursed down the aqueduct pillars. "I thought we might squeeze inside the aqueduct," he said. "But it's overflowing where the water goes through the wall, over there, see?" He pointed.

"We'd have to be fish to get through that," said Naaman.

Arah nodded. "I don't know what else to do."

Naaman thought, then brightened. He slipped past Arah and made his way back down the Via Principia, keeping in the shadows, though he was fairly certain the soldiers could see no farther in the pouring rain than he could. When they regrouped down the hill, around a turn in the road, Naaman began searching the ground.

"What is it?" asked Arah.

"Looking for something," said Naaman. He walked past a couple of ramshackle homes. "Ah!" he said, pointing. "There!" He trotted over to a large iron grate set in the edge of the cobbled street. He knelt and poked his fingers between the bars, trying to loosen it.

Arah joined him. "What's this?"

Naaman dug the mud from the edges of the square grate. "Just as water goes into the city, it has to come out. This is the sewer."

"How did you know it was here?"

"I've seen men urinating into it." He got a corner of grate loose and lifted it up.

"I'm not going in there," said Arah, wrinkling his nose.

"With all the rain, it's probably as clean as the aqueduct by now," said Naaman. "We just crawl up the pipe until we reach the next grating, and we're inside the city!"

Arah peered into the hole. A torrent of water was rushing past. "We'll drown!"

Naaman sat on the edge and dangled his feet in the water. "You want to help Jeshua, don't you?"

"We can't help him if we're dead."

"We might drink a bit of water, but we'll survive," said Naaman, lowering himself into the sewer. At first he was swept backward and a frightened look crossed his face, but then he found the bottom and spread his feet, steadying himself. He bent down, the water rushing past his chest, and squinted into the darkness. "I can see light! It's only a few rods."

"You mean furlongs," said Arah.

"Have faith!" said Naaman, smiling up at him

"This is faith?" asked Arah. "It feels more like suicide!"

"Same thing, sometimes," said Naaman, taking a step forward. Another two steps and he was gone. Arah sat on the edge of the hole,

debating. He was taller than Naaman, so if Naaman could stay above
the water, he could too. He lowered himself into the icy water. It was a
long, terrifying moment before he touched the bottom, and his sandaled
feet squished into softness, which he knew was not mud.

"Don't touch the walls if you can help it." Naaman's voice echoed
from the darkness ahead. Arah gingerly reached out and touched the
curved wall, which was spongy. The smell of feces filled his nostrils.
Pinching his nose, he slogged ahead through the rushing water. He
moved forward slowly, and after a dozen steps or so his eyes began to
adjust. He could see Naaman's silhouette ahead, so there must be light
beyond. After the initial shock of touching the residue caking the sewer
walls, he managed to touch it without gagging.

Then he heard a metallic scratching sound and looked up. Naaman
was pulling himself out of the conduit. In a few more steps Arah stood
under the open grate. Naaman reached down and helped him out of the
sewer.

They were on an unfamiliar side street, but they were indeed inside
the city. It was dark, but the nearly full moon glowed through the clouds
on the eastern horizon, casting gray shadows, even as the rain fell. Arah
held his hands up. The palms were black. He sniffed his cloak and recoiled. "I need a bath."

"How about a shower?" asked Naaman. There, at the corner of a
building, fell a cascade of water onto the stone cobbles below. Naaman
rubbed his hands together under the torrent. Arah joined him, and soon
they both stood under the waterfall, scrubbing themselves clean. When
they were finished, Arah's robe no longer smelled as much.

"It will have to do," said Naaman, trotting up the narrow, winding
alley, his feet squishing in his sandals. Arah followed, wondering where
they were. Suddenly, the alley met a broad east-west street, tiled with
rectangular flagstones set in a herringbone pattern. "The Decumanus!"
whispered Naaman. He pointed to his left. "The basilica is that way!"

Antipas settled himself on the carved throne atop the courtroom's
marble dais. The stone seat was uncomfortable. Arrayed in front of him
were Marcus and Neri, Ishmael and Hanock, and behind them a Jewish
worker who looked like he'd been beaten. At the rear congregated a

number of townspeople who had seen the commotion and followed the entourage inside the basilica. A dozen soldiers lined the wall at the rear of the courtroom. Water drizzled down the marble pilasters, pooling at the column bases. A drop of water landed on Antipas's foot and he moved it. "Neri," he said, "make yourself useful. Get me a cushion. I fear I shall be here awhile, if only because of the rain." Neri bustled off toward the offices. Antipas looked at the people standing before him. "I apologize for the lack of seating," he said, "but perhaps, if your legs are tired, you will all speak frankly and not waste my time."

General Actius stood in the darkness to one side, studying the people arrayed before Antipas. When they'd entered the basilica, he'd asked the king to exclude all but the interested parties. Antipas had demurred, saying, "Let the others in. When we're finished, they will tell the whole city that I've come to wage justice, not war."

Even with the wall sconces lit, the room was still too dark for Actius's comfort, and a group of hard-looking men was conversing across the room, largely in shadow. From the look of them, they were laborers, and they wore heavy woolen cloaks, perhaps hiding weapons.

Actius whispered to his junior officer to keep an eye on the men. Just then lightning split the darkness, and a peal of thunder tolled. Antipas smiled. "The gods have convened this court," he said, then remembering his heritage, he nodded toward the Jewish men. "And may Jehovah bless our deliberations this night."

Just then Neri reappeared, carrying under one arm a thick, brocaded cushion from Marcus's chaise and under the other a bundle of parchment. Antipas sat on the cushion and smiled at Marcus, who took it as an invitation. "Your Excellency—"

"Not yet, Marcus," said Antipas, raising his hand.

Marcus shut his mouth.

Neri handed the king a folded piece of parchment. The king opened it and studied the contents.

Actius took the moment to walk slowly around the rear of the gathered crowd, keeping his eye on the knot of men on the far side. Then he nodded for his junior officer to follow him out of the courtroom doorway and into the dark basilica nave beyond. "You saw those men?" he whispered.

"Yes, sir," said the officer. "Shall I remove them?"

"No. But in a half hour I want a hundred soldiers posted outside this building."

"Yes, sir." The officer trotted across the dark basilica, splashing through the pools of standing water.

Zoar elbowed Barak in the ribs. "Look!" A soldier appeared on the basilica porch, passed the guards, and ran swiftly down the steps. Zoar and Barak ducked behind the temple fountain. The soldier flew past them in a whisper of parted air.

"Will he deliver his message?" asked Zoar.

"No," said Barak, picking up his maul and starting after the man.

Zoar turned back and watched the soldiers huddling on the basilica porch, out of the rain.

"Soldiers!" whispered Naaman, pressing his back against the alley wall. They peered out into the forum, through the falling rain. On the basilica porch, several legionnaires in red cloaks were gathered around a lone, sputtering torch.

Arah pulled at his sleeve. "I know another way to the cisterns."

"He's not in the cisterns."

"How do you know?"

"Look at all the soldiers," said Naaman, nodding toward the basilica. "The king is inside the building—I'd wager Jeshua is too."

"Then we're too late!"

Naaman didn't know what to say. Maybe they were. He reached inside his wet cloak and turned the pouch around so Jeshua's stone touched his chest. It had the hoped-for effect: he felt braver. "Where are the rest of the soldiers?"

"I see enough already," said Arah.

"Look!" said Naaman, pointing. A soldier appeared from under the archway scaffolding and bounded down the steps. He turned north, disappearing past Jupiter's temple.

"There's your answer," said Arah. "He's going to the garrison to get the others."

"Look!" said Naaman. There, behind the temple fountain, a tall figure straightened and trotted after the soldier.

"Who is that?" asked Arah.

"Whoever he is, he's a giant," said Naaman. As they watched, another shape behind the fountain moved. "He's coming this way," whispered Naaman. They watched as the man ducked under the theater portico and trotted toward them. They pulled farther back into the shadows. The man stopped and disappeared through a door, closing it silently behind him.

"Who was that?" asked Arah.

"I don't know, but I don't think there is a play tonight."

"So why did he go into the theater?"

"Let's go ask him," said Naaman.

Zoar stood on the edge of the stage, looking down into the pit, where Joseph and Judah lay in six inches of standing water, being pelted by cold rain. Judah glared up at him. "I see the chill has not cooled your anger," said Zoar.

"Let us go!" mumbled Judah through his sodden gag.

"What was that?" said Zoar, putting his hand to his ear. "You say you want to join us?"

Judah shook his head furiously. Joseph sat nearby. There was no anger in his eyes. He was so calm, despite lying in the rain, gagged and bound hand and foot, that Zoar jumped down off the stage and pulled down his gag. "You have something to say?"

"We are not your enemies," said Joseph evenly. "You have nothing to fear from us."

"Now I know where Jeshua gets his reason," said Zoar. "But does Judah's anger also come from you?" Joseph shrugged. "Or perhaps he gets it from his mother," smirked Zoar.

"Perhaps you'd better gag me again, before I forget myself," said Joseph.

"Glad to oblige," said Zoar, replacing the gag. Joseph's eyes burned into him, and Zoar said, "No, he gets it from you. Good. If things go wrong, and we have to fight the Romans, we may need your anger." He jumped up on the stage, spoke briefly to Kemuel, and left by the door at the rear of the stage.

During Zoar's exchange with Joseph, Naaman and Arah slipped quietly inside the theater. They found themselves on the colonnaded portico behind the last row of seats, far above the stage below. Hiding behind a pillar, they watched as Zoar baited Joseph, though they could not hear their conversation over the rain striking the canvas tarps overhead. "It's Joseph, Jeshua's father!" whispered Arah.

"And his brother," said Naaman.

"Why are they bound?" asked Arah, starting forward.

"No!" whispered Naaman, restraining him. "If they could bind and gag two big men like them, they'll toss us aside like a couple of wet rags."

"Look! He's going," whispered Arah. They saw Zoar jump up on the stage, speak curtly to the guard, then disappear behind the proscenium.

Zoar entered the forum, ducking beneath the triumphal arch, out of the rain. He struck flint to a torch, which burst into flame, smoking wetly. He took a deep breath, pulled his hood up, and sauntered toward the basilica. When he passed the temple fountain, the soldiers on the basilica porch saw him. "Who goes there?" called one of them while two others ran down the steps, throwing their red cloaks back and unsheathing their gladii.

"Friend or foe?" asked one of the soldiers, stopping before Zoar.

"Friend!" said Zoar brightly. "I'm the watchman."

"What do you want?"

"I'm just checking on things, as I do every night."

"Everything is in order. Go home."

Zoar took a step forward.

The soldier barred his progress with his sword. "I said, go home."

"But I have to see if everything is all right," said Zoar plaintively. "I left plans out. They'll be soaked!" The soldiers looked at each other. "They're the *ethnarch's* plans," pleaded Zoar.

"I doubt he cares about them now," chuckled one of the soldiers.

"Is he in trouble?" asked Zoar innocently.

"Let's just say you might have a new employer tomorrow."

"Or none at all," added the other.

Zoar put on his most shocked look. "But whoever *is* ethnarch tomorrow will want those plans to be undamaged! Please!"

The soldiers exchanged a look. "All right," said one.

"Thank you! Thank you, kind sirs!"

"On your way," said the soldier.

"Thank you!" exclaimed Zoar.

"Go now," said the other.

"Thank you!"

"Now!" said the soldier, turning away in disgust. Zoar watched them walk back up the basilica steps, and a smile crossed his face. By the time he ducked under the arch scaffolding, the soldiers were none too glad to see him go. He'd thanked them over and over, as obsequious as a beggar, congratulating them on their glorious uniforms, fawning over their stature and strength, lamenting this terrible, bothersome Galilee weather, and hailing Caesar until they all, in unison, turned their backs on him.

Just inside the facade wall, Zoar crept over to the scaffold leg. His sledgehammer leaned against the nearby column. He reached inside his tunic and withdrew the parchment upon which he'd sketched the egg-shaped map of Sepphoris, inset with a cross indicating the main streets: the *cardo*, running north and south, and the Decumanus, running east and west. the city gates were marked by Xs, and tick marks indicated the number of men watching them. He ducked back under the scaffolding, waving the incriminating parchment. "I found it!" he said to the soldiers' backs. As one, they turned.

"Great," said a soldier, turning away again.

"I knew you'd be pleased!" said Zoar. "So will the ethnarch!"

"Whoever he is!" laughed another, also turning away.

Soon they were all ignoring Zoar again, and he tucked the parchment into his tunic and disappeared under the archway, into the blackness of the basilica.

TWENTY-TWO

High and Low

After reading it, Antipas put down the folded parchment Neri had handed him. He turned to Marcus and noted with pleasure that all color had drained from the ethnarch's face.

"Herod—"

Antipas raised a hand, then turned to Hanock. "You are Ishmael's chief steward, yes?"

Hanock nodded.

"Why were you imprisoned?"

"Antipas—" interjected Marcus.

Antipas frowned at Marcus, who held his tongue. When the king turned his attention back to Hanock, the plump man burst into tears and fell forward on his face. Marcus took a step back in disgust. "Come now, Hanock," said Antipas. "That's enough. Stop." Hanock lifted his head. Antipas motioned for him to stand, but Hanock would only get to his knees. His pudgy hands shook as he raised them toward the king, his mouth open. From deep inside, a tiny, hollow cry emerged, so weak and pathetic that Ishmael raised his hand to strike it out of him, then caught himself. Tears fell from Hanock's eyes, and great gasps of breath escaped him.

Antipas shook his head. "Why are you so disturbed?"

"Because . . . because . . . you . . . your . . ."

Ishmael snorted. "He lost your money," he said, glaring at his chief steward.

Antipas frowned at Ishmael. "My money? How did he get *my* money?"

Marcus stepped forward. "I gave it to him."

"Oh," said Antipas. "Then this is the financial wizard I've heard so much about."

"He came highly recommended," said Marcus, giving Ishmael a dirty look.

"So I loaned you money to finish your basilica," said Antipas, glowering at Marcus, who looked down. "But you, never one to leave well enough alone, turned the money over to a lender, to make even more of it. As if fifty talents were not enough." A gasp went throughout the room, and the Jewish laborers exchanged meaningful looks. "Yes," continued Antipas. "Fifty talents—a *kingly* sum, as I well know. And this financier, this miracle worker named Hanock—stand, man!—managed to lose it. Am I right thus far?"

Hanock slowly got to his feet, nodding.

Marcus raised his chin imperiously. "He says he gave it to someone named Ahmad, a merchant commanding a black galley, who was on his way to Rome to enter the money-trading business."

"Indeed," said Antipas. "I would say this Ahmad did as he promised—he has traded well for money—but I doubt we shall see his profits, or him, again." He looked at Ishmael. "Why did Marcus put you in the dungeon?"

"He's thinks I was behind the loss," said Ishmael.

"Marcus, do you really believe that?"

Marcus looked at Ishmael for a long moment, then shook his head. "I suppose not."

"Then why did you cast him into prison?"

"Because he had already bribed Hanock to implicate me," interjected Ishmael, glowering at Marcus. "He thought the dungeons might soften me up."

"And did they?"

"I enjoyed the peace and quiet," said Ishmael. "It was a sort of vacation, Your Eminence."

Antipas smiled. "Yet during your vacation, you may not have heard the good news."

"What good news?" said Ishmael, turning to Marcus, who took a step back.

"He can tell you," said Antipas, nodding at Marcus.

"Tell me what?" Ishmael's hand beat an invisible riding crop against his thigh.

"Go ahead," said Antipas. "Tell him."

Marcus backed up another step.

"Tell him," repeated Antipas.

"The king . . . for . . . forgave my debt," stammered Marcus.

"*What?*" shouted Ishmael, lunging for Marcus, who jumped behind a nearby soldier.

Two soldiers grabbed Ishmael, pinioning his arms.

"So I guess he *didn't* tell you," said Antipas.

"I meant to," squeaked Marcus from behind the soldier, who had his gladius drawn and was awaiting a sign from the king to strike Ishmael down.

"Well, that mystery is solved," said Antipas, clapping his hands. "But our work here is not yet done." He turned to Neri. "I found you in Marcus's dungeon as well. Why is that?"

"I lost a gold denarius he loaned me."

Marcus rolled his eyes and shook his head.

"And how did you lose it?" asked Antipas.

Neri blushed. "Gambling, I'm told. I'm not sure. I was drunk at the time."

Antipas laughed. "Foolish and embarrassing, to be sure, but, Marcus, my dear friend," he said, turning to the ethnarch, "is that something worthy of imprisonment? It was only a denarius, after all, barely worth counting, after all of the money *you* lost."

Marcus opened his mouth, then closed it.

"Nothing?" asked Antipas. When Marcus remained mute, Antipas said, "Neri, earn your keep. How many gold denarii would it take to equal fifty talents?"

Neri had already done the calculation. "Almost fourteen thousand, Sire."

Antipas whistled. "So why do you think the ethnarch, whose immense debt I freely forgave, threw you in prison, when all you lost was a single gold denarius?"

"I have no idea," said Neri flatly.

"I don't either," said Antipas, nodding. "Marcus, how about you?"

Marcus opened his mouth, but all that would come out was a faint, "I'm sorry."

"Well," said Antipas, "that certainly makes up for being cast into prison, doesn't it, Neri?"

Neri glared at Marcus but said nothing.

"And now, we're almost done," said Antipas, leaning forward. "Now, Marcus, perhaps you will explain this to me."

He held up the folded parchment.

Inside the theater, Kemuel followed Zoar to secure the rear stage door after he left. Naaman whispered a hurried plan to Arah, who crept along the portico to the far side of the theater. Naaman went to the main door, opened it slightly, and waited. When Kemuel appeared again on the stage, Naaman pulled his hood low over his face, slammed the door, and made a great display of walking down the steps, muttering to himself.

"Who goes there?" hissed Kemuel. Judah and Joseph squirmed on the wet ground, craning their necks to see who it was. With all attention on Naaman, Arah crept quickly down the far aisle and climbed up onto the stage, hiding behind the proscenium, where he had a good view of Kemuel's back as the guard watched Naaman stroll down the aisle. "Halt and identify yourself!" said Kemuel, putting his hand on his sword hilt.

Naaman raised a hand to acknowledge the command, but kept coming. Arah began crawling across the stage toward Kemuel. "They're doing it wrong, all of them!" said Naaman, gesturing toward the entrance.

"Doing what wrong?" asked Kemuel. "Who are you?"

Naaman walked past Joseph and Judah before pulling his hood back. He now stood face-to-face with Kemuel, who relaxed, seeing how unimpressive and short Naaman was. "Oh, those fools!" said Naaman, cocking a thumb over his shoulder. "Japeth and his men. They're right out in the open!"

"Japeth? I don't know any Japeth. Who are you?" Kemuel's hand tightened on his sword. Before he could draw it, Naaman rushed him, hitting him full force with his shoulder. Kemuel toppled over Arah's crouching form, flailing with his sword, and in an instant both Arah and

Naaman were on him. Naaman grabbed the sword and held it to Kemuel's neck. "I'm Naaman," he whispered.

Arah drew his own knife, jumped off the stage, and cut Judah's and Joseph's bindings. "That was foolhardy," said Judah, pulling the gag from his mouth and standing.

"And very brave," said Joseph.

"You're both right," said Arah, giving them a wan smile now that it was over.

Just then, Kemuel bucked Naaman off and jumped up. Naaman tackled him. In an instant Judah was on him and his greater size and strength made it no contest. Arah bound Kemuel's hands and feet while Judah held his knife to the man's neck.

Seeing a bloody gash on Naaman's cheek, Joseph produced a kerchief and handed it to him. Naaman didn't even know he'd been cut, and when he withdrew the rag and saw how much blood there was on it, his knees gave way and he faltered. Joseph helped him sit down on the edge of the stage. "Sorry," said Naaman, pressing the kerchief to his cheek, feeling woozy.

"Heroes have nothing to apologize for," said Joseph.

"What are you fellows up to?" asked Judah, prodding Kemuel.

Kemuel just glared straight ahead.

"The king is here in Sepphoris," said Arah. "He has his army with him."

"I saw no army," said Judah.

"They're at the crossroads," said Kemuel. "But we have a plan."

Judah shook his head. "Indeed. What is it?"

Kemuel raised his chin. "The ethnarch is inside the basilica being dismissed by Antipas. We're going to overpower the king's guards and then negotiate our wages with him."

"*Negotiate?*" laughed Judah. "Are we talking about Antipas?"

"Zoar knows what he's doing."

Judah rolled his eyes. "You're listening to Zoar? Did you stop to think about what happens when the legionnaires discover you're holding the king hostage?"

"He won't be a hostage," said Kemuel. "We're just going to talk with him."

"Will the army know the difference?"

"They won't even know about it until we're done. We'll intercept any messengers," spat Kemuel, "like we intercepted you."

Joseph kneeled and put a hand on Kemuel's shoulder. "What happens if a messenger comes from the crossroads?"

"I told you, we'll intercept him."

"And when he doesn't return? Won't that alarm the garrison?"

A dawning awareness lit Kemuel's face. He turned to look at Judah. "I thought—"

"You weren't thinking," spat Judah.

"At times like these," said Joseph, "I don't think there's much thinking going on at all."

While every eye was fixed on the piece of parchment the king held in his hand, Zoar crept through the courtroom doorway. The soldiers turned, their hands going to their swords. Zoar held up a wooden bucket. "Cleaning up," he whispered.

The guards exchanged a glance and nodded. Out of the corner of his eye, Zoar saw a good twenty workers scattered around the room. He made a display of looking up to the ceiling for drips. As he bent to place the bucket under a drip near a group of them, he whispered, "Be ready," and then he straightened and walked away, still scanning the ceiling for leaks. The soldiers shook their heads, noting that the roof was a veritable sieve and one bucket was a joke.

"Surely you recognize it," Antipas was saying to Marcus, holding up the parchment. He handed it to Neri. "Read it."

Neri unfolded it. "'To the estimable ethnarch of Sepphoris, the noble Marcus Pertinax, greetings—'"

"Skip down!" snapped Antipas.

Neri found the pertinent part, "'. . . you may rest assured that I will defend you against your self-styled king. May Mercury speed your success. I remain at your service, Calpurnius Piso, legate and governor of Syria.'" Neri looked up. "It bears his seal."

"Where did you get that?" barked Marcus.

"Be careful, Marcus, before you deny it," said Antipas. "I think you will agree that you have already received more than your fair share of forgiveness from me."

"It's an invention," sneered Marcus. "Neri's specialty. Look," he said, reaching inside his toga and withdrawing small piece of yellowed parchment. "Ishmael's bogus contract with Ezra of Nazareth."

"Marcus—" said Ishmael.

Marcus held the parchment up. "Neri forged this for Ishmael, to steal a merchant's warehouse and business. The letter from Calpurnius is just as false."

"That's not true!" said Neri.

Marcus held up the contract. "But you admit *this* is a forgery."

"Yes," said Neri. "But I didn't create it!"

"He's too humble," said Marcus. "Part of his job is inventing such things."

Antipas smiled.

Neri's mouth dropped open. "But it bears Calpurnius's seal! And there *was* a plot, Your Majesty! It involved a scheme to buy up Netofa estates and control crop prices." He climbed the dais steps and thrust the sheaf of papers onto the king's lap. "Here's the evidence! Letters of intent! Bills of sale!"

Antipas sorted through the papers, his face darkening. He pulled one out and held it up. "How did you get this?" he asked, glaring at Marcus. "The deed to my property at the Abel Springs?"

Marcus was stunned. He didn't know he even *had* such a deed. Then it hit him: Neri, the faithless cur and Antipas's spy, unable to find any real incriminating evidence against him, had done in secret what Marcus had just accused him of: he had forged the deed to the Abel Springs. Marcus stepped forward, raising his hands, "Your Majesty, this is a terrible mis—"

"I admit it!" shouted Ishmael, dropping to his knees, pressing his face to the floor. "It's true! We plotted against you, Marcus and I! Have mercy, Herod Antipas! Mercy!"

Marcus's mouth hung open in shock. Neri shook his head in delighted disbelief, aware that he had just received a most astonishing reprieve. Antipas watched Ishmael sobbing on the floor, then looked up at Marcus, who was shaking his head, glaring down at Ishmael. Antipas carefully folded the parchment and tucked it back into the sheaf of papers, dropping them on the dais by his stone chair.

"You meant to do me injury, Ishmael?" asked Antipas gently.

Ishmael, face down on the floor, nodded miserably.

"And Marcus was your coconspirator?"

Ishmael nodded again. "It was a mistake—"

"Fool!" growled Marcus. He tried to kick Ishmael but was restrained by the guards.

Antipas smiled. "Just a couple more questions before I pronounce judgment." He turned to Jeshua, who had been silent throughout the proceedings. "And your name is . . . ?"

"Jeshua bar Joseph, of Nazareth."

"And why were you in the dungeon?"

"I demanded that the ethnarch pay the workers."

Antipas studied Jeshua, impressed with his bearing, even though his clothes were torn and his face was bloody and bruised. Antipas turned to Marcus. "Why haven't you paid them?"

Marcus said nothing, but Neri spoke. "He has no money, Sire."

A shout erupted from the workers. Antipas gave Actius a look, and Actius nodded back discreetly. "Silence!" shouted Antipas. "I am listening to your representative."

"He's not our representative!" shouted one of the men.

Antipas turned to Jeshua. "You were elected?"

"Chosen, Sire," said Jeshua, "by the ethnarch. Ratified by the men."

Antipas studied Jeshua for a moment. "Why did they beat you?"

"For speaking the truth," said Jeshua mildly.

Marcus glared at Jeshua but said nothing.

Antipas nodded. "Yes, the truth can be painful—to both parties." He looked at the Jewish workers who were whispering among themselves. "A leader who tells the truth. You're sure he's not your representative?"

The workers were silent.

Antipas clucked his tongue, nodding at Marcus. "And how were you going to pay them?"

Marcus hung his head. "With the profits."

Antipas smiled. "Oh, that's right, the profits from Ahmad, the captain of the black galley, who sails to Rome as we speak with my fifty talents. Those profits."

• • •

Actius quietly excused himself from the proceedings and strode across
the darkened basilica hall. He ducked under the scaffolding and came
out onto the wide porch. The rain was letting up, though the low clouds
still dripped. The duty guard surrounded him. "What happened to my
junior officer?"

"He hasn't returned."

"I sent him to bring reinforcements," said Actius, frowning. "You,
you, and you," he said, singling out three soldiers. "I want a hundred
men surrounding this building in twenty minutes." The three soldiers
turned and dashed down the steps, disappearing into the darkness. Actius turned to the remaining soldiers. "Look alive! Something is amiss."
He went back inside the basilica, grasping the hilt of his gladius tightly.

Just inside the basilica, from behind a massive column, Zoar watched
the Roman general stride across the great, dark, many-columned hall.

"Someone's coming!" said Judah, running down the theater aisle.
"Quick! Hide!"

Joseph, Naaman, and Arah got out of sight just as the door at the
theater rear opened. A group of men, mere shadows, entered. A tall man
led them, shoving a red-cloaked soldier before him as they walked down
the aisle steps. From his place behind the proscenium, Judah watched
them approach and remembered Kemuel in the pit, bound and gagged.
His heart fell. *Stupid!*

"Ho, now," said a man, seeing someone lying on the ground. "I
thought there were two. What happened to your friend—" He rolled
the man over and jumped back. "Kemuel!" he shouted, drawing his
sword and scanning the shadows. He removed Kemuel's gag.

"Over there!" said Kemuel, nodding toward the stage. "Judah! And
others!"

The men drew their swords and advanced on the stage. Judah saw
no choice and stepped into view. Barak jumped up on the stage, shoving
the red-cloaked Roman officer before him. He fell at Judah's feet. His
face was a pulverized, bloody mess. Joseph, Naaman, and Arah stepped
out of the darkness, joining Judah.

Barak laughed. "Is this your army, Judah? A weakling, a boy, and an
old man?"

"One man is enough to stop a war," said Judah, "if the people have the wits to listen."

Barak shook his head. "No more talk—bind him!"

Several men started toward them, but Joseph threw his cloak back and brandished Kemuel's sword. "You will not." The men stopped.

"We're fellow tradesmen!" said Judah. "We shouldn't take up arms against each other."

"Then tell him to drop his sword," said Barak, nodding at Joseph.

Joseph, noting that the men were about to encircle them, dashed past Judah and in an instant had his sword to Barak's neck. The men fell back, surprised at his speed.

"He moves fast for an old man," said Barak, feeling the blade against his skin.

"Will you listen now?" asked Joseph, guiding Barak over to Judah.

"Listen!" pleaded Judah. "Jeshua and I agreed to the strike, as you did. We agreed that we've waited long enough. But we did not agree to start a war we cannot win!" He pointed at the Roman officer. "Stand him up." The officer was hauled to his feet.

Barak said, "He was on his way to bring the cohort."

"How many at the garrison now?" asked Judah.

The officer looked up. One eye was bruised closed. "Five hundred."

"In the legion, what happens if a soldier is killed by a noncitizen—a provincial?"

The soldier looked at Judah, fear in his eyes.

"Tell us," said Judah.

"For every soldier who dies, we are to kill fifty."

Astonishment coursed through the men.

"Rome rules by fear, not armies," said Judah.

"You're siding with them," spat Barak.

"I'm siding with *you*," said Judah. He looked around. "Ibhar, are you here?" Ibhar stepped from the group. Judah motioned him forward. "Who was in the dungeons?"

"First it was the steward. I don't know his name."

"Hanock," said Naaman.

"Then his master joined him."

"Ishmael," said Naaman, stepping forward. "He is my master as well. He and the ethnarch are plotting against the king, or so we believe."

"Then they threw Neri in there," said Ibhar. "And finally, Jeshua."

"And now they're all standing before the king," said Judah. "Consider it! When this is over, we shall probably have a new ethnarch—"

"Or a dead one," interrupted Barak.

"The truth is, we don't know what they're doing!" said Judah, nodding in the direction of the basilica. "Jeshua said more than once that this whole thing might resolve itself and no one need lose his life—not one Roman soldier, and not fifty Jews. Until we know the outcome of Antipas's judgment, it's foolhardy to do anything. It's wisdom to wait until your enemy reveals his plans, isn't it?"

Barak nodded grudgingly.

"Where's Zoar?" asked Judah.

Barak shrugged. "He said he had something to do."

"That's what I'm afraid of," said Judah, frowning.

TWENTY-THREE

Justice of Man and God

Antipas looked up, noting that the room had suddenly gotten quieter. "The rain ends and the time for testimony does as well," he said, scanning the crowd. "I will now render judgment."

Marcus glared at him with impunity—he already knew how things would turn out for him. His only option now was to appeal to the emperor himself, who was no friend of any of Herod the Great's sons.

Antipas nodded at Actius, who stepped forward. "Take the ethnarch into custody."

When Actius reached out to take him by the elbow, Marcus jerked away. "I am a citizen of the empire," he declared. "I demand a trial in Rome."

"So be it," nodded Antipas. "And you will have ample time to prepare your case in *my* dungeon."

"But I demand an *immediate* trial! You must send me to Rome!"

"In due time, dear friend." Actius and another soldier grabbed Marcus, quieting him.

"Now, Ishmael of Rimmon," said Antipas, motioning for Ishmael to stand.

Ishmael, however, overcome with fear, shook his bald head. He'd been on his face since his outburst five minutes ago. He'd hoped that in that position Antipas would forget about him.

"Stand!" shouted Antipas, making everyone jump.

Ishmael clambered to his feet.

"Your confession moves me to compassion," said Antipas gently. "But unlike Marcus, who has his emperor to judge him, you have me as your king and I will judge you." Ishmael started sinking to his knees in despair. A sharp look from Antipas straightened him. "As plots go," said Antipas, "this one was rather . . . inconsequential. Apparently, all you wanted was land—including my land. You weren't plotting my death, were you?"

Ishmael shook his head furiously. "No, Your Majesty, just land, and not even your—"

"Just the land," repeated the king. "Well, since we are both Jews, you will be pleased to know that I shall use the Law of Moses to affix your punishment."

Ishmael's face went white.

Antipas knew what was going through Ishmael's mind and gave it time to sink in. Then the king smiled and looked up piously, quoting: "'And thine eye shall not pity; but life shall go for life, eye for eye, tooth for tooth, hand for hand, foot for foot.' I imagine that also includes land for land. Therefore, the amount of land you attempted to wrest from me will be taken from you and *given* to me."

Ishmael's eyes opened wide.

"Ah," said Antipas, smiling. "It was *that* much, was it?"

Ishmael shook his head slowly but didn't reply.

"So," said Antipas, "I will choose from your estate the parcels that please me most."

Ishmael started sobbing. Hanock watched him in horror. He'd never imagined his master could be so humbled. Disgust filled him, and he took a step back. Then he looked up at Antipas and saw a greater truth: his fortunes would soon mirror his master's.

Antipas said, "And now, Hanock, since you are the cause of all this, if I know anything about human nature, you are now Ishmael's *former* chief steward." Hanock fell to his knees, but he knew it was pointless to plead or beg. He simply hung his head and awaited judgment. Antipas continued, "But because your incompetence has aided me in learning of your master's treachery, I owe you something, so I will give you some advice: at all costs, avoid the money trade."

Hanock looked up in surprise. He would not be beheaded after all! Then he glanced over at Ishmael, saw the naked hatred in the man's eyes, and knew Antipas had just given Ishmael permission to punish him in any way he chose. Hanock gulped and nodded at the king.

"And now, Neri," said Antipas, turning to the scribe, "what shall we do with you?"

Neri had been recovering the parchments Antipas had let fall to the dais steps. He looked up. "Pardon me, Sire?"

Antipas clucked his tongue. "You might want to pay attention—this concerns you." Neri put the parchments down. "Good," said Antipas. "I expect you to finish this 'administrative center.'" He extended a hand, intercepting a falling drop of water. "It needs a better roof. And pay the workers what they're due."

"With what, Sire?" asked Neri.

"I care not," said Antipas breezily. "That is your responsibility."

"Mine?"

Antipas chuckled. "You were so busy gathering up your parchments that you missed the main point, Neri. Of course it's your responsibility. Paying the workers is always the responsibility of the *ethnarch*."

Neri's jaw dropped. He shook his head.

"Are you saying you don't want the job?" smiled Antipas.

Neri shook his head again.

"Well, which is it? Do you want it or not?"

Neri blinked and looked about. Marcus was glaring at him hatefully. Ishmael was standing, shoulders slumped, staring at the ground. Hanock gaped at him.

But Jeshua was smiling.

Neri looked up at the king and sucked in his stomach. "Yes, Sire, I do want it."

Antipas nodded. "Just don't make the same mistakes Marcus made."

"He'll make all new ones," said Marcus flatly.

Antipas looked at Neri, who just shrugged, dismissing the snide remark.

"Judicious," said Antipas, smiling. "A good quality in an ethnarch." He signaled Actius, who hauled Marcus toward the courtroom door. Antipas descended the dais, removed a torch from a wall sconce, and followed Actius and Marcus into the dark basilica nave.

It took four soldiers to collect Ishmael and Hanock off the floor, one under each man's arms to support them. Ishmael had not yet realized he'd escaped with his most valuable property—his life—intact, but Hanock knew his master would soon regain his wits and the moment he had his riding crop in his hand again, Hanock would feel it. Between one dragging step and another, Hanock decided he'd had enough of Galilee. Once he cleared this cursed city, he would go where he didn't know a soul. A fresh start, poor as a beggar, but he would be alive.

Neri had to run to catch up with the king as he strode across the darkened hall. "Are you leaving, Sire?"

"Yes," said Antipas, splashing through a puddle of water. "That reminds me," he said, frowning at Neri. "There is to be just one dungeon in Galilee—*mine*—understood?"

Neri nodded.

Zoar was crouching behind a column near the facade wall. He heard echoing voices. At the far end of the basilica, barely visible between the columns, came a group of people, the king's general hauling Marcus along, leading the procession. Antipas followed, holding a torch. Zoar picked up the sledgehammer and adjusted his grip, looking over at the scaffold leg. He took one last look up. Though the darkness hid them, the spandrels were up there on the top tier, waiting. He took a step toward the scaffold and coiled himself to swing.

Jeshua was walking behind Ishmael and Hanock when he saw movement by the scaffolding. He broke into a run, pushing past Hanock, shouting, "Look out!"

Actius and Marcus were frozen in place under the scaffolding, looking back over their shoulders, wondering who was yelling and why. Zoar swung the sledge, and the shims flew out from under scaffold leg, one striking Actius's foot. He looked to his left just in time to see Zoar race past him.

The lower section of scaffold shuddered, wooden supports shrieking as they bent and snapped. Far above, a spandrel the size of an oxcart slid down a plank, was deflected by another stone, and tipped off the scaffolding onto a voussoir arch stone, dislodging it. The scream of breaking wood pulled Actius's attention from Zoar's fleeting shadow to the darkness overhead, where another spandrel fell through a snapping plank, thudding against the massive keystone, moving it an inch. Actius peered into the darkness overhead. Dust rained down, blinding him. Far above, the arch voussoirs, with no spandrels in the wall to keep them from moving, slipped back a little, and the keystone dropped another inch. A plank flipped up, dropping another spandrel, which collapsed the upper scaffolding. Marcus and Actius jumped at the sound as the facade wall shuddered and the great keystone slipped from its slot, hurtling toward the ground.

At that instant, Jeshua slammed into them from behind, knocking them through the archway.

A few feet to the rear, Antipas got up on one elbow and raised his torch. He had been knocked to the ground when Jeshua bolted past him. In the dim light, he could make out the scaffolding collapsing amid the thunder of stones as they struck the floor in rapid succession. An immense spandrel block hit the marble floor, bounced, then careened against a scaffold leg, splintering it. Wooden scaffolding shards as long as javelins arced toward Antipas, who ducked, barely avoiding being impaled.

Then a thunderclap and the keystone hit the ground with a crash that shook the building. Antipas felt dust raining down on his head and looked up. Far above him, in the darkness, a stone architrave beam shifted on a column top. Next to him, a pillar base shifted, and a crack like black lightning raced up the column. Antipas scrabbled backward as the spandrels continued to fall out of the darkness, bouncing off the marble floor with bone-jarring *thuds* and hurtling themselves toward him. A terrible grating cut the air, and finally the voussoirs slipped from their places in rapid succession, bringing the rest of the arch with them, the wall following. Stone dust boiled up and engulfed him.

As he was thrown out of the building by something or someone, Actius's head glanced off the base of a porch pillar. The ground under him shook, and he stumbled to his feet, certain he was in the middle of an earthquake. A flood of blood poured from his forehead. Marcus lay in front of him, not moving. The guards he had posted had fled to the bottom of the steps, looking up at the shaking building, their eyes wide with fear. Down a few steps, a burly dark-haired man, the shadow he'd seen inside, staggered to his feet.

A deafening roar of rending stone jerked Actius around, and he watched as the arch voussoirs hit the ground in staccato succession. He dived to one side as one bounced off the keystone and arced crazily through the air, end over end, striking a pillar behind him, taking a huge chunk out of it. Seventy feet above, the triangular pediment shifted and stone shards rained down on him. A plume of dust billowed out of the archway, its tendrils reaching out for him. Actius crabbed backward, then felt the marble under him shudder. He looked up. Through the swirling dust, he saw the entire facade wall coming down, stones hurled to the ground as if by giants. He got to his feet, grabbed Marcus by the toga clasp, and dragged him down a few steps. The whole building was shaking, and he was engulfed in smoke.

Someone inside was yelling, "Assassins! Assassins!" Actius turned and saw the burly man crawling slowly down the basilica steps. Actius limped down and grabbed him, whirling him around. Zoar had a short, curved knife in his hand. Actius jumped back, reached for his sword, but it was not in its scabbard. Zoar lunged at him with the blade, and Actius recoiled, narrowly avoiding it. Zoar circled slowly, his eyes fierce. Blood poured from a huge gash across his nose. Actius took a step back and tripped over a stone. In a flash Zoar was on him, the knife at his throat. Actius grabbed at the knife with his bare hand and felt the blade cutting into his palm. He screamed, blood coursing down his wrist. Then, suddenly, Zoar's hand went limp and the blade fell to the ground with a clatter.

Zoar collapsed on top of Actius, an arrow point sticking out of the front of his neck. Actius pushed him off. Zoar's hands flailed at the bloody arrow tip, unable to grasp it. A wet, bubbling sound came from his throat, and his eyes were wide with surprise. Actius looked down at his own bloody hand, badly cut. "The king!" he said, slumping to the ground. The little remaining light was soon overwhelmed with darkness.

Inside the basilica, Jeshua pulled himself out of the rubble and got to his hands and knees. Someone was yelling "Assassins!" and he went toward the sound, almost stumbling over Neri, who lay on his side.

"Are you all right?" asked Jeshua, helping him to a sitting position.

"What?" asked Neri, cupping a hand to his good ear. "I can't hear you!"

Jeshua looked the scribe over for injuries. He leaned toward Neri's ear. "Where's the king?"

Neri shook his head. Jeshua looked around. Amid the rising dust, he saw a tiny circle of haloed light. He felt his way along, stumbling over man-sized chunks of broken stone, and found Antipas sitting, his back against a cracked pillar, shaking his head. His torch guttered on the marble floor next to him.

"Are you all right?" asked Jeshua.

Antipas nodded and, inexplicably, laughed.

Barak hid behind a theater portico arch, biting his fingernail, thinking. Suddenly, what sounded like a tree being snapped in half over a giant's knee yanked his attention to the basilica. A second later, Zoar burst through the arch, followed by the screeching of breaking wood and thudding explosions as stones began hitting the ground.

Barak grabbed his maul and trotted across the forum, paying no heed to the sentries, who were running down the basilica steps, their eyes wide with fear. The sequence of events that followed slowed him, but he never stopped moving toward the building, scaling the broad steps, and an instant after Zoar fell from the archer's arrow, Barak dragged Marcus's body behind a column, unseen by any of the soldiers.

Now he peeked out. Down a few steps, a soldier was wrapping a bandage around the general's cut hand. Actius was ashen and going into shock. Someone inside the basilica was shouting, "Assassins! Assassins!" Several workers were creeping up behind the soldiers on the steps, who were gaping at the tumble of stone and the drama involving Actius and Zoar.

"I have him," shouted Barak, and the sentries turned toward him.

"The assassin?" asked one of them, even as he stepped over Zoar, who still clutched blindly at the arrow, coughing blood.

"I have him!" repeated Barak, and suddenly the sentries were surrounded by workers with drawn knives and swords.

Five Roman swords clattered on the ground.

• • •

Jeshua picked up the torch and peered through the darkness and dust, looking for other injured men. Most of the workers, who were well back from the arch, had escaped unharmed, except for one who was hit by a flying stone shard. He lay unconscious, another man bent over him. The soldiers quickly found and encircled Antipas. When Jeshua returned, they pointed their swords at him. One of them continued to yell, "Assassins!"

Antipas said, "Enough! We know!"

The soldier nodded and resumed his wary scan of the darkness.

Jeshua said, "Is everyone accounted for?"

"Everyone important," snorted Antipas, pushing his way past the men encircling him and grabbing the torch from Jeshua. Turning to the soldiers, he said, "Let none escape." The soldiers moved off into the darkness toward the workers. Antipas turned to Jeshua. "If there was an assassin, and if he's not buried, he's outside. Let's go." He nodded toward the hill of rubble that was once the facade wall. From behind them came shouts. Someone cried out in pain. Jeshua turned, but Antipas pushed him forward. "You stay with me."

They found Neri where Jeshua had left him, sitting, one hand clutching his damaged ear, the other pressed against his chest as if to see if his heart was still beating. Jeshua helped Neri to his feet. "You first," said Antipas, gesturing them toward the tumble of stones.

They began climbing the rock pile, Jeshua leading the way. The stones shifted under their feet. Twice Jeshua had to reach back and grab Neri to keep him from falling. Above them, in the dust-shrouded darkness, an architrave shifted, raining pebbles and dust down on their heads. "Move faster," said Antipas, goading Neri forward. "I don't want to die looking at your fat behind!" Jeshua reached back and took Neri's hand, pulling him up onto a huge spandrel, but Neri hesitated, unable to find a foothold. Antipas shoved the torch into Neri's rear, making him jump and cry out. Jeshua pulled him up onto the spandrel, out of reach of Antipas's torch, if only for a moment.

They finally summited the broken wall and looked out over the colonnaded porch. Just beyond the fall of stones lay Zoar, his hands weakly scrabbling at the arrow in his neck. The Roman sentries huddled at the foot of the stairs. Actius sat against a pillar, white as a sepulchre. Marcus was nowhere in sight.

Antipas and the others descended the fall of stone. He pushed his way between Jeshua and Neri, holding the torch up. The sentries made no move toward him. "Well?" he said angrily.

"Welcome," came a voice behind him. Antipas turned, and there was Barak, holding Marcus up before him, a knife to his neck. Marcus appeared to be either dead or unconscious.

Antipas turned and saw that none of his sentries bore a sword. Then forty workmen stepped from behind the pillars, and in a moment he was surrounded. "Actius!" he shouted.

Actius opened an eye but didn't move.

"Not much help, is he?" said Barak, handing Marcus off to another man. He crossed and glowered down at Antipas. "And don't worry about your army—they're going to be delayed."

"Delayed but not prevented," said Judah, coming up the basilica steps with his father and a dozen Nabateans. Salim held a curved scimitar, as did the other Arab men.

"Take him!" yelled Barak, grabbing the king and pressing a blade against his throat. Salim's men quickly made a perimeter around Judah and Joseph, facing outward, their scimitars ready. Barak's men encircled them, their swords drawn.

"I don't know who to bet on," said Antipas.

"Shut up," said Barak.

Judah looked up at his brother, who had been grabbed by two men. One held a knife to his side. "Jeshua, are you all right?"

"Yes," said Jeshua.

Neri was shoved to the ground between the two groups by Kemuel. "Here's the culprit."

"That's the scribe, fool," said Barak, nodding at Marcus, who had revived and was now supported by two men. "We have the ethnarch."

"He says *he's* the ethnarch," said Kemuel.

Barak looked at Antipas, who shrugged. "Things change."

Barak frowned at Marcus. "Then he dies." Kemuel unsheathed his blade and moved toward Marcus.

"Kill a Roman and we all die!" said Judah, blocking Kemuel's way. "Is that what you want?"

"We want our money!" shouted Kemuel, kicking Neri, who rolled down another step. Jeshua jerked loose from those who held him and helped Neri to his feet.

"Is that what this is about?" asked Antipas, straining against Barak's knife. "Money? You brought down the basilica and nearly killed me for *money?*"

"Destroying the basilica was his idea," said Barak, nodding at Zoar, whose struggles were quickly diminishing. He lay sprawled across two steps, his bloody hands still clutching the arrow protruding from his throat.

Antipas slowly pulled Barak's knife down and turned to face him. "He was acting alone?"

Barak nodded.

"Is that the truth?" asked Antipas, looking at Jeshua.

"Barak is many things," said Jeshua, "but he's not a liar."

"If that is so," said Antipas, "then justice has been done and you have no reason to fear."

"We are not afraid," said Barak, pulling the blade tighter against Antipas's neck.

"I am willing to forget this ever happened," said Antipas evenly.

"Why should we trust you?" asked Barak.

"I am also many things," said Antipas coolly, "but I do not meddle in affairs that don't concern me. It's how I've stayed alive, my giant friend." Barak snorted. "I've already ordered your new ethnarch to pay you." Barak turned to Jeshua for confirmation.

"It's true," said Jeshua.

Barak turned the king loose and grabbed Neri, practically lifting him off the ground, holding his knife up before the scribe's terrified face. "When?"

"I don't have any money right now," squeaked Neri.

Barak started shaking Neri like a rag doll. Antipas stopped him. "Yes, he does."

At that moment, Ishmael and Hanock summited the fall of stone, followed by several soldiers. When they saw Antipas surrounded by workers with drawn swords, a soldier yelled, "Assassins!"

"Shut up," said Antipas irritably. "Sheath your swords." He turned to Barak. "I will keep my word," he said. "See to it that you keep yours."

Barak nodded but still held Neri by the throat.

Antipas nodded at Marcus. "You may redeem yourself at any time, Marcus."

"I doubt that," said Marcus flatly.

"Then I will help you," said Antipas, turning to Neri. "Marcus will not need his villa anymore, as he is moving to Rome."

Marcus stamped on the floor, his face bright with rage.

Antipas pointed at Neri. "My counsel is that you sell the villa and use the proceeds to pay these men—especially this tall one."

Neri nodded. Barak released him and he fell into Jeshua's arms, one hand going reflexively to his damaged ear. Suddenly, he noticed something that had escaped him until this very moment. He cupped a hand over his good ear and exclaimed, "My king! My king!"

"What?"

"I can hear! I can hear!"

"So can we, Neri," said Antipas.

"No!" exclaimed Neri, looking around at the sea of angry and uninterested faces. "I've not heard in this ear since . . ." He stopped, noticing one man in the crowd who was not looking at him like he was a pathetic, fat joke. Jeshua.

And then Neri remembered. Inside the basilica, after the wall fell, when Jeshua was looking him over to see if he was injured, he'd momentarily cupped his hand over Neri's damaged ear and whispered something, which of course, Neri couldn't hear. Neri's mouth dropped open. "I can hear," he said quietly. "I can hear, Jeshua."

Jeshua nodded.

"Then hear this," said Antipas. "Decide right now what you, as the new ethnarch of Sepphoris, intend to do about these men's wages."

"I will sell Marcus's villa and pay the workers," declared Neri, loud enough for all the men to hear, delighting in his own hearing as well. Then he turned to Marcus. "And I will repay you its value. I was always faithful to you, right up until the moment you threw me in prison. Even though the king commanded me to spy on you, I never told him anything of value."

Marcus looked at Antipas, who shrugged.

Neri turned to Antipas. "Marcus recently told me how your father remained faithful to his lord, Antony, in his war against Octavian. And when Antony lost, and Herod was brought before Octavian, he boldly proclaimed that just as he had been faithful to his former lord, so would he be faithful to his new lord."

Antipas smiled. "My father *was* faithful to Octavian, wasn't he?"

Neri nodded.

"You may make a ruler after all, Neri," said Antipas. "And you, Marcus, might still have a few coins in your purse when this is all over."

"I doubt it," spat Marcus.

Neri then turned to Jeshua, his eyes glistening, still unable to believe what had happened. He touched his ear, which was still a scarlet nub, then snapped his fingers. At the joyful sound, he grinned broadly.

"When do we get paid?" shouted Barak angrily. He glowered at Neri, who just smiled up at him, unable to believe his good fortune.

Jeshua answered for Neri. "Why not now?"

Neri gave him a puzzled look. "Right now?"

Jeshua nodded. "I'm sure Marcus has a bank account."

Again Marcus angrily stamped the floor.

Neri snapped his fingers again, and his smile grew. "Yes!" He pointed at Judah. "You! Take two trusted men to the bank and get what you are owed from Marcus's accounts."

"I'll take the two most trusted men I know," said Judah, putting his hand on his father's shoulder and pointing at Jeshua. "My father and my brother."

"Your father, yes," said Neri, "but not your brother. We're not through here yet."

Jeshua nodded, and Judah and Joseph turned and walked down the steps, followed by a number of cheering workers, torches held high.

"They'll rob me blind," lamented Marcus, watching them go.

Antipas snorted with pleasure. "Justice everywhere tonight!" He turned to Neri. "You trust them?"

Neri looked at Jeshua. "If he's Jeshua's brother, my lord, yes, I trust him."

"It's your city," said the king. "Do what you will!" He clapped Neri on the shoulder and turned to Barak. "If never before and never again," he said solemnly, looking up at the giant, "tonight let our words be true. You will be paid, and I shall take my army home to Tiberias."

"Not to return?" said Barak, finally sheathing his knife.

"Not over this," said Antipas. "I'm too busy building a city to watch one be torn down!" He started down the steps, motioning for the soldiers to bring Actius and Marcus along. The workers parted before him, and Antipas found himself in front of Arah, who stood before him, dripping wet but chin raised proudly. "Ah!" said Antipas. "The water carrier. You followed me here?"

"No, Sire, I followed him," said Arah, pointing at Jeshua.

Antipas turned and looked at Jeshua. "What did you say your name was?"

"Jeshua!" cried the workers.

Antipas turned back and saw that Arah had knelt before him. He looked back and noticed that Jeshua was also kneeling, as was Neri. In a moment, all the soldiers and all the workers were kneeling before him. Antipas surveyed them for a moment, then threaded his way between the rough marble blocks dotting the muddy forum, followed by his men and Marcus.

When Antipas had disappeared into the darkness, Neri raised his hands and spoke to the crowd. "Tonight you showed wisdom. Tomorrow I shall show wisdom as well." He saw Zoar's dead body on the steps and turned to Jeshua. "I want you to continue as worker representative, if your men will support my decision."

The workers cheered, and Jeshua was clapped heartily on the back. Someone shouted and the crowd looked toward the bank. Judah and Joseph were hauling a heavy, gilded money chest out onto the porch. The remaining workers, hearing the siren call of gold, ran toward the bank. Neri turned to Jeshua. "Even with Marcus's loan, I'll still have to tighten my belt a little."

Jeshua patted Neri's bulging stomach. "I believe you have a few notches to spare."

Neri laughed, delighting in the sound even a barb made in his good ear. Then he sighed. "I suppose my baths will just have to wait a while longer."

Out of the corner of his eye, Jeshua saw Naaman standing in the forum below. "Perhaps not, Sire," he said, waving Naaman forward. Naaman bowed low before the ethnarch, shaking and cold in his wet tunic.

"Who have we here?" asked Neri, surveying him.

"A friend of Jeshua's," said Naaman.

"The ethnarch and I were discussing finances," said Jeshua. "He may need your help, Naaman."

"My help?"

Neri doubted the man had a lepton, much less a denarius. He raised his hand. "Thank you, but—"

Then Naaman understood. "I have money!" He pulled out his pouch and poured the contents onto his palm. The little black stone came out first. The large silver talent rolled out after and came to a rest on top of it.

Intrigued, Neri pushed the silver coin aside and picked up the stone. "And what's this?"

"A gift from Jeshua," said Naaman, looking down, embarrassed. Neri held the stone up, looking thoughtfully at it. "It's just a stone, Your Honor," said Naaman.

"I doubt that," said Neri. "A gift from Jeshua is a very valuable thing," he said, touching his nubbed ear. "Even more valuable than an entire trunk of silver talents, don't you agree?"

The sincerity in Neri's voice made Naaman look up. "Yes, Sire, I do."

"If it was offered, I would rather have the stone," said Neri, handing the little black pebble back to Naaman. "But as it was not, I will take the coin and finish my baths. And I will repay it, with interest." He tucked the talent into his girdle and patted his stomach, satisfied.

Naaman clutched the black stone in his fist. "Then we are both pleased, Sire, to have the friends we do." He winked at Jeshua and turned and walked proudly down the steps, his chin held high and narrow shoulders thrust back.

Neri turned to Jeshua. "Quite right. A friend is the most valuable currency of all." He paused, thinking. They were alone on the basilica steps. He leaned toward Jeshua and asked, a little sheepishly, "Do you think, Jeshua, that a man as rich as you would ever need another friend?"

Jeshua nodded and clapped Neri on the back. "Always, Neri. Always."

TWENTY-FOUR

Night and Day

I don't think he's coming back," said Zerah, picking up a pair of Hanock's sandals and examining them. "Do you suppose he'd mind . . . ?"

"He might," said Naaman, shaking his head. It wasn't right to go through the man's possessions—he'd been gone only a few days.

"Sure he will," said Zerah, trying on the sandals and lacing them up. "He'll come back. And when he does, Master Ishmael will forgive him!" He laughed, shaking his head.

"Ishmael will recover his fortune," said Naaman, folding one of Hanock's silk togas and placing it on the bed. "He's very smart."

"Have you seen him?" asked Zerah.

Naaman shook his head.

He hasn't been out of the house in days," said Zerah. "The backs of my legs itch like they know they're going to get switched."

Naaman nodded. He knew that feeling.

Suddenly, a loud voice split the air. "Zerah!"

The two men looked at each other. "Ishmael!" cried Zerah, jumping to his feet and looking for a place to hide. "Don't let him hit me!" he wailed, clutching at Naaman.

Naaman sighed, resigned. "He'll be too worn out after beating me."

"Zerah! Where are you?" shouted Ishmael's voice. Naaman opened the door and looked out. Ishmael was standing in the doorway to their room, down at the end of the row of servant quarters.

"Master," said Naaman.

Ishmael turned and strode toward him, a new leather-wrapped riding crop gripped tightly in his hand. He stopped at the doorway and peered around Naaman. "Where's Zerah?"

"Here, Sire," said Zerah, cowering behind Naaman.

Ishmael glowered down at Naaman. "What did you tell him about the other night?"

"Nothing, Master," said Naaman, trying hard to keep his voice steady.

Zerah nodded. "He wouldn't say a word about it, Master."

Naaman noticed that the crop had stopped tapping against Ishmael's leg, always a bad sign. He steeled himself. "I figured it was your business."

"My business," grimaced Ishmael. "What's left of it." He pointed his crop at Naaman. "I understand you loaned Neri the talent Hanock gave you. Is that right?"

"Yes, Sire."

Ishmael shook his head. "See he doesn't rob you, young man."

"Yes, Sire," said Naaman.

"But I'm impressed," said Ishmael, surveying Naaman. "Thinking on your feet—that's a good quality. Careful with money, also good. And you weren't cowed by Hanock—all good, good." He looked thoughtfully at Naaman. "Hanock is not returning," he said at last. "Finally showed some brains. But when I find him!" The riding crop sang through the air before Naaman's face, causing him to shudder. "And I will! Black galley, my hide!" He looked through Naaman for a long moment, then said, "I guess I'll be needing a new chief steward."

Zerah straightened. "Yes, Sire?"

Ishmael ignored Zerah and looked at Naaman. "Tired of horses yet?"

"No, Sire. I love them," said Naaman.

"Well, I hate to separate a man from work he loves, but you're my new chief steward."

"But, Sire!" interjected Zerah.

"Shut up, you!" growled Ishmael. Zerah shrank into the background.

Ishmael glowered down at Naaman. "I don't think you'll have much trouble managing an estate as small as mine is now!"

"You'll build it up again, Master," said Naaman. "It's your gift."

Ishmael looked at Naaman. "Plain speech—another plus. Good. Now, get your things. You'll move down here, to Hanock's room. Go!" Naaman took off at a trot toward his new life.

Ishmael glowered down at Zerah. "What do you know about horses?"

The sun was not yet up when Dinah took her place in line at the spring. She adjusted the jar on her hip and brushed aside a long black tress. Then she saw him, standing near the front of the line, head down, two water jars at his feet. She noted the curve of his neck, the way his hair curled over it, and she felt her heart leap. But she didn't move. She had made such a mess of things. What started out as a simple attempt to show that she was not like other girls—the water jar prank—had resulted in a deep gulf between her and Judah, and now she didn't know how to bridge it. She could have forgiven him at the beginning, if he'd just apologized for presuming she loved him back, which she did. She knew it was foolishness to be angry at him for stating the truth, but when she saw the certainty in his eyes, it was just one more example of men making decisions for her. It was bad enough that her destiny was to be a man's property, but to have him say it right to her face?

It took her a week before she could think about him without gritting her teeth. But when the anger faded, it was replaced by regret, because she really *did* love him. And it was this inner turmoil that made it impossible for her to even think about talking to him. She found herself gritting her teeth again and took a deep breath to calm down.

Judah picked up the jars and advanced another step. She noted a scab on his left elbow and knew it probably had something to do with the events of last Sabbath night. She'd heard how Judah had helped regain Esther's warehouse, how he had turned the Nabatean workers into friends by finding them work in Sepphoris. After leaving Esther's that day with her mother, she was so proud of Judah that she didn't hear anything Tarah said against him for the rest of the day.

And yet Judah did not come to tell her about it. Then, a few days ago, Judah's little brother James told her that Judah had almost single-handedly stopped a plot by the ethnarch against the king! And still he did not come to tell her about it. Dinah knew why, for James let slip just moments later that he'd told Judah it was Dinah who had been emptying the water jars.

"What did he say?" she asked fearfully.

"He said he didn't care," said James, hanging his head. "Sorry."

Judah moved up another step. *He didn't care.* Too much had happened for him to care about a mere girl now. His life had been at risk, and he'd moved beyond concerns of the heart. From now on, he'd be like other men: too busy or too smart or too self-important to talk to a woman. She was astonished at how much the idea hurt. Her heart actually *ached,* and she found it difficult to breathe. And now, just ten feet away, Judah stood, oblivious to her existence, where just a few weeks ago he had professed to all the world that he loved her and would someday marry her.

"Dinah, honey, move up," came a woman's voice behind her.

Dinah picked up her clay jar and stepped forward, and when she looked up, Judah was looking back at her. Their eyes met, and he turned away without a smile or a frown.

It's true. I don't matter to him anymore, she thought miserably. She put her hand to her breast, amazed at the pain she felt there. Her breaths came in spasmodic gulps, and she thought she might faint. *Wouldn't that be a show?* she thought. *Fainting dead away right in front of him!*

She looked up. Judah had turned away, but Dinah recognized the tilt of his head. He was thinking, and with Judah, action would soon follow. He was getting ready to leave, to walk away, and she knew that unless she did something right now, he would leave her life forever. She set her jar down and walked up the line. Sensing her presence, he turned. The look on his face was inscrutable, and Dinah wished for the old Judah back again, the one who shouted his heart to the world and didn't care who heard. They looked at each other for a long moment, then, on an impulse, she picked up one of his jars and marched toward the head of the line.

"Here we go again," said someone.

Dinah nudged the woman at the basin aside and filled the jar, then walked back to Judah. "It was me," she said, handing the filled jar to him. "I emptied them."

"I know," said Judah.

She turned to go, but Judah caught her sleeve. "It was a good joke."
Dinah's fear turned to anger, and tears filled her eyes. "It wasn't a joke!"
Judah nodded. "I know that too."

"What do you mean, 'you know'?"

"You were right, Dinah. I'm sorry."

"Sorry for what?"

"The things I said that day. I'm sorry I said them."

Dinah felt a catch in her throat. "You are?"

He nodded.

She looked at him, all hope dissolved. "Oh," was all she could say.
She turned to go, but Judah still had her sleeve.

"I promise I'll never say them again."

She looked up into his face, her chin trembling. "You won't?"

"Not unless you ask me to."

A tear rolled down her cheek. "I'm not asking," she said, her voice
quavering.

"Good," he said. "Then I'm not saying."

"Good."

"But if *somebody* doesn't ask, I think I'll burst." Judah smiled at her.

"I'm asking!" said a woman behind him, and several others laughed.

"Tell her!" said another.

Judah looked around, noting the women's smiling faces. Dinah
looked up at him. When their eyes met again, she nodded. "Well," said
Judah, "since *someone* asked—"

"I'm asking," said Dinah quietly, brushing the tear away and taking
his hand.

Judah's heart started beating again. It had stopped long minutes ago
when he'd heard someone speak Dinah's name in the line behind him.
He leaned closer. "You won't be embarrassed?" Dinah shook her head,
tears flying. Judah took a breath. "Dinah, I love you."

He wanted to kiss her then, but they were not engaged and it was
not permitted. Then the woman next to him said, "It's all right. I'll
chaperone!" So Judah leaned forward and gave Dinah a peck on the
cheek, their first kiss.

"All right," said the woman, seeing the look in both their eyes.
"That will do."

She went to separate them, but Dinah reached out and pulled Judah down to her, whispering in his ear. "I love you, Judah bar Joseph. I always have." She kissed his cheek and drew back. "And I always will," she said, tears rolling down her cheeks. Then she was bustled away by the chaperone.

"Does this mean I have to fill the jars from now on?" called Judah after her.

"Yes!" came a chorus of women's voices, and Judah turned.

He was first in line.

Jerusalem's white sandstone walls glowed warmly in the setting sun. Esther urged her weary legs up the last of the stone steps. She must reach the Sanctuary before it closed for the day. She was tired, but her heart was full to bursting with happiness, for today she would keep her promise.

She reached the topmost step and looked up. The Temple walls rose high above her. She hurried into the passageway which ran under the southern portico. Her cane clicked on the stone pavers as she hobbled toward the light at the far end. A steady stream of merchants and money changers flowed past her, their labors finished for the day.

Emerging into the Court of the Gentiles, Esther gaped in wonder at the Sanctuary complex emerging like a gemstone mountain from the granite prairie of the expansive court. The Sanctuary itself was sixty feet tall, constructed of brilliant white marble, with columns and accents of solid gold. As Esther walked toward it, the sun slowly slipped behind the western portico, leaving only the highest reaches of the Sanctuary glistening in the slanting sunlight.

Black smoke from the sacrificial altar billowed high above the Sanctuary wall. Through the smoke Esther could see the Antonia fortress in the northwest corner of the mount, taller even than the Sanctuary itself. It housed five hundred legionnaires, who marched out onto the wall parapets during holy days, their lances a reminder that even the House of the Lord was under siege.

It would not always be that way. Someday the Messiah would come and overthrow the yoke of bondage, but in the meantime, the Jews must serve Jehovah under Rome's critical eye. Esther stopped at the low balustrade surrounding the complex and read the sign chiseled into stone prohibiting any non-Jew from entry.

The Sanctuary complex sat upon a raised stone platform of several steps. The two bronze doors of the eastward-facing Gate Beautiful stood open, guarded by two burly sentry-priests, who made inquiry of each person entering as to their lineage. Esther approached them and re-cited her genealogy back four generations until they raised their hands and bid her enter.

Passing through the gate, she found herself in the Court of the Women, which was colonnaded on all four sides. At the far end, the Nicanor Gate stood open atop fifteen semicircular marble steps. Beyond the open gate, perched high upon a rough stone foundation, was the bronze altar itself, its four huge horns smeared with blood from a long day of sacrifices. Flames leaped high as a priest tossed a lamb's entrails into the fire and dark smoke boiled into the azure sky. The acrid smell of burning flesh filled the air. Esther craned her neck. Beyond the altar rose the Sanctuary itself, its monumental golden doors now being closed by a phalanx of barefoot priests in white robes.

As a woman, Esther was not permitted any closer than just outside the Nicanor Gate. She was last here five years ago, with Ezra, for Passover. She stood in this same spot as he carried the Pascal lamb up the steps and handed it to a Levite, who scaled the altar ramp and gave it to the priest for sacrifice.

Now, as she watched from the Court of the Women, several Levites closed the massive bronze gate. She turned and found herself facing a tall, regal-looking priest with flowing white hair. "The day is ending," he said, gesturing toward the exit.

"I have an offering," said Esther.

"No more sacrifices today," said the priest.

"Mine is not a sacrifice," said Esther, showing the priest her bulging money purse.

"Ah!" said the priest, nodding. "Do you have a preference?" He gestured about at the pavilions built into the four corners of the court: the Chamber of Wood (donations for keeping the altar burning); the Chamber of Oils (for keeping the Temple lamps filled); the Chamber of

Nazirites (to support people who consecrated their lives to God); and the Chamber of Lepers (where the healed came to certify their cleanliness to the priests).

Esther pointed at the Chamber of Lepers. "I too have been healed."

Kohath, the white-haired priest, nodded and led her to the pavilion. Inside, a young Levite in his midtwenties was sweeping the floor. "Lamech," said Kohath, "this woman would like to make an offering."

Lamech gave Esther a broad smile. "How can I help?"

"You can accept this," said Esther, handing her coin purse to Lamech, who almost dropped it, unprepared as he was for its weight.

"It must weigh fifty minas!" exclaimed Lamech as he lugged the heavy purse over to a table. "Are you sure?" he asked, turning back.

"Of course she is!" asserted Kohath. "She brought it here, didn't she?"

"How much is it?" asked Lamech, opening the purse.

"Two hundred Tyrian shekels," said Esther proudly. "The Lord has blessed me."

"I can see that!" said Lamech. It was enough to feed a village for a month. "What happened?"

"Lamech!" chided Kohath.

"Sorry," said Lamech, bowing his head.

"Not at all," said Esther. "I'm proud to tell it. Before my husband died, he was taken advantage of by an evil rich man."

"Aren't they all?" said Kohath, shaking his head sadly.

"After Ezra died, this man took all I had!"

"What happened then?" asked Lamech.

"Faith, young man!" crowed Esther. "Faith that Jehovah would hear the prayers of an old woman and give her justice. And he did!" She stamped her cane on the tiled floor forcefully. "Everyone said to accept my lot. Even Jeshua cautioned against hoping for too much. Well, God heard my prayers and changed the heart of the ethnarch, and I have come all the way from Galilee to give thanks!"

"Where in Galilee?" asked Lamech.

"Nazareth."

"And this Jeshua you mentioned . . . he lives there too?"

Esther squinted at Lamech. "You know him? The carpenter?"

"Perhaps," said Lamech. "If it's the same man, he was working last year at the Qelt Inn on the Jericho Road. How is he?"

"They made him worker representative on the construction of the ethnarch's basilica."

"That doesn't surprise me," said Lamech. "No matter how big the crowd is, Jeshua stands out, doesn't he?"

"Who are you talking about?" interjected Kohath.

Lamech turned to him. "You remember the carpenter who built the addition on the Qelt Inn? We were there when the Samaritan arrived with the injured man—the fellow who was set upon by robbers. He was badly hurt and Jeshua healed him. It was a miracle."

"I don't remember any miracle," snorted Kohath. "The man got better, that's all. Might have been feigning his injuries for all we know. You shouldn't be so credulous, Lamech." He shook his head. "Miracles! Those days are past."

Esther looked up at Kohath and jutted her jaw. "Excuse me for saying so, but that's not true. That same Jeshua he is talking about is also the miracle worker in my case. In fact, he had something to do with this!" She shook the money bag emphatically.

"Well," said Kohath, reconsidering. "That kind of miracle is hard to gainsay."

Esther thought she now understood the imperious priest quite well. She turned to Lamech and smiled. "I see we know the same Jeshua. What is your name?"

"Lamech."

Esther made a mental note to remember the young, slender Levite, so she could tell Jeshua about him. She turned to Kohath and smiled. "So, will you accept my offering?"

"Yes," said Kohath, nodding. "We will. And God bless you."

"He already has!" said Esther, striding triumphantly out into the courtyard.

"Imagine that," said Lamech, watching her go, shaking his head. "Jeshua."

"Yes, imagine that," said Kohath, opening the leather purse and running his hands through the coins.

Neri sat on the edge of the filling bath, his feet dangling in the water, which came out of the metal pipes hot and clear, filling the room with thick clouds of glorious steam. He looked down at the shimmering mosaic image of Neptune on the floor of the bath, seated in his clamshell throne.

"What do you think? Do you like my bath?" Neptune glared up at him through the water. "Come on, I know you like it." Neri laughed and snapped his finger by his ear. He still hadn't gotten over the delight of his restored hearing, and now the world was a much kinder place. He heard whispers across the room now and was happy to discover that just because people talked in low tones, it didn't mean they were mocking him.

His first month as ethnarch had gone well. He kept the books as he always had, and without Marcus's skimming and thievery, he had more than enough to meet expenses. He was even able to give the basilica workers a small bonus for their patience in being paid.

Judging disputes was more difficult. On his terrifying first day in the judgment seat, Neri looked out over the assembled crowd and detected skepticism on their faces. He doubted his own abilities and was trembling with fear when Jeshua entered through the big double doors at the back of the room. With his appearance, peace descended upon Neri and his mind cleared. *Just do the right thing*, he thought, taking a breath. *Just be fair.*

The first two petitioners stepped forward and pleaded their cases. Neri listened with both ears—what a blessing!—and pronounced a judgment that was met by astonished silence in the room. He thought perhaps he'd made a mistake, when suddenly both petitioners nodded agreeably at each other. A murmur swept through the assembly, and Neri felt the skepticism dissipate, replaced by a collective sigh of relief: the new ethnarch intended to practice justice.

At that moment, Neri felt good, and he smiled at Jeshua, who smiled back, turning to leave—each had his own work to do.

Neri leaned back, feeling the warmth from the hot water rising deliciously up his legs. His mind once again returned to that rainy Friday night when Antipas came to Sepphoris to unravel Marcus's plot. When Neri had finally crawled into bed the next morning, exhausted, he'd lain there staring at the ceiling, unable to sleep because of one important, unanswered question. So he'd gotten up, put on his clothes, and trudged back over to the basilica, his eyes red and stinging from lack of sleep but his mind whirling and frenetic, unable to rest.

On his desk just inside the office door sat the stack of parchments he'd handed to the king. Neri searched through them for the deed to the Abel Springs, which Antipas had held aloft. It was the proof that had caused Ishmael to fall to his knees and confess everything. Neri went through the stack three times but was unable to find the deed. His heart was sinking, as it was a key piece of evidence against Marcus and Ishmael. Finally, pushed far back between two heavy leaves of parchment, appeared a small folded parchment, which he carefully smoothed out on his desk.

It was blank.

Neri looked up in wonder. He snapped his fingers in recognition. *That old fox!* he thought, shaking his head.

He tucked the parchment into his girdle, went home, and slept straight through the day and night until the next morning, when he arose and began to govern Sepphoris as its new ethnarch.

As he nestled into the hot bath, Neri snapped his fingers again. *If you're going to deal with Herod Antipas, you'll have to be wise, Neri,* he thought. *Wise as a serpent.*

Arah was out in the middle of Lake Gennesaret in a little boat with no oars. The sky was black with clouds. A sharp wind caught his woolen hat, and it sailed off into the air. He hung on to the gunnels as large swells lifted and then dropped his tiny boat into deep gray troughs. Rain began to pour down, drenching him. A mighty wave lifted him up again, and lightning lit the sky, and in that illuminated instant he saw another boat far off, its white sails luffing and snapping in the rain-laden wind. Immense waves crashed over the bow. Some of the men on board were bailing furiously while others clung to the mast in fear.

Arah shouted, "Over here! Over here!" but the men gave no notice. Curtains of rain obscured the boat, then it was visible again, and then it was gone. And then, as Arah's little boat crested a wave, about to be hurled again into a deep trough, he saw something. A man in a red cloak was walking on the water toward the other boat. Then a great swell swallowed the scene, and when Arah's boat emerged again, the man and the boat were gone. A hand was shaking him. "Arah? Arah? Wake up, boy."

Arah opened his eyes. His father, who had been dead for years, was sitting on the edge of his sleeping pallet. "Father?" croaked Arah in astonishment.

Philip nodded. "Time to get up, Son. Fill the jars."

Arah sat up and was surprised at how small the bed was. It was his old pallet, stuffed with straw ticking, and he had the little blue blanket his grandmother had made, which he had worn out years ago and thrown away. He looked down at his hands, which were small and pudgy. "I'm little," he said, looking up at his father.

"Not too little, I hope, to do your chores," said Philip, tousling his hair.

"Father?"

"Yes, Son?"

"Where are you?"

Philip smiled. "I'm with God, Arah."

Tears filled Arah's eyes. "Are you happy?"

Philip nodded.

"Do you miss us?"

"Yes, Son, I do."

"Will we see you again?"

"Yes, Arah."

"When?"

"Not for a long time," said Philip. "You have many things to do yet."

"What are they?"

Philip smiled. "You will find out. Now get out of bed and fill the jars." He stood and walked out the door.

"Arah? Arah?" came a voice.

Arah opened his eyes. Micah, the grizzled old field worker, was sitting on the edge of the bed, shaking him gently. "Time to get up, Son. Fill the jars."

For an instant, Micah looked just like Arah's father. The same dark hair, ruddy complexion, and kind blue eyes. "Father?"

Micah smiled, his tooth gleaming. "No, Arah. It's just me, old Micah."

The dream slipped away and tears filled Arah's eyes. "Oh, Micah, I saw my father—he spoke to me!" He hugged Micah, tears spilling down his cheeks.

"What did he say?"

"That we'll meet again!" Arah sobbed against Micah's chest.

Micah held the boy gently. "Our greatest hope, Arah," he whispered. "Our greatest hope."

"You came," said Antipas.

Sadoc's head jerked in the direction of the sound, and he groped his way through the darkness toward it. "I had little choice, Sire," he said. "You commanded me."

"That I did," said Antipas, turning up a lamp. Golden light filled the room. The king wore a purple robe and a jewel-encrusted crown, and he held a heavy gold scepter topped by an eagle. "Do you know why I summoned you?"

"Yes, Sire," said Sadoc, slowly unwrapping the slender black leather *tefillin* ribbons winding down his left forearm. Then he untied the knot securing the tiny inscribed box to his forehead. He wanted to take the tefillin off before the guards started beating him. Finally, he pulled his white linen tallith back, exposing a thick crop of peppery black hair. "I am here to confess my guilt," he said, bowing.

"Yet there is pride even in your confession," said Antipas. "Remarkable."

"Sire?"

In a sudden, fluid motion, Antipas swung his heavy scepter, striking Sadoc on the side of the head. The rabbi crumpled to the floor in a heap. Antipas descended the throne steps and sat on the lowest one, placing the scepter across his lap. Sadoc looked up at the king, stunned. Blood trickled down his cheek.

"I am Herod Antipatros, tetrarch of Galilee and Perea," said Antipas. "One day, I shall be king of the Jews." He leaned forward. "I forgave Ishmael because of his great wealth, most of which is now mine. You have been implicated in his scheme. I might also forgive you," he said, studying the rabbi, "but you have nothing I need."

Sadoc managed to get to his knees. His head felt split wide open, and he struggled to undouble his vision. "I would serve the king," he said, touching his bloody temple gingerly, trying not to slur his words. "In any way he desires."

The two little tefillin boxes, each containing four verses of holy scripture, lay on the floor between them. Antipas picked up the boxes, which trailed long ribbons. "Really?" he said, turning them over in his hands.

"Yes," said Sadoc, his eyes also on the sacred objects. "In any way."

Antipas set the tefillin on the floor. He stood and placed his boot heel on the boxes, crushing them, his eyes never leaving Sadoc. "In *any* way?"

Sadoc stretched himself facedown on the ground, pushing the ruined tefillin out of the way, his fingers mere inches from the king's heavy boots. "I will serve the king of the Jews," he said humbly, tasting blood at the corner of his mouth.

Antipas smiled down at him. "Yes. You will."

Jeshua awoke suddenly. Perspiration dewed his brow, and his chest heaved as if he had just run a great distance. Slowly, the terrible dream dissipated. The Jezreel Valley. The armies, poised to fight under a full, blood red moon. His name on every tongue, a curse or a prayer. The weight of responsibility crushing his soul. The burden. The coming darkness.

He felt the rough pine bark against his back, which ached from sleeping sitting up. He slowly rose, feeling as old as the world, and reached for his staff.

And there, just a few feet away, standing shakily on a rock, was a lamb, no more than a few weeks old, a tuft of grass in its mouth, chewing thoughtfully, looking at him. Jeshua put his hand out, beckoning. "Little one," he whispered, "what are you doing out here? Don't you know there are wolves about?" He picked up the lamb and nuzzled it to his cheek, stroking its soft fuzzy coat. In that instant he realized that the darkness had receded and he felt better than he had in months. He looked out over the Jezreel Valley, peaceful in the hazy morning light. He stretched, rotating his neck, luxuriating in the sense of lightness that now lifted him. He thought his feet might actually leave the ground, he weighed so little. He looked down at the lamb in his arms. "I understand. One soul at a time, and though the world be destroyed, many souls will be preserved." He looked heavenward. "Thank you, Father."

He strode off down the path, holding the tiny lamb in his arms.

• • •

"Why are we here?" asked Judah, frowning.

"It will take just a moment," said Jeshua, ducking under the stone arch. He picked his way between the markers and climbed the hill. Judah followed. They stopped at a recently whitewashed sepulchre. A spray of wild flowers, now dead, lay before the rounded entrance stone.

Judah pinched his nose. "Is this——?"

Jeshua nodded, reaching into his tunic, withdrawing two small, white stones. He handed one to Judah and placed the other on the sepulchre. "Father," he whispered, "receive your son with love."

"Zoar doesn't deserve our honor," frowned Judah, dropping his stone on the ground. "He was an evil man."

"Yes, he was," said Jeshua, picking up Judah's stone and placing it next to the other one.

"Then why honor him?"

"Because he had a wife and children he loved and who loved him and miss him now. He was a leader of men and a talented artisan."

"But he tried to kill you."

"Yes," said Jeshua. "And he will not be the last."

The sadness in Jeshua's eyes forbade a response, so Judah just squeezed his brother's arm.

Jeshua smiled wanly. "Are you ready?"

"You really intend to go?"

Jeshua looked higher up on the hill. Above the rooftops, a red flag flapped in the warm evening breeze. The sun was setting in a blaze of golden summer light. "When the flag comes down, it begins. We should hurry." He started up the hill.

Judah followed him. "I still don't think Father would approve."

They entered the city by the south gate and walked up the *cardo*, dodging vendors closing down their stalls. The forum opened up before them, and they skirted Herod's Arch and passed Jupiter's temple, where the fountain bubbled quietly. The finished basilica came into view, its six white porch columns gleaming gold in the setting sun. The rebuilt facade wall rose behind the columns, and the two immense golden doors stood open, revealing the dark interior. Far above, carved into the triangular pediment, was a frieze of Minerva holding a judgment scale.

Jeshua turned to the right. "Look!" Atop the tall theater wall, the flag was coming down. They headed toward the portico, where a line of people waited to enter. Soon they were inside, looking down the sloping aisles at the stage far below. Seats were filling rapidly, and they were surrounded by the buzz of conversation. They walked down an aisle and found a likely row. As they seated themselves, Judah saw Neri and Naaman in one of the first rows, far below them. He nudged Jeshua, pointing. "Has the ethnarch lost weight?"

"Perhaps he's too busy governing to eat."

"Then may he be half the man he once was!"

Just then, Neri turned, saw them, and nudged Naaman, who looked up. They smiled and waved. Jeshua and Judah waved back.

"I'm very excited," said Jeshua. "Think of the dramas that have unfolded here."

Judah nodded, remembering his rescue by Arah and Naaman in this very place. "I'm sure it will be exciting," he said. "How could it not be?"

Then, on the stage below, a trio of men stepped from behind the proscenium and put silver horns to their lips. A fanfare filled the evening, silencing the crowd.

Jeshua leaned forward to see what would happen next.

The Carpenter Teaches

One evening, as they sat around a small fire, Peter turned to Jeshua and said, "Master, if my brother offends me, how many times must I forgive him? Is it seven times, as the rabbis say?"

Jeshua shook his head. "No, Peter, not seven times, but seventy times seven."

Noting his disciples' astonishment, Jeshua said, "My friends: the kingdom of heaven is like a certain king, who called a servant before him for an accounting. And the king said, 'I loaned you ten thousand talents, and the time has come for you to repay.'

"But the servant could not, and the king commanded him to be bound and sold, along with his wife and children, to pay the debt. But the servant threw himself on the ground before the king and cried for mercy, saying, 'Have patience with me, Lord, and I will pay you all that I owe.'

"The king was moved with compassion, and he removed the servant's bonds and forgave him of the debt. And the servant fell to the ground and worshiped the king."

Peter and the other disciples nodded their approval, and Jeshua continued. "But then that same servant left the presence of the king and found a fellow servant who owed him a hundred denarii. He grabbed the man by the throat, and said, 'Pay what you owe me!'

"And the servant fell at his feet and cried, 'Have patience with me, and I will pay you all that I owe!'

"But the servant would not listen, and he cast his fellow servant into prison until he would pay the debt.

"Now all this was seen by other servants, and they were angry, and they went and told the king what they'd seen. And the king called the servant before him and said, 'You wicked servant! I forgave you the huge debt you owed me because you begged me. Why, then, didn't you take pity on your fellow servant, when I had compassion for you?'

"When the servant answered nothing, the king was angry, and he cast the servant into prison, to remain there until he should repay all his debt to the king."

Then Jeshua looked at his disciples and said, "If you would have God forgive you of your trespasses, you must forgive others theirs."

Now it was just a few days before Passover, and as they crossed the Jordan into Judea, Jeshua felt his long journey finally coming to an end. This would be the last time he would go up to the Holy City, and there he would openly declare his doctrine, to whatever consequences might come.

As they walked up the dusty road, Jeshua spoke to his disciples about the coming of the kingdom of God. He encouraged them to be prepared and to have faith, saying, "In a certain city there was a judge who did not fear God, nor did he regard man. And one day a widow came before him, saying, 'Avenge me of my adversary.'

"But the judge would not, and the widow went away grieving. But the next day the widow came again, and again he sent her away without justice. And the next day she came yet a third time, and still he refused her pleas.

"But, undaunted, the woman still came daily, pleading for the judge to give her justice, and he became weary of her pleas, and thought in his heart, *I will give her justice, not because I fear God or man, but because she tires me with her continual pleading.* And so he gave her justice and avenged the wrong done to her, and she went away rejoicing."

Then Jeshua stopped and looked at his disciples. "Now, if even a wicked man will grant justice to someone he neither knows nor regards, how much more quickly will your Father in Heaven answer your prayers?"

Acknowledgments

Thanks are in order to the many people who helped create, critique, and construct this book. My mother, Virginia, and my sister, Bonnie, read early drafts and shared helpful ideas. My friends Doug, Lex, Natalie, Jan, Irene, Linda, James, Julie, Carol Lynn, Bill, and Lisa also listened to the story or read the manuscript and offered suggestions on improving the story.

The folks at HarperSanFrancisco also deserve my thanks. Lisa Zuniga oversaw production, developing the beautiful book you are now holding. Priscilla Stuckey made sure the prose was clear and the moon phases were correct. Carol Lastrucci proofread the manuscript, Joseph Rutt did the interior design, and Jim Warner designed the cover. Mark Tauber, Terri Leonard, and Michael Maudlin have created an environment at HarperSanFrancisco where excellence is both the goal and the reality. Roger Freet and Margery Buchanan masterminded the marketing, Jennifer Johns publicized it, and Jeff Hobbs saw to it that the book found its way onto the shopping shelves.

My friend and editor, Gideon Weil, helped me shape the book into a solid storyline with a complex but plausible plot and a satisfying solution. He encouraged me when I was discouraged, challenged me to improve and streamline the story, and always voted for more Jeshua on the page. The result is indisputably better than I could have managed alone. Thank you, Gideon.

My pal and agent, Joe Durepos, is an inspiration. His knowledge of the writing business is profound, his wisdom unassailable. On even the most serious subjects, there is always a twinkle in his voice, and he always lifts my spirits. He's also a good husband and father, and for that alone I'm proud to know him. Thanks, Joe.

Finally, I'd like to thank Jeshua bar Joseph, who has been a generous guide to me on life's rigorous road. He always leads the way, lifting the lamp of enlightenment, beckoning me onward. When I stumble, he helps me to my feet. When I lag behind, he waits for me. He listens attentively to both my grumbling complaints and my shouted joys. He is a trusted fellow traveler, and my heart's hope is that one day, when we are once again face-to-face, he will call me *friend*.

Kenny Kemp
San Diego, California